When the trials begin,
in soul-torn solitude despairing,
the hunter waits alone.
The companions emerge
from fast-bound ties of fate
uniting against a common foe.

When the shadows descend,
in Hell-sworn covenant unswerving
the blighted brothers hunt,
and the godborn appears,
in rose-blessed abbey reared,
arising to loose the godly spark.

When the harvest time comes,
in hate-fueled mission grim unbending,
the shadowed reapers search.
The adversary vies
with fiend-wrought enemies,
opposing the twisting schemes of Hell.

When the tempest is born,
as storm-tossed waters rise uncaring,
the promised hope still shines.
And the reaver beholds
the dawn-born chosen's gaze,
transforming the darkness into light.

When the battle is lost,
through quake-tossed battlefields unwitting
the seasoned legions march,
but the sentinel flees
with once-proud royalty,
protecting devotion's fragile heart.

When the ending draws near,
with ice-locked stars unmoving,
the threefold threats await,
and the herald proclaims,
in war-wrecked misery,
announcing the dying of an age.

—As written by Elliandreth of Orishaar, c. −17,600 DR

FORGOTTEN REALMS®

THE SUNDERING

THE COMPANIONS
R.A. Salvatore

THE GODBORN
Paul S. Kemp

THE ADVERSARY
Erin M. Evans

THE REAVER
Richard Lee Byers

THE SENTINEL
Troy Denning

THE HERALD
Ed Greenwood

FORGOTTEN REALMS

ED GREENWOOD
THE HERALD

FORGOTTEN REALMS®

THE
SUNDERING

Book
VI

THE HERALD

©2014 Wizards of the Coast LLC.

Published by Wizards of the Coast LLC. Manufactured by: Hasbro SA, Rue Emile-Boéchat 31, 2800 Delémont, CH. Represented by: Hasbro Europe, 4 The Square, Stockley Park, Uxbridge, Middlesex, UB11 1ET, UK.

Printed in the U.S.A.

Prophecy by: James Wyatt
Cartography by: Mike Schley
Cover art by: Tyler Jacobson
First Printing: June 2014

9 8 7 6 5 4 3 2 1

ISBN: 978-0-7869-6460-4
ISBN: 978-0-7869-6549-6 (ebook)
620A4360000001 EN

Cataloging-in-Publication data is on file with the Library of Congress

Contact Us at Wizards.com/CustomerService
Wizards of the Coast LLC, PO Box 707, Renton, WA 98057-0707, USA
USA & Canada: (800) 324-6496 or (425) 204-8069
Europe: +32(0) 70 233 277

Visit our website at **www.dungeonsanddragons.com**

For Lindsay Cote
Who fits well a tale of standing up for what is right
And enduring and persevering when all is in tumult
To come trudging out the other side into a better world.

THE HERALD

And when morning mists lift over the bloody field
where the vultures and gorcraws have come to feed,
then comes the herald, tabard all bright, revealed
that life go on, with victor and vanquished decreed.

—from "Comes the Herald," a ballad by Tethra Tantalusk,
Bard of Triel, composed circa the Year of the Haunting.

CHAPTER 1

The Triumph of Night

"THE NIGHTS ARE GROWING LONGER, AND BETIMES THE EARTH shakes!" young Lady Wyrmwood hissed, leaning forward in her excitement and granting the table a splendid view of the six linked silver dragons arrayed on fine chains across her décolletage. "What does it *mean*? Are we all *doomed*?"

The younger nobles around the table leaned forward in shared excitement, but several older ones rolled their eyes or muttered disparagements.

"Doomed, doomed—always doomed!" gray-haired Lord Garonder Illance remarked. "We've been 'doomed' since before I was born. Thankfully, the gods work slowly. Even more slowly than unsupervised servants."

Lady Wyrmwood regarded him with finely honed scorn. "Dismiss my views at your peril, Lord Jaded Seen-All! Things are *happening* beyond these walls, outside our fair city—things that could well shake every last high castle in all the world! The nights *are* growing longer, believe you me!"

An elder lord at another table turned in his high-backed chair with a sigh of exasperation. He harrumphed to indicate his minor embarrassment at knowingly breaching etiquette—even in a club like this one, open to all with coin enough to pay ruinous prices for platter and goblet—it was customary amongst well-bred highborn to give no sign of having overheard something not addressed to them. And then he growled, "Of *course* things are happening beyond these walls; we're at war again! I'd have thought you might have noticed! Aye, it's Sembia, and it's *always* Sembia, but the battles do affect the prices of everything, which is to say the fortunes of us all.

"And, aye, the nights are indeed getting longer. Yet strange things happen in the world every day; the lengthening nights may have nothing at all to do with the wild news that's been reaching us—or even the real troubles. Still less do longer nights mean any sort of inevitable 'doom.' The ground-shakings have all but stopped, and they mean volcanoes erupting, not gods walking!

"All of this gloom-talk reminds me of the fights in my youth among the high priests of this city, over what certain movements of the stars meant. Each one seemed convinced the stars 'proved' that *their* deity was going to triumph over the others. And yet, where are we now? No god has triumphed over all others, and the stars still move. So please, let us hear less of inevitable doom!"

"What? Stars *move*?" A young lordling frowned in disbelief from a table at the back of the room. His father shot him a look of contempt.

In the darkest corner of this exclusive upper room in the Memories of Queen Fee, the most fashionable and expensive club of all the clubs that overlooked the great Promenade in Suzail, the battered mountain of a man known as Mirt hid his rising interest behind a large and nigh empty goblet. If there was one thing apt to make nobles of Cormyr fall abruptly silent, it was being reminded that commoners—or worse, outlanders—were present and listening to them.

And if there was one good reason why a man who should have been dead a century ago, who'd been a lord himself in a different time and place, would spend far too much coin to drink with this lot of bores and snide highnoses, it was to overhear interesting things. Things that could be turned to his advantage.

Things that made Mirt feel as if there was any sort of reason to go on living at all, in this unfamiliar and darkening world.

Literally darkening. The night seemed on the verge of engulfing all, war erupted across the lands, and each day brought news of new strangeness. Stars fell from the sky; folks proclaimed themselves Chosen of this god and that, and gathered armed hosts to battle other self-proclaimed Chosen; and monsters boldly stalked farm fields and high streets night and day—*pah*.

'Twas like a bad dream.

But enough, the nobles were still gabbling. Of course.

"Lord Haelrood," young Lady Wyrmwood was loudly telling the room, "I *gladly* accept your correction, for does not your care for this matter—your noticing the lengthening nights, and thinking on what it might mean—ride muster to my *point*? Grim portents are everywhere, the world around us darkens, and some great reckoning is at hand!"

"Great reckoning? I had *no* idea the Wyrmwoods had been dodging the royal tax takers," Lord Harflame commented mockingly, from behind the decanters of fine Tethyrian rubyfire he'd been steadily emptying all evening. Club rules forbade doxies from entering the upper rooms, so rather than cradling a playpretty in either arm, he'd brought a perfumed glove from each of the two waiting for him, and perched them atop the decanters as boastful trophies for all to see. "A *great* reckoning coming, indeed!"

"Display not your ill breeding further, sirrah!" Lady Wyrmwood spat. "I speak in all solemnity, caring for fair Cormyr above all—and we *are* at war, are we not? Or did you hide off in the countryside and do nothing to defend Suzail?—but beyond our borders, mindful of the fate of the vast world that cradles us all! Mock me not!"

"Ah, but you offer such a splendid—dare I say 'juicy'?—target, my *good* lady—"

"Harflame, *enough*," old Lady Rowanmantle snapped, secure in the weight of her years and the formidable reputation she'd built over those many seasons. "What you dare or do not dare, and whether Lady Wyrmwood is correct or not, are alike neither here nor there. Your dares are your own amusements and follies entirely, but she fears for the future of our realm—and with good reason.

"War ravages our land once more, and I hear Cormyrean fights Cormyrean—something that even a *child*—if not a noble lord—must see can have no good ending for Cormyr. Moreover, since you seem for some inexplicable reason to need the reminder, 'tis the duty of nobility to ponder and fear for the future of their land, for that *is* their responsibility and their daily business. Or should be. As *true* nobles well know."

Silence fell in the wake of that biting rebuke, and Harflame went pale and thin lipped. He sat back and reached for one of his decanters.

"Our realm has troubles and tumult enough," another old lord muttered, "but wars are raging everywhere, on our soil included. We *should* worry. The lass speaks truth."

One of the young ladies sitting with Lady Wyrmwood burst out eagerly, her eyes large and dancing in her fervor to be a part—at last!—of important matters, "Fabled Myth Drannor stands besieged! And there's talk that gods long thought dead and gone are awakening! And Chosen—or folk believing they are Chosen, or base pretenders claiming to be Chosen, and those are all one when it comes to the damage done—of every deity, demigod, and half-forgotten place spirit are everywhere, toppling thrones and raising armies and murdering those who stand against them, or whose gold or fancy hats they covet."

"A bad time," Haelrood agreed heavily. "A bad time indeed."

THE HERALD

Lord Snelgarth slammed down his twentieth empty goblet of the evening and snorted, "*I* think it all began when some sages started talking of the World Tree, and were allowed to go on doing so. Madness, sheer madness. Give me the Great Wheel, and I know where I stand. Give me order, and the rule of kings, and laws and good roads and warm indoor privies—"

"And clean water," Lady Rowanmantle put in firmly.

"*And* clean water, aye, Lady, well said, so long as servants and peasants are taught to *use* it occasionally, upon their own persons—and I can live out my life content, worrying myself over the trifles my very safety gives me the luxury to raise into grave concerns. Caring about gossip and fripperies, secure in the knowledge that the Realms is as safe as it can ever be, life solid and sure for most, and peace preferred to war by sane folk. Not this 'world all afire' stuff. I'm too old for it."

A darkly handsome stranger who'd just strolled into the room, a goblet and a sealed flask of the choicest Shaldaunsan glimmerfire in his hand, nodded at Snelgarth and murmured, "Me, too."

Various nobles looked up at the sound of that smoothly cultured, purring, unfamiliar voice, but—not recognizing the face, and so judging the man an outlander—made no reply.

Into the resulting silence, as he unhurriedly crossed the room, the newcomer added, "Yet some old ways still hold true now as Marpenoth begins in this Year of the Rune Lords Triumphant—and just who are *they*, now? Feuds, hatreds, and the desire for revenge keep many of those of elder years alive and active rather than sinking into their dotage, as such things always have."

"True," Mirt granted, waving a hand at the empty chair across his table, as the man reached the back wall and discovered no handy vacant seats. "And which lord are you?"

9

"Manshoon," the darkly handsome man replied quietly, dropping into the proffered chair and using a thumbnail to unseal the glimmerfire with the ease of long practice. "Once, I was High Lord of Zhentil Keep. Just as you were once a Lord of Waterdeep, Old Wolf."

Mirt's eyes narrowed. "Now *that's* a name I've not been called in many a year . . ."

Manshoon shrugged. "Old glory, older secrets. Yet you tarry here, in this pretty kingdom of knights in shining armor, great green forests, and foolheaded nobles. Why?"

"'Tis as pleasant a place to die as any, and the lasses are passing fair."

"I'd noticed you partaking of their company, yes," the darkly handsome man almost purred, over his goblet of glimmerfire. "Yet wolves can never content themselves with mere dalliance. Surely you have greater concerns."

It was Mirt's turn to shrug. "Don't we all? Or pretend to, to justify our idleness? What concerns you, that you have time enough to listen to idle nobles prate and blow wind?"

"The Chosen of the gods concern me, as it happens. Specifically, that they now seem as abundant as wild-breeding rabbits, underfoot everywhere, all running about in confusion—save those who're being rounded up and imprisoned."

Mirt's eyes narrowed. "Oh? By whom?"

"A god who wants to feed on their power, of course," Manshoon replied. "The question is, which one? Obvious candidates leap to mind, but I like to be sure."

"And the gods aren't talking to you these days?"

"The mantle of Chosen is one I've never accepted."

Mirt shrugged again. "Most of us never even receive such an offer."

Manshoon sipped glimmerfire. "Do shepherds ennoble their sheep?" He set his goblet aside, and added, "I confess to be harboring

10

growing curiosity as to your own standing, Old Wolf. Do you tarry here because someone divine asked you to? Are *you* a Chosen?"

Mirt smiled thinly. "Old wolves never tell."

Manshoon sighed. "Yet you just have, haven't you? Ah, but deeds press and time races on." He rose, drained his goblet, and set it down beside the flask. "Enjoy," he said, turning away. "I must see a goddess, about the fate of a world."

Mirt lifted bushy eyebrows. "What—again? What a *dashing* life you lead!"

The onetime lord of Zhentil Keep threw a scowl back over his shoulder, and was gone.

Mirt regarded the glimmerfire calmly, and resolved to take it with him, not touching a drop, and hurl it into a foundry fire. When the smiths were at a safe distance, of course.

The Manshoons of this world, he thought, are capable of *anything*.

Amarune heard the old man's approach long before she saw him, in the damp, deep forest: slow and careful but heavy footfalls. Nor were his the only footfalls she could hear.

There were others out there in the thick stands of trees, quieter than he was—and moving cautiously closer.

She shot a swift glance back into the tomb behind her to see if her companions had heard.

One wise old eye met hers just long enough to wordlessly tell her they had. Yet they kept to their work, seemingly unconcerned, so Rune kept to hers.

Not that she turned her back on the forest for an instant.

She'd thought nothing more dangerous than deer would disturb them here in this small but forgotten forest tucked into the rolling hills southeast across the Chionthar from Elturel. Too small to even be shown on most maps, and old and tangled and untouched by woodcutters. Well, so much for her judgment.

The old man came into view at last, ducking out from behind the trunks of trees as fleetingly as he could until he climbed the last leaf-covered ridge and bobbed up into the open.

At first, she pretended not to notice him, though anyone not deaf would have heard his coming, this close at hand. Heavy boots stalking with care through the rotting leaves, old stones, and dry dead ferns, not more than a dozen strides away.

She cast one swift glance in his direction through the fall of an errant lock of hair that always escaped her browband, just to make sure he carried no bow.

There was no sign of one, so she returned her attention to her work, not looking up again.

After all, he was just one man, and she could hear the wheeze in his breathing—and no matter how many others were skulking unseen out in the trees, the tomb had thick stone walls girt with much earth and gnarled tree roots, and only this one door.

Rune kept on scraping away the muck of centuries with her trowel. Gods, but small furry forest things shat a lot. And went to a lot of trouble to gnaw twigs and weave them into nests that—

"Well met."

The old man's greeting was flat and unfriendly. The sort of "Well met" a warrior tosses before him like a gauntlet, in challenge. He might as well have bluntly demanded to know her name and what she was doing—

"Who are you, and what's your business? Here in the tomb of a wizard dead these three centuries?"

Rune straightened slowly to face the man, brushing her hair back from her face. Her two companions kept right on with their cleaning, bent over in their respective dark corners of Ralaskoun's crypt. Leaving this to her.

"Tennarra," she replied, giving the name she usually used when dealing with strangers. "I am, as you can see, cleaning."

The old face was unfamiliar, adorned with old scars, and more unfriendly than ever. "Aye, girl, but *why*? Most folk leave wizards' tombs well alone. Are you a tomb robber? Or one of those who seek to raise the dead?"

Rune gave him a frown back. "Neither. I work to cleanse tombs and bless them, so the dead won't rise and walk as liches."

The old man nodded. "Wizards itch to walk, aye. But they don't need help. Come out of there."

He wore homespun, and over it a leather jack that had once been part of some modest warrior's war harness. A belt knife and a short sword rode at his belt. He was burly, and had hands as hard as his face, but no gauntlets, and nothing drawn and ready.

"Come away *now*," he snapped, stalking closer. Rune could hear other footfalls in the forest now, to her left and right.

So could her two bent-over companions; she could tell from momentary pauses as they turned their heads to listen.

Rune sighed and drew back into the crypt. Away from its mouth, where she could be rushed from either flank or easily shot down with arrows. Into the damp, musty darkness of the unlit stone room with its plain, high stone-block casket, like the altars in many a way shrine.

"I said come out of there!" the old man snarled, drawing his sword.

Amarune backed along the casket, moving to her left. "The wizard Ralaskoun never married, and died childless. He can have no kin. So by what right do you tell me what to do and not to do, old man? Who are *you*?"

The old man ignored her question, advancing on her slowly. He'd taken but three slow, menacing steps when five men waving swords suddenly burst into view, three rushing out of the trees and bushes behind him to charge straight at Rune, and one coming around either front corner of the crypt to race along its walls right at her.

"How many?" one snapped at the old man, as he sprinted past.

"Her and two feeble old women behind her, inside," the old man called, as the first swordsman reached Amarune—and hacked at her face viciously.

She sprang back, flicking her trowel full of twigs and old dirt into his face, and swept out her dagger. Trowel and dagger were feeble defenses against a broadsword, but—daggers came whirling past her ears out of the crypt behind her like darting wasps, and the swordsman thrusting ruthlessly at her was suddenly shrieking and clutching at his face.

Which meant he left his throat unprotected.

Amarune rushed forward to cut it open, but another dagger flashed past her arm from behind her and got there first.

Gurgling and spurting gore, the hilt jutting from under his chin, the swordsman sagged back into another rushing up right behind him, into a brief, stumbling collision. More swordsmen were heading the other way, rushing around the massive stone casket in the other direction—to promptly crash to their knees, gurgling and clutching their throats, though the flying daggers had come nowhere near them.

The foremost swordsman had fallen; Rune watched the second go down with the swarm of daggers stabbing at his head from all directions.

Beyond them, the old man had planted his sword point down in the trampled ferns, and was raising his hands to work magic.

Rune drew back her trowel for a throw, but he, too, was suddenly clutching at his throat and struggling to breathe, his eyes and then cheeks bulging as his face slowly went purple—and he toppled like a felled tree.

Silence fell. Rune trotted swiftly around the wizard's casket to make sure all of their assailants were down. They were—and by the time she'd returned to the mouth of the tomb with the crone who'd been working on that side of the crypt, the other crone was standing in it, head lowered in concentration and hands spread.

They stopped and waited. It wasn't long before the first crone's head rose, eyes opened, and hands fell. "No one with a thinking mind near. Hold silence, though."

She turned to look at the other crone. They met each other's eyes, nodded, and lifted their arms in smooth unison like two tavern dancers embracing phantom lovers on a stage, both shaping empty air as if caressing it. Then they murmured wordless whispers of concentration and effort . . . and the forest in front of the tomb seemed to fade away beneath sudden, swift-spreading mist.

Mist that was neither damp nor clinging, but tinged with a luminous blue radiance. Mist that made Amarune's hair stand on end all over her body. Including up her nose.

Fighting down the urge to sneeze, she asked, "I recognized the war-daggers spell, but El, what did *you* do to them?"

"A very old and ruthless spell. Expands the tongue swiftly, and chokes its victim. Doesn't work on most mages these days, as the incantations they speak linger just enough to guard their tongues against such meddling. Everyone else, though . . ."

That crone had straightened to become a white-bearded, beak-nosed old man, gaunt and sharp eyed. The other became a tall, shapely woman with long, flowing silver hair that moved restlessly around her shoulders as if stirred by many breezes, or as if each tress had a snakelike mind of its own.

The man was Elminster, the ancient and infamous Sage of Shadowdale, and the woman was Storm Silverhand, the legendary hearth mother of the Harpers. Archmage and harpist, both fabled

Chosen of Mystra. Traveling companions many a novice mage would not have dared to even approach.

Nor tarry within half a realm of.

Rune smiled a trifle bitterly. For her part, she hardly dared step out of their sight, for fear some fell foe watching them from afar would pounce on her and rend her with claws or spells or magic before she could draw breath to scream.

She'd been helping them as an unskilled laborer helps master crafters, handing them what they needed, cleaning up in their wake, and doing grunt work. Dirty dishes, for instance. She'd seen a lot of those, these past three tendays, as they trudged the backlands, from tomb to tomb and ruin to ruin, from overgrown and forgotten altar to hilltop way cairn. A young woman and two feeble old crones, ostensibly cleansing and blessing old graves to prevent undead from arising from the earth—but in truth, rebuilding the Weave.

It was like a vast and invisible web or intricate tapestry, its strands torn and snarled, whipping restlessly in the shifting winds and in need of anchoring.

Which was what they were doing: crafting new strands of force to bind the Weave to the few wards that had survived the ravages of the Spellplague, and repairing others that could be salvaged until they could serve as anchors. This tomb was one of a handful of unscathed wardings. Mystra or no Mystra, war or fresh spellstorms or wrathful Chosen or not, a stronger Weave meant a stronger world in the time ahead.

This mist now hiding the forest was no ground fog born of dampness nor weather magic, but something El and Storm had just spun from the wards of Ralaskoun's tomb to hide them from anyone magically spying from afar.

"Come back into the shadows," Storm bade Amarune. "We must take a look at our enthusiastic would-be murderers."

"Brigands?"

El shrugged. "Those three, perhaps. But the old man who confronted ye, and this last of the sword swingers, here . . ."

He spread his hands in a way Rune knew was calling on the Weave to dispel all enchantments, stripping away disguises as well as protections and contingencies.

Looking down at the result, he nodded grimly.

"Shadovar. Minor arcanists, to be sure, among the least of Thultanthar. Thine own magic outstrips theirs. Possibly they sought magic in this tomb, and wanted no one else getting to it first."

"Or possibly, they were hunting us," Rune said quietly.

Elminster shrugged dismissively, but Storm looked past him at Rune and nodded, slowly and silently.

"This is not the first time these last few months Shadovar have been observed seeking magic," the Old Mage murmured. "I wonder what they want it for?"

"Shar's preparing her mortal armies to conquer all they can, and destroy what they cannot?" Storm hazarded.

Elminster sighed. "She's been doing little else these last few centuries." He shook his head. "Would that more of the gods would take up some *hobbies* . . ."

He sighed again, looked around the dark tomb, and announced briskly, "We, however, still have *our* work to do. So we can move on to Heatherhill and see what's left of Galmark Tower. Good wards it had, back when Vangerdahast was my 'prentice."

"El," Storm said gently, "we won't be able to do this Weave work in hiding for much longer. Things *are* getting worse across the Realms, not better. If half the gossip we hear is true, Chosen—or those who proclaim themselves Chosen, however deluded they may be—are being murdered as casually and as often as men stamp on cockroaches . . . and all too many of their slayers kill in the name of this god or that. All too often, Shar."

17

El grunted. "Mayhap, bu—"

He broke off midword and crouched down hastily. Amarune turned to peer at him, startled, and saw that he was hiding his face in his hands. Hands that were returning to the knobble-jointed and age-spotted look they'd had when he was playing crone. Storm was resuming her crone shape just as swiftly.

The light in the tomb was changing. Rune turned to stare at the mist—and discovered it gone, the forest back at her feet again.

The two bent old crones scuttled back to the corners of the crypt, wheezing and humming, to resume cleaning as if they'd never stopped.

Amarune went from startled to frightened in one chill instant, realizing what she'd just witnessed.

Someone from afar had just magically turned off the wards, so as to see and hear everything inside the tomb.

"Who—?" she started to whisper, then hastily swallowed her words, and asked the rest of them to herself, in the silence of her own thoughts.

Who has the power to do that?

She stared at the crone she knew was Elminster. Just for a moment, one eye met hers—and one hunched shoulder lifted and then fell again, in a shrug.

Elminster didn't know. And dared not try to find out.

Rune stared into the depths of the forest for a moment, feeling very alone and yet very watched. By unseen, unfriendly eyes.

Then she drew in a long, shuddering breath and bent to use her trowel to collect all the dirt and twigs she'd flung in the face of the man who was lying, very dead, right beside her.

She tried not to look at him. Or the second dead swordsman, beyond him.

Not that avoiding looking at things made them go away.

Even young children knew that.

Did archmages?

18

CHAPTER 2

A Darkness in Thultanthar

EYES OF FLAT AND BALEFUL PLATINUM REGARDED THE MAN BELOW the dais coldly. "Am I understood?"

"Y-yes, Most High."

"Good. Go."

The man went.

Telamont Tanthul, Most High of Thultanthar, suppressed a sigh. He was getting tired.

And these days, when he grew weary, his temper shortened.

He was getting old.

His lips thinned at the thought, causing the next Shadovar agent marching into the chamber to hesitate, measured footfalls faltering momentarily.

Telamont let his mouth go calm, forcing himself to *almost* smile, and stared the man down, keeping his face expressionless.

The agent went pale, but kept coming.

Telamont quelled another sigh. He had ordered these reports, but had now heard enough of them in unbroken succession to grow weary indeed—and the agents yet waiting to make theirs were still lined up clear across the city from the other side of that door. The door of his—well, call it what it was, an audience chamber.

An overly formal place he seldom used, but that suited his purposes just now. A great long and high chamber sheathed in gleaming white marble, that at its rear rose to a dais where a high-backed seat fashioned of one great piece of gleaming black obsidian stood facing the door. A huge bare metal table flanked the throne on the right, and the *tammaneth* rod floated upright in the air in the corner far behind to its left.

Telamont's only amusement of the long day had been watching each pair of eyes—those of every Shadovar agent entering the room to make their report—dart to the great black rod, hurriedly look away from it, and then try to keep their gazes locked on him.

They all wanted to know what it was.

What it was, was a great black rod—studded down its length with black spheres enclosing empty, dark glass globes—that floated vertically off the floor in that corner.

That was all they needed to know about it, for now. As for the rest, let them speculate. And fear.

Fear was a handle that moved many men.

Even the best agents of Thultanthar. Who were, after all, men. Of greater lineage and learning than the lower, coarser rabble of Sembia and Cormyr and the lands beyond they might be, but underneath . . . still human. And beneath all airs and graces, humans were still clever beasts. Talking herd animals.

Witness this long queue. Shadovar agents filing in, one at a time, for an audience with their Most High. They'd come rushing back to report their successes in murdering all sorts of Chosen, across the world, at his command.

A herd, none quite daring to be first—but frantic not to be last once they knew one of their fellows had returned to Thultanthar.

Telamont spread his hand to the latest arrival, silently gesturing for the man to speak.

He cared little about the details. Even if he'd gone hunting himself, or sent someone whose competence he could truly trust, like Aglarel, some Chosen would escape. Others would be inspired to think and call themselves Chosen for the first time, in days yet to come. A few would even have real standing, however paltry, in the eyes of some god or other.

Nor would any of this long line of worms dare to honestly tell their Most High how many Chosen had eluded them, or why.

He was most interested not in their achievements, but in the alacrity of their obedience, for busy Shadovar are Shadovar too enwrapped in their work to accomplish elaborate treacheries.

He asked this latest one the same question he'd asked them all, and received the same answer. "Oh, no, Most High, I have been most careful to adhere to your clear command, and have *not* tried to work any magic that touched another's mind, oh, no."

Telamont believed him.

All of the agents, in turn, had assured him of that.

His memory told him this one's name was Laerekel, and that he was one of Thultanthar's better agents. Diligent and loyal—to a Most High who showed no sign of weakness, at least. Show no weakness, yet display not your every weapon, as the old saying put it.

Telamont knew well that his keenest weapon was his memory. Without it, he'd have fallen from his high place centuries ago. Dragged down by those waiting for the chance.

Yet none who'd tried had lasted long enough to succeed, or try a second time.

He recalled what he wanted Laerekel to do next, crisply gave the man those orders, and dismissed him, as he had all the previous agents.

It took him some minutes, sitting alone on his throne, facing the open doors and pondering darker matters, to realize Laerekel had been the last agent of the day.

At *last*. He stood up, gestured to the guards to close the great double doors, and turned away.

Not that he would trust them. He never did.

Where he was headed was hidden behind two successive sets of doors he'd close and seal himself, with spells few of the mightiest arcanists of this city could breach, even with much time and trouble.

He did not want to be disturbed.

The inscription was pitted with age, but had been graven deeply enough that the words could yet be read: *Handramar Ralaskoun*.

Above the wizard's name was a sigil unfamiliar to Amarune. Ralaskoun's own. Below it was a rune she'd become familiar with this past year: the sealing rune that kept magic pent in and the dead at rest, the one she privately thought looked like three entwined and amorous snakes.

Rune used an improvised brush made of tufts of dead pine needles to finish cleaning out the inscription, not looking up when the bent back of the hunched-over crone who was Storm came swaying up to her.

Then brushed against her.

Rune tried not to stiffen as Storm's touch sent magic crawling through her, but knew she'd failed. So she feigned a coughing fit instead, as Storm's clear, sharp, and cool thoughts lanced into her mind.

This mindlink magic will enable us to converse by thought, so long as we keep close together. Say nothing *that will betray who we really are. We'll depart this place soon.*

Rune almost nodded, but caught herself just in time. What shook her was not Storm's words, but the fear that flared clear and cold behind them.

She hadn't known that, after all her centuries, Storm could still feel that afraid.

The Most High of Thultanthar stood in the last and innermost room of his sanctum, dim and dark and private. The room he had just sealed himself in.

With every step away from the dying fire of the seal he'd just cast on the last door, the floor faded under his boots, and the darkness grew.

This most secluded of his spellcasting chambers was as dark as the void, and almost as cold. Telamont could feel its chill stealing into him as he strode on, seeking the place where the floor would be entirely gone, and it would seem as if he was floating.

The void swallowed echoes, so they came back strangely, and then muted, then not at all. When he reached the right spot, he waited, feeling the cold slowly and silently claim him, visualizing a serene and beautiful feminine face of dark beauty, whose eyes were utter pits of darkness.

My Chosen, the familiar whisper came to him, from everywhere around yet so close it seemed he could feel her icy breath in his ear, *have you completed the task I set you?*

"Which one?" he dared to ask.

He did not quite dare to add the bitter thought that flared in him then: my sons are not endless in number.

Had he dared, he suspected the Mistress of the Night would merely command him to sire and rear more, orders that would come wreathed in cruel laughter.

One more task, that would be, among the many that continued, both large and small. The one that had recently consumed most of his time was the hunting and slaying of Chosen. All Chosen but

Shar's own—especially the Chosen of Mystra—were to be destroyed so her ambition to finally command and reshape the Weave in her image could unfold unchecked.

Is the training of your special agents complete? Are they ready?

Shar did not sound angry, merely eager.

Telamont swallowed despite himself. He hadn't realized how strong relief would feel, flooding through him. "I trained five. Doing so slew one; another engaged in treacheries and was eliminated; a third was found lacking and again was destroyed—but two are ready."

Good. Use them as I have commanded. You are to leave the slaying of Chosen to the underlings you have already set to the work, and take up the task of seizing and draining the mythal of Myth Drannor and the mighty wards of Candlekeep. You shall use the power they yield up to gain control of the nascent Weave, so I can transform it into a new and more powerful Shadow Weave.

Telamont managed a smile. "To give You dominion over magic everywhere."

Of course, Shar replied, and was gone, leaving him falling through the icy void.

The tomb was somewhere behind them in the deep, trackless forest. At least seven ridges back . . . or was it eight?

Rune helped the two bent, waddling old crones on, over tree roots and through the slimy mats of dead leaves between. They trudged with slow and grunting care through the trees, setting many small unseen things to scurrying away into hiding behind the moss-girt trunks and the fallen, toadstool-infested hulks of long-fallen duskwoods and felsul.

El, she dared think at the noisier of the two old women with her, *who are we hiding from?*

The Sage of Shadowdale sighed heavily. His reply, when it came, was grim.

Neither Storm nor I have any idea who compelled the wards from afar—but whoever did so has more power than either of us possesses.

We want to get to cover. Quickly. Storm's thought was just as gloomy. They *were* upset.

Rune suppressed a shiver, and helped them hasten on. Slowly.

Telamont suppressed a shiver. He *still* felt cold.

The bone-deep chill took longer to leave him every time.

The doors of the audience chamber were closed, so he'd made the dais itself glow with enough amber radiance to let the two men standing before Telamont see their Most High as more than the deepest shadow, like a dark flame on the throne of black glass.

It suited him for those summoned before him to see his face and feel his power.

They faced him impassively, all dark and slender menace. Silent and still, as watchful as two cold-eyed snakes.

Maerandor and Helgore, the two agents he'd trained, wizards he'd plucked from youthful ambition and raised right past the ranks of the arcanists, forging them personally—and separately— into blades as deadly as he could manage in the far too little time he'd been given.

Still, they would have to do. Time waited not even for the gods, despite what those deluded fools who called themselves "chronomancers" were wont to believe.

He watched them give the *tammaneth* rod the briefest of curious glances, then fix their gazes on him. He smiled inwardly.

Curiosity is a razor-sharp blade with two edges and no hilt. It slices us even as we wield it, yet we cannot resist swinging something so sharp.

He passed his hand casually over a particular spot on the left arm of the throne, causing the secret way in the wall to the left of him to slide open, and watched them both start to look in that direction, then school themselves to keep their gazes on him.

Better and better. He'd forged them well.

He locked eyes with Maerandor and ordered crisply, "Depart at once for Candlekeep. Follow the plan; it stands unchanged."

Then he turned to Helgore, and commanded, "To Myth Drannor. You know what you are to do."

He looked meaningfully at the way he'd just opened. Turning from him and seeing the great doors they'd come in by standing closed, they took the hint and strode across the room, departing by that secret way.

He passed his hand over the arm of the throne again, closing the way behind them, and permitted himself a sigh.

Then rose in haste, fighting down another shiver.

Age was riding him down at last.

Was it time to become even less human, and so cheat the ravages of the passing years?

Would he be able to snatch the time it would take for the exacting, painstaking process of becoming a shadow lich, in this spreading chaos and tumult? Or did she have other ideas?

Perhaps he should pursue some of the alternatives. What sort of a life did a floating skull enjoy? Skinless, bodiless, reduced to little more than malice and sinister whisperings . . .

How far from that am I right now, really?

Those dark thoughts took him down from the dais and, striding unhurriedly, to the great double doors. His will made them swing open at his approach, heavily but in velvet silence.

His will then made his staff appear out of nowhere in his hand as he walked.

Well, at least *some* things still obeyed him without pause or question.

Aglarel was waiting for him just outside the doors. Of course.

Aglarel, tallest of his sons and bareheaded but resplendent in his obsidian armor, was the commander of the Most High's personal bodyguard—and the closest thing to a trusted friend in Telamont's life for too many years to count now.

He fell into step a careful half stride behind Telamont, as usual, the faintly purple crackling of his armor's ward surrounding Telamont's own invisible mantle. Nothing short of a falling spire from one of Thultanthar's loftiest towers should be able to reach the Most High through their combined wardings.

Not that anything in this city had dared to try, for some time.

Yet there would come another attempt someday. One always did.

Aglarel did not ask where they were heading. Wherever his father desired to go, he would walk escort unless ordered away.

Truth to tell, Telamont enjoyed his company.

"You sent your two new wizards off on their first assignments?" Aglarel asked casually.

"Yes," Telamont told him flatly.

No more words passed between them as they walked the length of the long and deserted forehall. Although they were alone, Aglarel tirelessly peered this way and that seeking trouble, as was his habit.

They came out into the round reception hall with its lofty and magnificent vaulted ceiling, where guards stood at attention, carefully impassive. Telamont turned left.

"You're not going to tell me what those missions are, are you?" Aglarel asked calmly.

"Not yet," Telamont replied, his tone matching his son's.

Together they strode through a hall of gloom and shadows where their footfalls echoed as if across great distances, and there were no guards. Beyond themselves, there was no one at all.

They proceeded in calm silence through an archway, to emerge into a room lit by the soft, steady purple glow of magic, and crossed it to another archway opening into deeper darkness.

They were halfway down the long passageway beyond, walking in darkness no mere human could have navigated through, when Aglarel ventured, "In order to protect you properly, Father, I would like to know the reason behind your sudden prohibition on using magic that attacks minds, or contacts them at all. Working blind is . . . unsettling. And dangerous."

"So is suffering damage to our own minds, whenever we use such magics," Telamont replied. "And that's what recently began to occur. If you try to read minds a dozen times before nightfall, you'll go to bed a far lesser arcanist than you were this morning."

"Who's behind this?" Aglarel's voice was ever so slightly sharper. "Surely we should all know everything we can learn about such a peril, so as to deal with it swiftly, before all else."

Telamont looked at him. "Have you never wondered why for so long I forbade all attempts to bring Hadrhune and your brothers back from death?"

"I presumed it was to avoid any chance of those who make undead their thralls—such as the one called Larloch, and Szass Tam of Thay—extending their influence among us. I take it I was wrong."

"You were right, but a new reason has been added to that. What most call the Spellplague, this continuing chaos of the collapsing Weave, does not mean the Weave is dead. Holy Shar would not seek its capture, were that so. Lesser wielders of magic than we went mad, or had their brains literally melt or explode, when the Spellplague began. Those greater wielders of the Art who still live are far less sane than they were. And now, lurking in the Weave, are fell sentiences that prey on us—on all of Shade—when we work magic that contacts other minds. For a time, Hadrhune was one of these lurkers. They yet include some of your fallen brothers and rival arcanists, of this city and others."

"They died, and yet still live?"

"Their minds are caught in the Weave. They seek to regain full life. They need more life-force, depth of will, and scope of mind to forcibly take over a capable living person. Their best road to doing so is to plunder minds they know. So they wait for us—and when we work those sorts of magic, we lay ourselves open to them, and they stealthily rob our minds of some power, every time. It's happened to you. To me. To most of your brothers, perhaps all."

Aglarel stopped, mouth agape. "How is this *possible?*"

Telamont shrugged. "None can ever fully understand the Art. Yet when I seek to compel the Weave, to conquer it locally and claim it for Shar, it resists me as it always has. Which means Mystra yet survives, or enough of her Chosen, to offer resistance."

Aglarel's face hardened. "Which is why they must all die," he snapped. "More than that—be utterly destroyed, minds shattered and severed from the Weave. I am going to be so bold as to guess you have sent your two agents to bring us closer to that goal."

"So much is obvious," Telamont replied. He spun around to stare into Aglarel's silver eyes, their noses almost touching. "I tolerate all the intrigues, petty treason, and misbehavior of your brothers and lesser citizens of our city so long as they stray not from that goal. Every last creature of Mystra, and the vestige of that goddess herself, must perish utterly. We cannot rule this world, else. And in time to come, through patient achievement that ruins not the prize we seek to claim, rule it all the worthy among us *shall*."

That last word was said with icy firmness, ere the Most High turned on his heel and strode on.

"The worthy among us," Aglarel muttered, lengthening his stride to catch up to his father.

"Tell me, how many of us are worthy?"

"All too few," the High Prince of Shade replied curtly. "It's why I went on siring sons."

CHAPTER 3

The Silent Harp

I CAN'T *BELIEVE*," RUNE PANTED, AS THE TWO THOUSANDTH BRAMBLE of the day whipped across her face, drawing yet more blood, "anyone has passed this way in the last generation or so. *Owww.*"

Dry and dead thorncanes crackled as she forced her way through them, marveling again at the lithe grace of the silver-haired bard ahead of her, whose shapely behind and muscled back she'd been rather grimly following for what seemed a very long afternoon. Of course, when your hair can reach out like a dozen strong arms to pull branches, vines, and brambles apart, it's a lot easier to travel thick, trackless wilderland woods in the unmapped beyond, to be sure . . .

"Not long now," Elminster murmured from right behind her. They were far from Elturel, in a forest reached through an ancient portal Amarune couldn't have found again if she'd wanted to. This forest was thinner and higher than the one that held Ralaskoun's tomb—which was seven days behind them now—on rocky and rising ground.

They'd been climbing higher for some time, and right then were ascending a steep, lightly forested slope where loose stones underfoot were only outnumbered by growing things that bristled with sharp thorns. Rune was very glad she'd worn thigh-high boots, or her legs

31

would have looked as if she'd fought a long and hard battle against halfling children armed with thornsticks.

The air around her smelled of sharp spices she couldn't name that were probably drifting from the seedpods they'd been disturbing. There was nothing stealthy about their crashing progress, but their surroundings certainly seemed remote and overgrown, and, well, forlorn.

Storm came out into a small glade floored in thick moss, beneath the shade of some gnarled hurthar trees. Ahead, the soft green carpet underfoot ended and bare rock thrust up from the earth into a tumbled cliff of sorts, rising out of sight. Before them, as Rune and El joined the bard, in a cleft between two thrusting tongues of ancient rock, stood a head-high mound of stone so overgrown with clinging creepers—and, yes, more thorns—that Amarune could barely make out that the mound was a cairn whose upper reaches were worked and finished in smooth blocks that supported something tall, thin, and carved from a single block of stone. A statuette of some standing figure? No . . . a *harp*!

A high-prowed hand harp, of the sort successful bards and elves played, and few others could afford.

"What *is* this place?" Rune asked. "Some safehold sacred to the Harpers?"

El and Storm both gave her wry half smiles.

"In a way, 'tis indeed," Elminster replied. "This is the tomb of the Lady Steel, one of the founders of the Harpers. Too long ago." He sighed, shaking his head at the overgrown harp, then added briskly, "'Tis warded; we should be able to hide here."

Rune peered around. "Here? Under these trees, in the open? If it rains, we're going to get drenched. And I'll bet that cliff will become one giant waterfall." She looked down at the soft, thick moss under her boots. "Takes a lot of damp to keep moss this lush."

"So it does," Storm agreed serenely, "but we won't be out here, under the stars, soaked in the night mist. When Dath died, we didn't just leave her lying on the ground for wolves to tear apart, you know." She plucked some creepers aside to lay bare more of the carved stone harp, and murmured, "Dathlue Mistwinter. You'd have liked her."

Amarune murmured wistfully, "I'm beginning to mourn the loss of so many people I was born too late to meet. Truly." She collected the gazes of both of her older companions, and added firmly, "But that *doesn't* mean I want to meet their ghosts. Echoes of the fallen beyond counting are caught in the Weave, aren't they?"

Elminster merely nodded. Then he lifted one hand to her in a silent beckoning, and led the way around the overgrown cairn to the cliff behind.

Where Rune found herself looking at many deep clefts in the old and weathered rock, none of which looked larger than her arm or deeper than the length of her body, even if she could somehow sink through solid stone and lie flat.

"Is this more Dale humor?" she asked lightly, and quoted the old jest: "'Pray, my lord, what see you? For I see only rocks and trees. Look again, for there is more. I see it not, Lord, what is it? Trees and rocks, of course. Trees and rocks.'"

El smiled thinly. "I remember the lady minstrel who first said that, and set highborn and backwoods folk alike to laughing. But as it happens, those words are pertinent. Look again. Hard. Right there."

Amarune followed the line of his pointing finger—and gazed at the rocks he was indicating.

They were just solid stone. Yet . . .

Hard, he'd said, so she stared at them hard. For an uncomfortably long time.

Whereupon they seemed to *ripple*, subtly.

Ripple . . .

"You have the Gift," Storm explained softly. "You can see what most cannot. Some of these rocks are the wards playing at being solid stone, and most are truly stone. To someone who commands no Art, all of them will feel the same."

Then Storm stiffened, and murmured warningly, "*El.*"

The old archmage nodded calmly and strolled to where he could put a hand on Rune's and Storm's elbows from behind.

"I'd noticed too," he muttered. Amarune felt magic flood silently through her from Elminster's touch, leaving her tingling all over. She felt the prickling in her nostrils that meant every hair on her body was trying to stand on end.

Then the world in front of her exploded in a blinding flash, and something smote her so hard she flew through the air, crashing through branches in a raging hail of shredded leaves and splintered twigs that whirled her into a nest of groaning, swaying boughs high in the tangled meeting of two hurthars.

Men were screaming—raw, throat-stripping, keening howls of agony. Through a blur of tears she saw mens' arms clawing empty air in pain, their helpless bodies dancing in spasms outlined against an angry, roiling glow of risen magic. Two of those dark silhouettes abruptly vanished—and from somewhere near at hand she heard Elminster snarl a short and angry incantation and *felt* him pull at the Weave, with the same sort of beckoning gesture he'd made to her.

And suddenly those two men were back where they'd been standing before, looking startled.

No, terrified.

"Minor arcanists of Thultanthar," Elminster identified them, more weariness than anger in his voice.

Behind the two he'd dragged back from wherever they'd teleported to, the other men who'd been hiding behind the wards of the tomb collapsed silently to the ground, dropping weapons and looking very dead.

"And the swordswingers who run with them, like browbeaten dogs," El added, shaking his head.

One of the arcanists hissed something, deft fingers weaving a pattern in the air that Storm sliced to ribbons along with several of the man's fingertips, her sword so swift that the man never saw it. The tip of his tongue exploded in blood as she cut it on her backswing.

Then she and the man she'd just wounded were flung aside like two rag dolls, as magic erupted from deeper in the unseen tomb and smashed into them—a tongue of devouring force that sheared a path of destruction through the trees. It would have stabbed at Rune, caught in the tangle of still-swaying boughs, had it not struck the harp cairn and rebounded from it back into the tomb—evoking a startled curse, and the brief clacking thunder of many tumbling stones.

"*That* ward, I spun when I was stronger than I am now," El muttered in satisfaction, striding to the other arcanist and lifting his knee into the man's crotch.

The Shadovar cried out in startled pain and fell into a crouch, clutching himself—and El swarmed all over him, dagger out. The air around them flared as a frantic spell rebounded from Elminster back onto its caster, leaving the arcanist sobbing and staggering. He went down in abrupt silence when the old archmage slammed the pommel of his dagger down on the back of the man's neck, leaping into the air to add force to the blow.

"Ye think me foolish enough to go about with a mantle spell that reflects only one attack?" he asked the crumpled heap contemptuously, turning to walk right into the seemingly solid rock that masked the tomb.

The cliff silently swallowed him.

Rune discovered she'd been biting her lip and holding her breath. She let it out gustily and hastened to clamber down out of the trees, wincing at the pain in her battered limbs. Oh, there'd be bruises! Happy dancing hobgoblins, every damned time she went anywhere with these two, she got battered about as if she was a—

Storm came limping out of the tattered trees, sword in hand and blood on her cheek. Exasperation flared on her face when she saw Rune hastening to the ground alone.

"He went in there, didn't he? Ever since Alassra . . . thinks he's invincible . . ."

And in a whirl of long silver tresses, the Bard of Shadowdale plunged into the fissured cliff face, and was gone.

Leaving Amarune to peer wildly at the rocks and trees all around her, this way and then that, seeking any foes. Hearing and seeing nothing, she cautiously went to the cliff, at exactly the same spot she'd seen Storm step through it, and . . . just kept walking.

The tingling was as if a storm of sparks had plunged into her, stabbing at her eyeballs and racing up her nose and down her throat. She screamed, or tried to, but she couldn't move, couldn't make a sound. Could only plunge on, sightless, her whole world a blinding cloud of raging sparks that shook her body until her very teeth rattled. Her fingernails felt as if they were coming out, her innards groaned, her tongue undulated involuntarily—

She was through, and reeling in dank darkness, standing on a floor of smooth old stone that seemed to yaw and pitch under her, refusing to stay still.

A strong hand caught hold of her arm, just below the shoulder, and steadied her.

"Easy, now," Storm reproved. "Most of us learn wards and attune ourselves to them, instead of trying to rush through them like a bull at rutting time."

"But," Rune gasped, "you just *vanished*, and left me there, all alone! Wasn't I *supposed* to follow? If I'm to stand with you and in time take over from you, how can I—?"

"Ye speak level-headed truth, as usual, lass," Elminster said glumly, from somewhere in the darkness ahead of her. "Yet we're all too late. The Shadovar lying in wait had no inkling—*this* time—that we can rebuff more than one spell. Or that while Thultanthar hid on the Plane of Shadow, this plane's lesser wielders of the Art might just have built wards stronger than overconfident young arcanists can spin or anticipate. If he hadn't thought to amuse himself by shattering Dathlue's marker . . ."

"So his own spell came right back at him," Amarune interpreted, "and—what? He hurt himself?"

"His magic shattered her casket, and its shards, caught within the wards, had nowhere to go, and so raged around inside it. Shattering some of his limbs, by the looks of all this blood. He took himself back to wherever he came from just before I could get to him and finish him."

"Finish him?" Storm shook her head. "El, don't fool yourself. We were fortunate. If they'd been a little more patient, and let us step into the tomb before attacking us—or just resisted the urge to hurl spells first, and stuck daggers into us instead . . ."

Elminster waved a hand, and a dim radiance kindled all over the walls of what Rune could now rather blearily see was a small stone room with a round dais at its heart. A dais now strewn with stone rubble and yellow-brown shards that might have been very old bone. More rubble lay scattered across the floor beyond it.

The Old Mage's face, as he gazed at Storm and Amarune, was grim.

"Ye're right, as usual," he admitted. "We were lucky to prevail."

He looked down at the ruin of the casket. "Dove used to camp here, when harsh winter weather caught her in these parts . . . ," he murmured, as if to himself. "Where is she now, I wonder?"

Amarune gave him a sidelong look. "Dove?"

In reply, he lifted his chin and said firmly, "We can skulk about mending the Weave here and there no longer. We're hiding from no one. Time is, as they say, running out."

"Running out before what?" Rune asked.

El regarded her thoughtfully, and she burst out, "No, *don't* stand there deciding what to tell me and what to keep secret. I can't give what feeble aid I'm capable of if I don't *know* what's going on! Damn all the gods, Elminster, hear me: every last woodcutter and farmer and cook across all of Faerûn deserves to know what's going on!"

Elminster kept on looking at her expressionlessly for what seemed a very long time, and then smiled a wide, fond smile, shook his head at her in seeming admiration, and growled, "Ye humble me, lass. Ye do. Well, then, the short of it is this: the agents of Shar are proceeding boldly to carry out the wishes of the Dark Goddess."

His face changed, and he raised his arms, closed his eyes, and added, "A moment, please." Then he muttered something fluid that sounded Elvish, but that included not a single word Rune had ever heard before.

The tingling rose within her again.

"What're you—?"

"He's twisting the wards," Storm murmured in Amarune's ear, "just as he did back at Ralaskoun's tomb. To hide the three of us from anyone magically watching and listening from afar."

"So this little council will be ours, and ours alone," El added.

"'Council'?" Rune asked wryly. "Is that what centuries-old archmages call the moments when they grandly decree what will be done, and everyone else listens?"

Storm chuckled. "I've no doubt you'll make a great successor, Amarune Lyone Armala Whitewave, if . . ."

"If you can keep me alive long enough?"

The Bard of Shadowdale winced. "You've less learning to do than I'd thought."

"If ye've stopped trying to be clever and tart-tongued for a moment or two," El said to Amarune, sounding more amused than severe, "hear my decree. We must leave off this Weave work for now, and turn all of our efforts to stopping the agents of Shar."

"And if we fail?"

"If Shar succeeds before the Sundering of Toril and Abeir is complete, *she* will forever be the goddess of magic, her name written in the renewed Tablets of Fate, and darkness and shadow shall spread across Faerûn and hold sway forever."

"Enslaving all intelligent beings, and pitting them against each other for her amusement," Storm added quietly.

"For her sustenance," Elminster corrected. "She feeds on pain and loss, on the keeping and sharing of secrets, and on what is forgotten when rememberers are slain without passing on what they know. Despair and oblivion and what she calls the Cycle of Night. Life will become an endless intrigue of cabals battling each other for survival and dominance, inspired and commanded by a goddess who wants them all to fail and fall. The Endless Night, as the Mad Bard of Netheril called it when Shar whispered it to him, more than an age ago."

Amarune shuddered, despite herself. "All right," she told the two Chosen of Mystra, "you've succeeded in frightening me. Again. So rather than wallowing in despair or grimly assuring each other that we *must* not fail, or the world is doomed, tell me something useful. Such as: in light of all that, what do we do now?"

"I," Elminster told her without a moment's hesitation, "must go to Candlekeep. Alone."

"Why?" she asked bluntly, in such perfect mimicry of his tone that Storm grew a wide grin.

"If there is a key to rebuilding the Weave—something that would swiftly restore most of the great tapestry of interwoven forces, at a stroke—it lies hidden in Candlekeep's library, or survives nowhere at all. I must find it."

"How do you know such a power, or process, or whatever it is, exists at all?"

"Mystra herself once whispered as much to me. And told me the explanations were hidden—well hidden—in Candlekeep, and that I was not to seek nor concern myself with them, unless doing so became crucial to preserving everything she stood for. And she *is* the Weave, so . . ."

"So, it's time," Amarune agreed. "You know, leaping about bare-skinned while busily hurling bottles at brawling nobles in the Dragonriders' was *so* much easier . . ."

"Ye are far from the first to voice such sentiments," the Old Mage told her dryly. "Though not all that many of Mystra's Chosen have been mask dancers. Khelben and I lacked the figure for it, to be sure."

"You at least got to wear a mask," Storm told Rune. "Laeral and I never did."

"Laeral and—? This I *have* to hear!"

"Later," Storm told her firmly. "Save the world first, remember? I rather suspect, if the Shadovar are after wards—and they sure look to be—they'll head for Candlekeep sooner or later."

Elminster nodded. "And if anyone can aid in holding the great wards of the keep against them . . ."

Rune rolled her eyes. "No lack of confidence in *this* particular tomb, is there?"

Elminster chuckled. "Blood of my blood, say rather that it's a task I'd not want to saddle anyone else with. While I'm, ah, sporting amongst the monks, both of ye must go to Myth Drannor, to aid the elves in withstanding the siege."

40

"Agreed," Storm said simply. They both looked to Amarune.

Who shrugged her assent, because she knew not what else to do. If she ran into a Sharran who wasn't a priest or a shade, she probably wouldn't even recognize them, and so could be surrounded by foes at any time and not even know it. And how would she even go about deciding where and how to fight the Dark Goddess and all her servants?

"What if—?" she began, but fell silent, startled, as Storm put two swift fingers across her lips.

The radiance in the room had abruptly died, leaving them in darkness, but a moment later a damp wilderland breeze blew around their ankles, bringing with it the faint light of day from outside.

Someone from afar had snuffed out the wards. Again.

El reached out a hand and pulled Rune down to her knees. He and Storm crouched on either side of her, both of them suddenly crones again.

"Are *you* doing this, so you need not answer me?" Rune whispered to him, exasperated.

Elminster shook his head, looking grimmer.

And frightened. Again.

The smell of the sea was strong here, amid these dark and ancient rocks that rose like the prow of a great ship above the endless thunder of the waves. The rocks crowned by the gigantic and many-towered monastery of forbidding stone. Candlekeep was called a fortress in blunt truth. Grim and crude compared to floating Thultanthar, but impressive enough when towering high above him, as it was now. It would have been disconcerting to stand in this place when the earth still shook often, as it had all spring and most of the summer.

Something Shar had wrought, he'd heard. But then, one heard a lot of wildness at times like these. Like Yder sending warriors to defend the Hall of Shadows!

Thinking of which . . .

Give yourself to the shadows.

Maerandor smiled, and did that. One moment he was a dark-clad man, and the next he was roiling shadows, shifting and drawing away into the darkness of the clefts and hollows in the rocks all along the unseen barrier.

The ancient wards of Candlekeep were legendary and many layered, peerless in power. Not living things like mythals, but accretions of layers upon layers of spells, some of them knit to others, and some of them embroideries and extensions of simple, mighty magics hoary with age and as enduring as mountains.

Here, prickling his cheek with their nearness, they pulsed with power. Throbbed with the deep currents of spreading heat thrown off by sullen magma through miles of rock, with the tug of the tides, with the fury of the waves crashing on the shore it crowned, with the warmth of the sun on its towers and the rocks around it . . . and with the slow, ponderous might of the turning world.

A might that was lessening, just now, thanks to the Mistress of the Night. Though the wards remained a shell very few besieging armies of mages could hope to shatter—and not more than a handful of archmages.

However, he was not here to make war on the wards from outside.

He was here to creep through them, a shadow amongst shadows, making use of the very spaces that kept one spell from flooding into the next and bringing them all crashing down in an uncontrollable torrent of raw, wild spellfire. How could a brick wall keep out a man who could pass through mortar?

Oh, there were a few spells within the wards that made war on shadow magic, but they had been worked by wizards dwelling in a world that did not know mortals could become shades—and had become shades—and what such shadowed folk could now do.

Wherefore he could make his way through the wards and live. Though it would be a slow and agonizing process and would deliver him inside the walls naked and shorn of any active spells.

Maerandor sighed, gave himself to the wards, and let the pain claim him.

Only his will would hold him together through what followed.

But then, without a will greater than the best forged steel, no Art adept of Thultanthar lasted long enough to claim the title of arcanist, let alone to become a shade.

Nor yet the personal agent of the Most High of the city.

Maerandor smiled again. By the time he was finished forming it, that smile was all that was left of him.

The rabbit stew would be good—Storm had a way with sauces—but the wind was like icy daggers slicing at them, as it whistled between the rocks. Here in this rocky wilderland the gods alone knew exactly where, somewhere near the eastern border of Cormyr, well up in the backlands away from the coast.

Amarune shivered one more time, and shook her head in exasperation. She was about done with hiding her aggravation.

"Well if this mysterious spy is watching us from who knows where, surely they can see *me*—as I've not gone around disguised for one moment—and figure out in a short instant that I've ditched two old crones somewhere. Crones they probably already know are—were—you and Elminster."

Storm nodded. "Yes."

"So why are we just marching along as ourselves now? What was the *point* of all that, four months of Weave work in tombs and old ruins and standing stones and that old mill and the broken bridge and—and all the other places I've forgotten already?"

Storm stirred the pot, and told it serenely, "The point was to keep anyone spying on us as confused as you've been. So they'd watch to see what we were up to, figuring all the Weave work was a cover for something else, rather than attacking us. So we went on strengthening the Weave unhampered. Until these last few days."

"And El, is he strolling across the lands, pipe in mouth, wearing his usual old robes?"

"No. He's still in disguise. Many guises."

Rune crooked an eyebrow. "So he matters, and we don't?"

Storm nodded. "Precisely. Until there's a Mystra again, he matters more than any other mortal alive in the world." She grinned. "A role he's used to, I'm afraid."

"Is that why he's so insufferable, so often?"

Storm chuckled, gave Rune a twinkling smile, and murmured, "I've met worse. Most old wizards are *far* worse." She sipped at a ladleful of stew, nodded her approval, and announced, "It's ready. Your cup?"

Rune held out her battered belt mug. "So we'll be walking all the way to Myth Drannor as the Bard of Shadowdale and her sidekick, the lowly mask dancer from Suzail? It's early in Marpenoth, yes, but snow *could* come any day."

"Unlikely this year, but yes, it could. And yes, we'll be walking, unless you'd prefer a disguise. Yet we *are* the decoys, and I must warn you that my magic isn't much. My disguises run more to costumes and smudged faces and mimicry than magic."

"No, I've no particular trouble being myself," Rune informed her dryly. "Seeing as myself has a good chance of persuading a certain

Lord Delcastle to accompany me. If you can spare the time for us to detour and visit him."

Storm gave Rune a wide grin along with her full and steaming mug. "We can indeed, and he'll be right welcome. His sword will come in useful, his arms will make you happier, and I wouldn't mind a bath and a good bed in Suzail for a night, before we all troop off to die."

Rune stopped with the too-hot mug close enough to her lips to sip from, and asked quietly, "You mean that, don't you?"

Storm sighed. "I hope not. But yes, I fear I do."

In a dark and deserted wardrobe chamber in Candlekeep, full of winter cloaks, high boots upturned on angled racks, scarves hanging on pegs, and shelves upon shelves of caps and gloves, a deeper darkness drifted oh, so slowly, coalescing into a pool of shadow. A pool that rose to stand like a man, shook itself, peered cautiously around the room to make sure it was empty of monks, and then coughed.

Maerandor shook his head again, irked with himself. Though he was far from solid yet, his phantom jaws ached from the smile he'd been foolish enough to shape ere roiling into shadow.

Idiot. A small thing, yet small things could get one killed, even in Candlekeep.

Hmmph.

Especially in Candlekeep.

He stood stock-still at the end of a line of cloaks, his back to a wall, and listened hard. But there were no sounds of anyone nearby. He could smell old, worn leather, but no trace of mildew, and that confirmed he was inside the wards, which fought and killed molds and mildews. It was why the monks went outside their fortress to dine in the open fields below when they wanted to enjoy cheese.

That was just one of many, many mundane details he knew about the monastery, thanks to years of Shadovar spying—and, of course, what the minds of captives had yielded up less than willingly. Right now, however, he had to use what he knew of the monks themselves. The senior monks.

He had to find and murder the right monk.

Klaeleth or Norldrin would be best. Chethil would do, or Guldor or Aumdras. Cooks and warders, men of learning and years, who were respected but did not command, who saw to their own duties and walked their own ways in the vast old fortress. Monks who knew how to momentarily open a way through the wards without damaging them or alerting others that such a breach had been made.

A cook would be best, being as Maerandor of Thultanthar was hungry. Worming through the wards was *exhausting* work.

A dark and silent shadow in the darkness no normal man's eyes could penetrate, Maerandor drifted to the door, and through the gap beneath it.

It was time to be a-murdering.

CHAPTER 4

In the Halls of the Endless Chant

I T MIGHT HAVE BEEN WISER NOT TO USE ONE OF THE OLD GATES, but the Great Shield was up, and the gates of Candlekeep were firmly shut to the outside world in these times of war and tumult, no matter how valuable the tomes that supplicants waved under the noses of the monks who guarded the way in. Moreover, this latest doom coming down on Faerûn wouldn't wait forever; Abeir and Toril were more or less apart already, even if most mortals knew nothing of such matters but wild rumors.

And, no less importantly, his feet hurt.

"Besides," Elminster muttered to himself darkly, "ye gave up on being wise centuries ago. About the time ye decided to do something about the magelords, back in Athalantar."

Athalantar, the vanished kingdom he was the last prince of. Not that anyone beyond sages and a handful of elves remembered more than its name, these days.

For that matter, he doubted very much anyone still alive—beyond, again, a handful of elves—remembered the gate he intended to use, which lacked side posts these days, or even a marker. One merely stepped between these two leaning boulders—in a crouch, if ye were human sized—after hooking around yon first stone in just the one direction—so—and murmuring "Ama*lae*roth" in the right intonation, at the right moment.

Which was . . . *now.*

Here on this brisk morning of the ninth of Marpenoth, in the Year of the Rune Lords Triumphant. The year 1487 in Dalereckoning. Not a bad day, if one didn't mind chill winds, but winter—real winter—would be coming soon.

So, behold, one step took ye from the hills near Elturel past shut and guarded doors and warily watchful monks, to the tunnels that riddled the root rocks beneath Candlekeep, well down beneath the silent, endless thunder of the wards.

Where it was dark rather than sunlit and breezy, startlingly so after the open air, but his nose told him he was in the right place. Elminster stood in an ale-hued gloom lit faintly and fitfully by palely glowing fungi, the soft and flowing sluglike growths that fed on the, ah, aromatic cesspool outflows.

Aye, he wasn't in the undoubtedly warded and dragon-guarded warrens that descended into the Underdark, but a far smaller, parallel webwork of passages, old cellars, and cesspools, carefully kept separate from the caverns that linked with the Realms Below. Three gates opened up into the monastery above—gates that even the most senior monks who led Candlekeep today knew nothing of. Their predecessors had known how to keep secrets, and spirit away written references, as well as any Chosen of Mystra.

So El doubted he'd meet with many traffic jams on this particular way up into the great fortress of learning. Wading through chest-deep sewage was never a popular pastime.

He pulled off his boots, moved the flask of oil from his belt into one of his boots to keep it upright and handy, and started disrobing, stuffing everything he took off into the deepest crevice he could find.

He would miss those boots. Comfortable boots were always hard to come by. Usually it took years of trudging in discomfort, aches and blisters and worse, to break them in. But most of the monks wore soft leather slippers that gave no cushion at all against the cold, hard stone . . .

Bah. Give thought to such luxuries later, after the rapturous fun of the moment. He began working oil into his hair, his beard, everywhere—nostrils and eyelashes last.

The oil would help the sewage slide off him more easily, afterward. There was a side sump that carried the water down from the baths, which joined the main cesspool outflow in the cavern with the large stripe of quartz down its walls. It should serve as a shower . . .

Carefully he lowered himself in, and started wading.

Back in the brown stuff again . . .

Mystra forfend, but the monks were spicing their fare more highly. And eating more cabbage too.

Clear proof of their diligent guardianship. Less food was arriving from outside, forcing them to rely more on their larders and what they grew themselves—and for some reason known only to the gods, cabbages thrived atop crumbling stone towers, hereabouts. It would be interesting to learn why they'd raised the Great Shield.

His progress was slow, foul work. Two caverns in, he felt the wards crackling and thrumming in front of him, thickening to prevent a living intruder so imbued with magic—the workings of his hectic centuries—from passing through them.

He'd added to these wards himself a time or two, and knew how they interacted with the Weave. That was the key to slipping through them; making himself so "of the Weave" that the wards would take him for it, and not for an old, naked man trudging through the cess . . .

49

El set about losing himself in the Weave, his body becoming more smoke and shadows than solid, sewage falling away from what it could no longer cling to. As a silent, patient cloud, he advanced, crossing another cavern before he felt the silent thunder of the wards behind him rather than around him, and let himself—slowly again, a gradual and patient shifting—slip back into solidity before someone or something might detect his use of magic.

It was a cavern later when his cautious feet struck something hard and solid, under the turgid brown flow, where there should have been nothing. Something El thought he knew, and had even been expecting, before he'd gingerly felt it up and down enough to identify it.

The body of a man, extra clothes knotted to his arms and legs and neck that had been wrapped around sizeable stones.

A corpse weighted down with stones to keep it submerged and hidden. Almost certainly a murdered monk. Well, well . . .

Two caverns later, he encountered another. Then another.

These two were in shallower sewage than the first, and El took the trouble to drag them to where he could haul their heads out and wipe at them to see if he recognized them.

He did. Two monks whose faces he knew. The name of one—a man from the far, far South beyond Faerûn who had coal-black skin, and who'd always spoken sparingly—he couldn't recall, but the other was a freckled, red-bearded onetime trader from Tharsult.

"Dalkur," Elminster muttered aloud, as the name rose out of his overcrowded memory. "Wrote a beautiful hand, as swift as some folk breathe."

He let both bodies slip back down under the reeking brown current, and waded onward thoughtfully.

Oh, monks died and their brethren in Candlekeep didn't trouble to let the wider world know. They kept to themselves as a matter of course. A great many folk in Faerûn had no idea there were women among the monks, although there had always been, simply because the Avowed of Candlekeep hadn't bothered to let the world think any differently. Aye, monks could die and the world not be told about it.

Yet the penitent dead weren't buried by being weighed down and hidden in sewage, and for years he'd had his own spies among the monks, and so had the Harpers, the Lords' Alliance, and half a dozen less savory cabals and alliances . . . and if there'd been many losses among the Avowed of Candlekeep, some word of it would have leaked out.

Nor had any of the bodies been there all that long. Moving excrement that mixed with air as this flow did was far from a preservative.

No, these monks had been murdered and then impersonated, or he was a shade of Thultanthar. So others were as interested in what was inside Candlekeep as he was.

"Well," he muttered to himself, "this makes matters slightly easier. Undoubtedly I won't be the only impersonator. 'Twill be interesting when I run into my double."

Dalkur would do. Close enough in height and build . . . aye.

El found the bathwater sluice and tarried there, letting its chill waters thoroughly rinse away what he'd been wading through, as he concentrated on calling up every last memory he could of the freckled monk's voice and manner and looks.

Andannas Dalkur, once of Tharsult, before that from Secomber. From once-mighty Athalantar . . .

This changed matters, to be sure. Repairing the Weave in a hurry was still of utmost importance, and the secrets Khelben had hidden about how to do that were here if they survived anywhere, but it now seemed he had numerous competitors in the hunt for those secrets, and dealing with them must come first. So, add a few more steps to this most crucial of missions—and in that, why should it be any different than most of his tasks? There were *always* more steps to everything than ye thought there'd be, at the beginning. El chuckled and scrubbed his scalp with his fingers, trying to get the last of the sewer stench off himself. His freckled, bony-jointed, sunken-chested new self.

He failed, of course. It'd be the baths for him, once he stole a robe from the spare stores nigh the stables. And a good roll in mule dung in one of the stalls that hadn't been mucked out yet, to cover one stink with another. *Then* the baths.

And then it would be time for the new false Andannas Dalkur to find the older false Andannas Dalkur in the halls of Candlekeep.

If that other impersonator didn't find him first.

Ah, Norun Chethil. *The* cook among the cooks of the Avowed, and foraging alone in the deepest back pantries. Ideal.

Maerandor waited until the cook—a stout man, like most who tasted as they went—was bent over and rummaging through cobwebs at the back of a shelf in search of the oldest jars of preserves—oysters in spiced oil, as it happened—because they should be used first.

"Come out of there, you skulking rat of a jar," Chethil grunted, smooth crockery spinning under his stubby fingertips. "*Hah*! Got you!"

That sounded like too good a cue to waste. Maerandor silently solidified right behind the monk. And pounced.

The moment his fingers closed on Chethil's throat and head, the Shadovar put all the weight of his body and the speed of his bound into one swift, ruthless wrenching.

The cook's neck broke with a soft, sickening splintering, the man's arms writhing wildly enough that Maerandor had to fling out a hasty foot to kick one jar of oysters back onto the shelf before it could fall and shatter.

Then Chethil went limp. His slayer held him in a grip like unyielding steel, keeping the dying man immobile and alive for as long as possible.

It took but a moment to awaken the right magic and invade the dimming, helpless mind. *The wards, reveal all you know of them . . .*

Ah, much indeed. *The wards, tell more!* The kitchens had their own doors through the wards, which were opened when it was both safe and needful to use such swift alternatives to traders' wagons coming up the Way of the Lion to the gates. That wasn't often.

Tell more! Ah, and these gates were there and there and there, opened thus and so and with these safeguards . . .

Chethil's next culinary work would begin three chants from now, after visits to the cellars that held onions and leeks and peppers, then up to the tower where the greenleaf was flourishing in the window boxes.

Yes, let's have where all the cellars and pantries are, and what they all hold. Aha, yes. There were no keys to lock any of the deep back pantries, but few of the monks knew their ins and outs, and only a handful ever went to them. Unless Chethil took longer than three chants to appear in the kitchens, no one would come down seeking him. The apples many monks liked to sneak for themselves were a good five levels above.

Chethil's undercooks were the monks Rethele and Shinthrynne, merry young women Chethil was fond of and whose jests and lively converse the stout cook heartily enjoyed—even if dusky-skinned Shinthrynne was from the hot jungles where they had strange ideas about fiery seasonings, whereas Rethele was from upcountry Impiltur and thought dry thistles made fine salads. They'd both be in the kitchen right now, making sauces and dicing marrows . . . and they knew what he'd gone to fetch. So he must depart the pantry with three jars of oysters.

What did Chethil know of the rest of Candlekeep?

Huh. Just about all of it, though no monk alive had been in all the turrets of the main keep. Some of the turrets had been walled off for centuries. Chethil had lived much of his life within Candlekeep's walls, and had walked the well-worn route of the chant for the first score or so of those years.

The cook's mind was darkening fast, his anger and fear mere dull echoes, his formerly frantic thoughts a slowing, drifting chaos as he slipped away.

Maerandor bore down, seeking what he needed to feign the man himself. Favored sayings, habits, hues, hobbies, Norun's own preferred food.

Ah, *that* caused a last flare in the fading mind. Chethil himself detested ale and smoked meats, and loved strong cordials and the marinated lizard dishes once popular in Var the Golden . . . back when it had still been Var the Golden.

Back when . . . back when . . . the last life faded in a flickering, and all of Norun Chethil became a "back when."

Maerandor lowered the stout body. Good. He'd plundered more than enough from the monk to fool others that he was Chethil. Once his body was an exact match for the cook's, of course.

He stripped the monk with unhurried care, so as not to damage the man's robes. A simple apron, the usual clout, a truss—so Chethil was sensitive about his growing girth—and the usual soft leather slippers. A leather-bound chapbook on a neck thong, for the taking of notes. Cookery notes only, it seemed.

Maerandor worked several spells to change his body into an exact copy of the dead monk. That was the secret to a superior disguise— layers of spells, not just one.

Then he dragged the corpse to a closet that Chethil had known had once been a long-dead predecessor's private wine cellar, stuffed it inside, and latched the door.

Time to call on what he'd just learned about opening a door in the wards. With the same patient calm, he did what Chethil would have done to open the wards, enabling himself to emerge momentarily among the purple-black northslope rocks of the ridge Candlekeep rose from, and retrieve the thorn-and-wax-sealed metal coffer Maerandor of Thultanthar had brought with him and hidden there.

After returning to the deep back pantry, he used Chethil's belt knife to slit the seal, slicing aside the thorns the worms found poisonous, and opened the coffer. Inside were two flesh-devouring worms of the sort that consumed vermin in Thultanthar. Both as long as his forearm, glistening black, and plump, their segments rippled with hunger. Opening the closet he'd stuffed the dead monk into, Maerandor poured the worms onto the corpse's chest and firmly closed the door.

Shut in for long enough, they'd not just strip the skeleton bare, they'd gnaw the monk's bones to powder, too.

All very tidy. Now, three jars of oysters and a detour to a particular cellar to collect the wine he knew Rethele and Shinthrynne liked to sip when the ovens grew hot and the sweat started to stream.

The fewer monks left, the less resistance. And the Most High wanted no magic wasted and lost in fighting when it came time to drain the wards of this place for Thultanthar. So, his own task was to eliminate any who might fight against that draining. And Maerandor had a reputation to maintain. He did swift, efficient work.

All of which meant it was high time to bring about Candlekeep's downfall.

Elminster hadn't visited Candlekeep often, and had never stayed long. There'd always been so many pressing tasks to do, things he couldn't neglect or delay. Yet many times he'd wanted to tarry in this most lore-filled of monasteries, drawn to the rooms and rooms full of grimoires and spellbooks and histories and every other sort of book he'd not had the time to sit and really enjoy. Even with twelve centuries to find time enough in.

He was drawn to them now, but knew better than to wander and search shelves and so be noticed as behaving oddly. Dalkur had been an intense devourer of tomes on just one "enthusiasm" at a time, only to turn to another after a handful of years, rather than a voracious reader who enjoyed variety.

Though he had no idea just what Andannas Dalkur's current enthusiasm was, El knew his best course would be to casually select a book, take it to a quiet corner table somewhere near where it had been shelved, and peruse it with care. While listening and watching what was going on around him among his fellow Avowed, without appearing to do so. He had to know what the current tenor of daily life was like among the monks, and to spot any sign of an impostor, or collusion, or some swiftly approaching planned violence.

Besides, it was high time for a little reflection. His mind had been swimming in the Weave and concentrating on repairing and augmenting it for so long that he needed to think again of daily life in Faerûn, and what he needed to watch of *that* to be warned of trouble in time. If, that is, he might possibly snatch time enough to deal with all the troubles he should do battle with.

He knew better than to seek one of the inner rooms that housed books of powerful magic or inestimable value, which could only be examined with the permission of the most senior and highest-ranking monks, and in their presence.

If fate, the conspiracies of others, and the whims and striving of the gods were going to allow him time enough to accomplish what he sought to do here at all, then there would be time enough in the days ahead to seek out and read through everything his longtime colleague the Blackstaff had written, that had found its way here or been placed here deliberately by Khelben. Just now, something less precious would arouse less suspicion in any impostor seeking the same lore he was, and so would do just fine . . .

He turned into one of the smaller chambers that opened off the Everwinding Stair with an open archway rather than a door, gently ignored several monks who were deep in books at the study tables with the same eyes-down silence with which they ignored him, and selected Archemusk's *Trends in Approaches to the Art*, its thousand-odd well-worn pages shedding their crumbling edges with the same enthusiasm he remembered from when the book had sat in a wizard's tower in upland Amn more than six hundred summers ago.

It was large and heavy, bound with ironroot panels clad in black peryton hide, and El cradled it in both hands as he shuffled to the vacant back corner table, sat himself down, and relaxed into the gloomy, dusty *patience* of Candlekeep. There was a glowing globe hanging dark and motionless in midair beside one of the older bookcases, whose graceful serpentine side pillars differentiated it from its later neighbors. The globe detected El's arrival and drifted gently over to hang behind his right shoulder, a gentle radiance kindling within it. When it was bright enough, El glanced up at it, and it stopped brightening and held to a steady level of glow.

Archemusk was a beautiful calligrapher, his hand fluid and flowing, generous with ornamental swashes—which more than atoned for the utter lack of limning. There were no illustrations, beyond depictions of runes, sigils, and the drawn arrays of the complicated castings that were popular after Netheril had fallen, and then again in the earlier 1100s. Everything in black atharnscale ink that never faded, so it all sprang out at his eyes fresh, dark, and crisp even though the pages he turned were mottled brown with age.

El—Dalkur, he must think of himself only as Dalkur—passed over the early sections of the book, having little taste for reading again the utterly fantastical admiration Archemusk had held for the magelords of Athalantar and the early self-styled "emperor wizards" who'd left ravaged Netheril behind them to conquer this or that corner of Faerûn.

Once Archemusk had reached the founding of Thay and the earliest squabbles over what magic was of which school, things grew interesting, and El settled in to read—with half his mind, anyway. The rest of him pondered what little he'd heard and seen of Candlekeep thus far.

The Endless Chant was just rising into audibility, still far off in a distant tower, and the chambers around him held the usual number of monks and books, in the usual near silence.

What was different was the atmosphere of the place: tension.

A tension he'd never felt in Candlekeep before.

He turned a page of Archemusk's writings, hearing again from memory the dry and superior voice of the man, though Orold Archemusk had been dust for two centuries now, and listened to the chant draw slowly nearer. It sounded smaller than he remembered, as if there were fewer novices marching behind the Chanter, chanting in plainsong unison as they traversed the long, familiar, smooth-worn circuit through the great monastery.

As the chant swelled, El thought of all the rooms around him, both the walled-off towers and those in use and lined with books. Monks shuffling silently from chamber to chamber, cowls shading their faces, lost in thought. Inevitably, he found himself wondering how many foes were among them, lurking within these thick and ancient stone walls.

Intruders like he was, wearing the faces of monks they'd slain. Waiting for . . . what?

The chance to steal or seize the mighty spells of centuries past? Or the magic of the monks of Candlekeep? Come to think of it, he'd not seen any magical rods thrust through the belts of the Avowed since his arrival, though that habit had once been usual. On the other hand, he'd not yet laid eyes on any high-ranking monks . . .

Or were the disguised intruders just hiding from the war and tumult outside the fortress, judging the ancient monastery to be the best refuge they could think of to ride out worse things that might well be coming?

Or were they here to try to harness the wards of Candlekeep for some fell purpose? Or find the same secrets of the Weave he himself sought?

High time to think about such things, or at least about how he should best proceed to learn more about them, indeed. Without, of course, seeming to do so.

El turned pages as if seeking something. He stopped when he found one of the casting arrays drawn out, with its triangles and radiating lines and encircled runes of power, and peered at it, pretending to study it intently.

While he really stared right through it, and let himself feel the Weave. It was bright and many knotted around him, of course, yet he saw it through ale-brown smoke of varying thickness: the wards.

Here in the old fortress that was the heart of Candlekeep, the wards shaped and constrained the Weave, binding it into walls and floors and the many-layered domes of surrounding force.

Making it hard for him to send unseen spying arms of his awareness anywhere within its bounds without having to fight the Weave—and making his presence and intent obvious to anyone attuned to the wards. As all of the older and higher-ranking monks were.

Which meant he'd have to do things the old way. Use spells only when absolutely necessary, and otherwise use his feet, his eyes, and his thinking.

Hmph. All of his failing faculties.

The chant was much nearer now. It *was* lesser than it had usually been during his visits, with fewer voices raised in the chanting. He knew the prophecies of Alaundo as well as any monk here did, and it was surprising how few of them had come to pass, and so had been dropped from the chant, since his last stay at Candlekeep.

The chanted words were clearly audible now.

"One shall rise out of thorns and fire, and seven shall be the swords that cleave to him, seven the crowns he binds together. One shall fall from the skies, and free dragons from their dungeon, and they shall scour the lands for their imprisoner. One shall—"

"Pray excuse, Brother," a voice murmured from the next table, a man's hand, palm down, moved gently into Elminster's field of vision and stopped, hovering as was the custom, waiting for a response.

El put his finger down on an inscription in the upper right of the casting array as if to tamp the spot down in his mind, stiffened his oldest and least detectable mantle spell to shield himself from an attack, and looked up—into a kindly, anxious face. "Yes?"

It was a monk he'd met only once before, when the man had been much younger. Myndlar. Of Athkatla. Ah, yes, this was the monk who believed dragons sought to steer human thought by writing books, purporting to be human women, and by sending dreams to humans who'd established reputations as writers.

"Archemusk, yes?" Myndlar asked eagerly, yet timidly. "The page before that array . . . does he mention Aravril as having claimed that several Netherese archmages hid by taking wyvern shape? Or was it the half-elf Talastaril who made that claim?"

"Neither," El replied from memory, turning back a page, and adding hastily, "I *think*." What he knew to be true might well not be what Archemusk had written . . . but in this case, it was. The book mentioned Moranveril of Myth Drannor as having seen archmages take the shape of wyverns, in ruins deep in Raurin—Moranveril who shortly thereafter vanished, and "was seen no more by anyone."

Myndlar studied that passage for a long moment, then nodded, thanked Dalkur, and returned eagerly to his own reading, flipping the pages of three open books until he found several passages to compare, in light of what he'd just learned.

Typical behavior of a monk of Candlekeep, when not dealing with a monk of exalted rank or one known to be difficult. And not a word, look, or hesitation that might suggest he viewed Dalkur with the slightest suspicion.

El turned back to the casting array, found the inscription he'd put his finger on, and went back to thinking.

If the old stiffneck hid anything coherent anywhere for others to find, it will have been here. And I *know* he wrote everything down, in flowery full—know it as sure as I know my own name. His pride would demand nothing less.

Aye, he had known Khelben Arunsun through and through, just as Khelben had known him. Which is why they'd never stopped arguing with each other, or going about things in very different ways, yet never stopped working for the same cause. Even if not always together, or without deliberately getting in each other's way.

Now, the question was, had Mystra imparted secrets of the Weave to Khelben greater than the understanding of its great tapestry one Elminster Aumar had reached?

And if she had, had anyone else suspected as much, and come here looking for them?

61

A bell so deep throated as to be felt more than heard tolled then, just once.

In response, more than one stomach in the small chamber rumbled.

El hid his amusement at how swiftly his fellow monks set aside their books and departed the room.

Food for thought seldom triumphed long over food for the belly.

"So, Old Wolf, we meet again," purred a voice Mirt hadn't expected to hear in a place such as this. Here in one of the dimmest and farthest of the discreet upper rooms of the Dusty Knight, an establishment of far less than savory reputation that graced a dirty back street halfway across Suzail from the Queen Fee.

Manshoon stood in the doorway, tall, thin, and as darkly handsome as ever, his cloak swirling as he drew one gloved hand along his belt to rest on . . . something Mirt didn't recognize, that looked both magical and menacing.

Mirt gave the women seated around him silent looks that suggested it would be safest if they left the room, right now. Experienced night-coin takers all, they melted out of the room by the three side doors in a few swift and quiet moments, leaving the onetime Lord of Waterdeep alone with the cloaked vampire who'd ruled both Zhentil Keep and Westgate in his time.

Under the table, Mirt readied some handy magic of his own. "You our first patron?" he inquired gruffly.

"'Our'? You co-own the Dusty Knight now? My, you *do* move swiftly!"

"Not that quickly. The ladies and I have just formed a go-to-patrons venture. To cater to citizens and visitors who'd rather not be seen coming here."

Manshoon strolled into the room and shut the door. "Promising—if you can get word to the right ears in the right manner—a warm, safe haven in these times of tumult."

Mirt fixed his unexpected guest with a suspicious eye. "Aye. And would a safe haven be the subject of your current hunt?"

Manshoon lowered himself into one of the vacated chairs across the table from Mirt, took up the decanter from the table and an unused tallglass, and drawled, "Not particularly. Say rather, I prefer to move from good vantage point to good vantage point—the better to watch unfolding doom—for entertainment's sake. Rather than plunging into the fray."

"Until?" Mirt asked, interpreting the pitch of his guest's last few words.

"Until the Shadovar, at least, have made their move."

"Ah. The archmages of the floating city, who now rule Anauroch. Again, some are saying."

"The same."

"You're acquainted with them?"

"I've learned enough to decide on my present, ah, course of inaction."

Mirt accepted the return of the decanter, filled himself a glass, and asked dryly, "So does a certain Manshoon have any plans to refound, or take over, a certain Brotherhood, or Black Network—or whatever it's called these days?"

The vampire smiled. "Another year, perhaps."

Mirt set down the decanter and asked, "After Elminster has made his own intentions regarding the continued existence of the Zhentarim, and your blossoming career, in particular, clear?"

Manshoon paused with his glass almost to his lips and asked coldly, "And why would I concern myself in the slightest with the doings of that ancient and overblown hedge wizard?"

Mirt shrugged. "Mayhap 'twould be that he seems to go looking to thwart you, and whenever you and he cross blades—or spells, or whatever wizards do when they fight—Elminster always seems to win."

"Always *seems* to, yes. Thanks to Mystra. Truth be known, his so-called triumphs often make things worse for us all. He's Mystra's doomsman, her destroyer. Her herald, showing us the darkness before she rides in to rescue us all with her divine benevolence and light. He doesn't even see how badly he's being used. Or worse, perhaps he does see it, and is too insane to care about the damage he does."

Mirt nodded calmly. "Did it never occur to you that Mystra might be using you just as she does Elminster? Herald and dark herald?"

Manshoon gave the old man a coldly level look. "I see Lords of Waterdeep regard heralds in rather a different light than the rest of us."

"'Rest of us'? There are more of you? I seem to recall hearing about a war of many Manshoons that . . . took care of that."

The vampire sneered. "Believe what you want to believe, Mirt. The truth is seldom so tidy."

Mirt raised his glass. "At last, something we can agree on. I'll drink to that."

Mockingly his guest toasted him, and they sipped in unison.

Mirt sighed gusty appreciation of the vintage, set down his glass, and observed, "I'm sure you'll eventually get around to telling me your reason for troubling to seek me out—here in the less than publicly prominent Dusty Knight."

Manshoon smiled. "Soon."

"Shall I save you the dallying? You think I'm working with Elminster, and want to know what he's up to right now."

"My, old wolves retain sharp wits."

Mirt shrugged. "That may or may not be, but this particular Old Wolf isn't working with Elminster, and hasn't the faintest where he's gone or what he's busy with. He's meddling, of course, but as for where and why . . ." He shrugged again.

"Spells to compel truth are things even young apprentices can master," Manshoon remarked idly.

"If you want to waste one just to learn I'm speaking truth, be my guest." Mirt combed his beard with calm fingers, found a fragment of garlic hardbread crust from his last meal, and ate it with gusto. "Isn't it a trifle . . . dangerous, being this candid with me?"

The vampire smiled again. "You're no fool, Old Wolf. You know prudence. I, too, am no fool—and have more than enough magic to fry the brains of any lord or aging rogue who crosses me."

Mirt matched his guest's cold smile. "You mean you have more than enough magic to try."

Manshoon set down his glass. "And there you take the inevitable step too far, old man. A bold stride into foolishness, to be sure. Wise men know better than to push the likes of me. We push back."

The spell came across the table without warning, a boiling darkness that flared up and lashed out at Mirt's face like a wide-fanged snake.

Only to rebound with a bright flash, parried by an unseen mantle spell that turned it back entirely upon Manshoon, whose startled grunt soared into a shriek of pain before—

The chair across the table from Mirt held only silence, and a thick tendril of rising, drifting mingled smoke and mist.

"Contingencies," the Old Wolf muttered disgustedly. "Wizards never do taste the full consequences of their folly."

He reached for the decanter. Once he'd raised it, clearing his field of view, he could see that the blackened seat of the smoldering chair across from him was now cracked right across.

"Still as overconfident as ever, I see," he observed to the empty air. "Did it never occur to you, Lord of the Zhentarim, that someone who's survived as long as I have might—just might—have fallen into the habit of anticipating rather obvious danger, and preparing for it?"

The rising, fading mist offered no reply, but then, Mirt hadn't expected it to. He filled and promptly drained his glass, in one long gulp.

And then shrugged, reached across the table to pluck up Manshoon's abandoned tallglass, and drained it, too.

CHAPTER 5

A City So Fair It Must Fall

Lminster settled on a larger but quieter chamber as
his preferred study area, and had returned Archemusk to the
shelves in favor of Traethur's frankly speculative *The Art in the
Ages Ahead*. Amusing reading, some of it, to one who knew more
than most.

More than he should, some would say.

Yet never enough, he and his Alassra had always agreed. He felt
the familiar stirring ache of grief as she came to mind, and set it
aside with cold deliberation.

Not now, he thought. I have a fresh and more pressing disaster
on my platter.

By which he did *not* mean the monastery meals. They were better
than he recalled them being.

Aye, after three days of settling in, Candlekeep was both the same
as he remembered it, and different. The same deep but somehow
listening silence, the same unseen-in-darkness high ceilings in some
chambers and low stone vaultings in others. Bare stone floors worn
smooth by the passage of many, many soft slippers down the centuries, every wall—even those lining the short flights of stairs—covered
with crammed-full bookshelves.

Physically, it was the same great fortress of learning. What was different was the mood.

The serene *patience* was gone. Silent acceptance had become silent tension.

The monks were wary. Not just troubled by news of the fresh disasters and devastations of a world in tumult beyond their walls, but disquieted by what had befallen within them.

Disquieted enough to talk about it all. So without any mind touching, El had readily been able to learn what had happened in Candlekeep during the past year.

Some monks had disappeared, just slipping away from the monastery on errands, strolls to take in the air, and so forth, never to return. Others just . . . weren't there at chant or meal or prayer. Gone, with no one having seen them depart, and not to be found when they were searched for. Others had fallen out of view for a time and later returned without tenable explanation, sometimes refusing to say anything at all.

Some of those latter had come back changed. Fearful and withdrawn, furtive and looking ever over their shoulders.

The nights had grown increasingly longer, with no explanations to be found in any tome—but hundreds of dire hints and cryptic possible references. As day after day, war and cataclysm wracked the lands outside Candlekeep's walls. The monastery had been besieged several times by frightened wealthy folk at the gates pleading for refuge and offering vast sums to pay for it. Even more frequent arrivals had been the envoys of many rulers, guilds, costers, and trading alliances, and even dwarf clans demanding the Avowed of Candlekeep share what they knew of battle magic, warding, and mending magic, in this time of ever-increasing troubles. Then had come an actual invasion, by a force of devils led by a wizard who commanded them in the name of Asmodeus, who'd gotten inside the walls to maraud through the fortress itself.

It had all been too much. The world outside seemed to be trying repeatedly to plunge these halls of learning into the strife and tumult raging through the lands.

The senior monks had come to a decision with a speed that in Candlekeep verged on the obscene, and hastened to raise the Great Shield, that seldom-raised heart of the wards that let only sound, light, and air pass, and to all else was like a great dome of force, a mighty wall to keep the world out.

And so the Avowed had physically and magically barricaded themselves inside their ancient fortress, seeking to keep the outside world at bay.

They were frightened and upset, for it was not a matter of simply ignoring the surrounding lands in favor of prayer to Oghma and pursuing intensive study and writing. The world kept knocking at the gates.

Even the Great Shield had been tested. Someone had taken to lobbing boulders over the high walls, and although these had been easily turned back by the wards, what sort of wanton destroyer would do such a thing?

Then, just days ago, a dragon—a *dragon!*—had arrowed out of the skies to try to wrest open the top of one of the keep's walled-up and abandoned north-facing towers. Why that particular tower, and what it might contain, were matters of pure speculation to the current monks. The gigantic black wyrm had almost reached its goal thanks to the woman riding it. No one had recognized that rider, but her magic had forced back the Great Shield so far that the mightily flapping dragon's straining claws had almost raked the tower's spire before Great Reader Asmurom had used a Rune of Warding to hurl both dragon and rider into another plane of existence.

Those runes, personally bestowed on the monastery by Deneir and Oghma, were precious and irreplaceable. There were now, so far as the Avowed knew, only four of them left.

And who had that dragonrider been? And his what—*what*—had she sought?

Elminster had no better answers than the bewildered monks, and well understood their consternation. If the armies besieging Myth Drannor marched on Candlekeep, just how long would the Great Shield stand? And how long would the remaining handful of Runes of Warding last?

He could craft replacement runes, as it happened, though doing so was neither swift nor easy. Yet if confronted as to where he, Andannas Dalkur, had been, it gave him a ready answer: He'd been off alone searching the many, many books of Candlekeep to find instructions for raising a rune he knew to be coded and hidden therein—knew because he'd found tantalizing fragments of four separate writings, by different sages, and just needed to follow the cryptic clues to find the other parts of the four processes. Should he find them, he would of course have to experiment with actually crafting the rune, and such perilous experiments were traditionally done in the deepest caverns beneath the keep itself.

An excellent excuse for what he'd really be doing—which was, of course, seeking the writings he needed to rebuild the Weave, all at once rather than in painstakingly slow and piecemeal mendings here, there, and everywhere. Mendings that took much too long to rescue Faerûn from its current tumult.

If he'd had a leisurely lifetime ahead in which to study, he could have just read his way through book after book—for his Mystra and Mystryl before her, not to mention Azuth and Savras and even Selûne and, for that matter, Jergal, had instructed many mortals in Weave work down the unfolding centuries, and even the gods might not know how many mortals had taken up quills and written of what they'd learned.

Yet that siege wouldn't last forever, and Shar had been draining captured Chosen like an insatiable devourer all year long, and so he lacked time to do much of anything properly or carefully. As usual. Which meant he had to seek out the writings by one man he knew had understood the Weave, and set down instructions and lore for later readers to find: Khelben Arunsun. His longtime colleague, the strict bark to his sly bite. They'd been very different men who'd shared all too little common ground, but if there was one thing El could trust in, it was the Blackstaff's magic.

If he could find it. All he had to do, among all these thousands upon thousands of bound volumes and even more scrolls, was find those Khelben had written, rewritten, edited, or penned under names other than his own. Unfortunately, having detested the man's stodgy, plodding, and dogmatic style, he'd paid as little attention to Khelben's writings as he could. Which meant he could recall just six titles, knew of the existence of another ten or so . . . and remembered the contents of just two books, one of which would be no help at all in his present quest.

While impostors among the Avowed around him hindered him or even sought to kill him.

Just once he'd caught a glimpse of the other Andannas Dalkur from afar, across the central courtyard of the monastery, but the other monk had hastily turned away, pulled his cowl up over his head, and vanished through a door into a maze of passages that could have taken him almost anywhere within the fortress.

Lurking in hiding.

Elminster smiled wryly. As he was, himself—and judging by the bodies he'd found, more than one other might be doing as well, here in this great, gloomy stone pile of a monastery.

Lurking in hiding, while war and chaos raged and reigned all around.

There was a lot of that, these days.

It wasn't much of an army camp. Tents huddled here and there in the seemingly unbroken forest. Even with all the felling for firewood and the digging of dung pits, the trees were so old and vast that the disturbances of the besiegers seemed lost among them. Those hidden and scattered tents actually formed a great ring around Myth Drannor, but far enough back from those soaring towers as to be out of earshot of the endless singing, that wordless chorus of song and chiming that was strangely alluring. And deeply unsettling. Elves *were* different, and the world would be a better place when they were all eradicated.

Not that his mission here would accomplish that. It would, however, put an end to the damnable singing.

Helgore of Thultanthar strode through the encampment undisguised, his cloak flapping, and shifting tongues of his own darkness traveled with him like so many striding shadows. Mercenaries aplenty were huddled around their cookfires and snoring in their tents. All of them seemed to be following orders: every tent had its pair of armed and watchful sentinels, standing back to back staring out into the dark forest, well away from the fires—and the light of every fire was shaded by shields driven into the earth at angles to form walls. Blackened shields of the older, heavier sort not favored in battles these days formed the bed of each fire, to keep flames from spreading and burning out the besiegers.

The sentinels watched Helgore as he passed, but not one of them was unwise enough to challenge him. The lone walker's dark skin, emanation of shadows, and his face—two bright eyes staring out of roiling shadow—told them he was a shade, and his purposeful, even swaggering gait betokened high rank.

He should have been stopped and questioned, at the very least, but the hireswords weren't looking for traitors who were shades.

Helgore's lip curled. They should have been.

The sharp wits, forethought, and ruthlessness of Telamont Tanthul might prevent open rebellion, but the Shadovar Helgore had known all his life were constantly scheming to advance themselves and discredit others, and to let the princes of Shade know and see as little as possible of their true ambitions and deeds. *Everyone* had hidden wealth and weapons, and plans for a life outside Thultanthar that began with a swift escape from the city. And everyone was learning all they could of the suddenly tumultuous world around their city, with an eye to making use of what they learned for their own private advantage, in ways large and small, despite any plans for conquest the Most High might proceed with.

Helgore himself wouldn't have dreamed of crossing the Most High in the smallest detail or degree, but he wouldn't—couldn't—have sworn the same for any of his fellow Shadovar. Even Maerandor.

Hmm. Perhaps *especially* Maerandor.

Helgore thrust that darkly amusing thought aside. What was ahead needed his full attention. The camps were behind him now, and he was heading up into the trampled clearing where wounded mercenaries were tended to, and those held in reserve were assembling. Swordcaptains gave Helgore hard and suspicious stares, but he ignored them, striding on toward the din of battle and the flaring, moving glows amid the trees that marked where elven armor was being tested. The hard way.

The front lines were within sight, not that the darkness of deepening night and all the trees made it easy to actually see anything.

Myth Drannor was more tended forest than it was buildings, and entirely lacked walls, moats, ditches, or any of the other usual defensive barriers besiegers faced when attacking most cities.

So this siege was an endless series of running skirmishes in the deep forest, often fought amid ancient trees with not a building in sight. At first, the Shadovar-led army had set fire to the forest to try to scour the battlefield bare and drive the elves out, but the smoke had proved deadly, choking the besiegers more than the elves—who had no doubt devised spells to protect themselves against forest fires long ages ago—and lending elf strike bands ample cover to move around, pounce, and slaughter.

Closer to the fabled elf city, the mythal prevented small fires and dampened large ones, making burning anything down nigh impossible. And in the vast forest, the elves were in their element. In the fray they melted away into the trees seemingly at will, often racing lightly aloft through the countless boughs. They knew which glades were now disguised deadfalls that would plunge unwary invaders down into the yawning cellars of vanished or overgrown buildings. And there were all too many such ruins, remnants of the halcyon days when Myth Drannor had been larger, brighter, and home to all races, the fabled City of Song of flourishing art, growth, and harmony among all peoples.

So it had come down to the Shadovar trying to bury their foes under sheer numbers, wearing down the far fewer elves but taking horrific losses as they slowly, ever so slowly, drove the defenders back. Losses that made the hireswords—men mustered from many lands, whose good pay could, after all, be spent only by the survivors—ever more wary and surly, and all too apt to retreat or take no chances at all rather than press hard in the fray and perhaps shatter the elf lines.

The Most High was both methodical and calculating, but his cold and unhurried calm did not mean his patience was endless. Myth

Drannor had to fall, and had to fall soon. Unfortunately, the city's mythal was itself the prize, so the quick victory stroke of assembling the arcanists of Thultanthar and hurling their Art against the mythal to destroy it and end this strife in a swift cataclysm of utter destruction was out of the question. Rather, this must be done the slow, hard way, sword to sword and hurling only small battle spells that would not threaten the mythal.

And so it fell to Helgore to be Telamont's dagger unlooked for, to stab at the belly and groin of a foe whose attention was kept elsewhere by this endless hacking and stabbing amid the trees. Helgore's task was to drain and destroy baelnorn after baelnorn, robbing Myth Drannor of its wise and mighty magical guardians who might well be able to control the mythal with adroit and precise spells to keep it as a shield for the city while also turning it into a sword against the Shadovar-led attackers. Just why the Most High valued the mythal so highly, demanding it go undamaged while swords ran red with gore within and beneath it, was none of Helgore's business. In truth, he cared not.

His concern was to destroy baelnorns so swiftly and thoroughly that the Most High would be mightily impressed even though he was the source of all the weapons and training that made Helgore able to do so, the undead-destroying spells and the gem.

The high loregem, to be precise. How Telamont Tanthul had come by the seemingly ancient *selukiira*, Helgore had no idea. Again, not his affair.

What mattered to him was that it functioned as a passkey to the mythal that was all around him now, its embattled verges giving the deep forest an eerie silver-blue glow.

A handful of outnumbered elves had just been forced to abandon the trees around, as hundreds of fresh mercenaries had fallen upon them, hacking tirelessly. The Myth Drannans had fled into a deeper tangle of trees, and the besieging hireswords had rushed right after them. Giving Helgore the moment of relative peace and privacy he needed.

Shrouding himself in the usual instant of thickening darkness, like smoke suddenly tumbling through the air close around him, he put his back to the trunk of a large, old, and leaning duskwood tree, and looked all around to make certain no one was watching— or worse yet, readying a bow, spell, or charge for him. Seeing no watchers, he quickly unsealed a warded belt pouch, then drew out and unwrapped a cloaking scrap of black shadow-imbued cloth to reveal the long and sparkling loregem. Its facets winked at him as the rainbow tourmaline caught the silver-blue light of the forest. He held it up—and swallowed it.

It was hard and pointed, and hurt going down. And, he decided after a few cautious moments, didn't make him feel one whit different.

Yet as he worked a spell that transformed him from a man to a long, fat black serpent and began to slither on through the trees, Helgore was aware that a certain tension that had been building around him as he'd walked closer to the elf city, a sometimes-crackling thickening of the air and the very blood in his veins, was suddenly . . . gone. The mythal was no longer fighting him; he could proceed freely. The gem was working.

Helgore tried not to pay attention to the momentary cascade of faint memories that were not his, now welling up within him. Elf memories, of course.

He didn't want to know which proud elf House this *selukiira* had come from, didn't want to know what the pointy-eared, sneering posers thought about and valued and did. Let the gem inside him be a key and nothing more. It wasn't *his* high lore, and he wanted no part of it.

Helgore glanced around again, peering out of the darkness he'd shrouded himself in to keep nearby eyes from seeing he was eating a gem and taking snake shape. There was still, so far as he could tell, no one watching.

Good. The Most High had warned him that the high loregem would mark Helgore as a foe who must be destroyed to any elf who saw it. If no elf had seen it, what was coming just might be a little easier to accomplish.

He needed to find a way down into the underground levels of old Myth Drannor. Down to the oldest elf family crypts. Blasting a hole amid all the tree roots would draw unwanted attention and probably spend a lot of magic getting nowhere near where he wanted to be. Finding a chasm opened in previous fighting would be much easier. And slipping into such a handy hole unnoticed would be best.

The first furious assault had created—or rather, revealed the hard way—more than a few such holes, but Helgore, hidden away in inner chambers of Thultanthar under Telamont's exacting tutelage, had been told rather than seen this.

Nor did the eyes of his serpent shape afford the sort of vision he was used to. He needed height, and he needed it now.

He slithered up the nearest tall tree to look around.

Ah! There, and there, and over *there*, too. The farthest one looked the most promising. It was the largest, and had a few faint, distant, and steady magical glows visible in its depths, suggesting that it opened into some broad expanse.

He slithered back down the tree and glided to that farthest chosen hole, keeping to cover and not hurrying. Right now, cloaking himself in self-created darkness—if the mythal allowed him to do so at all—would certainly draw attention to his presence.

Let the elves spend their spells and ply their swords against the mercenaries, instead of hunting him down. That's what the Shadovar armies had been hired for, after all.

He passed over many bodies, some of them too cooked by spells to have started to rot. Most were human, sprawled and butchered, but there were elves, too, and more of them the farther he went.

Between two massive serpentine duskwood roots, most of the way to the hole in the forest floor he was heading for, he came upon what looked to him to be an elf knight—a splendidly armored warrior, a female. Her helm was damaged—the visor torn aside and the spear that had claimed her life still buried deep in her face, thrusting up out of it like a leaning sapling—but the rest of her was more or less intact.

Helgore reared up and took a long, careful look at her, seeking to capture in memory her build, her hair, and the precise hue and shaping of her boots, gauntlets, and armor. Its plates overlapped here and there, and were especially graceful here and over here—and he needed all of this, every last detail, tamped down in his remembrances so as to be able to shift his snake shape into an exact likeness of her when he reached the bottom of that hole.

Or even earlier, if the way down should prove to be a damaging plunge for a snake but climbable by a slender, armored elf.

He slithered on, his advance scaring small, scuttling things amid the leaves into relocating elsewhere. A good thing; their presence argued against elves waiting in concealment nearby to pounce on a snake as long as any three of them.

He reached the ragged edge of the pit, where a part of old Myth Drannor had collapsed under spells and furiously battling elves and men, to reveal older chambers and passages below. Most folk thought of dwarves, when it came to delving beneath the earth, but elves had hollowed out chambers aplenty here, and shaped and rearranged living roots as carefully as any exacting palace gardener, so as to build their city as much beneath and in the living earth as above, within trees and atop their interwoven branches.

He could see enough to be certain this wasn't just one large underground chamber whose ceiling had fallen in. No, there were *streets* of chambers down there, leading off into buried darkness. Yes, what he sought would be somewhere down there.

Even better, the way down looked to be straightforward, and was. Roots trailed down into the gloom like half a dozen cables, and a serpent could coil around them and proceed along them with slithering ease.

So he did that, and when down on a floor of moss-girt earth, with not a flagstone in sight, Helgore sought a corner of a room he'd seen from above, that would be sheltered from most spying gazes from both the forest above and from surrounding underground areas, and became the likeness of that elf knight.

Rising up slender and shapely, with armor that made no sound as it moved because it was part of him.

Helgore flung up his arms and twirled around on his toes like a dancer, to settle into the feel of this new body and how it balanced and moved.

Better and better. His vision was his own again, and this body had a catlike grace he favored.

He headed off down the largest of the underground passages, seeking archways surmounted by House sigils, the traditional entrances to the burial crypts of high elf Houses.

Shouts and the clang of swords came faintly to him from behind and above, from the opening where the forest had fallen in, but down here it was strangely quiet and deserted, with no sign of mercenaries or defenders.

Helgore walked a long way in the lilting, silent gait of his new shape, along a tunnel-like, curved-walled passage that gently wended to the left and was festooned by an intricate web of exposed roots.

He halted in an instant when he saw movement ahead—but not quickly enough.

The elf who came toward him was tall, imperious, and wearing a high-collared robe. No baelnorn, but a male of still-vigorous years, whose eyes and hands glowed with risen magic. He seemed to be alone.

"Embruara of Duemethyl, what brings you here?"

That challenge was far from friendly, but Helgore shaped his lips into a tremulous smile.

Get close, and then . . .

Rune shook her head in silent wonder at the sheer beauty before her.

Storm had led them through a gate behind a tapestry in the back room of a toy shop in an unfashionable part of Suzail. One step past that hanging—a faded working of blue unicorns sporting with satyrs in a wooded glade—she'd been plunged into the familiar sensation of gently falling through an endless void of warm royal blue.

Yet her next step had been here, somewhere far enough from the capital of Cormyr that the damp sea air was gone and a cool mountain breeze was in its place. A somewhere that looked out over an endless forest, as the moon rose bright and clear, bathing everything in silver.

Under Selûne's silvery light, beneath a sky studded with twinkling stars, the land below seemed so tranquil.

"As pretty as the kiss of a princess," Arclath murmured, from behind her. "And as misleading as the honeyed tongue of a dock trader."

"That, Lord Delcastle," Storm agreed gently, "has been said a time or two before. In my hearing, by folk standing right here, arriving when the weather is fair. Sometimes, the winds howling over this height would freeze your heart and set your teeth to chattering before you could wax so lyrical. I'm afraid it's more than a fair walk from here to Myth Drannor. The mythal keeps closer ways closed."

"Where are we, exactly?" Arclath asked, looking back over his shoulder and seeing the distant many-spired rock wall of the Thunder Peaks rising to the stars.

"Right here," Storm teased, and then added, "This is Downdragon Tor. Named for the dying fall of a red dragon onto this height, after a midair death struggle between two such wyrms, one summer when I was young."

"Four years back, or five?" Arclath replied swiftly.

"Oh, you *are* a sly gallant, sirrah," Storm reproved him fondly. "Don't make me regret dragging you from your hearth and wine, now."

"So 'sly gallant' means base flatterer?" Amarune asked her lover archly.

Lord Arclath Delcastle shrugged. "The words used pale before what is heard and understood, as always, ladies. Pillory me not, I but speak fond foolishness to the two greatest ladies it's ever been my honor to escort anywhere."

Storm and Rune looked at each other. "Base flatterer," they agreed in crisp unison.

Arclath sighed. "Outnumbered and vanquished," he declaimed mournfully. "Lead on, Lady Bard. As impressive as the view may be, I doubt a desire to tarry here is what moved you to drag me from idle luxury into sword-ready danger. 'A fray that will probably mean your death' was how you described it, as I recall."

81

"Yet you rose, buckled on your blade, ate a handwheel of cheese in two bites while you dragged on your boots, and came with us," Storm reminded him.

"'Twas the 'us' that carried me into whatever imprudence you might have commanded, not the spice of danger," Arclath replied. "Speaking of which, lead on, Lady of the Harp."

Storm smiled. "Now *there's* a nice name I've not been called before." She looked at Rune. "You chose a well-spoken one."

Amarune smiled. "I chose the best. Or rather, he chose me. Rather persistently, as I recall."

Arclath winced. "Shall we revisit my style, or lack of it, later?"

Storm was already heading down a narrow, winding path that clung to the weathered rock walls of the tor. In the steepest spots along it, steps had been carved out of the solid rock. They followed her down into a wild wood of rock creeper vines, old and jagged rocks, and struggling felsul and quarr trees.

"Where are we heading? Within Myth Drannor, I mean?"

"Dlabraddath, first." Catching sight of Rune's puzzled look, Storm explained, "The part of the city that was open to all races in elder days. Since the city was rebuilt, it's been where commoners of low coin dwell, sell, and buy, keeping shops for wealthier folk to flock to. So its defenders won't just be elves, and we run a lower risk of being lightning bolted on sight by the nearest high mages."

Arclath winced. "I'd forgotten their fervent dislike of the likes of us."

The woodland path they followed cut around a towering stand of duskwoods and out into the open where a small fire—lightning, probably, and no more than two seasons ago—had cleared a slope down to ashes and blackened spars that were the tusklike remnants of trees.

They traversed that slope, and others beyond, then nine or more rolling, wooded hills, to emerge at last on a height where Storm stopped and flung out an arm.

Amid the trees stretching out below were a few slender spires of towers, and nearer jutted up three separate keeps that looked like the turreted gate towers of Suzail.

In a great ring around these buildings were the tents, campfires, and glittering weapons of a vast besieging army.

"Behold," Storm announced, in a voice that had a clear bitter edge to it, "Myth Drannor! A jewel ruined and rebuilt and ruined anew more times than it should have been. That now bids fair to fall once more. Because to some fools, a city so fair must be made to fall."

"I—I—am hurt!" Helgore gasped. "W-where am I, exactly?"

"Right here, Lady Duemethyl. In the Promenade of the Fallen. A place I am charged to guard, where you should not be."

"Oh," Helgore murmured, feigning injury and dazedness, swaying as he staggered nearer to the imperious elf. "Oh, dear . . ."

He put one hand to his head, moaned as if in despairing pain, and felt blindly for the elf barring his way, or the nearest wall, or something solid to cling to.

Shaking his head and murmuring wordlessly to himself, he sensed rather than saw the elf smoothly step out of the way to avoid being touched, and raise a hand festooned with rings that winked and glowed as he called on the magic within them.

So he'd have to strike now, and this was as close as he was going to get.

His back to the imperious elf, Helgore made the forearm and fingers of the hand that were most hidden from the guardian grow longer, and slipped the incantation of the vampiric spell Telamont had taught him into his mumblings.

It tingled down his lengthened arm, and he spun around and lunged, willing his arm longer still.

The guardian shouted and flung up both hands, bright magic lashing out—but the tips of Helgore's longest two fingers brushed the recoiling elf's elbow for an instant.

And that was all that was needed.

The roiling radiances of the spell lashed out, red and purple and edged with black, washing over the shouting guardian, whose shout had time only to soar in fear into a sort of startled mew before it abruptly ended.

The guardian staggered back, and Helgore cast one swift glance down the promenade to make sure there were no witnesses. Seeing only empty darkness, he looked back at his victim, the tingling in his arm becoming a numbing explosion of silent spasms, and watched as the spell raged up the elf's body, draining the guardian of vitality, blood, and moisture, the eyes becoming two dark pits above a vainly gasping mouth.

The doomed elf sagged as his life-force poured into Helgore, who stood over him watching in satisfaction.

Well, now. Drain enough elves, and one could live forever, yes?

The guardian collapsed into a puddle on the floor, mere shriveled skin over bones.

Helgore broke off his spell before it was entirely done in his haste to shape himself into an exact likeness of this imperious elf as Helgore had first seen him, hale and frowningly alert, before he forgot any details of the guardian's appearance.

He thought he'd succeeded well enough, but truncating a spell has consequences. When he turned away, the puddle on the floor stirred, tugged eerily as if connected to him by invisible cords, and then . . . the skin of his victim flowed away from its bones.

Helgore looked down at it with interest, then regarded the sprawled bones. Anyone walking down the passage could hardly miss them. Which might raise an alarm and hamper him, before he was done with his work here. So these bones should go, or at least be put somewhere a trifle less in the way.

He looked up and down the promenade, seeking handy hiding places. Every doorway along the way was set into its own alcove, and there were scores of them, a long curving row of closed stone doors graven with House sigils, each of them its own dark byway. He kicked the bones into the darkest corner of the nearest, and turned away.

In his wake, the skin of the elf he'd just slain slithered after him like an obedient dog.

CHAPTER 6

Time to Loose the Prowling Beast

WELL, LORD DELCASTLE?"

Arclath looked his ladylove up and down. Not that it was easy in the dimness of the deep forest all around them and through the darkness that now clung to her. Her face was entirely hidden; he could just make out the gleam of her eyes through what seemed a roiling cloud of smoke.

"I prefer to see what I want to kiss," he told Storm. "Just to avoid broken noses and chipped teeth, you understand. Yet I won't deny this shadowy look has a certain exotic allure." He looked at Rune. "Tell me, does it tickle?"

"No," she replied with a chuckle, "and that's a good thing, being as she's started on you already."

"What, and didn't even buy me a drink first?"

"My, but what passes for humor among nobles is . . . *interesting*," Storm commented darkly as she strolled around Arclath, studying him critically as her illusory darkness built around his shins like swirling smoke, and started to drift higher. "Seldom amusing, but interesting."

"We learn from the very best," Arclath assured her affably. "Jesters, bards, and Elminsters."

Storm's reply to that was a snort. Ere she stepped back, looked him up and down, and pronounced, "You'll do. We look like three Shadovar arcanists showing our true selves so the motley mercenaries we've hired from all around the Sea of Fallen Stars and beyond will recognize us, and not put swords or crossbow bolts through us."

"By accident," Arclath amended dryly.

"By accident," Storm agreed. "Now let's get going. It's a fair hike through yon army. One piece of advice, if I may: Lord Arclath Delcastle of Cormyr, *try* to keep your mouth shut. You don't sound Netherese enough to fool anyone. Let me talk, as the two of you do the murmur, mumble, and 'stare silently' routine."

"By your command, Marchioness," Arclath agreed with sardonic formality, falling into step behind Rune. Rune chuckled again.

Ahead of them both, Storm was already striding purposefully onto the little path that led to the latrines and on down into the encampment below.

As they passed the expected aroma, Arclath wondered for the fourscore and second time why soldiers always seemed to dig their latrines *uphill* from where they'd be sleeping—but keeping in mind Storm's command, he wondered it silently. Crossing Storm was best done for very good reasons, and as seldom as possible.

The camp was the usual confusion of men trotting in various directions all at once, laden with firewood and weapons and grimly important looks, but it was quieter than most. No officers were shouting urgent orders.

Not that any were needed. The siege had settled into a daily grind of fighting in the trees, slowly wearing down vastly outnumbered defenders who couldn't replenish their losses.

The three false Shadovar walked straight through it all unchallenged, heading for the clang of sword on sword, the occasional brief flashes of spells, and the smoke drifting from where fiery spells had set trees aflame.

Arclath set himself to wondering again. This time as to why exactly this age-old, merry woman with octopus-like living hair the hue of polished silver was taking them straight into the heart of the thickest choking smoke.

Rune was coughing already. Storm turned, murmured something, and touched her throat, then kept right on turning until her long fingers tapped Arclath under the chin.

He blinked. There was still smoke all around them, so thick it was getting hard to see, and he could smell the sharp, acrid burning in his nose—gods, *up* his nose—but the tickle in his throat, the searing that threatened to set him choking, was just . . . gone.

"How—?" he blurted involuntarily.

"Magic," Storm purred in his ear. "Pray *silence*, Arclath. Not for all that much longer, but for now. Please."

Her unseen hand captured his, and a thigh that, by what was belted around it, almost certainly belonged to his Rune brushed against his. Storm led them both by the hand down a little slope, into the blinding heart of the thickest smoke.

Arclath could see nothing of their surroundings then, not even what must have been a large, gnarled old tree trunk as he brushed—scraped—past it. The world around them was lost to view, entirely hidden in smoke.

Storm stopped suddenly. Her arms proved as strong and immobile as iron bars, abruptly halting Arclath and Amarune as they started to walk obliviously on.

"Down," she murmured nigh their ears. "Sit down, then lie down, trying not to lose hold of my hand."

I couldn't if I wanted to, Arclath thought ruefully, doing as she'd commanded and saying nothing. She is *so* much stronger than I am, this Lady Bard, I can scarce believe it. She looks in good trim, yes, thewed as well as buxom, but I do believe that if she ran to meet a galloping horse, and they crashed together, it would not be the horse that raced on unchecked. Ye *gods*, she has a grip like thick forged steel.

He couldn't see Rune, but knew she'd laid herself down on the ground on the far side of Storm, just as he'd now done.

Abruptly, that iron grip relaxed and his hand had its freedom back, but he could feel what seemed to be a dry lapping wave flowing over his chest and arms, tracing the shape of his torso. Soft and yet firm, a manyfold caress at once reassuring and yet at the same time clearly bidding him, without a word being spoken, to remain still.

Storm's hair, those long silver tresses that moved like so many serpents with minds of their own.

Their owner was murmuring something soft and low, strange words that bore the hum of power. An incantation.

As it came to an end Arclath felt suddenly rigid, hard and cold and somehow at the same time detached from himself, distant from the smoke-muffled din of battle. He *couldn't* move, not a muscle, even his breathing came with a struggle, through a tightening chest and throat.

And now, he was tight all over.

Helpless. Immobile on this battlefield sharp with the stink of charcoal, of trees gone half to ash and brush scorched away into windblown cinders.

Storm's hair was gone, her reassuring touch absent too . . . and now the very ground beneath him had left him.

He rose into the air, ascending smoothly. Straight up, if the eddying and swirling smoke around him could be trusted.

And then he was rising no longer, but sliding forward through the air, horizontal and feet first, scudding along rigid through thinning smoke . . . yet into air that was somehow *thicker*, heavier and yet alive.

His heart thudded and the air all over his body jutted out on end as a tingling within him grew and grew and . . . he was briefly aware of a soundless burst and a roiling of impossibly bright blueness, a spray that washed over him like water yet left no wetness upon him that he lanced through as lights flared and pulsed silently around him and then were gone in his wake.

The air thinned, and the thrilling, tingling vitality left him—left behind in that place in his wake where the air had been thicker and heavier. Suddenly Arclath knew what had happened. The mythal. He'd just flown through the magical walls of Myth Drannor without harm.

Not alone, of course. Storm had done it and was with him, and somehow he could feel Rune beyond her, the three of them arrowing on in unison.

Over flashing swords and struggling men and elves, and what was briefly a grisly carpet of the sprawled and bloody dead below, ere they all raced into a dark, riven shell of stone, and slowed as abruptly as if an unseen giant's hand had barred their way and started to drag them down.

Down they sank, through what had been a magnificent upswept tower before boulders the size of warehouses had been hurled into it, to crash against and then through its walls. What was left of the tower was a mere shell, broken open to the sky and all down one flank.

They sank past a collapsed floor hanging in tatters, and amid the wreckage he saw more bodies, many so battered and smeared that they were more bloody splatterings on the old stones than corpses. Beyond that was another floor that no longer existed and sweeping stairs, which lay shattered and dangling in splintered claws, ending in nothingness. Then they sank past a mirror, in which Arclath saw not a silver-haired bard flanked by two younger humans, but three ballista shafts, the great sleek iron war lances fired like giant arrows by wagon-sized ballistae.

Then they passed into deeper darkness, as a great stone floor rose to meet them, and the jagged roots of the tower walls hid the forest battlefield from view.

And they were human again, stumbling as their feet met shattered flagstones and abundant strewn stone rubble atop that floor.

Storm's strong arms steadied them, and Arclath couldn't keep himself silent any longer. "Ballista shafts? You fired us into Myth Drannor disguised as *ballista shafts*?"

"Flew us, actually," the Bard of Shadowdale murmured. "Yes. And through the mythal—*the* Mythal—yes. Some centuries back Elminster showed me how to pass through it without visible display or taking harm. So . . ."

She raised a warning finger to her lips and tilted her head warningly in the direction of the stairs leading up out of the dimness around them. Down them had come a clinking sound. They listened to it in silence, and when no sounds of someone moving closer came, Storm leaned close to Arclath and Rune and added a quieter whisper. "Welcome to the besieged remnants of Myth Drannor. Specifically, to the ruins of an old watchtower recently shattered by the besiegers, in the part of the city where all races mixed: Dlabraddath."

Arclath and Amarune gave each other reassuring glances that became an embrace. Lord Delcastle wasn't just reassured to see his ladylove's face and know she was unharmed, he was reassured to find Storm's conjured darkness gone, so he could see Rune at all.

"And now?" Rune asked Storm, from the sheltering warmth of Arclath's arms.

The ageless bard smiled rather impishly. "Now we try to slip out of here into the city proper. Which probably won't be all that easy."

Arclath gave her a wry half grin. "Why do I *know* you're right about that?"

"Possibly because you've learned the trifling beginnings of a sense of how the world works during your years thus far, Lord Delcastle," she replied, as haughtily as any dowager duchess of Cormyr.

Arclath grinned at her. "You've never stopped being a marchioness of the Forest Kingdom, have you?"

Storm smiled back at him. "I've never felt the need to stop. It comes in useful. Briefly and every century or so."

Rune sighed. "If you two ornaments of belted nobility are *quite* finished being arch . . ." She indicated the stairs with an elaborate flourish that would have done the most flamboyant servant proud.

Storm chuckled as she strolled to the worn stone steps. "Lady Delcastle, you're a fellow belted ornament now."

"*Don't* remind me. Bad enough that I seem to be some sort of echo of Elminster."

Storm snorted. "I've heard similar sentiments a time or two before, from others."

"And what befell those others?" Arclath asked.

"They're dead. Of passing years, not some sort of curse or inevitable lurking doom. Now *belt up*, I pray you. This *is* a battlefield, remember?"

And with that, Storm led the way up the rubble-choked stairs, her silver tresses holding swords and daggers at the ready and swirling out to probe the walls, steps, and ceiling ahead.

Beams had fallen, to lean and slope in a crazy maze, but the lady bard picked her way calmly through them, stepped delicately over a crushed body from which a lone rib jutted up like a dagger, and headed for a narrow strip of daylight where a door stood ajar, jammed half open by what had fallen on it from above.

The two young Cormyreans joined her, halting abruptly as she flung out a wall of silver tresses like a barrier in front of them. More of her hair had drifted past the edge of the door to hold up a polished silver vial from her belt to serve as a mirror.

Storm studied what was reflected in its tiny side, sighed so softly they could barely hear her, and drew her hair back in around her into a sedate mane that would arouse no comment until she passed someone who happened to notice its sheer size; it was as if she was wearing a large trader's carrysack down her back, but all made of solid hair.

She shot them a silent, severe "Behave!" warning look over her shoulder, then stepped smoothly around the door.

They came out into leaf-dappled sunlight and found themselves in a field hospital of sorts, a litter of cots among the roofless remnants of a hall that had been attached to the tower. On all sides wounded elves lay in suffering silence or murmuring pain, tended by elves, half-elves, a dwarf, and two humans.

One of those humans was a lame, badly limping barrel of a man, a warrior or former warrior by the looks of his sword scars and the filthy remnants of what had once been a leather war harness. Standing in the path that led down from the tower door through what had been the main aisle of the hall, he turned quickly at the sound of footfalls in the rubble before the tower door, snatching at a long, wicked dagger at his belt and growling wordless challenge like a dog.

At his first sight of Storm he froze, jaw dropping open in astonishment that became a wide smile of joy. He left off drawing his dagger to put hands on hips and stand and stare, grinning.

Storm strode toward him serenely, having seen his jovial, crude and worldly wise sort a time or thousand before.

"Hoy, now!" he exclaimed. Then, catching sight of Arclath striding just behind Storm, he grinned. "Snuck off into the tumbled stones for a bit o' privacy, hey? Well, can't say as I blame—"

The warrior broke off as he espied Rune behind Arclath. He sidestepped, leaned, and peered hard to make sure there were only three people coming toward him out of the fallen tower where there should have been no one. He hadn't seen any women among the besiegers before, but . . .

Then his leer returned, even more broadly. He gave Arclath a wink and growled, "Well, if some jacks don't have *all* the luck in fair Faerûn! Still, if you're man enough . . ."

"Crude oaf," Rune commented, but almost fondly.

The man chuckled. "Well, lass, if you ever wear him out, keep me in mind, hey? Thardyn Hammerhar; 'the Hammerer,' they call me, and it's not for—"

"Your subtlety," Storm completed his sentence for him dryly, striding past. "Now, where is the coronal most likely to be found?"

"The *coronal?*"

"Yes," Storm said crisply. "Ilsevele. Or Fflar, if he's not too busy fighting at the moment."

The man gaped at her. "Who *are* you?"

"Just one of many you should treat a trifle more politely," Storm replied gently, as several of her long silver tresses darted out to encircle the wrist of a half-elf healer at a nearby cot, and forestall his stealthy drawing of a dagger. She whirled to confront him.

Thardyn Hammerhar grabbed again for his own dagger—but froze once more as he felt Arclath's sword tip at his throat. The young noble watched him sternly from right behind it.

Amarune stepped past them all to regard the rest of the wounded and those tending them, and announced, "No trouble, please. We are not here to do you harm." She raised her hands as if she was a mighty—and calmly confident—archmage, and stood waiting.

Behind her, the half-elf healer tugged with all his might, but couldn't make his sword arm more than tremble in the grip of silver hair that was suddenly as immovable as a wall of iron, as he and Storm stared expressionlessly into each other's eyes.

More of her tresses were moving, doing other things. One of them was plucking up a stone, a shard of the ruin, and holding it beside her face, in front of his gaze.

Still other tresses reached out as gently as a windblown feather to a wound that was seeping blood through its bindings, to return blood smirched, and with the wet gore draw a symbol—two vertical lines bracketing two identical ovals—on the stone.

Storm watched the eyes she was gazing into closely, but saw no recognition there. Her tresses smeared the blood across the stone to obscure the symbol she'd made, and she released the healer.

Arclath watched. Had that been a Harper rune, or an old sigil of the elves? He knew better than to ask Storm, even as he tried to fix the symbol in his memory for later. If there *was* a later . . .

"Ilsevele?" Storm repeated, to all of the silently watching, astonished healers. "Fflar?"

One of the elves among them shook his head a little helplessly, but offered her a bowl. "Broth?"

"An acceptable alternative," Storm replied with a smile as dazzling as it was sudden.

He'd seen the monks frowning after him as he'd hastened back out of the kitchens. Obviously, it wasn't like Chethil to journey down into Candlekeep's extensive cellars and forget to fetch back anything at all needed for the evening meal. Not to mention something so large, obvious, and awkward to carry as *onions* . . .

95

Maerandor shrugged. His fellow workers in the kitchens would be noticing other small and no doubt odd changes in their senior cook, henceforth; he couldn't help that.

He took care not to look back as if he was checking to see if he was being followed. The creaking door at the head of the second stair he'd be taking was all the alarm he needed; if he heard it not, there was no pursuit.

Not that he cared overmuch, though it would have been *very* inconvenient to have to kill Rethele or Shinthrynne just now, and be saddled with even more cooking.

All he needed was long enough to hasten along this old, well-worn hall, and back up the other stair into the Long Passage—he could tell it was deserted just now because he couldn't hear the Endless Chant echoing along it—to do what must be done next.

Before he returned in triumph to the kitchens with the sleeves of onions he'd hidden ready earlier, that is.

The passage was indeed deserted, and here was the stretch of wall he sought. Here where the everglow was strongest. He slid the hood off the old candle lamp, raised it, and started scorching and blackening the stone with care, making a certain mark—two vertical lines bracketing two identical ovals—*thus.*

And it was done, that swiftly. He spun around and strode back to the stair that had brought him there; standing back and taking time to admire your handiwork was an apt-to-be-fatal mistake of the rash and inexperienced.

He knew it stood out dark, fresh, and clear behind him. The symbol that would alert other monks who'd been subverted by the Shadovar long ago that it was at last time to rise, and act.

"Act" as in eliminating all other monks and seizing control of the monastery. With no monks left to try to wield the wards against foes—such as revealed Shadovar, when the time came—the wards would hum unaltered, and could be drained all the more easily. And that time would be soon.

So, now, take the next step closer.

Maerandor smiled as he went to fetch his onions.

Time to loose the prowling beast.

Its lack of wrinkles had told him that Andannas Dalkur's face seldom wore a scowl, to say nothing of a frown, so Elminster took care not to let his inward frown reach the borrowed face he was wearing.

It was the twelfth day of Marpenoth today. Which meant he couldn't deny that it was taking him a very long time to uncover which tomes Khelben had secretly taken a hand in crafting, or written outright, without being overly obvious about it.

It was taking him even longer to *find* any of them.

Might even take him forever.

Thus far, he'd laid eyes or hands on not a single one.

In room after room, he'd found the titles he knew to look for were missing. Even *The Beneficial Flows and Their Mastery*, a book the monks often copied for various rulers and civic officials because it was so exhaustively practical a work on sewers, drainage, and fertilizer. The keep had owned more than thirty copies of that particular tome . . . yet he could find none of them.

Obviously someone who'd arrived in Candlekeep before him shared his conclusions about Khelben—that the Blackstaff had hidden clues within his works here at the keep. Possibly in the form of invisible-under-normal-circumstances magical writing, or more likely by means of a skip spell that—once triggered by the utterance of the right word or phrase, or the touching of the right sequence of separated words on a particular early page of the book—would illuminate specific words of the text throughout the book, in a particular sequence, to form different sentences than met the eyes of any casual reader.

He had come to this hunt too late. Someone, or someones, had struck first, removing the books he sought.

Still carefully not frowning, El did not turn away from the shelf that hadn't held the Arunsun-penned tome that should have been there, but instead peered along it, as if interested in the nicely bound dross that filled out its run. He could feel the weight of suspicious scrutiny from behind him, like a spear boring through his back between his shoulder blades, and from his left, like the searing flame of a too-close fire. There were multiple monks in both directions, apparently lost in their own silent, contemplative study of various tomes he'd already noticed weren't by Khelben.

He had taken great care, of course, not to obviously search for any book, least of all title after title by one author, and had broken off seeking Blackstaff books to peruse all manner of unrelated tomes whenever he thought he was in the presence of a monk who was the double of any of the bodies he'd found . . . yet some time ago he'd become aware that certain of the monks were covertly watching him.

Regarding him with increasing suspicion.

So now he feigned finding something that delighted him. He reached out and seized a tome with a loud and pleased, "Aha!"

His find wasn't entirely a random book; he'd pounced on a volume that had nothing to do with Khelben, but that was old enough, and written by someone who dwelled in the right location in the Realms, to have *possibly* had something to do with Khelben. The Blackstaff's publicly known offices, residences, and concerns, that is.

Tucking the tome under his arm, El scurried out of the room and down a back passage, departing the busier areas of that part of Candlekeep.

His find happened to be something that should be required reading for all practitioners of the Art, and that thieving guilds and cabals often stole on sight: *Shield and Sentinel: Observations on Warding Magic*, by Alais Maeraphym. Not a spellbook, but a workbook of half-spells and incantations that could augment the well-known castings. Useful and well written; Alais had been a warm, affectionate woman, and her prose was too. A book any novice wizard would lust after.

He hurried along dimly lit back passages and down worn but little-used stairs, heading deeper into the rocky roots of the monastery, where the spellcasting caverns were. And that very haste caused someone behind him to hurry, and so make a few little noises—scuffs and scrapes of soft leather soles on stone. There, again. Yes, someone was following him, he was sure of it.

Skulking, taking care not to make overmuch noise or show a light, but stalking him, to be sure.

El smiled tightly, and kept on going, slowing now so as not to lose his shadow.

"I thought I'd be done saving the world by now," he murmured to himself, closing and barring the one door he could so fasten behind him, to force his foe to take a longer way around. "Saving, heh. No shortage of overweening arrogance here . . . yet that *is* what I do, and know it. I strive for the better, albeit all too oft by lawless or ruthless means. Yet I can't stop, not until my oblivion comes."

He descended another stair, and added, "Because what I do must be done, and aside from the bare handful of my fellow tested and true Chosen, I can trust no one else to do it. No one."

Through another door, down a long, sloping passage, the air growing noticeably cooler, and around a bend into the first of the caverns.

"Aye, it must be done, and I am the only one I can trust to do it. As many a tyrant has believed, of course."

The cavern was empty. He crossed it in haste, hearing the first distant echoes of his follower, thwarted by the door he'd fastened closed, pelting down a distant stone stair. "So carve the headstone: 'Elminster Aumar, Better Tyrant Than Most.'"

Another passage, with another, larger cavern, loomed ahead.

"Or should that be: 'More Deluded Than Most'?"

This cavern too was deserted, its usual amber radiance shining down on the silent emptiness. El strode across it to the leftmost of the two doors set into its far wall, and found it locked. Murmuring a cantrip he'd learned more than a thousand years earlier, he went through it as swiftly as if he'd had a key.

And passed into another passage, which sloped gently, with three caverns opening off it before it hooked around and descended into a fourth.

The second cavern, with its natural pillars of fused stalactites and stalagmites, would be best for his needs. Its door proved to be locked too, but no matter save the dark thought: when had the monks of Candlekeep taken to locking the deep spellcasting caverns?

El selected where he'd take his stand, shelved the workbook in a crevice clear across the cavern, returned to his chosen spot, and calmly sat down on a rock to wait, holding his hands up as if he was cradling a tome.

He did not have to wait long.

He'd closed the cavern door in his wake, so its opening would give him some moments of forewarning. Albeit soundless forewarning; it seemed hinges were kept well oiled down in the cool depths of the keep, these days . . .

The door opened.

El kept on studying his imaginary book, his attention on it and not on the robed and cowled figure coming toward him with slow, silent care.

Knife in hand, of course. No matter that the blade and the hand holding it were hidden well inside a flared sleeve; the movements were unmistakable to one who'd seen them so often, down the centuries.

Elminster's spell mantle was, of course, waiting.

When the man was about six strides away, El looked up at him calmly.

"Aye? Is there something?"

The monk made no reply, but charged, free hand reaching out to clutch at or sweep aside El's own arms, knife held back for an upward, gutting stab.

El rose to meet the charge—then sat down abruptly, kicking out.

The monk bent and slashed, but the force of his rush and the sudden absence of his target had him overbalanced; he was on his way over Elminster, headfirst into the unyielding stone spur that had served the Old Mage—and so many monks before him—as a seat.

His vicious slashing sliced only empty air as El's feet slammed into his shins and boosted him upward, but where the dagger raced through El's invisible mantle it left a purple glow in its wake.

Poison.

Of course.

That hue told him the mantle could neutralize it if it got into him, but—

The man sprawled with a desperate grunt, managing to slam his chest against the stone and not his head, but he was winded—and El's hard kick sent the poisoned dagger spinning across the cavern to clink and ring against a distant part of its rough stone walls.

While the man was still convulsing, El landed on his back with an agility and back alley ruthlessness that was odd indeed for Andannas Dalkur, landed two swift blows that should briefly numb the man's arms at the elbow into near uselessness, slid one arm around the monk's throat in a choke hold, and set his fist against the base of the man's skull, where it could do much damage with the swiftest of raps.

"Well met," El purred sardonically into an ear that was suddenly very close to him, and sent his mind into the monk's with a ruthless thrust of his will. It was neither a polite nor a good deed, mind-reaming, but when one is at war with the proverbial fate of Faerûn in the balance . . .

"One leans on an overused excuse indeed," he murmured aloud to end that thought, as he met his first real resistance among the murky half-seen thoughts of his attacker's uppermost mind, and bore down hard.

The murkiness became a dark gray wall, like dirty wood smoke but as unyielding as iron. This mind was magically shielded. Again: of course.

Yet some things he could see more than feel. This wasn't an impostor impersonating a slain monk of Candlekeep, but a genuine Avowed who'd spent years within these walls. Corrupted by the Shadovar long ago, and for years a spy for them, reporting back what was said, read, and done within the monastery.

The man was . . . was . . . Naerlus was his name. So, what could be gleaned from the shielded mind of Naerlus? Press on here, and there, follow what the mind tried to hide, pursue the deepest darkness through the silent smoke . . .

A face, seen again. And then again.

Important, then. A face cruel and hard and not one El had seen at the keep, but coming to mind in the memories of the increasingly frightened Naerlus repeatedly as El fought to worm his way through the shield.

Was that face associated with the monk's thoughts of the Shadovar? Yes!

Latch onto the face, then, drag it nearer and clearer, and see what surfaced, dripping and entangled, with it . . .

The Shadovar speaking, smiling bleakly—the only smile Naerlus had ever seen on that cruel face, as the cruel-faced man did something important . . . bestowed something important . . .

Looking down as a gloved hand put something into the reluctant grasp of Naerlus . . . the poisoned knife!

Who was to await the sign to use it . . . "The serpent uncoils at last."

The Shadovar's cold voice uttering that pass phrase was overlaid and echoed by a far more recent whisper, said by a passing monk who had his cowl down—Naerlus hadn't known who, and hadn't dared turn to try to find out, but a book had erupted from within that monk's nearest sleeve, spine up, and had been used to point at . . . Andannas Dalkur!

So recently, then, had this slayer been set at his heels.

The pass phrase had alerted Naerlus that it was time to use the poisoned blade to slay a person indicated by the one giving the phrase. Which led nowhere. Unless . . . was Naerlus aware of anyone else working for the Shadovar at the keep? Or did he suspect anyone else? Had Naerlus ever seen the cruel-faced man speaking with any other monk?

Elminster bore down, mind-smoke swirling.

Then something angry crimson and hot and mighty surged to meet him out of that mind, power the monk's mind couldn't have held, power that shouldn't be there—

El broke his mind free with a shiver, suddenly icy cold yet drenched with sweat, and so *just* eluded a mind-thrust that would have slain him.

Someone had become aware of what he was doing, and—or, no, *someones*. More than one mind, and uncaring of what befell poor

Naerlus, to burst into his mind and come racing up through it like that while shaping a deadly mind-thrust, leaving him a reeling, drooling idiot—

Naerlus, still caught in Elminster's grasp, flung himself suddenly sideways, with a roar like an enraged lion, to slam Elminster against the sharp and very hard cavern wall, breaking the Old Mage's grip.

And whirling to grab at an ankle and come up with—a second knife.

The air shone a sudden and vivid purple in its rising wake—so this fang was as poisoned as the first—as he came at El fast, his face trembling and twisting between maniacal glee and a sort of bewilderment, as the unseen others tried to control the monk's mind, and got in each other's way.

Elminster didn't wait for them to reach accord and smooth cooperation. He darted to one side of the monk, ducking past the poisoned dagger, then turned, grabbed the monk's knife arm with both hands, at elbow and wrist, and turned the force of the monk's charge into a rush at the cavern wall, dagger foremost and locked in an extended position. Let the dagger be broken or knocked free, or the fingers that held it shattered . . .

It struck unyielding stone hard enough to strike sparks, with a shriek that became two high ringing clangs as it spun away.

The rest of the monk slammed into the wall, then bounced free. Naerlus broke out of El's grip and turned with a snarl—to drag out yet *another* knife.

Ye Watching Gods, how many daggers did monks of Candlekeep carry around, anyway? He'd best be hard and careful if any minor disputes arose over who got to read a book first! Why, the—

Naerlus came for him again, blade in hand and quivering lips mumbling something that sounded very like the faltering and choking beginnings of an incantation.

Elminster feinted a grab for the knife, and when Naerlus slashed at him, landed a punch that snapped the monk's head aside—letting El grab the wrist that held the knife, thumb firmly on the nerve that would make the knife hand numb and force Naerlus to let go of his weapon.

He dug in with his thumb, and with his other hand caught Naerlus by the throat.

"My apologies, Avowed of Candlekeep," he murmured as the eyes above his tightening hand grew wild with fear and pain, "but I have this aversion to dying just now, when—"

The knife tumbled from the monk's numbed hand—and Naerlus stopped trying to claw the hand that was strangling him away from his throat and used that hand to make a wild grab for his weapon.

A grab that became a lunge that dragged Elminster off his feet—but ended in a sagging stumble that became a slow collapse to the floor.

El saw blood welling between the monk's fingers. His hand had been laid open on the edge of the knife.

The poisoned knife.

Even as El twisted around on one shoulder and scrambled to his feet, two monks came into the cavern, their faces hard and unfriendly. They took a few steps in opposite directions to get well apart from each other, planted their feet, and started to work spells.

Deadly spells that had the same obvious target.

Elminster Aumar had time enough to sigh.

CHAPTER 7

A Prince of Peerless Sorcery

S TAND ASIDE," THE DARKLY HANDSOME YOUNG MAN TOLD THE
guards coldly. "As the son of Lamorak Tanthul and grandson of
the Most High, it is my right to have an audience with my grandsire."

The guards barring his way to the tall, closed doors of the palace
at Thultanthar's heart kept their faces impassive. "Even so," the elder
one replied, "our orders are clear. No one may pass."

"*You* have no right to stop me. I say again: stand aside. Or I shall
do what is needful to clear my way to the Most High."

"Calm yourself and wait here, while we send word of your arrival.
It may be that the Most High will see you, but it is not within
our power to freely admit you through these doors. Stand, please,
while we—"

"No. Get out of the way!"

The guarded doors opened, and Prince Aglarel Tanthul looked
out, his face like stone.

"Or what, Draethren Tanthul?" he asked. "Is there something
wrong with your hearing, or your wits? 'No one may pass' seems
clear and simple to me; why does it not to you?"

"As the son of your brother Lamorak, and a prince of Thultanthar
in my own right, I *demand* audience with the Most High. So much is

106

my right—and not something you can deny me. So you too, should stand aside." Draethren raised one hand and moved his fingers in the weaving gesture that Shadovar used as a warning of their sorcerous power and their willingness to use it.

"Admittance denied," Aglarel replied flatly, folding his arms across his chest. "I am aware of the strength of your sorcery—and of your temper. You are on the verge of raging right now. Why should I let you get one step closer to the High Prince?"

"Where did you get the idea that my loyalty to the Most High or Thultanthar is any less than yours?" the young prince snapped back. "How do I know you haven't slain him and are just preventing me from discovering that? Now stand aside. My sorcery is more than sufficient to compel you—or destroy you."

As if that threat had been the order for an often-practiced military maneuver, Aglarel and the two door guards spread out in front of the doors to get apart from each other, and raised their hands as if to cast spells.

"Your estimation of your own might, young prince," Aglarel said quietly, "is more than mistaken."

Draethren's eyes blazed, but he backed up a step, darting glances at the three Shadovar arrayed against him.

"Stand aside and let Draethren, son of Lamorak, pass."

That cold, calm, and unexpected voice came from the darkness behind Aglarel—who stiffened at the sound—through the open doors.

"I could not help but overhear the *polite* salutation Prince Draethren employed to seek audience," Telamont Tanthul added.

The door guards stepped aside, and Aglarel turned to regard his father, who added gently, "It is always a mistake to dismiss the young and rash as of no account. For the day always comes when they are."

Aglarel inclined his head with an expressionless nod, and stepped back to let a wisely silent Draethren step past.

Then he fell into step behind his triumphant nephew, to escort him into the chambers within, but the Most High of Thultanthar, already on his own way back down the passage to deeper chambers, met Aglarel's eyes and commanded firmly, "Leave us."

Aglarel lifted his head in a silent signal of surprise and reluctance, but stopped right where he was—until a silent inclination of his father's head signaled him to advance and close an inner door.

Leaving Telamont Tanthul alone with Draethren, son of Lamorak.

Who was drinking in his first sight of the audience chamber without it being thronged with guards and more senior Shadovar. Deserted, it seemed both smaller and more imbued with watchful menace. Was it because of the towering seat of obsidian that seemed to loom over the entire room? Or the great black sphere-studded rod hovering upright in its corner?

Or the vast relief map that Draethren had never seen before. The metal table on the other side of the throne from the floating rod was bare, but its top was a single, irregularly sculpted black mass. A model of the lands between Anauroch and the Sea of Fallen Stars—complete with tiny floating cities hovering above it, and here and there little glows and lines of radiance that—Draethren peered—yes, denoted magical wards.

His grandfather regarded him with something that might have been wry amusement in his eyes. "You've never seen a map before?"

Nettled, Draethren shook his head and waved a hand as if to brush away both the question and all thought of maps, and burst out, "The city is *moving*!"

Telamont turned to study the map. "Our home is a flying city," he replied mildly. "Flying cities . . . fly."

"Yes, but why? My father set me the task of altering the life-drain spell to affect ward fields—and no sooner do I begin to achieve real progress than you whisk us away from the warded tomb of Anlathgrus, the only handy ward we can sacrifice. With every passing moment we get farther from the tomb, and my work is at a standstill!"

Once begun, the rage that had been simmering inside Draethren for too long boiled over. "Surely the finished ward-drain spell will enable us to use the portals, overwhelm the elves, and so take Myth Drannor in far less time and losing far fewer swords than wearing it down in a protracted siege! Is that not *why* you *wanted* a ward-drain spell?"

The Most High bent to peer closely at a particular city—possibly one of the Sembian ports—and asked, "Can it be that the son of Lamorak, the most vaunted sorcerer among the younger princes, has forgotten how to magically take himself from one place to another?"

Then he straightened, turned to face his grandson, and asked, "Why confront me, when you could simply return to the tomb and pursue your vital work?"

Draethren flushed. "I—I don't want to be away from Thultanthar at this crucial time."

"As the kin you most desire to destroy are all within it?"

The son of Lamorak slowly went pale. He opened his mouth to frame a cold and scornful protest, but found no words under the dark weight of Telamont's knowing look.

"I have been aware of your intended treachery for some time, Draethren," the Most High told him calmly, "but I should warn you that now is not the time for it. You will find my tolerance rather low."

The air in the chamber suddenly darkened and swirled, until it seemed as if many vast cloaks were gliding soundlessly through the air, circling the young Shadovar sorcerer—cloaks that had fangs.

"W-what do you mean?" Draethren stammered, finding himself eyeing them and hastily forcing himself to look back at his grandfather.

"Every one of my sons, at one time or another, has judged the elders of this city cruel and ignorant fools whose deeds and policies will soon doom Thultanthar itself. In turn, all of my grandchildren have, quite independently, come to embrace the same views. I have grown quite used to it. Some, regrettably, grow imprudent in their actions. Did you *never* wonder what happened to your elder brother Tantoras?"

"The accident that befell him was . . . no accident," Draethren muttered. "I have always known that."

"Yet you learned nothing from that knowledge? Then you are more foolish than I'd thought. That you despise your elders has been clear enough for some time now. Young princes of Thultanthar are seldom subtle—and even less often able to hide their aims from their older kin. Thankfully, most of them eventually come to see that working together for the good of our city is preferable to defiance and poorly thought-out, airy schemes."

"How is moving so *slowly* to conquer best for Thultanthar?"

"Those too hasty to snatch prizes often damage what they grasp for. Why bleed the lands that shall be ours in pointless warfare, when we can work smaller violences and steer those realms into our control without all the destruction? Lay waste when you must, but never casually ruin or consume what may be useful in time to come."

"I do not see in such lofty platitudes any justification for idle inaction."

"Draethren," his grandfather said grimly, "you do not *see*. Now go, and think on what I've said, as you perfect that ward-drain spell for us all. You may even live long enough to grow wiser."

The son of Lamorak stared at his grandsire for a long, silent time, then nodded curtly, turned on his heel, and strode out of the audience chamber.

As he swept past the door guards, he took care to ignore the trace of a smile hovering on the lips of his uncle Aglarel.

His grandfather's coldly contemptuous smile was like an icy dagger between his shoulder blades at every moment of that long, lonely walk.

The Most High of Thultanthar indulged himself in a cold little smile as he watched Draethren go. Then he awakened one of his rings to bolster his mantle before he turned his back on the young fool.

He really did want to study his map right now. The ever-shifting Weave had been collapsing for a century, yet somehow it never crashed entirely, nor faded away—and increasingly it seemed to him the reason for that seemed to be its many small local anchor points.

Some of which were here, here, and *here*.

Could it be that to truly understand the Weave, and come to govern it, one had to know *all* of its anchors, and so see how to best grasp it?

Telamont recalled with distaste his utter failure to bend the Weave to his bidding the last time he'd tried to work with it directly, rather than calling on it with spells. It had been like trying to grapple with a great wave crashing over a harbor rampart, or a gale that was shattering stout trees—and it had crashed over him in a great dark whirling that left him helpless to influence it or even work any magic at all, shattering him into an oblivion that had taken a long time to recover from.

He sighed. To find and mark every last anchor of the Weave, not to mention the moving ones that were creatures, would take a handful of days less than forever, and . . .

He smiled sourly. If Draethren thought matters were taking too long right *now* . . .

Telamont let his wraith-slaying mantle fade back into invisibility, and called on the little ward that cloaked the room to carry his words to Aglarel, outside the doors.

Fetch the next hotheaded young traitors. Dethud's daughters, I mean; I'm well aware our kin harbors a large and growing collection of the seditious. Those two are easier on the eyes than the Prince of Peerless Sorcery who just marched out of here.

Aglarel was close enough to the open door for Telamont to hear his snort of amusement, even before he leaned in to give the Most High a nod.

The two female elves facing Storm were as tall as she was, and more splendid of face and figure. They had a presence to match her own.

Yet the senior Myth Drannan elf—a male who strode between the two female guards, to the fore, and stood a head taller than them all, and as straight as an upright grounded pike with robes wrapped around it—was grand enough to awe even Arclath Delcastle. Arclath and Amarune were sheltering behind Storm and holding hands for comfort, as she faced the haughty Varorn Irrymgalis, Steward of the Southern Gate.

She was trying to offer her services—and those of Amarune and Arclath—in the defense of the city, and it was not going well.

The steward was clearly dubious.

"A longtime Chosen of Mystra, an untried young woman of uncertain magecraft, and an equally young member of the restive nobles of Cormyr," he said dismissively, his careful courtesy somehow anything but. "You must appreciate that our usual suspicion of

N'Tel'Quess who serve other masters before our coronal, within our city, is necessarily heightened now, while we are besieged. Tell me, how is it that you passed through the foes surrounding us, if you are not of them, or sent by them?"

"Magic," Storm replied dryly. "And a little base guile. Elves are not the only dwellers in Faerûn to indulge in either of those things."

Varorn's gaze went colder. "I have little patience for bandying words with children, and even less so with those who offer me evasive answers."

Storm gave him a sad smile. "I felt old when your grandsire Imlarren first asked me to dance, here under the leaves in Shimaeren's Glade—when there still *was* a Shimaeren's Glade. Yet your prudence is only right, in time of war. So many of my fellow Chosen have fallen and yielded their fire and their knowledge to me that my magic is better now than it was but a short time ago. It sufficed to hide our true natures from the army that besets you, and enabled us to pass over the fighting unrecognized."

"Through the mythal? Human, tell a better lie!"

"The mythal knows me, Varorn. I had a hand in its repair."

"That's hardly a better falsehood."

"It's the *truth*, son of Orblyn. And if you knew the true character of my companions, you'd not so swiftly dismiss—"

"Ah, but I do *not* know them. Nor you. Only the words you offer me, words so far beyond belief that I can scarce—"

"By the First, Var!" interrupted one of the female elves. "We need every sword, every spell, every healing hand, every pair of eyes—and you spurn this brave handful? If you're suspicious of them, our spells can see their thoughts, true likenesses, and root natures easily enough. Even if they came awash in mischief, they'll hardly have time to indulge in it, if we put them to fighting in the trees where the Shadovar hirelings press us!"

Arclath sidestepped to peer past the haughty elf lord at the exasperated female. So that must be Narya Ilunedrel, whom his mother had once met and grudgingly spoken highly of . . .

"You do not command here, Narya," Varorn snapped without turning.

"Nor do you," said a new voice, deep and grim.

Fflar Starbrow Melruth, the High Captain of Myth Drannor, came into the chamber, lurching in weariness, his armor scarred and stained, reeking of sweat and blood and the emptied innards of those who'd recently died on his sword.

Striding past Varorn, he regarded the three newcomers for a long, silent moment, and then said, "Be welcome, all of you. As Narya says, we need every sword, or Myth Drannor is doomed."

In the silence that followed, every pair of elf eyes in that room held the same knowledge.

Lord Arclath Delcastle was too polite to voice it, but could read it loud and clear:

Myth Drannor is doomed anyway.

Dethud's daughters were the sort of tart-tongued and darkly beautiful femme fatales who preferred to have the world think they passed their time in the languid sway of indolent boredom and were incapable of being awed or impressed by anything their mere elders did or wrought. Yet the High Prince of Thultanthar was amused to see how their eyes darted around the audience chamber whenever they thought he wouldn't notice. Their restless gazes passed over the table from which his conjured map had vanished, and returned again and again to the towering throne and especially the *tammaneth*

rod—despite the glass globes enclosed within its black spheres being empty and dark.

How fearful of their High Prince they truly were was difficult to discern beneath their purringly arch manner, but Telamont knew that to threaten or bluster would never be the right approach with these two. Not when Lelavdra and Manarlume were together, at least.

"Your manipulations of the rising arcanists of our city have not," he informed them dryly, "gone unnoticed."

"And so?" Lelavdra voiced what Manarlume merely signaled with one scornfully arched eyebrow.

"And so," Telamont continued, "I have certain special tasks in mind for you both. Your first service for Thultanthar; your path to earning trust and reputation and real power."

He paused for their questions, but they merely shifted their poses and waited in half-smiling silence for him to continue.

Cool young things, indeed.

"You will not find this work to be a stretch from your habitual . . . entertainments," he added. "You are to secretly form a club or group that meets for drinking and intimacies, behind closed doors, and invite any and all ambitious arcanists to join. Make the proceedings seem exclusive and attractive, so that your contemporaries will seek to join."

"And then do what to them?" Manarlume purred.

"And then befriend the most suspicious of them. Seek to gather even the slightest hints of disloyalty to Thultanthar, and of any secretive schemes."

"*All* of the ambitious arcanists?" Lelavdra pouted. "Some of them are frankly . . . slimy. Others, hardly men."

"All," the Most High replied calmly.

"Seducing the least loyal and biddable of Thultanthar—sharing ourselves intimately with every last one of them—is hardly a duty

Tanthuls expect to be asked to perform," Manarlume observed. "I prefer to choose my partners." She gave Telamont a sly look. "As you have no doubt already learned."

By way of reply, he regarded her in impassive silence.

After a moment, she asked softly, "And if we refuse?"

"New princesses of Thultanthar can be sired easily enough," he observed calmly. "You will not be remembered. Save as warnings to others who may contemplate such disobedience."

"Are our lives worth so little, Most High?" she asked, her voice quiet but dark fire rising behind her eyes. "Advance this or that nuance of your latest scheme, or be casually destroyed?"

"I do nothing casually, nor do I embrace 'latest schemes.' I advance Thultanthar always and unstintingly, in many ways. Such is the duty of all Tanthuls." Telamont's voice was conversational, and for the first time he felt they were a little afraid of him. "As for the worth of life, those who do not strive toward goals are hardly alive. Not that I've observed any lack of striving in either of you."

"You *have* been watching, haven't you?" Lelavdra asked archly.

"Of course. How else could I know the work for which you are best suited?"

"Your words," Manarlume observed calmly, "strike true. Shall we begin immediately?"

"It is why I summoned you now, and not a day ago."

"Then we should take our leave and begin."

Telamont nodded. "I have no doubt you'll enjoy this work. It will be preferable if you work together rather than as rivals."

"Your will be done, Most High," they murmured in chorus, and withdrew, sultry grace in every gliding movement.

Telamont watched the doors close in their wake, and muttered, "Neither of you are quite as expendable as you believe I consider you. Yet."

The steam rising from the stewpots in this dim corner of the lengthy Candlekeep kitchens dripped off the walls. Just as the sweat of Maerandor's own hard work dripped off his nose.

He stepped back with a sigh and wiped his hands dry. When chopping with a cleaver this sharp, even if the cleaving was being done just to parsnips, dry hands were a must. He wiped the cleaver's worn leather grip for good measure, hefted it, and stepped forward to the chopping board again.

And then stiffened, to freeze with cleaver raised and no parsnip menaced, as an unexpected hand touched his shoulder, then slid down his back and started to massage the stiffness there.

For an instant, Maerandor was whirling, hands darting up to slay—and in the next instant, he was forcing himself to stop and relax, shuddering under the caressing fingers.

"Locks of the Binder, Norun, but you're upset! What's wrong?"

It was Shinthrynne, and her voice held the soft concern of a friend. Not a lover. Good, that was a complication he didn't want. Lovers noticed when you slipped out of bed and away.

Not that he knew where Chethil's bed was. Shar curse and shatter. That hadn't been among what he'd been seeking in the dying cook's mind.

And of course, should have been. *Why* was life so full of "should have beens"?

Maerandor feigned a cough, then growled, "Apologies. I—" He coughed again, and it was genuine this time. The spices down this end of the kitchens were catching at the back of his throat.

Ah, but he *had* been getting stiff, and hadn't yet noticed it. The Southerner's long, slender fingers were digging deeper into his back now; she was *good* at this. He hastily started to pay attention to just where and how she was kneading, in case—

"Right, old snapjaws, now you do *me*. Stirring batter is much harder on the back than a little bending and chopping."

"Of course," he agreed, and found himself facing a truly splendid back, curving muscles flanking a long, sinuous, and deep line of spine. Shinthrynne wore only a light smock, smudged here and there with flour and a few stray petals of parsley, and he dug his fingers into it and tried to emulate what she'd just been doing to him.

"Hoy, lovers!" Rethele called, from the far end of the kitchen. "The thrummel and the dagh will be sticking and scorching in a trice, and I'm stuck down here stirring my goldaevur! Stir now, and fondle later!"

"Sorry," Shinthrynne called back, and was out from under Maerandor's fingers in a lithe instant.

Leaving him quelling a sigh. Good. Too much more of that, and his loins would have been more than just stirring.

And he had no idea how things stood between these two amiable young women and the senior cook of Candlekeep.

Well, at least he knew what thrummel was.

Men stank as they rotted. As did their dung pits, and the smoke of their cooking fires when left untended to burn refuse and nearby shrubs and saplings. Thin threads of reeking smoke were drifting through the trees as Storm, Amarune, and Arclath trudged warily along through a deep and soaring forest that was still beautiful, despite the war that had come to it, and was all around them now.

There was a faint, ever-present singing too. An ethereal, wordless rising and falling chorus that was by turns mournful and filled with exultation. Despite what looked like wild forest, they were within the City of Song.

Or what had once been Myth Drannor, before its fall and rebuilding on a smaller scale and now this siege.

Just now, the three companions were walking in a little dell that held no bodies or combatants. Just the three of them, walking among the tall trees.

"One hears so much errant nonsense about fell wizards energetically engaged in dooming the world, that one shrugs the words off like an ill-fitting cloak after a while, and pays no attention," Arclath remarked. "Lately, of course, the rumors and reports have come darker and wilder with each passing month. Tumult across the world entire, mountains thrusting up and seas draining away, dragons falling from the skies and scores—nay, hundreds—of mortals proclaiming themselves Chosen of this god or that, and rushing here and there plundering things and destroying things and mustering armies. Yet tell me now—the wizards of the city that floats above Anauroch are behind this siege, truly?"

"*Floated* above Anauroch," Storm replied. "Thultanthar is somewhat nearer now."

Lord Delcastle rolled his eyes, then fixed them on his beloved. "So, a city of ancient archmages hovering above us, blotting out the sun as they enthusiastically hurl dark and mighty spells down on our heads . . . we *are* doomed."

Amarune Whitewave looked back at him and rolled her own eyes. "We are *all* doomed in the end, my lord. The trick is to make the journey from birth to doom as delightful as possible."

"Base philosopher!" he reproved her fondly. "I left my warm hearth and—dare I say it—splendid wine cellar for *this?*"

He waved a dramatic hand at the vista of burning trees and rushing men and elves, the din of battle rising loud from the still-unseen front line of the fray beyond.

"No," Rune told him, "you left hearth and goblet for *this*." She ran a hand down her curvaceous front and gave him a wink that was just this side of a leer.

"Right," Storm observed briskly, "I believe it's now *my* turn for some eye rolling. By all means bill and coo, you two—but on a battlefield, time for such dalliance must be earned. The hard way."

She cast an arch glance Arclath's way. "As a noble lord of the Forest Kingdom should know well, if he's been raised properly."

And with that, the silver-haired bard led the way over a ridge cloaked in dead, fallen leaves and a deep, rich emerald carpet of moss, heading for the fighting.

"But of course, Marchioness," Arclath replied mockingly, following her. Amarune strode at his side, a dagger out as she darted swift glances in all directions. He looked at her admiringly, still secretly in awe that this mask dancer who'd stirred him with her looks and spirited flippancy for years, and turned out to be as fierce and staunch a companion as any man could wish for—not to mention brighter than he was and of the blood of an infamous, age-old wizard—loved him.

Oh, many a tavern dancer or shop drudge had leaped at the chance to wed a noble of Cormyr, or even become a lord's kept, cloistered mistress . . . but his Rune liked his company and wanted to be with him.

And he wanted to be just where he was now: right by her side, no matter what befell, and even when they were both aged and aching, unsteady and frail and wrinkled.

"Arclath Delcastle," his ladylove said warningly into his ear, her dagger-free hand pinching his cheek and jolting him out of his thoughts, "if you don't stop simpering at me, you're going to walk straight into yon tree!"

Arclath blinked at her happily, heard Storm sigh deeply and then chuckle, from just ahead, and found himself staring into the frowning face of his beloved.

"Arky, could you take a break from being a love struck lord for the next little while?" she asked. "I want you to live to see nightfall, not get butchered by the first man with a sword you wander within reach of!"

The Fragant Flower of the Delcastles shook his head and groaned, "'*Arky*'? Really? *Must* you?"

"Well," Storm put in, pinching his other cheek, "if it keeps you alive, Arky dear . . ."

"*Nooo!*" Arclath cried, giving Rune a glare. "How can I buckle a swash with heroic confidence, knowing my foe is sniggering at facing 'Arky'?" He swung around to face Storm, and snarled, "Still less, 'Arky dear'!"

The bard smiled impishly, long silver tresses stirring around her as if a freshening storm breeze was rising. "A grave matter indeed, Arky dear. We must discuss it over flagons of something suitable, after we—"

Something large and heavy and aflame came hurtling through the trees to crash down, bounce, and roll onward in a whirlwind of smoldering leaves. In its wake, there rose a ragged shout as motley armsmen charged into view through a tangle of trees—trees out of which fell an elf in mottled leaf-and-leather armor, limp and dead.

"—break this siege, and hurl back these hired swords, clear through Sembia and into the sea!"

And with her silver hair spreading out as wide as four men and clutching a dozen swords she'd plucked up from amid the fallen, Storm Silverhand strode to meet the onrushing men.

With a yell, Arclath roused himself and sprinted after her, to come up on the bard's left flank. Rune gave him a wink and a grin and headed for Storm's other flank.

And with various contemptuous shouts and snarls, the dozen-some mercenaries charged to meet them, blood-drenched blades in hand.

Helgore strolled along the dimly lit halls as if he belonged there. His elf guise was gone, banished in his draining of that meddling elf guardian, but he cared not. That fool's shed and empty skin was still slithering along in his wake, but it was more amusing than annoying, and might even prove a useful distraction if he met other elves.

Not that they seemed to come down into these cool, damp, endlessly curving passages often. He'd been exploring for a long time now, with neither a sighting nor a challenge. Still, during a siege, anything could happen.

It was surprising how extensive these underground ways were. Elves were popularly thought to love fresh air and green growing things and the out-of-doors, not stone-lined holes in the ground. Was such terrain not dwarf territory?

Myth Drannor had been a city where many races were welcome, so perhaps these underways were unusual for elf cities, but surely the elves would have considered their dead sacred to themselves, and not let dwarves dig out and tend the vaults where the elves laid their ancestors?

If the crypts were as extensive as they seemed—given that he'd walked a long way now, along passages and past many doors that presumably led to many rooms—then taking Myth Drannor might be a longer, harder endeavor than the Most High and all the princes had thought. He kept a conjured spell-shield moving along ahead. It would float along, silent and invisible, until it met the sort of magic awakened by intrusion—and then it would flare into sight, warning him and hopefully shielding him from the worst of whatever erupted.

Hopefully.

His task would have been far easier if he'd been able to find any sort of map of where the crypts of the high elf Houses were, but the team of junior arcanists who had promised as much and had plunged in to find such a thing with enthusiasm had turned up nothing at all.

Helgore was beginning to suspect no map existed, save in the minds of each family of elves, knowing where their ancestors lay, and probably the neighboring crypts. Still, finding a crypt almost certainly meant finding a baelnorn, for the strange elf undead were guardians bound to the crypts of their families.

Guardians whom he was here to destroy.

So they couldn't manipulate the wards against Thultanthar, in ways the arcanists and even the Most High just didn't have time to unravel and thwart. The baelnorn had to be gone, and soon.

Which meant he could do what he loved to do most: slay ruthlessly and viciously.

Helgore smiled in anticipation, and flexed his fingers. The Most High had given him spells that should rend baelnorn with ease, and after his long, cruel, exacting training, he *ached* to lash out at something.

Ho, now, what was *this*?

Ahead, his shield had flared blue and come to an abrupt halt, the seemingly empty air in front of it thickening into a blue curtain.

Well, more wall than curtain, though it rippled like a hanging tapestry. He thrust at his shield with his will, forcing it to move forward—but it merely quivered, as if caught fast in a titanic spider web.

Helgore chuckled, enjoying the moment, and dropped into a catlike stalk, focusing all his senses in a straining effort to see and hear everything as he advanced slowly. There could be pit traps beneath his boots, death waiting to plummet from above, deadly spells lurking . . .

Or nothing at all. All was silent in the passage save for the small sounds of his own progress, his faint breathing louder than the gentle breeze ghosting past his ankles. He came up to his shield and thrust his hand through it, at the blue wall—a vertical patch of air that was only opaque and blue where the shield touched it, and mere dimly lit emptiness everywhere else.

His fingers felt the chill prickling of arisen magical energy, flowing endlessly up and down, forming the wall.

So was it a barrier to him, or just active magics such as his shield? He withdrew his hand, got out the long, needlelike poniard sheathed down his left forearm, and extended it. It bore small enchantments to keep away rust and resist acid, and to glow when a wielder willed it to, so it was magic.

Would this blue wall just block his way, or try to visit some harm on him? The *selukiira* was awake too, thrumming subtly as he leaned nearer to this wall.

The long dagger thrust into the wall as if it weren't there—and a moment later, it wasn't.

The wall was gone as abruptly and as silently as if it had never been there, his shield racing forward unopposed—only to wink out with a little sigh, destroyed by something unseen.

Helgore frowned. No doubt he'd just set off some sort of magical alarm, but who would answer it?

Somehow the warding magic felt old, not something cast recently to warn of current besiegers bursting up from the Underdark or through the crypts into the city . . .

He stepped forward with slow caution, into utter silence.

"That's close enough, human. I have little reason to love or trust Netherese. Your most accomplished spellcasters are rash, to put it politely, and those of less mastery—the Tanthuls, for instance—are a danger not just to your own cities, but to all the world."

The voice was as calm as a gently reproving mother's, not as cold and harsh as might be expected from the words spoken.

Yet Helgore, peer as he might, could not see its source. So he kept on advancing, very cautiously now, his dagger in one hand and the other raised and ready to hurl a mighty spell.

"So you serve a Tanthul, and hail from Thultanthar, and are here to work ill."

Blue flames erupted out of empty air to dart at Helgore's eyes.

He turned them aside with a frantic spell, just in time, and fell back with a snarl. "Who are you? Show yourself!"

The air a little way down the passage rippled as if a curtain was being parted, and there was suddenly a very tall, impossibly thin elf lord facing him—floating with feet together, off the ground, legs nearly skeletal. Helgore could see ribs, arm bones . . . the flesh cloaking them was translucent, and he was seeing the male elf's bones right through it!

"I am Thurauvyn Nathalanorn. Guardian Undying of House Nathalanorn. Just as you are an arcanist of Thultanthar, hight Helgore. Helgore Ulitlarathulm. Sent to destroy bael-norn. My, my."

"And you know all of this how?" Helgore asked softly, not wasting breath in denials, but making sure his strongest ward spells were awakened.

"The *selukiira*. Telamont should have warned you about that. If he knew about it at all; Telamont Tanthul always was a careless, too-hasty youngling. Who considered those working for and with him expendable tools."

Helgore wrenched the loregem free and flung it aside.

The baelnorn winced. "Such vandalism is . . . distressing. Unworthy, even of young and foolish humans drunk on their burgeoning mastery of the Art."

It looked past Helgore, gazed at the empty elf skin slithering closer to him, and repeated more sharply, "Unworthy, indeed."

The slaying spell whirled up out of nowhere to blast Helgore with roaring emerald flames of fury.

CHAPTER 8

The Three Who Wait in Darkness

THE FIRST FEW BLADESINGERS STORM, AMARUNE, AND ARCLATH had come rushing through the forest to reinforce had given them startled looks, and a high mage of Myth Drannor had shot them a look that was frankly hostile, but once the mercenaries came swarming through the trees in earnest to fall upon this handful of elves defending this particular wooded knoll of Myth Drannor, there was no time at all left for anything but frantic hacking, running, and parrying.

The elves were every whit as agile as Rune, who was used to being the most nimble in any fray, but Storm Silverhand awed her.

A whirlwind of long silver tresses snatching up swearing besiegers and dashing them against trees, or trammeling their swords and maces, the bard seemed to float through the battle, at the heart of the thickest fighting as mercenaries rushed in to try to overwhelm her.

Twice it seemed they'd manage it, as even Arclath—who was plying his sword in one hand and a captured blade in the other, both arms red to the shoulder with gore that wasn't his—was beaten back from trying to reach her so he could guard her back.

Shouting murderously, the mercenaries closed into a ring around her, thrusting with bills and glaives, hacking with hand axes and blades, nigh burying her with their bodies.

And twice, a moment of silver-edged silence fell, all local din and clangor muted, as every hiresword was snatched off his bloody-booted feet and flung away from her, seemingly in slow motion, a startled open-mouthed tumbling that became a swift and brutal splattering of hurled bodies against unyielding trees. Moss and bark were torn away by rebounding broken bodies, and in a rush all the sound returned, most of it shrieking or raw howling of pain, amid the groans and wet thudding of bodies bouncing and landing.

Leaving Storm standing alone, the fire of risen anger in her eyes, her long slender sword raised and ready as she sought the most formidable-looking nearby foes—and launched herself at them.

"*Challenge*," she'd snarl if their backs were turned, then she'd set her teeth and swing. In the ringing shriek of blades crashing together that followed, more than one contemptuous veteran battleblade was driven back on his heels, shaken and astonished. A few of them lived long enough for that astonishment to give way to fear, but as Storm apologized to one falling corpse, "I'm in a hurry."

The third time the besiegers sought to overwhelm her, they came at her from all sides as she fenced and fought, dancing and whirling to keep from being taken from behind. Rune and Arclath fought shoulder to shoulder, trying to reach her but barely managing to hold their own ground. And then four hulking warriors came rushing at Storm in unison, glaives lowered in a deadly wall of long gutting points, shouting at their fellow mercenaries to get out of the way.

Those deadly, gore-smirched points were almost under her sword arm before the silver silence came again.

Arclath and Amarune gaped at the muted ballet. The charging warriors were hurled up and back, glaives almost raking Storm's chin as they flew skyward, gauntleted hands clawing at unhelpful air all around. Saplings swayed as men crashed into them, falling leaves swirled, and—the sounds of the nigh deafening battlefield rushed back, battered besiegers fleeing wildly, some of them limping or crawling.

"How do you *do* that?" Rune demanded, as she came up beside Storm. Who gave her a smile far friendlier than her blazing eyes, and shook her head.

"Not a spell I can teach you," she panted. "Called on the Weave. Like El does, more than he spouts incantations, these days." The bard grounded her sword and leaned on it, fighting for breath. "Soon, you'll feel how," she added.

Louder panting and gasping could be heard all around them, as exhausted elves sagged back against trees, or wearily thrust steel through the throats of dying mercenaries.

"My thanks," one of them called to Storm. "Your fury made all the difference."

"Prowess," another corrected, bent double in his fight for air. A bladesinger who looked so like him that she might be his sister stroked his shoulder as she passed, heading to where she could keep a wary eye on the retreating besiegers.

Yet it seemed that this corner of the woods had been left to the defenders of Myth Drannor for the moment.

Storm watched one of them turn over the body of a fallen elf, then grimly let it fall back. But not before she'd seen what the living elf had—a face and throat in bloody ruin, flies buzzing thickly.

The surviving elf looked up, met her eyes, and shook his head. "Lhaerlavrae," he murmured. "She should have lived and laughed for centuries more."

He got to his feet, the tears coming, and wandered away almost blindly, embracing the trees he blundered into as if they were the comforting arms of kin.

"Heavy losses," a bladesinger sighed. "Heavy losses."

Storm went and laid a comforting hand on her shoulder.

The elf smiled up at her, and covered the bard's hand with her own. "We usually rush around in battle, pouncing on foes and then melting back into the trees, using our oneness with the forest and nimble swiftness to make our numbers strike the foe as hard as if we were thrice or more what we truly are—but here, where we must stand and defend, we take losses. Too many losses." She shook her head. "Every day, too many of us fall. This can't go on."

"Every bowshot of forest, every spire of the city lost to the foe is a greater death to our race," one of the high mages snapped at her. "We stand and fight!"

Storm sighed and said to him, "This battle is not about defending courtyards and elegant spires, nor yet wild forest that can all be recaptured or rebuilt. You are fighting for the survival of Fair Folk in these lands. Come sunset, the coronal or Fflar won't care if you stood your ground or rushed about pouncing and retreating, but only that you still hold Myth Drannor—and that as many elves as possible are alive to do so. Do what works best, to set these mercenaries—who fight for coin, not their lives or their people—to flight. Mere ground is not sacred."

"You are not of our people," the mage replied coldly. "You do not see things as we do."

"This is not even your fight," another high mage put in.

"We've been defending this forest, this great city, for longer than you have been alive, human," said a third. "Do not presume to tell us how to conduct ourselves in battle."

"As it happens," Storm replied mildly, "I was defending this city—and the forest all around us, here—when it was an overgrown ruin, and none of you were to be seen anywhere near here. I know this to be firm truth, for I knew everyone who ran with Alok Silverspear, and knew them well." She raised her voice so all the elves around could hear, and added, "Your lives are worth more to all *Tel'Quess* than this little ridge, or that stand of shadowtops yonder. So keep moving, striking from the trees and running on, to strike again. The trees can't move, so do the moving for them. If you stand your ground against so many, you'll die."

"School humans, human," the first high mage sneered, and turned away. Storm shrugged and bent her attention to a wounded bladesinger.

"They're coming again," Arclath warned, peering through the trees.

"Help me get her to her feet," Storm told Rune, who rushed to aid the bladesinger.

"There, amid the *artraela*," the first high mage ordered. "We'll meet them there."

Arclath hadn't heard the Elvish for "duskwoods" before, but it was obvious what the elf was pointing at. The other high mages were already heading for it, picking their way over moss-girt tangles of long-fallen trunks with a fluid grace he envied.

Only a handful of the other elves were moving with them. The rest looked at Storm, as she and Rune got the shuddering bladesinger up between them, and either moved to form a ring around them, or melted back into the trees.

"*D'khessarath!*" the nearest high mage swore. "Heed!" he cried, and pointed at the stand of duskwoods.

Silent elf faces looked back at him, but no one obeyed.

He whirled to give Storm a glare. "This treachery is *your* doing!"

She arched an eyebrow. "Treachery is a strong word, from one leaving wounded to the nonexistent mercies of the foe."

"Insubordinate defiance of discipline wins no wars," he snarled, and whirled away from them to hasten for the duskwoods.

Storm sighed. "Too many *Tel'Quess* are sounding more and more human, these days."

Beside her ear, the wounded bladesinger tried to chuckle, but it turned into a gasp.

The elves around them peered at the advancing besiegers, then looked to Storm uncertainly.

"Go," she said firmly. "Into the trees, to move swiftly and strike shrewdly at the foe and then withdraw again before you can be surrounded and overwhelmed. Go!"

One warrior looked at the wounded bladesinger and then at Storm, anguish in his face. "I—there is no honor—"

"Win more honor by staying alive and fighting on," Storm said softly, "warriors of Myth Drannor. Do not let your fallen have died in vain. I say again: go."

They went, some shaping salutes to her—and they were barely gone amid the trees in one direction when rising shouts and the crashing of trampled ferns and brush from another heralded the arrival of the foremost mercenaries.

"Leave me," the bladesinger panted. "Save yourselves!"

"No," Storm replied firmly, lifting the elf with her hair and settling her gently against the scorched and blackened trunk of a forest giant that had been blasted away. "Here, against what's left of this shadowtop. Rune, to my left—Arclath, my right. We'll do as yon fools want, and make a stand." She glanced at the onrushing besiegers. "There are only about threescore of them."

"Meaning?" Arclath asked with a grin.

"They don't stand a chance," Storm told him grimly, her hair lifting from her shoulders to writhe, each tress lashing like the tail of an angry lion, as she took a step forward and let her hair rise into a great restless halo of full readiness.

"Here we go," Rune said to no one in particular, as the yelling mercenaries crashed through the last few strides of brush and fell upon them.

The two false monks were hurling their spells already, magics that told him they were powerful wizards indeed—arcanists of Thultanthar, most likely—as they stared at Elminster across the spellcasting cavern with looks that mingled hatred and sneering triumph.

There was time for him to elude death, but only just. An escape that concerned only himself and the Weave immediately around him, and though it meant agony when done so swiftly, it could be done in mere moments.

If you were a master of the Weave.

And if his mastery failed now, or he was an instant too slow, he would be as dead as if those spells struck him . . .

Elminster gave himself to the Weave, pouring himself into it in all directions at once, throwing back his head and trying to scream in utter silence. The *pain* . . .

And by the time a fell emerald glare flared to visit death upon him, and a forest of slicing force blades hissed into being to rain down and make that demise doubly sure, Elminster was a mere seeing sentience in the moving air.

There were many who muttered that the Sage of Shadowdale was a great bag of wind, and El reflected wryly that they'd only been wrong about the "great bag" part.

"You *must* tell me how to manage that," Amarune muttered, as the sounds of the siege suddenly came back to them—and various broken mercenary bodies slid bloodily down trees all around them, to crash limply to the forest floor.

"If I have to try it much more often," Storm whispered raggedly, her face gray, "you may just have to learn it on your own."

She sagged, and Arclath leaped to catch her before she fell. She leaned gratefully on his arm.

"I'm not the Weave master Elminster is, or some of my sisters were," she said grimly. "I was always more interested in people. Speaking of which . . ."

Flinging out her hair to clutch at tree trunks like a drunken man keeping his feet by grabbing onto anything and anyone handy, she set off through the blood-drenched forest toward the stand of dusk-woods. Most of the mercenaries had come at Storm, but more than a few had gone crashing up the nearby slope into the duskwoods.

"Well?" Arclath asked, glancing at Rune and then at the blade-singer who nodded her approval of their departure. He started to pick his way over downed trees and fallen elves after Storm. "How fared our oh-so-friendly high mages?"

"This," the bard replied heavily, as he and Rune caught up with her, "is bad."

The small stand of duskwoods looked like the nest of some gigantic forest carnivore, a great, untidy ring-shaped heap of bodies— besieging mercenaries, most of them, but at the heart of it, elves.

Including every last one of the high mages, who'd been overrun and cut down. Storm looked from one to another of their slack, staring faces amid all the blood, and shook her head.

"Small wonder there are so few high mages, and fewer as the years pass."

Now naught but roaring wind, Elminster blew himself across the cavern, racing at the two furious and almost certainly counterfeit monks who'd just sought his death. Seeking not to slay them—though momentarily blinding them and driving them down to cowering helplessness was both tempting and useful if he wanted to get well away—but just to escape.

They cowered as he came howling at them, clapping their hands to their faces, but still, the air in front of Elminster was glowing and changing. He knew the two cowering mages had had no time to work other spells. So was there a third foe, hitherto hidden and—?

Wind or not, he was ensnared.

The air had become a net, formed in but a handful of instants.

Formed from the wards of Candlekeep, and by one of these two monks kneeling before him. A forming that had been done by calling on the Weave.

And as he felt the tightening net, its shape was all too familiar. It had been snatched so hastily into being by someone working with the Weave as Elminster himself had trained them to do.

Which meant one or both of these two monks almost had to be Chosen of Mystra he himself had trained.

He was nigh certainly facing one or two of the Seven Sisters.

El forced the net away with an ease he'd learned twelve centuries ago. Its creator fought him, but it was as if she was tugging vainly on the string of a kite he had clutched firmly to his chest. With the force of his will, El twisted the net inexorably into a magical wall against any other spells these two might send against him.

The struggle made the wall shimmer once or twice into visibility. Behind its protection, Elminster took on his own usual ancient and bearded shape.

And watched astonishment dawn across the faces of the two monks.

"Your turn," he told them calmly.

Reluctantly, they took on their proper shapes too, and he found himself facing two tall women he'd treated as his daughters, long, long ago.

Sisters, tall and furious. Alustriel Silverhand and Laeral Silverhand Arunsun.

Laeral was the first to break the silence. "El," she asked grimly, "why are you here? What are you up to?"

"I'm seeking Khelben's writings, as ye very well know, to try to find out what *he* was up to. Because it's time."

"It's *past* time," Alustriel corrected. "It was past time the day you turned against Khelben, and we Moonstars."

"I 'turned against' no one," El replied sternly. "*I* followed the bidding of the Lady we all serve—or claim to."

"We have *all* obeyed Mystra," said Laeral, "and continue to do so. You reared us, El—do you not know how much we love you? Do you think we would have taken different paths without her blessing, and still remained her Chosen? You were closer to her than the rest of us, and know full well she revealed things to you and gave tasks to you that she did not share with us—can you not accept that she did the same with each of us, and that she chose not to reveal it to you?"

"Nor can any of us roll back the years and undo what has been done and said," Alustriel added. "We three stand here now. Is it to be war between us, or common cause?"

"That will depend," Elminster said wryly. "Are we agreed in this much: that Shar seeks to destroy Mystra and remake the Weave as her own? And that if she succeeds before the Sundering of Toril and Abeir is complete, *she* will be named the goddess of magic on the Tablets of Fate, and darkness and shadow will hold sway in the Realms forever?"

Both sisters nodded.

"We are," Laeral confirmed, "and it is now our turn for asking, Elminster. I ask again: why are you here?"

It was time for full truth. El cleared his throat and began.

"I've worked with the Weave for more centuries than I care to remember, and have labored on it mightily these last seven years, mending and restoring it. Yet rifts and roilings recur in it constantly; it has not collapsed, but is forever in peril of doing so. Where I was the meddler among thrones, mansions, guildhalls, and cottages, Khelben was the Weavemaster. If there is a key to restoring the Weave to stability, to rebuilding it to be the strong and pervasive web we once enjoyed, Khelben knew that vital secret and recorded it—and one of the places he *must* have hidden that record is here, in the great library of Candlekeep. I must find that key, master it, and restore the Weave."

He started to pace. "And if I can reason thus, so can any wise wizard. The Shadovar will come here—they have undoubtedly come here already, dwelling here as monks. While the wards stand, they can be rooted out and thwarted—but if the wards fall, the entire might of Thultanthar can be hurled against us, and all the lore stored here lost in the fray. I have slipped through these wards many a time, and know their strength, if not all their nuances. I can hold these wards up, if anyone can."

He brought himself to an abrupt halt, regarded them both, and said flatly, "*That* is why I am here."

Their frowns told him they were considering his words, but no more.

So he smiled and asked gently, "So why, ladies fair, are *ye* here? Posing as monks of Candlekeep, and moving or hiding all of the books I've sought? Are ye hiding the word of Khelben from the disguised Shadovar within these walls? Or just hiding from the Realms, as war rages, ravaging it?"

The two sisters looked at each other. Then Alustriel tossed her head and told him, "While you mastered the natures of all who dwell in Faerûn, and how best to sway and cozen them, and set about doing that so very well, Khelben foresaw the Sundering, and set about preparing for it."

She looked again at Laeral, who nodded, so she went on. "We have been monks here for more than a century, after arranging matters so the wider Realms thought us dead. Itching to act in matters large and small, yet keeping our silence and our secrets and learning the cold price of patience, to serve the greater cause. Making copies of the tomes here Khelben did *not* write, and sending them forth to other libraries, so that they might survive what is soon to come. Watching and waiting for the moment we must destroy Candlekeep."

"*What?*"

"What name do the elves have for us, El?"

"What do ye *mean*, 'destroy Candlekeep'?"

"What name do the elves have for the Moonstars, El?"

"*Answer* my—*Tel'Teukiira*."

"Yes, and what is written in *Amagal's Tome* about the *Tel'Teukiira?*"

El frowned. "That's one of the books I've been seeking these past days, and cannot find. I read it just once, centuries ago, and in great haste, seeking words of power that could compel elder dragons before they could ravage three kingdoms. *I* don't remember! So tell me: what *is* written in *Amagal's Tome* about the *Tel'Teukiira?*"

"The *Tel'Teukiira* will save us from the Three Who Wait in Darkness, the Prefects, and ourselves."

El gave them his best quizzical raised eyebrow. "Even so-called 'true prophets' get things plainly wrong, despite their habit of writing and speaking cryptically, for the gods are all too fallible. Ye've both lived long enough and seen enough to know that. Even if Amagal could see the future with clear precision—as even the gods cannot—how do ye know this is the time? And who *precisely*, for *certain*, are the Three Who Wait in Darkness, the Prefects, and 'ourselves'?"

"As it happens, Amagal did not see the future," Laeral said dryly. "He merely passed on a more ancient foretelling, purportedly uttered by Chauntea at her birthing, when Toril itself came to be—and Amagal mangled it while doing so. That older prophecy is thus: 'When worlds are sundered once more, and Toril itself stands in peril, only the *Tel'Teukiira* can save us from the Three Who Wait in Darkness, the Prefects, and ourselves.'"

"I can guess that the Shadovar have something to do with the Three Who Wait, but who are the Prefects? And who could Chauntea—if it *was* the Allmother—have meant by 'ourselves'? The gods?"

Both sisters shrugged.

El regarded them sourly. "All right, who did *Khelben* think 'ourselves' meant? And how did he—or the two of ye—come to conclude ye must *destroy Candlekeep*?"

"Do not think we have not debated this down the years, El," Alustriel told him ruefully. "Confronting Khelben, when we still could, as fiercely as you are confronting us now."

"More than once," Laeral put in sadly, "I wasted time disputing when we were abed together. Time I would give almost anything to have back now."

"We have argued it and argued it," Alustriel added, "and asked Mystra as much as we dared, and pieced together every hint we could find in what all the gods have said—Jergal in particular, hinted much—and threw all we could learn at Khelben. And he stood fast."

"So *what*, by the Lady's Secrets, did *he* believe?"

"That 'ourselves' meant those of us alive at the time, and the follies and mistaken beliefs that will lead us astray. The Prefects were what the senior officers of Candlekeep were collectively called by the monks beneath them in rank, at its founding; a term that soon faded into disuse and was forgotten. And we agree with you that the Three Who Wait in Darkness are probably Shadovar—and are certainly agents of Shar, for she *is* 'the Darkness.'"

Elminster nodded. "I find myself still waiting for a good reason Candlekeep must be destroyed. I have spent my life preserving lore so that the Art will not be forgotten, but flourish. If I am not to fall upon anyone seeking to smash this great storehouse of lore and destroy them utterly, the reason for my forbearance had *better* be good."

"Candlekeep's wards are the mightiest surviving wards on or under Toril. Myth Drannor's mythal is the greatest extant mythal. They are the greatest sources of stored magical energy in all the Realms—and both must be destroyed to keep their energies from Shar, and Telamont Tanthul, her most capable agent."

"Myth Drannor now, too? The mythal I helped raise so long ago, with so many dear to me who are now gone? Lus, Laer, have ye both gone *mad*?"

"We may well sound so, El, and believe me it grieves us to think of such great and lasting magics thrown down too . . . but hear us out."

"My ears attend ye," Elminster told them dryly. "Make it good."

Laeral gave him a sigh, then a smile, and then the words, "The elves of Cormanthor are a proud and truly noble people, but that pride is what it has always been—their greatest weakness. Most of them can't believe mere human arcanists, however skilled in sorcery, can defeat them. Yet they will never hold their city against what the Shadovar can muster against them. The monks in this great fortress around us are just as deluded; they trust in the wardings alone for defense. Telamont will seize the power here, then that of the mythal, and with it will tame the Weave and remake it into a true 'Shadow Weave.' And with that, Shar will finally become the greatest goddess she has so often boasted of being."

Elminster lifted his head as if to say something, but Laeral raised a forefinger to forestall him and added, "With the Weave augmenting the Shadow Weave and controlled by it, Shar will have a Shadow Weave that is more than an echo of the Weave we have served and strengthened for so long—she will govern the world with her Shadow Weave, and will be able to transform it into what she seeks. Oblivion. The world we know will become an endless night of hunting and slaughter, with all order and lore destroyed—and Shar exulting in the continual loss of life and all history forgotten, only the hounds that serve her knowing what they destroyed, and keeping those secrets within the ranks of those who serve her. It will be eternal nightmare."

"So you see," Alustriel added, "we must destroy the great wards here, and the Last Mythal there, rather than let them fall into Telamont's hands."

El shook his head. "Ye deem the elves weak, thanks to their pride, yet spare Telamont the same judgment. He has pride and overconfidence enough for any score of archmages."

"I know it will take some time to come around to seeing things as Khelben did," Laeral added gently. "It took us years. Years I'm afraid you don't have."

"Ladies, I very much doubt there are enough years ahead for us all, for there to be enough to bring me to thinking the old stiffnec—the Blackstaff was right in this. The old saying about 'defending the castle so fiercely that it was destroyed in the defending' comes to mind. In short, I have not heard such utter madness since Khelben was alive."

Laeral winced. "It has not been so long, El, that his death does not pain me. Please listen—"

"*Ye* please listen, the both of ye. Ye speak of destroying two of the greatest surviving magical treasures of our world, achievements that may never be replaced once they are gone, to say nothing of surpassed. Even if that vandalism means nothing to ye, consider the danger ye plunge all the Realms into if they are destroyed. Two great storehouses of active Art, brought down, will inevitably release such a flood of magical energies that the Weave would be torn to shreds. Every bit of it to fail would become wild magic, a spreading chaos that could well banish *governable* magic from the world. If ye thought the Spellplague was bad, imagine Toril and Abeir awash in unleashed and roiling power, yet with every last sentient being powerless to wield or steer any of it, because 'magic' as we know it has failed utterly. A second and greater Spellplague!"

Laeral shook her head and opened her mouth to speak, but El held up a forestalling finger and swept on.

"The two worlds will separate, aye, are sundering even now—and with the Weave gone, there will be nothing to safeguard any stability at all. Toril and Abeir were rocked by the first Spellplague, but what was left of the Weave still protected Toril then, like a tattered suit of armor. A suit, may I remind ye, that I have spent centuries strengthening and patching and fastening together ever more securely, which is why it survived at all when Mystra fell."

Elminster started to pace in his agitation, waving his arms like an exasperated tutor. "Without any protection at all, order cannot hold! The raging chaos of magic will strike all the Art stored in items—paltry sparks, but there are thousands upon thousands of them!—and all that unbridled energy must go *somewhere*! If the Srinshee is right—and I believe she is—both worlds will most likely collapse into uncounted shards, with all life on them swept away in tumult and agony. Do ye not *care* about our world, and everyone in it? What price victory, if we *all* die—and the Realms with us? What sort of triumph is that?"

"That will *not* happen, Old Mage," Alustriel snapped, "if we do as Khelben saw we must. You conjure dire fantasies, when you should face the truth. The Blackstaff studied this for *centuries*, and at first thought as you do, but then—"

"Made another of his misjudgments? The Lady knows I've made a generous share of grave mistakes, but Khelben made more of them, and stubbornly stood by what he'd decided, even after his folly became clear to all, longer than any mage not green and young I ever met. His stubbornness was his hallmark—"

"And his *strength*." Laeral's voice was as firm as a forge hammer striking iron. "Nor is this a contest of who's more worthy or more 'right.' In this case, this most important case of all, Khelben studied longer and harder than any of us, and reluctantly came to this one conclusion, and we agree with him. And you yourself have spoken of how the Srinshee promised to return in Myth Drannor's hour of need—so where is she, if that gravest hour of need is truly upon us?"

Alustriel spoke again, before Elminster could. "El, hear me: we have spent more than a century confined here, constraining our lives down to reading and writing and praying, to silence and holding back, to acting roles that chafe us, *because* we love the Realms too much to fail it. We will not be turned from this. The wards of Candlekeep and the mythal of Myth Drannor must be destroyed. Whether you stand with us or against us, this *must* be done."

There were tears in Alustriel's eyes now, and running down Laeral's cheeks, but their lips were firm lines of determination.

He found his own throat closing in grief, as he asked roughly, "And if I stand against ye both, what then, old friends? Foster daughters?"

Laeral lifted her chin. "Choose wisely, El. If you are not with the Moonstars, you are against the Moonstars."

El looked from one tear-wet face to the other, his face as sad as theirs as he used the Weave to spin down streamers of power from the mighty wards of Candlekeep, spiraling eel-like tongues of energy that became two cocoons of force to imprison Alustriel and Laeral.

He saw surprise in their faces—that became astonishment as they tried to command the wards against him, and discovered that his control overrode theirs.

He didn't wait to see more. Not that he'd ever seen the sense of wasting time in gloating, when there was something very needful that had to be done very swiftly if all this wasn't to end in disaster. He had to work a difficult spell of his own, and *very* quickly.

He got the incantation off, and the gestures, and it began. Half-seen movement in the air in front of him, the edges of fingers, darting and interweaving like a great school of fish swarming in the air. Ghostly hands, scores of them, disembodied and swirling in front of him in a shield of sorts.

The moment they were a little more tangible, he sent them racing at Alustriel and Laeral in their whirling, now tightening cocoons. Those streams of slapping, clutching, clawing hands should hamper any spellcastings they might attempt—and hold the two women fast if they managed to banish the cocoons.

They didn't try. Trading glances, they chanted the same spell in unison.

And shattered the ceiling of the cavern so it plummeted with a thunderous roar.

Elminster didn't bother to stare upward. He knew what he'd see. Tons of rock, hurtling to crash down on him.

CHAPTER 9

A Sword of Shadows

THE POWER OF THE BAELNORN'S SPELL WAS ENOUGH TO FORCE Helgore's body back, arching in the throes of a violent shuddering, but his wards wrestled with the emerald flames, holding them at a standstill. Should they reach him, they would consume flesh and tissue, and send burning magic racing through his veins; the wards told him that much as they roiled and recoiled a few finger thicknesses from his skin.

And then the spent spell fell away.

Leaving Helgore smirking at Thurauvyn Nathalanorn, Guardian Undying of House Nathalanorn.

Time for a little goading. Fun, but more importantly, this baelnorn might be made to reveal useful things ere he destroyed it.

He could see the arch-topped stone double doors it guarded beyond it—*through* it, actually—and could just make out the House symbol sculpted in relief upon them. A salamander wreathed in flames, entwined around a great fish with long, whiplike barbels and a jutting, many-toothed lower jaw. All wreathed and overlaid with sinuous vines whose many tiny leaves looked like ivy. So, fire and water? Pah, it could signify anything.

"So tell me, unworthy guardian," Helgore drawled, "why the world should remember House Nathalanorn? A few forgotten elves

145

who comported themselves with great pride, no doubt, as all elves do. But had House Nathalanorn any real grounds for such hauteur? Who were they, and what did they achieve?"

"Nothing one who comes to destroy and despoil cares about," the baelnorn replied coldly. "I'll tell you nothing that will aid you in finding other crypts or making any good use of anything you find here. I am sworn, beyond death itself. So much is, I grant, obvious, but I *am* speaking with a human."

"And we hairy, grasping, reeking barbarians are beneath you oh-so-superior *Tel'Quess*, is that it?"

"Race is not the major part of this. Youth and ignorance are. Grasping thieves and vandals of all shapes and natures are beneath the regard of House Nathalanorn," said the baelnorn, drifting a little nearer.

Helgore retreated a step in the face of its chill.

"There *is* no more House Nathalanorn, old fool," he told the undead guardian harshly. "You and your kin were forgotten an age ago, before the elves abandoned Myth Drannor to the forest, the roving beasts, and fell fiends. They remain forgotten now. I doubt if the precious coronal could name your family or recognize your blazon, if they were put before her now. You are not even memories—outside these few feet of passage and your own failing wits."

"I have little doubt we are as nothing in your regard, creature of Telamont. Nothing more than a stronger arcanist of your own benighted city is—and your interest is spent on such powerful beings as targets to be undermined and thrown down in time, to your own advancement. If that is a life you find worthy, revel in it. You will not find much company of worth, however, swimming with you in those waters."

Helgore shrugged. "I have no need of the adulation of others, dead elf. I *know* my place and my powers."

"Knowledge born of a self-delusion so mighty is sure and certain indeed," the baelnorn agreed caustically, drifting forward again.

This time, Helgore did not retreat, but took a deliberate step forward into the chill, his wards crackling and flaring purple in warning.

"It is past time I shattered your grating superiority, ancient fool," he said, showing his teeth to the translucent skull face. "So let it begin between us."

He drew back one arm as if to free it from sticky mud—and thrust it forward with crackling lines of purple-white lightning snarling from its fingertips.

The baelnorn regarded him expressionlessly from mere inches away, unmoving—and as unaffected as if his spell hadn't existed at all.

"So, have you begun?" it asked mockingly, after Helgore's lightning had died away. "Telamont is sure to be impressed by the swift and easy victory of his *most* capable agent."

"Still your tongue," Helgore replied venomously. "The tongue you no longer truly possess, yes? Just as you have lost all else of worth in your existence. Lovers, a body to love them with, kin, reputation . . . all gone. You chose to become nothing, and have achieved it. Congratulations."

"Your biting scorn is wasted, Shadovar; your understanding is so imperfect as to render your taunts laughable emptiness. I had hoped you'd furnish me some entertainment, but you are such a sad and hollow excuse for a Thultanthan arcanist—even among that wretched company—as to be merely a waste of time. Time that's precious only to you, for I have stepped beyond the demands of racing age."

"Undead thing," Helgore snapped, nettled despite himself, "be still. Your prattle is the wind of the tomb."

"Well, at least you know the poets," the Guardian Undying of House Nathalanorn said archly. "There may be some hope for you yet. However, you really should read more closely, being as you work with the Art. The proper words are: 'is but as wind from a tomb.'"

"Do you actually presume to toy with *me*, talking gatepost?"

The baelnorn chuckled. "Nay, nay, nay! There's an *art* to delivering an insult! This stiff, pompous snapping out of half-remembered barbed phrases wastes their cleverness and merely makes you seem more ridiculous!"

"Oh, *burn* you!" Helgore roared, and he lashed out with his most powerful spell.

He was rewarded by seeing Thurauvyn Nathalanorn reel back, red flames like dragonfire momentarily licking up one undead arm, as the baelnorn's barrier spell shattered like a great pane of glass, falling to crash silently to the floor in many thousand fading shards.

And then, as Helgore laughed in glee, the counterstrike came, and the world became an icy inferno of frigid needles piercing him in a score of places. Snatching Helgore's breath away, and all movement, and for one agonizing and seemingly endless movement, the beat of his heart.

Slow agony spread through Helgore like some sort of blind, bumbling caterpillar, and then—his heart fell back to beating with a sullen thud, the world rushed back to him as a place of eerie shrieking—his own, he realized dazedly—and he was falling, fingers writhing spasmodically, tongue undulating out of the side of his mouth as if flutteringly eager to be elsewhere . . .

He landed on his back with a crash, and bounced, arching in helpless agony and kicking up at the sky uncontrollably. The aftershocks of both spells rolled away along the passage floor in a shared sigh of fading, racing radiances, and then . . . silence fell.

A stretching quiet that was broken by both Helgore and the baelnorn saying, in almost-perfect unison, "Is that the best you can do?"

A moment later, horribly, they both started to laugh at the same moment. Dry mirth from the baelnorn, and wild hysteria from the living man.

Helgore found unfunniness first.

The forest was acrawl with bands of mercenaries hastening into the fray or trudging back to their camps to rest, and it hadn't taken Storm, Amarune, and Arclath long to trot straight into a collision with one.

In a trice, swords had been out among the trees, and Storm's long silver hair whirling startled hireswords into brutal thudding collisions with various handy blueleaf and duskwood trunks.

And then it was steel against steel, blades clanging and shrieking with the fury of the hacking.

"*You're* no elf!" the burly mercenary snarled into Arclath's face as they strained for supremacy in a clinch of steel, blades locked together and noses not all that far apart. "What in the Nine blazing Hells are *you* doing here?"

"Defending Myth Drannor from the likes of you," Lord Delcastle replied levelly, the veins standing out on his neck in his effort, as they shoved and set their teeth—and the arms of both men started to tremble.

"Oh, stop *toying* with your mercenaries, dear!" Rune muttered as she ducked past in the fray, hamstringing Arclath's foe in an instant as she went.

The man lurched sideways with a shriek that ended abruptly as Arclath's dagger flashed into his throat. As he collapsed like a load of dumped fish on the Suzailan docks, his slayer frowned at his lady's slender back, now plunging into a knot of mercenaries battling a lone bladesinger. "Hoy, now, was *that* sporting? Honorable?"

"I'm not here for sport, Lord Delcastle," she called back, driving the pommel of her dagger into the back of a mercenary helm so fiercely that it rang like a bell and spun half around on its wearer's head, blinding him. "And I think we've long agreed that I lack honor. I'm here to *win*."

"Hah!" a tusk-helmed mercenary jeered as he came crashing through the trees at the head of a fresh band of hireswords. "Then you're fighting on the wrong side! You and all these long-ears are doomed!"

"Doomed! *Doomed*!" various hireswords chorused, sounding like so many lowing sheep.

"Do you *mind*?" Storm complained, flinging the body of her most recent assailant away and moving to intercept this new force. Alone. "'Doom' was *my* battle cry, I'll have you know. A good seven centuries ago, I'll grant, but still . . ."

"Pah! Seven *years* ago, mayhap!" the tusk-helmed warrior spat. "Seven centuries, my left haunch!"

"That can be arranged," Storm told him sweetly, her tresses lashing out to hook around his elbows and ankles as their blades clashed, whisking him up and into the path of his charging fellows.

The tusk-helmed warrior's startled shout became a raw roar of pain as the glaive of a hard-charging hiresword thrust into his behind and tore on through. The glaive wielder was coming too fast to halt his charge or sidestep, and slammed right into the wound he'd just created, blood spraying in all directions.

As the stricken tusk-helmed warrior shrieked, the glaive wielder slipped in gore, slid right under the man he'd just wounded—and straight into Storm.

Or rather, into where she'd been. She'd sprung into the air, to come down hard with both feet on the sliding man, crotch and throat. Pinned, he managed a high-pitched strangling gurgle and a beached-fishlike thrashing ere a running bladesinger disgustedly drove a sword point in under his jaw.

By then, the mercenary charge had become a wary, scattered advance, hampered by the trees and Storm's fury. Myth Drannan bladesingers rushed to reinforce her, forming a formidable line that had more than one mercenary backing away.

When Amarune Whitewave arose from a tangle of three large and well-armored mercenaries, covered with blood but smiling, with her three foes lolling lifeless, and Arclath Delcastle came sprinting to her side with blood on his own sword and dagger, the mercenaries had tasted enough.

They broke and ran, leaving the human handful of Myth Drannan defenders unopposed. And trading weary smiles with the bladesingers who'd stood with them.

"A small victory," one elf muttered, "but victory nonetheless."

"Well said," Storm agreed. "'Savor victories whatever their size, and whenever they come—they are the little lights that brighten our days.'"

"Thaeruld Hraumendor," Arclath said approvingly. "From his *A Life Lived Adequately*. One of the better philosophers in my father's library. *Very* old book; I'm surprised you know it."

Storm gave him a dangerous look. "I knew the man, Lord Delcastle. When he was younger than you are, to boot."

"Ah," Arclath said, wincing. "Pray accept my apologies—bad manners to openly remind a lady of her age, very bad. In my defense, let it be said that my slight was entirely unwitting and unintentional."

Storm's look turned sly. "'Too many of our nobles, young and old, are headstrong self-centered louts, their every act unwitting of consquences, and uncaring of unintentional side effects.' To quote Baerauble, writing back in the reign of Tharyann the Elder. And yes, Lord Delcastle, that *was* before my time."

But Arclath was staring past her, through the trees, keeping his usual watch over the nearest mercenaries. And instead of replying to her sally, he frowned and scrambled a few steps sideways, over a softly rotten stump as large around as a good-sized oval dining table, to where he could see better.

"Well, Arclath," Storm asked gently as Rune joined her man, and he gave her an almost absent-minded hug, "what're the foe up to?"

"Much discussion," he replied. "Some of them are waving torches. Unlit, but by the way they're pointing them, I think they're debating trying to start a large forest fire."

"Much good may *that* do them. If there's one thing even young elves can master, it's firequench magic. Still, we should alert the best archers who can be spared from the lines. Fire setters have to tarry in one spot long enough to make superb targets—and if they try to use fire arrows, we can take down *their* archers. I—"

The faintest of rumbles arose, and the ground under their feet rocked. Out of a nearby hollow tree burst brief tongues of red flame, amid some ghostly shards of glowing light that faded to nothingness as they started to drift away into the air.

"What was *that*?" Arclath hissed. "Are the besiegers down below, blasting tunnels to get past our lines?"

Storm shook her head. "Impossible, with all the roots—see you the *size* of these trees around us?—that'd be in their way. Moreover, we humans and elves aren't the only things dwelling in this forest; the very badgers would be bolting up out of their burrows all around us, if any sustained tunneling was going on. No, that was something else."

She frowned. "Probably something ancient."

"Share," Rune suggested sharply. "I'm beyond tired of the 'I'm so old and wisely mysterious' act. Thanks to Elminster."

Storm gave her a wry smile. "Well, then, I'll turn to handing out sayings so hoary you'll roll your eyes: this is going to grow far worse, I fear, before it's over."

Rune obligingly rolled her eyes. Then gave Storm a glare and flared her nostrils like an angry horse.

The bard's sudden grin made her look like a young girl. "Oh, that's *good*," she said admiringly. "Wish I could do that."

Arclath sighed. "Ladies, *ladies*."

Storm and Amarune turned in perfect unison to give him the same flatly withering look. "Well," Storm remarked, "that's not your first slip of the tongue this day, and I suppose it'll be far from your last."

"Ah, the joys of growing up noble," Lord Delcastle observed. "Surrounded by spitfires. I'm quite used to it. And before you ask, know this: my mother could surround someone all by herself."

The agent of Thultanthar faced the baelnorn before the doors of the crypt it was charged to guard, and it was not the undead guardian who was the angriest of the two.

Helgore snarled wordlessly. This was taking too long, and he certainly hadn't expected the baelnorn to have managed to hurt him this much.

And he had so many more of them to find and destroy.

He'd just have to—but wait, the tiresome dead elf was declaiming his defiance again.

"I am Thurauvyn Nathalanorn, Guardian Undying of House Nathalanorn, and so long as any of me still exists, you shall neither pass nor prevail, human vandal." The hiss sounded fierce—and desperate.

"Well, then, baelnorn, we shall have to see about that continued existence of yours," Helgore taunted, with a heartiness he was far from feeling. There had *better* be powerful magic in the Nathalanorn crypt, because he might soon be in sore need of it. "You've proven to be little more than feeble bluster thus far, so it should not take me long, nor much effort . . ."

They both knew that was a lie, but his words at least made *him* feel better. This had not gone at all as he'd envisaged it, proud and confident that what Telamont had given him would allow him to sweep baelnorn to dust with a casual gesture, shattering their own baleful battle magics in an instant.

His most powerful swift spells for a fray were gone, spent in a duel that was taking far too long, and this damned undead elf was still standing, still defying him, still preventing him from taking one step nearer the door it guarded—and for that matter, down the passage beyond, seeing as this oh-so-annoying Guardian Undying of House Nathalanorn had decided it was guarding not just the crypt of its family, but the corridor outside the crypt doorway, from wall to root-laced wall.

So he couldn't even rush past it to blast other baelnorn he might catch unawares, and then return later to deal with this one. It was blocking his path like a castle portcullis. Damn it.

"Shar take you and rend you," Helgore muttered in the baelnorn's direction, though latest barrier magic swirled between them like smoke, hiding it from him except for two blue eyes that blazed through the gloom at him with crimson anger flaring around their edges.

If looks could kill . . . but they couldn't. Not the gaze of this ancient undead thing, at least.

And he *would* destroy it, would prevail here, if he just took care enough not to put a foot wrong . . .

He'd been impatient thus far, irked and letting his rising anger fuel overly swift and reckless attacks.

So it was more than time to try a little patience. First, another rash strike that the baelnorn would easily counter and sneer at—and in its wake, while its effects were still blossoming, three slower attacks: spell-serpents, those agonizingly slow lances of force that undulated through the air like swimming snakes toward a foe. Three, all coming at the undead elf from slightly different directions, while he kept it distracted and busy with swifter, more spectacular spells.

Yes.

He launched his rash strike—a spectacular spell that brought into being streamers of flaming acid, that he arced around to come at the baelnorn from all directions—and then, as the guardian's smoky barrier lit up under the assault to become a brightly flaring chaos Nathalanorn shouldn't be able to see through, Helgore created his three serpents, one after another in swift succession, and watched them begin their porpoise-like charges toward their target.

Whom he had to keep very busy, so the baelnorn wouldn't see its doom coming for it until too late.

He hurled a swarm of magic missiles. Puny darts that the guardian's barrier would almost certainly intercept and quell—but they were that many more twisting, racing, wheeling perils for the guardian to have to keep track of amid all the long, reaching tentacles of fiery acid homing in on it, in a tightening net that—

The magical blast that thrust at Helgore then was as sudden and powerful as it was unexpected, a speeding helix of force that tore through the barrier and snared the nearest acid streamers as it came, clawing them into itself and bringing them along as it—

Stabbed into Helgore's shoulder, laying open his chin to the bone as he frantically twisted his head away to avoid losing his face and likely his life as it hurled him off his feet and away.

Unfortunately, the far side of the passage was so close that he crashed into its unyielding stone with force enough to shake even his cocoon of warding magics.

155

The raw agony of it was worse than any pain he'd ever felt in his life before, and only his wards kept him from blacking out.

Which might mean he would manage to defend himself in the moments ahead and so cling to life, but certainly meant he felt it all. Every last raging flare of pain, as he bounced off the wall and rolled to a gasping, blood-drenched stop. His left arm hung limp and useless, his shoulder was just *gone*, and—

He could collapse his innermost ward into healing force, and he had to, no matter what the danger. If he got away from the baelnorn . . .

Helgore kicked feebly at the floor, trying to scoot himself away as he sat huddled and clutching his arm, rocking from side to side and moaning.

What was the baelnorn up to, anyway? Why hadn't it—?

Through streaming tears, as the dissolving ward flooded through him, sending relief enough that his shuddering body began to obey him again, Helgore saw . . .

That his serpents had reached the baelnorn and were searing into it, wriggling like hungry eels as they burned its undeath, boring in and up and through.

Translucent flesh sagged, seeming to melt, the baelnorn's mouth yawned open in a long and soundless scream, and it spent itself, falling from a thing with limbs and a head into a racing streak of glowing undeath, howling at him through its own fading barrier, racing at him in what expanded into a ghostly fanged maw fringed with many reaching taloned arms, talons that grew impossibly long—

And then faded away against his last, feebly flickering ward, and tore it down.

Baelnorn and ward vanished together, in small writhing snarls of nothingness that fell from him, to roll away, and fade as they rolled . . . across the suddenly dark and quiet stone passage.

He was alone. The Guardian Undying was no more.

Helgore lay there panting and staring into the darkness for what seemed a long time before he mastered the pain enough to work a restorative spell on his shoulder, sacrificing three lesser battle spells to fuel that healing.

It was longer still before he felt whole enough again to roll cautiously over and try to get up. As far as his knees, at least, to stare around at a passage that seemed strangely unmarked for all the raging magic that had so recently been hurled around in it. It was deserted. Dark and empty, with no elves racing to see what had made all the tumult.

And there, mockingly close to him, stood the doors of the crypt of House Nathalanorn that the baelnorn had guarded for centuries before his birth, and had fallen defending against him. Just as—if things went much better than this first bumbling assault—many other baelnorn would fall.

Wincing, for although the pain had fled to no more than a dull ache of reminder, his restored shoulder was stiff, Helgore got to his feet. His shoulder felt . . . *odd*. As if it wasn't truly part of him. It didn't seem to fit, somehow.

He shook his arm and flexed the fingers, numbness racing along them and then fading, as he studied the Nathalanorn House symbol. That entwined salamander and fish, amid a sinuous and clinging forest of ivy. At least, that's what it looked like, and he supposed there was no one left in the world to correct him about that now.

He had won.

Helgore permitted himself a smile, then walked a few cautious steps back and forth in the passage to make sure his body was his own once more. It was high time to, as the arcanists who'd first tutored him had been fond of saying, "Get on with it."

He hadn't much magic left, but *this* should suffice, right now . . .

He worked a swift magic, remembering to step aside as he finished, and had the satisfaction of watching the crypt door shatter.

The pieces, however, hung in place, hovering in midair, the broken edges glowing and pulsing with the angry blue racing glows of disturbed magic. So his way was still barred. Of course.

Helgore snorted. Misbegotten elves!

He spent the slightest of spells to sweep the shattered pieces of door aside, to crash down on the passage floor. Several of them slumped straight into dust.

Leaving him facing *another* set of doors. An inner pair that were closed and intact and seemingly not locked. These would, of course, bear an enchantment that would slay any non-elf—or any elf not bearing the right token—touching them, to prevent tomb looting.

So it would take *another* spell to . . . wait.

Helgore looked back down the passage the way he'd come, and there it was: the skin of the elf he'd slain. Rippling and lifting a little as he gazed at it, like a cat or quiet dog craving attention.

He gave the skin a wry little smile, worked a very small and simple magic—of the sort wizards these days called cantrips—and bent his will on it.

Obediently, it slithered forward, flowing to the doors and climbing them like some sort of animated, rearing leaf. At his direction, it wrapped itself around the pull ring of the inner doors, turned it, and pulled.

The doors opened in eerie silence, revealing the faint blue glow of a ward. By its light, he could see into the circular, dome-shaped crypt of the Nathalanorns.

He could see dozens of effigies on the floor. Or, no, they were the crumbling, ancient skeletons of elves, cloaked in magic that almost hid them from swift and distant scrutiny—magic that shaped the likeness of the dead as if they were alive but lying on their backs, asleep. Intangible effigies of magic, rather than the sculpted stone that adorned the tombs of some dwarves and humans. And—ahh— what he'd come for and had begun to hope hard for, in addition to the crypt ward itself, was there as well—small areas where the blue ward glow was more intense, unmoving spots centered on swords, hunting horns, harps, gauntlets, bracers, and breastplates interred with or upon the dead. Magic items.

Helgore looked up and down the passage again to make sure no one was approaching. Finding it as deserted and silent as before, he drew in a deep breath, settled himself into a comfortable stance, legs balanced well apart, and worked one of the longest and most intricate magics he'd ever been taught.

He was shaking with weariness when he was done, but if this worked, that would shortly cease to be a problem.

And so would whatever spells any baelnorn hurled his way.

Helgore smiled and held out both hands to what he could see of the crypt, as if it was a young child he was beckoning to run into his arms.

What stole out of the crypt was utterly silent, and slower than a child. It was more like a scent wafting through the air, inexorably drifting toward him, and up his arms—his fingers tingled as if struck by sparks, then went numb—into him.

Yes! His weariness melted away, his hair slowly straightened to stand quivering on end, his scalp lifted and prickled, his teeth started to itch . . . power was sliding into him, the force captured and stored by all those enchantments now becoming his, building in him, building . . .

Helgore stood silently, watching swords and harps and armor slumping to dust in the crypt as the magic left them and flowed into him, more and more of it.

The effigies faded, the bones slumped to dust, and the walls of the tomb cracked, long jagged lines moving across the hitherto-smooth dome, as the blue light grew fainter and fainter . . .

Until all of the power of House Nathalanorn was a visible blue-white line in the air, flowing into his embrace. And he was filling up, feeling the first rising discomfort as he swelled, on his way to bursting with energy—a discomfort that swiftly became pain, and that pain grew and grew . . .

He was quivering, a quivering that became trembling, that fell swiftly into uncontrollable shuddering. All of his wounds were gone, healed by the blue-white fire still sliding inexorably into him, but the boon was now agony, his skin starting to glow blue-white, his eyes turning to blue-white flames.

Blue-white fire spilled from his lips as he groaned, a long moan escaping from blue-white lips, a moan that started deep but rose slowly in pitch and urgency—

And then it was done.

The crypt of House Nathalanorn stood dark and empty, and Helgore Ulitlarathulm swayed and shuddered in the passageway, swollen with blue-white light that boiled and leaked out of him as he turned, lurching like a drunken man whose knees were too stiff to bend, and stalked like a zombie down the passage.

Drunk on power, swollen to gasping pain from all the energies surging through him. Heading for the next crypt.

It was surprisingly close to the one he'd just ravaged. This one had a device he recognized on its doors, an emblem that had been in the records that had been gathered to prepare him for his task. It was not something easily described—privately, he thought of it as the tangled collision of three harps—but Helgore knew it at first glance. It marked the crypt behind it as that of House Erembelore.

He lurched up to the doors, but no baelnorn appeared. So he fought the pain down to a few moments of precise control—and blasted the doors to nothingness, aiming sideways so if anything more shattered, it would be the stone of the doorframe, and nothing in the crypt beyond.

That brought out the Erembelore baelnorn, in a cold rage that Helgore was still in too much pain to indulge with high words.

He merely sent enough energy to make himself feel far more comfortable right through the undead guardian, a roaring that consumed it before it could utter a sound.

Helgore took five unsteady steps forward, right through the sighing, eddying, glowing dust that a moment ago had been an elf who'd spent centuries guarding his dead kin. He paused just long enough to make sure it was indeed gone, and not lurking as some sort of malicious remnant, and—fell headlong into the dim blue radiance of the last resting place of the Erembelores.

That hadn't been so hard, he thought dully, trying to collect his thoughts. The pain was almost all gone, and the dazedness that had almost overwhelmed him had been dashed out of him by his sudden meeting with the cold and unyielding floor.

He rolled over, almost absently spending a little more of his seized energies to banish the bruises of his fall, and settled himself on his back, listening hard.

There were no sounds in the passage outside, no sign that anyone had heard. All that was audible was his own breathing. Around him, the crypt was still and silent, the Erembelores sleeping the slumber from which no one awakens.

Good.

Now for the spell the Most High had devised just for him. Now that at last he had gained excess energy enough to fuel it, and didn't have the more pressing need to heal himself.

Lying on the floor, Helgore cast that magic with slow and exacting care . . . and just as slowly, something dark and edged in purple formed in the air above him, half seen and menacing.

The dark outline of a sword, floating horizontally. A sword large enough for a smallish giant, nine feet long and utterly dark, with no hint of light reflected back off metal—or of metal at all.

A Shadow Sword. Just as Telamont had crafted, and just as had formed when he'd first practiced the spell. Helgore released the stolen energy roiling in his body into it. Blue-white fire silently streamed out of him, flaring into brief tongues of flame, ere it vanished into the blade's all-devouring darkness.

Every moment brought relief, less pain, and the opportunity to relax. So relax he did, at last, indulging himself in a long moan of bliss.

Then Helgore rolled over and up to his feet, feeling marvelous. He chuckled and pointed the sword—and stood watching as it drained the wards and magics of this second crypt, family treasures sighing into little heaps of ash and dust as the Shadow Sword drank all their magic, effigies fading and the bones beneath them sighing into eddying dust.

This time, the darkness flared momentarily blue-white around its edges, seeming more solid and a trifle larger.

Then it subsided into darkness that verged on invisibility again.

Soon would come the time to slice at the mighty mythal above and around him with it, to sever it from most of its anchors so its energies could be drained quickly. Soon.

But not yet. To do so now would be to alert every elf of Myth Drannor to the doom yawning before them.

For now, the Shadow Sword would slay baelnorn and drink in more elven magic.

Helgore went hunting more prey. Haughty elves who'd lurked down here for centuries, serenely confident in their hollow achievements and service. The world was better off without them. Was better off without any toothless posers, least of all those who lorded it over humans as inferior barbarians, uncouth and dim-witted and . . .

Lip curling, Helgore stalked on. Following the passage around several scalloped curves, as the ancient way snaked around the mighty roots of age-old forest giants, to yet another double door carved with the device of an elf House. Its baelnorn faded through the closed doors to confront him.

Smilingly, he sketched a mocking bow.

"Who are you?" the undead guardian asked sternly. "You are no elf, and I fear you intrude here for no good or honorable reason. What is your purpose, smirking human?"

Helgore made no reply to this tiresome challenge, but merely willed the Shadow Sword forward. It glided down to transfix and drain the baelnorn in midspeech, destroying it before he had to lift a finger.

Helgore didn't bother to even look at the House carving this time. After all, what did it really matter?

Just another tomb full of dead elves, already forgotten. The sword drank them, and Helgore smiled and headed for the next crypt, his great weapon a silent silver line rippling with shadow in his wake.

Only to find his way barred, this time, by elves in armor. Faces furious, and hastening to form a line, swords out.

"Foul despoiler, your life is forfeit. Go greet the gods!" one of them cried.

"After you, elf." Helgore sneered, dropping to one knee and letting the Shadow Sword pass over him.

Sped by his will, it raced forward to devour.

Living, unliving, magic; what did it matter?

CHAPTER 10

No Shortage of Strife

O H," THE MONK SIGHED, SHOULDERS SAGGING IN RELIEF. "IT'S YOU. Sorry, Chethil, I thought you were—"

He tried to choke and sob in the same moment, and managed only a strangled *eep* as his eyes bulged, staring at Norun Chethil in shocked disbelief.

Maerandor chuckled. "And you thought that the head cook of Candlekeep could only kill with what he served forth on platters, didn't you? My, my, Wendarl, for such an old and wise man, you're as naive as a green young lad!"

By then, old Wendarl was sprawled at his feet, far beyond hearing jeers and witticisms, so the false cook fell silent. As was most prudent, considering that fighting had broken out in many of the rooms and passages around him. The other hitherto-hidden Shadovar agents among the monks had seen the sign he'd left, and begun murdering monks—only to encounter a few instances of suspiciously strong resistance. More than a few "monks" of the keep who seemed to have become powerful wizards and sorcerers when no one was looking.

Maerandor sighed theatrically. Truly, Toril had become a wallow of common deceit these days . . .

He took the time and concentration to make sure his personal wardings were ready to turn back both hurled weapons and mighty magics, then turned and walked away from the monk he'd just killed without a backward glance.

Wendarl had been a superb calligrapher in his day, but Faerûn held thousands of skilled scribes, and the sooner there were no monks left to hamper the cause of Thultanthar and the wards of Candlekeep could be delivered to the Most High, by far the better . . .

He still had no way of knowing who was friend or foe. Telamont had put into his mind images of the faces of the monks who'd been covertly slain and replaced by lesser Shadovar agents—but who knew how many of them might have been killed in their turn, and replaced by Moonstars, or ambitious independents?

After all, the legendary Larloch, mightiest of liches, was very real, might well be interested in all the magic within Candlekeep, and could well seize upon this time of tumult to try to take it all for his own.

Or for that matter, the renegade Chosen of Mystra, the Elminsters and Manshoons, were always on the prowl for more magic.

To say nothing of Szass Tam of Thay, or the mysterious Ioulaum and the shadowy mages who served him, or more than a dozen others the Most High had warned his arcanists to beware.

Telamont hadn't bothered to mention what he and Maerandor both knew—that even if every last one of these threats was accounted for and foiled, wizards lowly and mighty had a habit of lurking and waiting for opportunities to snatch powerful magic, and any one of several thousands of archmages could step out of the shadows at any time and make their own bids for the mastery—or swift plunder—of Candlekeep.

Nor were hedge wizards and archmages the only rogue dangers he must beware of just now. Long ago, Melegaunt Tanthul had warned several young arcanists that certain dragons thirsted for human magic, and had assembled their own secretive forces of agents to steal or seize spells and magic items whenever possible. Many of those agents would be long dead by now, and a handful of their masters, too, but wyrms lived long, their hungers ran deep, and agents could be replaced, generation after generation . . .

Maerandor had been one of those arcanists. Some of the others had been revealed as traitors to the Tanthuls, or driven by too-dangerous ambitions of their own, and were now dead. Others were missing, out there somewhere in Toril or elsewhere, on missions the High Prince had sent them on, or gone rogue and pursuing their own aims.

All of these perils meant damned near anyone and anything that hungered after magic could appear in these dim and dusty halls around Maerandor, and he had to be ready to defeat them. And swiftly, too, for while he was fighting one foe, he was necessarily inattentive to the plots and covert deeds of others, not to mention a trammeled, easy target for a second or third enemy—or just too preoccupied to see foes arriving, and what they might do and take.

Of more immediate concern were the known foes whose faces the Most High had shown him and informed him were here in Candlekeep, posing as monks. They had to be hunted down and destroyed, right now, before—

"Hold!"

That snarled command came from one direction, at the same moment a spell lashed out from another, catching Maerandor between them.

His wards flashed as the spell that had been meant to slay him was flung back at its caster in a shrieking spray of white sparks, leaving a monk reeling and moaning in pain. Maerandor turned a layer of his wards hard and solid, and used it to shove that man back against the nearest wall, pinning him there, gasping for breath and sobbing from the pain his own spell had caused him.

Then he ignored his attacker, to concentrate on the one who'd told him to halt.

"*You* hold," he commanded coldly, "or die."

Maerandor could see the monk who'd spoken. Who *should* be a fellow Shadovar, but . . .

"Send any magic my way, and you'll die horribly—and without delay," he added tersely, and lowered his wards enough to use a spell the Most High had given him.

It was a minor magic that identified persons Telamont had long ago magically marked—no guarantee of loyalty, only of identity; those the spell "found" would be arcanists of Thultanthar, no matter who or what they might now look like.

A silver flare kindled around the eyes of the man who'd challenged him, and in those of the man who'd just tried to kill him.

Which meant both were Shadovar.

"I speak with the full authority of the Most High," Maerandor informed them, "and you will accompany me now, and obey me as you would him."

He did not have to add "Or die." He made certain his quiet voice held that flat promise.

"And who are you," the one who'd challenged him asked sharply, "to claim the supremacy of the Most High? I've never seen you before; how do I know you're not one of these Moonstars, up to tricks? Or Old Elminster the Meddler?"

Maerandor gave the man a brittle smile. He'd been waiting for this.

And he was ready. Telamont had made certain he would be ready. The spell he was using to identify Thultanthans had another facet to it. The Declaration. He stepped back to where he could readily meet the eyes of both men, and used it on them.

Telamont Tanthul, High Prince of Thultanthar, was not a man who often raised his voice. He didn't need to, when his calm, cold, quiet voice carried doom enough. The Declaration was no shout, but the spell made it roll into their minds so powerfully that it might as well have been.

I am the High Prince of Thultanthar, and my word is law in Shade and all lands under the dominion of the matchless city of Thultanthar. I am Lord Shadow, and when I go to war, the mightiest arcanists of Netheril serve me, and when I am at peace, the most brilliant Netherese kneel to me and do my bidding and exalt my city. I am the ruler of the greatest city of Netheril, and I am the most powerful in Thultanthar. I am the rightful ruler of all Netherese; there is no other. Obey this my servant Maerandor, or face my wrath.

The mental echoes of that mind-voice had both men on their knees, half in awed obedience and half in dazed collapse, beaten down, by the time the last word smote them.

"Well?" Maerandor asked them, into the near silence of their labored breathing, his challenge barely more than a whisper.

They looked up at him like whipped dogs, wary and yet eager to obey. "I—whatever you command, Lord Maerandor," the unwounded man said hastily.

"Y-yes," the man still pinned to the wall managed, swallowing blood.

"Come," Maerandor snapped briskly, and he strode away, loosening his ward hold over the man and returning it to full defensive mettle.

He might well need it.

They stalked through a labyrinth of dim and cluttered chambers, walled in books and roofed in hanging maps, dominated by stout wooden tables and crude wooden benches.

Everywhere underfoot there were ribbons of sticky, starting-to-dry blood—and at the end of each one there sprawled the body of a monk.

Other Shadovar joined them as they went, none needing the hammer of the Declaration. Six, eight, eleven . . . Maerandor smiled, feeling powerful enough to swagger at last.

Which meant, of course, he'd best gird himself against real danger.

He let go of Telamont's recognition spell in favor of the far more widely known magic of true sight. It would go ill if he missed a real foe among the still-living monks he met.

They heard shouts, and more than one booming echo of a burst that was almost certainly a spell hurled in anger—but thus far, in room after room, they found no living monks.

So Maerandor turned and used his augmented vision on the Shadovar with him.

And with a grim and utter lack of surprise, saw that one of the purported Thultanthans was an impostor. That is, someone who must have murdered a Shadovar, impersonating a quietly slain monk.

For he could see now that this false Shadovar had a face Telamont had warned him belonged to one Saerlar Stormwyvern, a half-elf Moonstar.

Maerandor pointed and snarled, "A Moonstar! That one—kill him!"

There was a rush to do just that, as Stormwyvern's hands flashed through a desperate incantation—but before any magic could erupt, Candlekeep around them gave a mighty shudder, the stones rumbling and groaning so violently that everyone was flung off their feet.

Bouncing bruisingly, shouting in fear, or snarling out curses, the Shadovar bounced from wall to wall, shattering lanterns.

The great shaking seemed to be welling up beneath them, the floors bulging up and then falling back.

"Earthquake!" someone cried.

"We're doomed!" another Shadovar shouted.

"The ceiling's falling! *It falls!*"

A few stones and tiles and a lot of dust did fall, pelting and bouncing down, but no general roaring collapse came down on them.

Shockingly, though, the floating, magical glowing globes that provided general overhead illumination in this room of Candlekeep as in so many others all winked out in unison, plunging the chamber into darkness, as all around Maerandor, men grunted, grappled, and screamed as they were wounded—or stabbed to death.

There had been time enough, but only *just*.

The shield of force Elminster had spun from the Weave was large and curved enough to keep him from being flattened—as it was slammed to the floor and battered down by a thunderous deluge of falling rock, with him beneath it.

The roaring torrent became a syncopated hammering that gave way to individual stones crashing, bouncing, and rolling . . . and then to echoes and swirling dust.

Out of which Elminster's shield came whirling, hurled across the cavern with the full strength of the Old Mage's will and the wards of Candlekeep.

To slap Alustriel and Laeral as if it was a great paddle, batting them head over heels across the echoing expanse of the cavern.

El sought to pin the sisters against the rocks of the far wall—but skidding on knees and elbows, eyes flashing, they both called on the wards too.

Wards they'd been attuned to and living with far longer than Elminster ever had, wards now very familiar to them—and responsive to their will.

The shield racing at them slowed abruptly, came to a stop . . . and started coming back at Elminster, ponderously at first, but then with ever-quickening speed.

Elminster gave it a disapproving look, and it slowed abruptly. A ripple ran down his jawline, and the shield stopped.

And started back to where the two sisters stood side by side, glaring at him. They gave the shield a mental shove, and it shuddered, slowing abruptly. Elminster shoved back.

Alustriel's eyes glowed, flaring like two lamps, and the shield shook in the air. Elminster thrust at it with all he could call up from the wards.

And all light flickered and then failed, the cavern around them and under their feet shuddering as the Weave convulsed, shockwaves rippling.

El felt a drift of dust and fine sand falling on his face as Candlekeep groaned above him, a yawning slow and loud and deep, that fell into the rumbling of an earthquake.

He took six swift crouching steps to his right in the utter darkness—and that proved to be wise, because as the rumbling died and the magical radiances faded back into being, the shield was racing right at where he'd been standing.

And it was coming edge on, this time.

It swerved around in a slicing arc as Laeral and Alustriel saw where he now stood, and came at him again.

Elminster lifted his lip in a mirthless smile and strode to meet it.

The spell that would serve him best right then was already taking hold; a magic that would cleave the shield and anything else solid sent at him, leaving a path of emptiness before him wreathed in shimmering magical fire.

It did just that, smoothly slicing the shield asunder, and El left it seeking new things to devour as he used the Weave to call on the wards of the keep again, trying to bring down the cavern wall behind Alustriel and Laeral, so rubble would rain onto their heads—just as they'd sought to serve him.

His call became ineffectual tugging. They were using the Weave, two to his one, and their control over the wards remained firm.

The cavern wall didn't even tremble.

Not that they'd been idle. He raised his cleaving fire and tried to twist it to intercept magic, but it was still transforming when the spells they'd just cast tore through it and struck him—a roaring burst of flames enveloping his head and hands, as ice seared and rimed him below the waist.

El had to fight for breath enough to scream.

He writhed in agony, trying to cry out and blinded by scalding steam billowing up from the roiling, clawing meeting of fire and ice right across his chest. He was vaguely aware of falling backward, legs frozen and rigid, the silver fire within him leaping out of half a dozen raw wounds and licking up and down his limbs.

He landed hard and bounced, only his silver fire keeping his lower body from being shattered. He could not even squirm. Shudder, yes, but that was his ravaged body's doing, not something he could control. He lay there shaking and helpless, in whimpering agony.

"Sorry, old friend and mentor," he heard Alustriel say sadly, from somewhere close above him. "We didn't want to do this. We never wanted to have to do anything like this to you."

"Yet do it we must," Laeral wept. "Finish it, Luse. Finish him now, before we weaken and change our minds. Still alive, he's a peril forever. Do it!"

"I think *not*," someone else said then.

It was a cold and calm voice that Elminster had heard before.

"Oh? And who are you?" Alustriel asked sharply—and there followed an ear-shattering explosion.

"Is *that* the best you can do?" the newcomer asked contemptuously. "Truly, Chosen have become lesser beings than they were in my day."

"And when was that, bone lord?" Laeral snapped, and through swimming tears El was aware of a blindingly bright flash of emerald light.

The cold voice laughed. "You seem used to destroying far feebler liches. I am Larloch, the First Chosen of Mystryl, and her herald. Some call me the Shadow King. You may call me—Oblivion."

You grew used to the gentle singing of the City of Song after a time, Amarune had discovered. It was as beautiful and softly ethereal as ever, but it faded in your awareness to an ever-present background. Until something louder and more strident drowned it out.

War horns blared, deep and menacingly mournful, through the trees. Mercenaries' horns. They were coming now, a widespread crashing of leaves and dead twigs underfoot amid the thunder of many rushing warriors' boots, pouring through the forest in an all-out charge. The armies of Shade, striking in unison at last.

Converging not just on Storm, Amarune, and Arclath, nor the elves who stood with them, but closing in from all directions on the core of Myth Drannor that the elves still held, the war horns dying away in mournful echoes as a cacophony of shouts, war cries, and bellowed orders arose.

"Steady," Arclath commanded no one in particular, as he stood beside his beloved. Storm was on Amarune's other side, sword ready and the long silver tresses of her hair stirring around her shoulders like so many restless snakes. On either side of them stood a line of elves—a line only one defender deep, a pitiful handful to stand against so many onrushing mercenaries.

"Strike to disable," Arclath added quietly, "and let their fallen become a barrier we can defend."

Storm nodded. "Wise words, but—"

Then there was no more time for nervous talk. The charging mercenaries had reached them, roaring.

In half a breath the world became a confusing, bloody chaos of hacking swords. The shriek and clang of steel was deafening, birds fleeing from branches overhead squalling but utterly unheard.

Rune and Arclath stabbed and parried and sidestepped, but the footing soon became treacherous and they fell into the same attacks as their attackers—hacking wildly and frantically, like unskilled wanderers trying to cut their way out of a forest thicket. There wasn't room to do anything else; the few spears thrust high and tangled in branches overhead, their wielders reeling back, too wounded to keep hold of them. Blood sprayed blindingly in all directions as sword hands were lopped off and throats laid open, men reeled and fell, and . . . suddenly it was over, and the mercenaries were falling back.

Leaving mounds of heaped dead and moaning, writhing wounded behind them. Ruthlessly the blood-drenched elf defenders advanced to stab the stricken into silence.

Everyone was panting hard, covered in sticky blood—and Storm was working hard alongside the elves, tendrils of her hair plucking daggers from mercenary sheaths and swords from under bodies or out of failing hands, tossing the gleaned weapons back among the elf lines.

The besiegers hadn't gone far. They were within easy bowshot, through the trees, though no shafts were flying.

The surviving high mages had boosted the city's mythal to quench flames and slow arrows, spears, and other missiles in midair, but it had been done in haste, and they lacked skill and might enough for the augmentation to be permanent. The new abilities rode the age-old mythal uneasily, flickering and fitful.

174

A proof of this came hurtling: a spear arcing through the air from among the milling mercenaries. It deflected off a tree to crash to the forest floor, rattling and sliding . . . but didn't stop until it found heaped bodies.

"Our mages must be getting tired," a bladesinger panted, leaning back against a tree trunk beside Storm. "When they falter, so do the new mythal powers."

"At least the mythal work keeps them from getting underfoot when swords are swinging," Storm replied.

That brought a wry and weary grin to the bladesinger's face, but Storm didn't echo it. Rather, she turned and beckoned Arclath and Amarune, looking thoughtful.

"Come," was all she said as they left the lines. Arclath looked back warily at the mercenaries as someone among them started to beat a drum, but Rune laid a hand on his arm to gently tug him along.

Storm set a brisk pace through the trees, but they hadn't come far when two elves stepped from behind trees, blades in hand—long whipswords, barb-ended blades whose slender lengths flexed and sang—and faces unfriendly.

"Where are you headed?" one of them asked softly.

"To the high mages working on the mythal," Storm replied politely, not slowing.

The elves frowned, neither stepping aside. "How is it that you know—?"

Storm dodged between them with a liquid shift of her hips that lifted Arclath's eyebrows appreciatively, and murmured, "I was one of several who suggested the augmentations."

The elves started after her, but then stopped and sighed as Arclath went wide around them one way, Amarune did the same in the other direction, and Storm turned around to watch, from well beyond them now.

"It would be wiser, humans—" one of the elves began, but Storm shook her head and smiled.

"I've never quite had leisure enough to wait to become wiser," the silver-haired bard told the sentries. "I've always just had to go ahead and do things now." A few retreating steps later she added brightly, "'Tis our curse, we short-lived humans!"

Then she turned and hurried over a little ridge, to come down through duskwoods into a landscape of little lawns and grassy paths and curving stone walls amid the trees, where the wild forest gave way to soaring elven architecture.

Arclath and Amarune joined her, looking around in pleasure at the sweeping curves and spires of the City of Song. The fighting hadn't yet reached this far, but the litter of war was everywhere.

And so were the sentries. None of the elves who stepped forth to challenge the three hurrying humans had ready bows or spears ready to hurl, thanks to the mythal augmentations, but they were far less than pleased at "outlanders" seeking to get to the high mages, and Storm had to talk her way past sentry post after sentry post with increasing difficulty.

Arclath and Amarune kept their heads down and their mouths shut, knowing that without Storm—whom many of the elves knew—they'd have been attacked long ago.

For her part, though her voice remained gentle and courteous, it was clear from the increasingly flat brevity of her converse that Storm's temper was growing shorter and shorter.

"Easy, Lady Storm," Arclath muttered, as they finally won their way past a particularly rude sentry, and strode on. "Their ways are . . . their ways."

Rune gave him a withering look, and he shrugged sheepishly. Less than eloquent, to be sure, but . . .

"Thank you, Arclath," Storm told him softly, wrapping one long and shapely arm around him and squeezing. "I've never had much use for obstinate stupidity, but your point is taken. And your support appreciated."

Arclath struck a heroic pose that made her snort.

An instant later, something crashed through the limbs of some distant trees. Boulders plummeted and rolled, downed leaves and boughs crashing in their wakes.

"A catapult load," Arclath murmured. "I'd been wondering why they hadn't got around to that earlier. One could spread fire all too well . . ."

His words trailed away as he realized what the arrival of the boulders meant.

"Yes," Storm said grimly, seeing his face. "The high mages are failing in earnest."

"So, should we be hurrying?" Amarune asked. "Or is there really anything we can do?"

Storm sighed as the next sentries—a trio, this time—appeared from behind some trees ahead, and moved to intercept them.

"'One does what one can,'" she quoted the old saying. "'And the result must be taken as good enough.'" She shook her head, and muttered, "Though my sister Dove always hated that saying. Now I know how she felt."

The next load to rain down out of the sky and bounce bloodily, right in front of Storm this time, were the dismembered limbs and torsos of battle dead. There were some human remains, but all too much of it was elf flesh.

Fresh . . . and not so fresh. The staring, dusty-eyed heads were the worst.

The sentries recoiled from what spattered or rolled at their feet, and Storm sighed again.

It was early in the evening of this twelfth day of Marpenoth. Which meant that only the earliest and most eager of the idle and wealthy nobles in Suzail had found their ways to the Memories of Queen Fee.

So they could be first with the latest and juiciest gossip, of course.

"They're saying," Lady Shalais Wyrmwood burst out breathlessly, eyes dancing with excitement, "that Myth Drannor has fallen, and all the Dales too!"

"As even my great-grandsire often observed, 'they' say many things," Lord Illance said sourly. "Where's the proof? Lay before us some details, lass! A vagabond hiresword army has to be *paid*, remember! What they can seize from the elves and the Dalefolk is their own booty, theirs in addition to their promised coin. And last *I* heard, they hadn't been paid at the agreed-upon time, and were getting a mite surly about it. So before you have the fabled City of Song with all its proud elves *and* the Dales with their sturdy farmers overthrown, routed, and taken, hearken to this: I've noticed, down the years, that armies always win their greatest victories in rumor, and do rather less well on the battlefield."

"You'd not say that, Lord Illance," Lady Rowanmantle snapped, "if you'd seen the wasteland that was once the glittering heart of Sembia. Why—"

"And have *you* seen it, Lady?" came his frosty interruption. "Have you seen anything at all beyond what can be glimpsed from the highest towers in this city, in the last three decades? I think not. Wherefore you must needs rely on the same racing and loose-tongued rumor that so *informs* young Lady Wyrmwood here."

At the next table, Lord Harflame set down his goblet to sneer. "They'll be at our gates next! Run and hide your jewels *and* your best gowns, ladies!"

"Yes, and go about in our frilly scanties," old Lady Rowanmantle said caustically. "You'd like that, wouldn't you, Amondras? You always were a lecherous, drooling, tasteless *boor*!"

"Odds blood, what a sharp-tongued liar you are, Arletta! How would *you* know what I taste like, hmm? And were I as lewd as you claim, I'd even want to see *your* old dragon-scarred hide bared, whereas the truth of the matter is that I'm far more selective! Young Shalais here, Delaunthra yonder, and one or two others, not the whole aging herd of you!"

"*Herd*, Lord Harflame? *Herd*!?"

"Yes, 'herd,' to be sure. Although perhaps that's a disservice to my cows, who still yield milk and give me calves, and are on the whole far easier on the eyes, and most certainly on the ears, than you old battle-axes!"

Mirt hid a wide—and getting broader—grin behind his oversized goblet. This was better than a play! They'd be throwing food and dashing wine at each other next!

So as not to be noticed by anyone who might curb their tongue when reminded there was an outlander present, he settled himself a little lower in his seat in the darkest corner of this exclusive upper room in the Memories of Queen Fee. The most fashionable and expensive club along the Promenade in Suzail was sparsely populated just now, but then it was early yet. Many of the regular noble patrons were at home, with large and sumptuous meals and more than a few goblets of good wine still to get through, to fortify themselves for the serious imbibing that went on in the Fee.

Rank amateurs in debauchery to a veteran glutton and drunkard like the oldest living Lord of Waterdeep, but after all, these *were* Cormyreans; they went at such things far more lightly than in the Deep.

"Well," observed Lord Renstameir Haelrood, as he swept into the room with a club servant scrambling in his wake to retrieve his casually discarded, many-feathered hat and gilt-trimmed cloak, "I see you're all hard at work trying to dismantle each other's tempers and reputations, as usual, rather than concerning yourselves with the weightier matters that should ensnare the attention of us all. We'll find it hard to go on leading a kingdom if we find it destroyed beneath us on the morrow. Care you *nothing* for what's happening across Faerûn?"

"Such as *what*, precisely, Renstameir? Who or what is so thundering likely to destroy Cormyr overnight, may I ask?"

"You may, Lady Rowanmantle. Please do. Anything to keep Harflame goading you into being the old cows and battle-axes he so fondly likes to describe you as. Yet to keep matters from devolving down a dozen-some side lanes of distractions, name-calling, and riding favorite hobbyhorses, let me set before you these: the Great Rain has swollen the Sea of Fallen Stars so greatly as to restore its shores to something akin to what our grandsires remember, which means our own shores are flooding and may soon be sunken for good; priests of more faiths than I can keep track of are fighting among themselves over this or that detail of their gods, and this strife is widespread and becoming worse, so that we may yet have a score or more holy wars raging across all the lands; and it seems every third or fourth home or farm in every kingdom houses an ambitious person who thinks they are the Chosen of this or that god, and must go out into the world with fire and sword and claim the recognition of their deity by doing awful and great things that all too often seem to involve much bloodshed. Including killing others who claim to be Chosen. Something that may yet have the gods angered enough to do even more awful things to all of us."

Lord Haelrood sank into a chair with more sighing satisfaction than grace, and added, "I could go on, at length, but I need a drink. While all of you try to deny or dismiss everything I've just said so you can hurry back to arguing if Lady Such-and-Such is a trollop because she showed some knee through a slit in her gown two revels ago, or if Lord So-and-So's piles are larger and more painful than Lord Howsoever's. *Pah.* Can you not *see*, my lords and ladies? Toril around us is sinking into wild disaster—'cataclysm' is not too strong a word—and you care not, so long as the good food and better wine keeps coming. Well, the vineyards and herds and farm fields that provide such things may soon be laid waste, and then you will *have* to notice. Whereupon no doubt you'll start squabbling about which of your old rivals is really to blame, rather than all this rumor from afar about Chosen and Great Rains and disasters."

"Rains of frogs, forty nights of torrential downpours of blood, monsters coupling with other monsters to spawn as yet unheard-of stranger monsters, taxes going down, and—gasp!—nobles telling the truth," Lord Harflame recited to his goblet mockingly. "Whatever next?"

Haelrood turned on him. "So you mock, and think yourself oh-so-superior, and do *nothing*. Steward of the realm that you are, that we all are, we lords and ladies. Beware frightened commoners with pitchforks, Harflame. When they get angry and scared enough to go looking for something to stick their forks into, your ample behind will be right there in view—and *that's* when they'll remember they don't think much of the sneering old goat attached to it. I hope you can run faster than you can get up out of a chair here, after you've been guzzling firewine all night."

"I do *not*," Harflame replied coldly, "guzzle firewine. A *common* beverage. *I* guzzle Taerluthran." He held up his goblet, smirked, and added, "As I'm doing now."

Lady Wyrmwood surprised them all then by shooting to her feet, goblet in hand.

"Drink while you can, lords," she toasted the room grimly. "For war may yet come again to these very streets, and by then many of us may be a little too dead to drink."

Mirt had expected derisive jeers and laughter to greet these words, but instead a silence fell. And stretched, deepening, as lords and ladies exchanged glances and grew both pale and grim.

Well, well. Perhaps it wasn't going to be too late for Cormyr after all.

The deep blue-green forest around Myth Drannor had suddenly become a din of ground-shaking cacophony.

Catapult loads were crashing down on all sides now—huge boulders, heaps of fresh corpses, the trunks of felled trees, and the occasional smoking mass of firewood that the city's mythal had quenched in midflight—and more than one group of sentries were dashed flat before Storm and her Cormyrean companions could reach them.

"What's *that*?" Amarune shouted suddenly from behind Storm, and the bard whirled around in time to see the air to the southwest go from faint blue to blood orange, in a swirling midair stain that spread as if some unseen titan had splashed something orange from the southwest toward the center of Myth Drannor.

As they stared—it actually looked quite pretty, if one set aside all fear of what it probably meant—another and smaller part of the sky, off to the south beyond the roiling amber radiance, abruptly flared apple green.

"Magic, isn't it?" Arclath hazarded.

Storm nodded, looking grim. "Wizards—arcanists, rather—among the besiegers are hurling spells at the mythal," she explained. "Not doing much damage that I can see, but of course we must add the word 'yet' here, if we cleave to honesty."

"*Look*," Rune hissed insistently, pointing. In the distance, through the trees, the amber radiance flashed and winked back reflections from metal—metal on the move, and a lot of it. The invading army was surging forward.

"The elf lines must have been overwhelmed," Amarune concluded gloomily.

Even as Arclath nodded and turned to Storm to ask her what they should do now, the high, fluting calls of silver trumpets rang out from the tallest trees and spires at the heart of Myth Drannor.

The call telling the defenders to rally to the breach, and fight to hold the foe back.

Storm sighed, turned around with a wave that bade Arclath and Amarune to come with her, and answered that call.

CHAPTER 11

All Hail the Shadow King

Yes, Oblivion. A trifle boastful," the cold voice of Larloch added conversationally, "but such seems to be the style these days."

The archlich laughed, mirth that was almost immediately drowned out by a mighty roar.

Alustriel and Laeral screamed, and—

Suddenly the tumult and the cavern in which it had been raging were both gone, and Elminster found himself whirling silently through an endless blue void, tumbling and plunging down, down, down . . . to a brief flare of silver fire that transfixed him in utter spasming, gasping agony.

That faded as abruptly as it had come, leaving him panting, pain free and whole, but staggeringly weak, standing on an unfamiliar cold and dusty stone floor.

A brown floor, belonging to a cavernous, high-vaulted hall of brown stone. The very air around El as he swayed was ale brown and eddying, stale and tainted with the unmistakable reek of mildew.

Elminster blinked. He was facing a tall and slender figure in black robes. It towered head and shoulders above him.

He stared up at it. Into fell, old, and knowing eyes like two black, bottomless pools, set deep in a long, slender skull. For an instant, El was reminded of a bare, staring ox skull.

Then those dark eyes sharpened, and it was more like being impaled on two dagger points.

"Be welcome," said a dry voice from behind Elminster, "in the house of Larloch, the Shadow King."

El didn't turn to regard whoever had spoken—one of the Shadow King's liches, no doubt, serving him as herald or steward—but kept his gaze fixed on the eyes of the legendary Larloch.

Who stood confident and casual, flanked by a black staff twice as tall as Elminster, floating upright at the archlich's shoulder. It flared out from base to top, and was studded all along its length with the yellowing skulls of all sorts of creatures, from horned devils and demons down to small serpents.

A line of black-robed and glaring-eyed liches stood along the brown back wall of the chamber like the menacing members of a street gang, regarding Elminster as if he was a worm they itched to crush brutally in an instant.

Larloch made a casual gesture without turning to look at them, and they all hastily turned and filed out of the room through a modest door El hadn't noticed until then, behind the archlich's looming form.

"Your line, I believe, is 'Where am I?'" Larloch informed El pleasantly.

The Sage of Shadowdale shook his head, and found he needed to clear his throat before he could speak. "I was going to begin with 'Why did you save me?'"

Larloch smiled. "So we ride hard right at what is most important. Very well. I saved you, mage of Shadowdale, because you are the wisest and most capable of the Chosen—and always have been, with the possible exception of the Srinshee."

"And so? You've taken to collecting wise and capable Chosen?"

Larloch's smile went a trifle colder. "I need you, and the Realms needs you. You are the best tool at hand, to put it bluntly. And I cannot do this alone, for if just one spellcaster, in one spot, tries to call on the wards of Candlekeep to strengthen the Weave, the wards will surely collapse—like a man dropping and marring a long and heavy table he tries to carry from one end, whereas two men can readily manage the same transport, by lifting the table from both ends at once. The strengthening needs two of us, standing well apart, so we can draw on that part of the wards between us in a controlled manner, and so manage it."

El nodded. "And what," he asked carefully, "does the Shadow King—who weathered the Spellplague so handily—care about the Weave?"

Larloch tendered a cold, considering look, as if a pet had displeased him and he was reconsidering his acquisition of it.

And then he began to speak, leaning forward and speaking in earnest, as if El was a vital pupil who had to be clearly told something of utmost importance.

"Mystryl in my time, and two Mystras in yours, have been the goddess of magic—have *been* the Weave. The goddess Shar, in her pride and folly, believes that as Mystra is dead and there is still a Weave, the two are separate and can remain so. In this, she is wrong, but she also holds a belief that is correct: that control of the Weave, in the grasp of one with power enough, grants dominion over magic."

Larloch started to pace, the floating staff moving with him to always hang just behind his right shoulder.

"Her Cycle of Night failed here, and Sune defeated her attempt to have the Shadowfell flood into Toril and give her mastery over the other gods—have you not noticed that the tremors that shook the ground beneath your feet have now died away?—so Shar now desires to be the goddess of magic, and use it as her sword and war hammer and whip, to cause chaos and loss and destruction upon her whim. She believes this will deliver her from Ao and the order of things, by shattering that order, so the world shall become her plaything, under her absolute—and of course arbitrary—reign. Those sages who insist that we are all the playthings of the gods will finally be correct, to their despair, as we all learn what it is to be not the pawns of a more or less balanced group of many deities with opposing interests and techniques, but the pawns of one goddess. Who is mad, cares nothing for mortals, and exults in causing torment in all lesser beings. Some folk hate and fear magic for its devastating power. If Shar has her way, we will all hate and fear it, be we village idiots with no talent for the Art or archmages who might presume to challenge gods in our mastery of it. And we shall be but an afterthought to the Mistress of the Night, to be cast down and toyed with *after* she serves the other gods we venerate likewise. She wants to see gods suffer and despair, and slay themselves and each other, until she is the only god left, and her supremacy can never be threatened."

El nodded. This sounded like the Shar he knew, as much as any long-lived and alert mortal can come to know a deity.

Larloch came closer, his dark eyes still fixed on his guest as if they were blades or hooks that could pierce and hold sages of Shadowdale. "She will begin by subverting the least among the divine, while she manipulates the rest into making war on Ao. When he is destroyed or at least cast out of reach of our world, and the way he was sent sealed behind him, the ravaged survivors among the gods will become her toys, to be tormented at leisure, their destruction savored and prolonged. We mortals will be unregarded casualties in this endeavor, and only rise to her primary interest when there are no other gods—nor primordials, nor near-gods who might in time become gods—left, and the ways by which gods of other places might enter this world or influence it from afar are sealed or shattered."

Larloch halted right in front of Elminster, and points of light winked into being in many of the hitherto dark eye sockets of the yellowing skulls encrusting the floating staff—many fell and silent gazes that fixed coldly on the Old Mage, gazes that seemed to hold accusation and scorn.

"And all of this madness and wanton destruction begins with seizing control of the Weave. Working through her mortal servants whose ambition far outstrips their reasoning faculties—or they'd see the mad all-destroying folly they're attempting for what it is— yet who have skill enough in the Art to so serve. The arcanists of Thultanthar, who just might be numerous enough to achieve her first goal before they fail her or turn on her, as all of her previous magically mighty agents have done."

The archlich fell silent, and he and Elminster regarded each other expressionlessly as the silence stretched and deepened between them.

Finally Larloch asked, "Well?"

"Thy every word rings true," Elminster replied gently, "and I believe it. Yet what's befallen me down the years has schooled me to be suspicious of everything. Know that I am fully mindful of thy great experience and brilliance at the Art, yet feel moved to ask: how know ye all of this?"

Larloch nodded, betraying not the slightest hint of anger. "Telamont Tanthul, the High Prince of Thultanthar, is a vain man. As are many rulers, not to mention all too many archmages and archsorcerers. To me, he is one more arrogant young fool—and there's never been a shortage of those."

"A judgment he'll not welcome," El said dryly.

"His cold reception of it would not make it one whit less true. This self-styled 'Most High' has a habit of collecting trophies from those he's defeated—those he considers worthy foes, at least. One such is a ring he's proud of and wears all the time, as a mark of his defeat and destruction of a fellow Chosen of Mystryl, Araundras Othaun."

"And while he wears it, ye are closer to his thoughts than he knows," El concluded.

Larloch nodded. "While he wears it, I can see and hear what he does, though *not* touch his thoughts."

"And how came the ring to aid ye so?"

"A very long time ago, I doubted Othaun's loyalty to the goddess we both served—without cause, as it turned out—and altered the magics of that ring so I could eavesdrop on him." Larloch smiled mirthlessly. "Telamont has as yet not discerned this passive property of the ring. Much of his successes and survival, since Thultanthar's return to Toril, have been covertly aided by me and by those who serve me, often in light of what I have seen and heard through the ring. I saw Shade as a useful hand to shake many throats that should have been shaken long ago, without involving myself directly and publicly in current matters. Now, though, I have come to see differently. Now I see that Telamont *must* be stopped."

"As this shaking of throats will never end," Elminster interpreted aloud. "Progressing from specific targets to anyone whose downfall will benefit the High Prince or Thultanthar, and then to shaking every throat the Mistress of Night fancies shaken . . . which will eventually encompass every last throat that can be found."

Larloch's smile held not the slightest trace of mirth. "Precisely. So let me show you how best to call on the wards—so your control of them will triumph over that of Alustriel, Laeral, and the Prefects of Candlekeep."

"The Prefects . . . ," Elminster purred thoughtfully.

Rather than saying another word about the Prefects that so obviously intrigued his guest, Larloch smiled more widely and said, "Your mistake, thus far, has been thinking of the wards of Candlekeep as just local shackles that constrain the Weave into a specific order—which is, yes, what a mythal does. And, I'll grant, how you augmented the wards when you made your little additions to them."

Something overhead chimed very softly, but the archlich ignored it. "The wards seem to accomplish the same imposition of order that mythals do, but are far different in nature—being, for one thing, the untidy accumulated creation of so many diverse hands using differing methods and ways of seeing the world that no one examiner can now easily see how the wards accomplish what they do. So most individuals, if they can affect the wards at all beyond shifting matters from already-crafted setting to already-crafted setting, do as you have: they grasp whatever's nearest of the wards and tug on it as if turning the Weave to their will. That works, crudely, but can be easily and utterly foiled by anyone who knows more of how to 'work' the wards, as the monks say. The real monks, that is; watching the unfolding dance of covert slayings and impersonations has afforded me true entertainment, these last few years. So the proper way to bend the wards to your will is to . . ."

He waved one bony hand, and a glowing, moving image appeared in the air between them, showing a smaller and more silent Larloch calling on the wards with a particular technique.

The real Larloch imitated the actions of his image, and gave his guest a sidelong look. Obediently Elminster joined in, and together they briefly practiced alongside the animated image.

A bony finger wagged, the image winked out, and the Shadow King commanded, "Now you try working the wards in that manner, without guidance. I'll spin something that resembles the wards—thus. Now you grasp it and try to alter matters so the air of the warded area glows bright as day, and all sounds are muted."

El did as he was bid, thrice over, until he and Larloch were both satisfied the Sage of Shadowdale had mastered the technique.

"We are almost ready to return to Candlekeep," the archlich announced. "I can get us in through the wards without issue."

"Oh? How?"

"Who do you think renewed and expanded them, centuries ago?" Larloch asked, eyes twinkling. "Of course, I took the opportunity to make a few changes for my own benefit, in case I ever wanted to peruse a tome or two at my leisure."

"And have ye felt that want?"

"Many times, O man of many questions. Now, we'll need to begin by getting the Shadovar and the Moonstars to fight each other rather than us, to win us time to work."

"From what I know of both the Netherese and Khelben's cabal, they'll fight each other without any help from us," El replied dryly, "but I take it ye mean determine precisely where they're battling each other, so as not to see us—and attack us, on general principle."

The archlich nodded. "Precisely. We'll need to protect as many of the Prefects as we can too—the Keeper of the Tomes, the First Reader, the Great Readers and, only if they can be torn away from their duties without us spending overmuch time in doing so, the Chanter, the Guide, and the Gatewarden—because the more of them working with us, the more we can anchor and stabilize the Weave we're repairing, and minimize the risk of Weavefire, and it all going wild."

"Weavefire?"

Larloch sighed. "What *did* Mystra teach you and her other Chosen? Your Dove and your Storm prefer the sword to the Art, but the rest of you? I suppose, submerging herself into the Weave and becoming it, as Mystryl so long resisted doing, Mystra wanted no one to know that much about it, and so about her own vulnerabilities. Yes, Weavefire. Not like silver fire or the handfire novices conjure, nor yet spell-spawned walls of fire—Weavefire is when some part of the Weave is consumed by its own runaway energies, melting and shriveling like dry leaves in hot flame."

The archlich waved a hand, and another moving midair image appeared, showing Elminster just that. It did not look pretty.

"When your Mystra took you as a lover," Larloch told him, "she was putting the Weave into you. And she was putting you into it, making you a new anchor for the Weave. She did the same with the Simbul and others you never knew about. Using all of you because it was needful to keep the Realms from chaos. Just as you must now do what is needful. Which is to trust me a little more, and carry out my plan."

"And that is?"

"I'll send you back to Candlekeep with Telamont's sigil and secret words, and make your voice sound like his and your eyes look like his. His agents will believe you to be him; I'll give you their names and faces. Gather them and lead them into battle against the Moonstars, seeking to surround and contain Khelben's agents. When the fray is well underway, I'll snatch you out of it and back here—and we'll return to Candlekeep together and use the wards to seal off the warring sides. Those barriers won't last against determined spell hurlings, but should win us time enough to begin calling on the wards to mend the Weave."

El stared at Larloch for a long, silent time, then nodded and said, "I'll trust ye this far."

"Thank you. If all things work out well, you won't live to regret that trust. Rather, it will be time for Mystra's Chosen to raise the cry of 'All hail the Shadow King!' Or more likely not, from what I know of you Chosen."

And with those wry words, the lich stretched out a withered, long-fingered hand. "Receive, then, the names and faces you'll need to know . . ."

192

The war wizard was younger than Mirt had expected, his face pockmarked by one of the minor diseases that afflicted the young. Yet he carried himself with the quiet self-assurance of someone who wields both power and authority comfortably.

And Mirt had traversed so many rooms and guard posts, and spoken to so many courtiers to reach this inner room of the sprawling royal court building—hmmph, it looked larger than the damned royal palace itself!—on this chilly morning, that this lad must have *some* standing. Despite his pimples.

"It is less than usual for audiences of this sort between outlanders and the Wizards of War," the youngling began discouragingly, seating himself behind his desk and waving Mirt to a shorter, harder chair on the other side of it, "but—"

"It's 'less than usual' because you diligent agents of the Crown tend to come looking for us first," Mirt rumbled, glancing at the floor beneath the chair and the ceiling above it out of long habit, before settling himself into the seat with a grateful wheeze. "If we cause trouble, that is. From what I've seen hereabouts thus far, you lack resources enough to spy on everyone—common problem; had it myself—so the suspicious and known malcontents get most attention, and large-mouthed aging drunkards like me get dismissed as all wind and no dagger. A fairly accurate assessment, by the way."

The young war wizard's smile was a trifle pained. "We tend to prefer not to discuss specifics—"

"Courtiers behind desks never do. We all know—or tend to learn, the hard way—that words not said are easier to weasel out of. But come, lad, we'll be speaking of preferences and unusuals and difficult-to-says all day if our backsides and these chairs hold out.

Niceties have been observed, and you've sufficiently signaled yer inability to be blunt and yer superior position when dealing with outlanders. So to the point!

"Priests prate of the Sundering, and the world certainly seems in turmoil enough for nigh any doom crying to seem appropriate, even to the sea level rising to lap at the decking of yer docks down in the harbor here. And I've seen the turmoil among your troops. Purple Dragons marching out of the gates, armed Crown messengers riding in and out at all hours, guard posts reinforced everywhere . . . yet most of my evenings have been enlivened by sitting listening to nobles drink and dispute, and I've yet to hear one word out of any of them that suggests the palace is working with the nobility of the realm to strengthen Cormyr's defenses as all of this gets worse."

"Well, I hardly think these are the sort of matters they would discuss in front of an outlander. Still less are such topics appropriate for me to—"

"Oh, lad, lad, cut the free-flowing dung before it rises past your chin and *chokes* you! Even sitting here in Suzail, shuttling my backside between tavern, club, my rented rooms, and brothels, I've heard and seen enough to know there's strife over the throne, and the taking of sides, and the armies of Cormyr are armed and at war here and there and riding hard to some other place. How can I be of help? How can yer nobles, young and restless, as well as old and idle, make the realm stronger? Why aren't you *using* us?"

To Mirt's complete lack of surprise, part of the dark-paneled wall behind the young Crown mage opened soundlessly and two older war wizards stepped into the room, one of them spreading his hand in a swift quelling gesture to prevent his young fellow seated at the desk from replying.

"Forgive us," the visibly oldest of these two new arrivals—his hair was streaked white at both temples—greeted Mirt politely, "if we are skeptical of your motives. Defending the Forest Kingdom is *our* task. We ask ourselves, what aboveboard and honorable interest can an outlander, not loyal to the Dragon Throne, have in such matters? There are good reasons such individuals are not normally privy to our deliberations regarding the security of the realm."

"Fair enough to your latter, though I've always found that some public talk of security makes the citizenry feel better about any necessary daily bullying and serves as a warning to those who would do mischief, both visitors and homebodies. As to my motives, tell me if you find fault with my reasoning on this . . . if Cormyr falls or is weakened into civil strife, every sane inhabitant of Toril is the lesser for it. Yes?"

"Of course, but—"

"Lad," the unlovely mountain of man filling the chair on the supplicant's side of the desk told the senior war wizard rather testily, "there is no 'but' about it. I am—or was—a ruling lord elsewhere, and I tell you the best rulers are those who care not just for their domain, but all lands. For strife and disaster anywhere has a way of spreading, and sharing its pain, and so does peace and prosperity. If yer so all-fired worried about my possible disloyalty— though from what I've overheard, I could hardly be worse than some of yer Cormyr-born-and-bred-these-umpteen-generations nobles—then give me work where treachery is impossible or could do no harm."

"If we do, you'll inevitably see and hear and learn too much for the security of Cormyr," the second of the older war wizards replied flatly.

Mirt gave him an incredulous stare. "The Forest Kingdom's safety is *that* shaky? Truly? Well, it would seem to me that you have *far* greater problems than worrying about the deeds or motives of any individual outlander. And if they arrive in armies, their motives are a trifle obvious."

"Cormyr's safety and security are nowhere near 'shaky,' as you put it," the senior war wizard said coldly. "They are merely matters it is foolish to discuss, and needless to imperil in the slightest by involving outlanders."

"Not so," purred a new voice. "They are even weaker and more imperiled than Mirt suggests. I came to see to that, but found it unnecessary to do anything at all; the disaster has been waiting to happen here in Cormyr long before my arrival."

Everyone turned and stared at the smirking, darkly handsome man leaning into the room through another hidden door in the paneling.

"Well met," Manshoon added politely to Mirt. "Worry not; I'll not be sending any magic your way this time. Unlike the Forest Kingdom's Wizards of War, I learn lessons fast."

He turned his gaze to the three war wizards, and added gently, "You should heed this old man, you know. He's right. It's probably too late for your kingdom, but you war wizards may yet surprise me. By doing the right thing for once, for instance."

With a chuckle and a merry wave, he was gone, the paneling closed and looking as if there had never been a door there.

"Who—? How did he—?" the young war wizard stammered, but his elders were already starting to rush for the panel the unexpected visitor had disappeared through.

"*Don't*," Mirt growled, standing with unexpected haste to hurl his chair at the spot they were about to charge through. "He'll have left a nasty little spell trap behind. If no one does a dispel on that door and the passage beyond it—"

The chair bounced and clattered, the foremost war wizard batted it aside with a snarl, tripped over it and fell heavily, then bounded to his feet and snatched open the door.

The ear-splitting *crack* of many lightning bolts erupting from the revealed passage was still echoing in the room when the Crown mage's smoking body crashed off the far wall and fell to the floor, and the roast-boar-like smell of cooked human flesh started to fill the room.

Mirt sighed. "Men who say 'I warned you' are never popular, but I'm going to say it anyway. Idiots. I believe I'll go find some nobles who'll listen to me, and we can go and save Cormyr together."

The guards before the tall, splendid, and firmly shut doors of the palace at the high heart of Thultanthar were barring her way, but the young and darkly beautiful Thultanthan striding up to them with sultry grace never slowed.

In the end, the guards were forced to sidestep toward each other, until their hips almost touched, to physically block her from bursting between them and reaching the doors to the audience chamber of the Most High.

"You *may not* enter, Lady," one of them said sternly, raising a magical rod warningly.

She looked back at him steadily, and one raven-dark eyebrow arched in scornful disbelief—or feigned mockery of such emotion.

"Can it be that you do not know who I am?"

That goading question gained no answer, so the visitor said silkily, "I am Manarlume, granddaughter to the Most High. As such, I do not expect to find a door anywhere in Thultanthar closed to me. Ever."

"And yet," the other guard said gently, "we have our orders—and accordingly, this door remains closed. With all three of us on this side of it."

"Who gave you those orders?"

"The Most High himself."

Manarlume sighed, reaching a hand into her bodice, drew something forth, slid its chain over her head, and held it up.

"You *do* recognize this?"

She had the satisfaction of seeing one guard's jaw drop, and the other blink and then stare hard.

Small wonder. There were perhaps a dozen of these tokens in existence, small many-horned metal pendants bearing enchantments that could be felt—as a crawling, clawing presence—from some feet away. Given in secret by the hand of Telamont Tanthul himself, they granted immediate access to the High Prince of Thultanthar at any time, without dispute, explanation, or delay.

One of the guards did as he was supposed to—reach out and touch the token with a cautious fingertip, so its enchantment would show him the image of Telamont and affirm what it meant—but the other asked suspiciously, "How came you by this, Lady?"

"The Most High gave it to me, so I could reach him *without delay or dispute* if ever I saw the need," she replied crisply, "as I do *right now.*"

The two guards stared at Manarlume, then at each other. The one who'd touched the token reached behind his back, to the dagger sheathed at his belt there, and firmly depressed the stone set in its pommel.

That gem glowed momentarily as its magic flashed forth—a silent summons for the prince who oversaw the guards.

Aglarel arrived *very* quickly, cloak swirling. He was frowning as he strode, his hand on his sword. When he saw the token, he took it, jerked his head in a signal to the guards to open the doors—and as they swung open, stepped through the doorway, beckoning Manarlume to follow.

He ushered her to her grandfather in silent haste, gliding to a stop to stand watchfully right behind her, ignoring the hand she held out for the token's return.

The audience chamber looked different. It was still sparsely furnished with the high seat, the large and bare table, and the great black rod studded down its length with black spheres enclosing dark, empty glass globes, floating vertically off the floor in its corner. However, the High Prince of Thultanthar was busy watching the siege of distant Myth Drannor, gazing at a usually bare wall of the chamber.

The wall was aglow from corner to corner with many images, all of them views that looked down on the elf city from various heights. Scenes that were constantly moving—sometimes swooping. It was swiftly apparent to Manarlume that her grandfather was using spells to look through the eyes of birds flying over the besieged city.

Ah, of course. Scryings couldn't pierce the city's mythal from without.

Telamont turned from this glowing spell-spun tapestry of scenes, raising his brows in a silent question.

Manarlume met his gaze, then turned and pointedly looked at Aglarel—and then back at Telamont.

Who almost smiled. "Speak freely."

"Most High, among many petty transgressions and minor treacheries, we've found an immediate danger. The arcanist Gwelt."

"And he is dangerous why, exactly?"

"He's recruiting fellow arcanists who feel the ambition to replace princes of Shade!"

"As I told him to. Does he know you've discovered this?"

"No. That is, he may have his suspicions, but . . ."

"That explains the spell he cast on you. It's gone now."

"You *told* him to? But—"

"Granddaughter, you passed the test. Don't as swiftly lessen your standing in my eyes."

"Of course, Most High," Manarlume replied, and she looked at the floor.

"Aglarel, give her back my token. She'll have cause to need it again, I have no doubt."

As Aglarel did so, Telamont raised a hand to catch Manarlume's attention, and asked, "Tell me, what do your amorous arcanists say of two called Helgore and Maerandor?"

"That they are gone, undoubtedly on some secret mission or other for you, Most High. Most expect them to perish very swiftly—if they are not dead already."

Telamont's face betrayed no reaction. "Your arcanists are wiser than I'd thought."

Elminster found himself in a room he knew in Candlekeep, a lofty chamber whose walls bore gallery above gallery, each marking where an upper floor passed along the wall of the tall room.

He was standing face to face with Maerandor of Thultanthar.

Who was busily snapping commands at his fellow Shadovar, telling them to seek here and there and over *there* for Saerlar Stormwyvern. The half-elf Moonstar was nowhere to be seen, and had evidently vanished during the brief darkness accompanying the earthquake, as they'd all been charging at him.

"Most High?" Maerandor gasped. Then his face hardened, he snapped, "Can't be!" and his hands swept up to hurl slaying magic.

Elminster calmly drew the sigil Larloch had shown him in midair, and murmured one of the secret phrases.

This had *better* work.

CHAPTER 12

The Wards Our Shield These Long Centuries Passing

Staring at Elminster slack jawed in astonishment, Maerandor flung his arms wide, abandoning the spell he'd intended to hurl, and stammered, "M-my most profound and humble apologies, Most High!"

"Accepted," El replied coldly, and without the slightest pause, demanded, "Where are our other agents here at the keep? Revaerel and Tolorn?"

"Revaerel and Tolorn, Most High?"

"They have assumed the guises of the monks Hemmeth and Pelsrand, respectively."

"I—I know not. Forgive me, Most High, I didn't even know one of us was Pelsrand!"

El favored Maerandor with Telamont's best coldly disapproving frown, and watched the agent visibly cower.

He didn't give the man time to recover, but raised his voice a trifle so all the gathered Shadovar heard.

"We'll achieve more as a force rather than scattered skulkers," the false High Prince of Thultanthar decreed. "Let us go and find our missing two, then set out together to hunt down Moonstars. When we've scoured them out of Candlekeep, *then* it will be time to work on its wards. Properly, and with unhurried precision."

"*Die!*" a furious voice shouted, and a beam of ravening fire lashed down out of the dim heights of the room at Elminster.

Who flung himself headlong, down behind the nearest Shadovar. A moment later, the fiery magic incinerated the unfortunate Thultanthan.

As the deadly flames died away, the dead man toppling and then collapsing into swirling ash, the other Shadovar all whirled around and stared up.

To behold the Prefects of Candlekeep, standing on the highest gallery, frowning back down at them. Each monk was aiming a rod or staff, or holding up an orb—and every one of these enchanted weapons was glowingly awake with roused and ready magic. The highest-ranking monks of the keep had fetched the monastery's most powerful magics and come to make war.

They let fly.

Fire and frost and snarling lightning rained down, followed by the whirling chaos of more arcane deaths. Men screamed, convulsed, and died. Past the raging of unleashed magic, the fleeing false monks below—Elminster among them—could see tomes floating out into view from behind the shoulders of the Prefects, open grimoires and spellbooks from the libraries of Candlekeep, each wreathed in a rippling aura of risen magic. And from book after book, one by one, glowing beams shot down to immolate running monks below.

Elminster kept on crawling, trying to put solid stone between himself and what the Prefects could hurl. Preferably where he'd find a door out of this chamber straight ahead.

It didn't feel like the right time for parleys or explanations.

It seemed the Shadow Sword didn't care if it drank undeath or magic or the vitality of the living. Helgore had slain the last two elves by parrying their furious attacks while his dark conjured blade flew around to slide into them from behind—slicing into armor and flesh alike in silent ease, as if drifting through empty air.

Not that he'd resisted stabbing them when they were already dying. Shadow Sword or not, they were *his* kills. The latest in a count he'd already lost reliable track of, after a day of walking along in stone-lined underways, busily slaying.

Cormanthorian elves weren't so formidable, after all.

He looked around at all the lifeless darkness.

The glows of the armor had died with their wearers, leaving him alone in a corridor littered with dead elves and pools of their blood.

Helgore wiped his blade clean on a corpse's half cloak, sheathed it, and headed for the next crypt doorway. This was almost *too* easy.

He mind-guided the Shadow Sword to hang horizontally in the air, its star-kissed edge outermost, a dark and deadly barrier to anyone rushing up on him from behind. He willed it to flare its dark reach outward on either side of its blade as much as possible, to ensnare passing magic any elf might unleash at his back, and watched its darkness spread and loom obediently.

There. A shield nothing should be able to pass without his being warned.

Helgore smiled and went to the double doors of the crypt. Again, the device on it was unfamiliar, but really, what did it matter? One more forgotten family of elves too highnosed and haughty to have survived Toril's last few centuries. Even if one or two elves fighting in the forest above him right now still bore the same surname, they'd be dead soon enough. They all would.

Elves or titans, beholders or alhoon . . . none could stand against the arcanists of Thultanthar for long.

No coldly defiant baelnorn faded into view to challenge him. Well, perhaps some of them were learning prudence at last.

Helgore blasted the doors to pebbles and powder, enjoying the destruction. There were a few doors back home he'd not mind doing this to, so he could gloat over those cowering behind them ere sliding the Shadow Sword hilt deep through a few Thultanthans too haughty for their own good.

Yes. That was something to look forward to. After all, he knew the secrets of the Shadow Sword now. Telamont could hardly reach in and take away memories, so . . .

Well, now. Look at that. Riches at last.

Through the swirling dust, he could see many blue glows. Bright and strong, many layered . . . and mighty.

Oho. The Most High *would* be pleased.

Helgore strode forward. Yes, this crypt was packed with harps and swords and gauntlets—and all manner of gewgaws beyond his naming at first glance, each one of them aglow with the blue radiance of powerful magic.

This crypt was so crowded with loot that the dead lay not on their backs, but stood upright, the remains held vertical by magic that shaped truly lifelike effigies.

Helgore sneered. Well, they'd collapse into bones and dust swiftly and satisfyingly enough when all their magic was drained awa—

The centermost of the three effigies facing him had just opened eyes the hue of mithral flame, and stepped out of the soft blue glows to face him.

Copper-colored hair, pale skin, an elf female he knew from the training the Most High had given him—except that the real thing looked far angrier than Telamont's mind-portrait. He was face to face with Ilsevele Miritar, the Coronal of Myth Drannor.

Helgore stepped back hastily, ducking low and willing the Shadow Sword to turn and thrust into the crypt point first.

The coronal strode to meet it, blazing eyes fixed on him. "If you'd cared to learn some of the mysteries of the *Tel'Quess* before destroying them, Shadovar, you might have survived longer. The coronal can feel the breaching of any crypt in this city."

Whatever she unleashed then, howled into and through Helgore of Thultanthar's hasty wards and shieldings as if they didn't exist—and then into and through him.

He didn't even have time to scream as he met his doom.

So there was no one at all to see the coronal let the Shadow Sword slide into her and through her. Shuddering in agony, she embraced it, tugging at its great hilt to pull it hard against her breast as blue fire flared up around her in a snarling inferno.

And raged in that crypt mouth and out into the passage beyond, hot and bright and blue, racing away down the passage and then rebounding.

It roiled, spat, and became dimmer and smaller, fading . . . dying away.

When it was all gone, there was no Shadow Sword at all, and the coronal stood tall and unwounded, blue lightning crackling here and there in her copper hair, swollen with all the magic the sword had held.

Yet there was no pride in her face, only sorrow. She shook her head and went out into the passage, weeping softly.

Her tears glowed blue as they fell, dancing like little dying flames on the stone floor in her wake as she went, weeping for those now lost forever.

Deadly magic was still howling and snarling around the high-ceilinged chamber deep in Candlekeep, with dead or dying or frantically fleeing monks among it, and the grim Prefects of Candlekeep staring down from their balcony with the powerful tomes of magic floating around them, directing the death they'd just unleashed.

"Die!" the Keeper of the Tomes had shouted, and the echoes of his cry were still reverberating around the hall, borne on the roiling, spark-studded backwash of deadly energies.

"Die *yourself*," Maerandor muttered in reply as he finished his spell, locked eyes with the Keeper of the Tomes up on the balcony above, and unleashed death.

That end of the balcony vanished, the very stones becoming tentacles that should flail and batter even before they crushed and tore.

Farewell, Keeper. Good farruking *riddance*.

Other Shadovar spells were stabbing up at that balcony, too, and other monks up there were reeling. An orb exploded with a shriek and a bright flash, and Maerandor saw what was left of the monk who'd been wielding it stagger and then topple, now headless and armless . . .

The Most High was watching.

Maerandor smiled, chose another Prefect along the balcony, worked a deft spell—and killed the man. Harper or Chosen or Red Wizard impersonator, or genuine Avowed of Candlekeep consecrated to learning and Oghma the Binder . . . it mattered not. They all had to die, and the sooner the better.

Smiling a colder smile, Maerandor chose another target.

El had reached the doorway he'd sought, but didn't go through it. The Shadovar were both swift and obviously unimpressed by threats from massed old men on balconies who should have cast aside honor and struck first rather than hurling warnings from on high.

Now, every last one of the Prefects looked likely to be slaughtered in short order if nothing was done.

And if you want something done in the Realms, you call on Elminster . . .

Pah. El did a working he hoped no one would even notice that thrust an invisible tongue of the wards of Candlekeep straight across the room, right in front of this Maerandor of Thultanthar. The arcanist's next hurled doomspell should strike it and rebound right back on its caster—

Like *that.*

Grinning ruthlessly up at the balcony, Maerandor had flung a spell Elminster remembered from long, long ago. A magelord of Athalantar had been fond of that same bone-rend spell, the distinctive red-and-black cloud of grisly destruction as a living man's bones were torn right out of his body, bursting through flesh in an invariably messy explosion of wet spattering blood and innards.

The wet red heap that had been Maerandor looked no cleaner than any of the other victims El had seen.

Elminster looked down at what was left of the arcanist for a moment, then turned away. He'd seen little enough of Telamont Tanthul, but what he had taken in should be enough to convincingly feign being High Prince of Thultanthar for a little longer.

"Another traitor falls," he announced loudly, keeping his voice cold and calm, "failing himself and Thultanthar alike."

Shadovar were turning to him, listening. Telamont must have them well whipped.

"Leave these old fools for now!" he ordered. "Time enough to destroy them later, when the Moonstars are dealt with! The Moonstars who are creeping up behind our backs even now!"

And he spun to face the door he'd been crawling for, and blasted it open. Its shards were still hurtling and clattering down off walls beyond when he sent a second blast through the space where it had been—and blew apart an innocent statue, several rooms away.

"Spittle of Shar," he snapped, "I missed that one! *After him!*"

He pointed and then sprinted, not looking to see if any Shadovar followed.

Yet soon enough he heard them pounding along after him.

Every one of them. The ruse had worked. The Shadovar tore off through Candlekeep, away from the chamber of the balconies—and the dumbfounded Prefects.

This morning, the attacking mercenaries seemed endless. Even more numerous than the trees that stood all around this particular corner of the widespread fray.

Storm, Rune, and Arclath had been fighting for what seemed like forever, an endless deadly dance of swing, duck, dodge, parry, rebound from the numbing clang of blade on blade, and hack again. There were a score of besiegers to every defender of Myth Drannor, or even more.

Even given how many were being slaughtered with every panting, passing moment as the ring of attackers tightened around the city, yard by blood-soaked yard.

"F-fall back!" Arclath panted, slipping again on dead bodies underfoot. They were slick with blood, flies buzzing in profusion everywhere.

Not that he could hear the little pests. He was half deaf from all the clanging of blades striking blades or shields or armor, men shouting or screaming, raw dying shrieks on all sides. It had been nigh ceaseless, until a few panting moments ago.

Amarune flung out a hand to catch his shoulder and steady him. Gasping, he thanked her with a nod, and leaned on his sword, using it as a crutch to keep himself upright while he fought for breath.

This little lull in the fighting had come when the foe had fallen back to regroup. Which in this case meant drag the wounded away, reform survivors into new bands under the commanders who were left—probably all of them; these particular mercenary captains led from the rear—and in the meantime send fresh troops forward to pick up bodies and the dismembered, and fling them into heaps to clear some ground to walk on.

So they could all come charging up to the elf lines again.

Huh. Such as the "elf lines" were. There were perhaps a score of elves still on their feet, for as far as he could see along this ridge. And behind them all, there was no more wild forest, just the trees that sheltered and adorned the homes and garden terraces and soaring spires of Myth Drannor itself.

If the defenders retreated again, it would be the city itself they were yielding. Building by building.

"Sorry I got you into this, my love," Rune whispered into his ear, as they leaned together for support, both gasping for breath. "You could still be safe by your fireside, back at home."

"While you got butchered here without me? Never! After all, you'd haunt me over it—I'd never get a moment's sleep!"

"True," Rune whispered as she leaned against him. Forehead to forehead, they clung to each other, sharing their aches.

Storm had been helping elf wounded, and was now trudging back to meet them, with her hair, with *all* of her, drenched in blood.

Brow to brow with Arclath—who smelled as good as ever, she couldn't help but notice—Amarune watched the bard come slowly up to them, trailing a sword that dripped with gore. So Chosen got just as weary as mere mortals.

Somehow that was both discouraging and reassuring at the same time.

They'd all been fighting hard amid the trees for what seemed like forever, and everyone's arms—sword arms especially—ached and felt as heavy as castle stones.

"Kissing again?" Storm teased them, as she picked her way over heaped elf bodies to come up beside them. "You young ones never stop, do you? Don't forget to breathe, now!"

They were both still too winded to give her suitably arch replies, so Rune settled for a rude gesture. Storm chuckled and embraced her, hugging her and then massaging the younger woman's shoulders. Rune groaned.

Arclath smiled at them both fondly—as a war horn blared far off in the trees.

From far back in the enemy ranks somewhere.

He peered in that direction. The besieging mercenaries seemed endless; Arclath could see banners swaying among the trees as their bearers clambered over roots as high as tables, moving closer. The farthest banner was distant indeed.

He sighed, and leaned a little more heavily on his sword. There were too many mercenaries, too great a host for the surviving defenders to hold for long.

But then, he'd known all along that without far superior magic to hurl on the battlefield, Myth Drannor was doomed. It wasn't a question of if the city would fall, but when.

The banners were moving again.

"They're coming," he muttered. "Are there any elves in reserve, or is it just this handful of us to hold back an army?"

Storm looked back over one shapely shoulder, then told him, "No, there's another handful coming. I'd say Fflar is standing more or less alone against the mercenaries attacking the far side of the city. He's sent most of his command to join us."

Then she added, "Excuse me. Stay where you are."

As Amarune and Arclath watched, the bard plunged down the steepest nearby slope, into a little pit ringed by the heaped dead—and shook herself like a wet dog, all over, her long silver hair thrusting itself out straight and stiff like a pincushion.

The heir of the Delcastles hauled Rune hastily down, so only a fine rain of blood fell on them like a mist, rather than a huge wet wall of it.

When they scrambled up again, to peer at the advancing mercenaries—who were thankfully coming with wary slowness, not shouting and charging—the Storm who joined them had hair that was silver again, clean of blood. The rest of her, however, was still besmirched.

"*That's* a neat trick," Rune told her. "Show me that, when we have time."

"Gladly," Storm agreed, as she raised a hand in greeting to the elves hastening to join them.

"Lady Storm," the foremost warrior greeted her with a wry smile. "Well met. It's been a few summers."

"It has, Velathalar. Good to see you again. Are those with you likely to take a suggestion from a human, or are they more interested in trumpeting their precious honor and so dying in their own way?"

Arclath was greatly amused to hear that a dumbfounded male elf said "Eh?" in just the same tone of voice a male human did. But recovered, he had to grant, faster.

"Why?" Velathalar grinned. "What suggestion are you apt to make?"

"That we retreat, right now, to just *there*, where the fallen end, so we can stand on sure footing while the mercenaries struggle on the dead underfoot."

"Wise," the elf agreed, "not that honor will agree." He whirled around to snap an order to the elves with him. "Back! Back to where the footing's clear!"

211

"*What*?" a taller, older female elf snapped back at him. "And surrender soil of our city without even fighting for it? Where is your *honor*, Velathalar Muirdraevrel?"

Velathalar turned and gave Storm an "I told you so" look that was so clear and comical that Rune found herself giggling.

Despite more mercenaries than she could count mounting the last corpse-strewn slope with bills and glaives and spears ready in their hands that even now were being lowered to menace her.

"*My* honor," Storm told the elf, before Velathalar could begin a reply, "comes from staying alive to win more of it, in days and months and years ahead. You do all *Tel'Quess* more service if you live to fight and defend beyond the next few minutes. If you're fighting for grass and trees, why these, just here, in particular? Once you're dead, you'll never again be able to defend any of them."

The bard hadn't raised her voice, but her hair was stirring around her shoulders, and her words carried to every elf along the ridge. Magic or Weave work. And most of the elves pulled back a few strides to open ground.

"They're here," Arclath said warningly, as he backed carefully to join them, Rune at his side and Velathalar guarding his other flank.

The angry elf looked at Storm, and Storm gave her a sunny smile in return.

About then the elf realized the two of them now stood alone, a good three or four paces ahead of all the other defenders. She grimaced, sighed, then turned and retreated with more haste than grace. Storm stood behind her, guarding her back all the way—as the mercenaries reached the end of where they'd dared to clear bodies aside, and broke into a stumbling charge across the heaped and slippery bodies, with ragged yells that mingled into a general rising roar.

And the din of battle broke out again, metal clanging on metal, laced with screams and grunts and yells. Storm's tresses thrust forward like tentacles, wielding hand axes and daggers and at least one stolen mercenary spear, and the elves of Myth Drannor fought alongside her with a lithe agility that Arclath had already learned he had to keep from watching, lest he be fascinated for an instant too long and pay for his distraction with his life. The elves were skilled and fighting for their home—but they were also weary from days of fighting. No matter how many mercenaries they slew, the motley human hireswords just kept coming, in a great sea of helms and shields and breastplates, flooding through the trees in a flow beyond counting, a surge of bodies trampling their own fallen that forced the outnumbered defenders slowly back, and back again, and then into a hasty hacking scramble along the ridge to keep from being cut off and buried in thrusting enemy blades, and . . .

"Fall back!" Velathalar shouted, too beset by attackers to snatch at his horn. "Sound the retreat!"

High, fluting horns promptly did just that from behind the foremost elves, then larger and more distant horns took up the blaring call.

Storm's hair curled around three throats from behind, and snatched that trio of Velathalar's attackers off their feet; he used the respite to swiftly slash the other two and clamber up a heap of dying men he'd helped to build, to bellow, "Back, and rally!"

He shouted it twice, and by some magic of Storm's, his second shout rolled through the trees like thunder. A glowing banner promptly unfurled atop a rise to the east, as a rallying point—but out of the trees beyond the mercenaries came a black, howling cone of biting jaws and raking claws, pouring through the air just above gleaming, bobbing mercenary helms to pounce on the banner.

The rise became briefly a dark cloud of swirling death and tatters of banner, but then the air turned bright, and the claws and jaws were beaten back, fading to nothingness.

Storm's face, as she fought, turned grim.

The city wards should have stopped that Shadovar spell; it shouldn't have taken a counterspell from an elf in the fray.

The inevitable end was coming much faster than she'd feared. Hereabouts, in this particular battle, perhaps in her next panting handful of breaths. Despite all the reinforcements Fflar had sent.

Elves who could not be spared, so if they fell here . . .

And in the end, she must do her utmost to preserve Amarune, and take her far from this, no matter what else happened or who fell.

She thought all of this without one moment of hesitation in her deadly dance of ducking, twisting, lunging, and leaping, sharp blades of steel thrusting and slashing at her constantly, many blows so heavy that sparks flew at every parry. She slew mercenaries with the same brutal ruthlessness they were trying to use on her, and they were falling in their dozens and scores, shoved onto the blades of those behind them, kicked to make them fall and trip their fellows, stunned from above by branches groaningly spell-bent for a moment, and beset by hails of fallen weapons flung in their faces by Storm's tireless tresses. This was to the death, with no parleys nor ransoms, no chivalrous agreements for breathers or chances to retrieve the wounded or the dead.

Mercenaries were dying at a sickening rate—yet elves were falling fast too, and soon there'd be too few to hold any ground here at all, and the battle would be into the city streets and flying bridges, catwalks and room after splendid room of the homes and mansions that—

"*Arclath!*"

That anguished shriek nigh deafened Storm, and she whirled with her heart sinking, afraid that whatever had befallen Lord Delcastle, whom she had come to love and respect, would drive his beloved so mad with grief that she'd run right onto mercenary steel uncaring, or not seeing her peril at all.

And saw Arclath staggering back with a blade through his neck, the snarling mercenary who'd driven it there already dying, his fierce snarl sagging into bulging-eyed and agonized disbelief as a furious woman had leaped on him, her thighs now wrapped around his shoulders—and one of her daggers hilt deep in his nearest ear, her other dagger slashing at the man's sword arm as if its blade could slice right through plate armor if it just struck often and hard enough.

Rune was going to overbalance, her weight dragging herself and the mercenary she was riding down, down atop the already dead and dying underfoot, and there were three mercenaries with well-used swords already lurching forward, ready to hack and stab . . .

Storm sprang to meet them, slashing viciously at faces and putting her shoulder into the chest of the first one, to topple him back into others and win space enough for Rune to come crashing down atop her mercenary without getting impaled on a reaching blade.

Storm sent her hair lashing out in all directions, to blind and to ensnare sword wrists and to tug at ankles and elbows, heedless of the pain as some of her hair was torn out by the roots.

Rune was down, crashing atop the mercenary she'd slain, his sword in Arclath and his dagger flying free into the air, and Storm sprang over her and landed on her toes right in front of the mercenaries she'd wounded and sent falling. She spent a precious spell to whirl up a dozen fallen weapons into a clanging, darting wall of slashing steel to keep back the mercenaries coming up behind those she'd felled, and spun around to try to get to Arclath.

Rune was there first, of course, sobbing and crying his name and trying to hold her man up—but stumbling helplessly to the ground with him. Or rather, thudding down onto the heaped bodies of the dead and dying. Storm shouldered her aside, to corral Arclath's head in one hand, and kiss him long and hard on his blood-drooling mouth.

As she brutally tore the sword out of his neck.

"*What're you do—*"

Rune stopped in midshriek as she saw silver fire leaking from around their joined lips.

Storm was holding Arclath up, kneeling over him, and in her strong but shaking arms Amarune saw her man writhe and stiffen. His eyes flared, momentarily becoming two silver flames.

Then he shuddered, arched—and fell back out of Storm's embrace, shaking his head and moaning like a bewildered child in pain. His eyes were his own again, but trailing smoke as they wept blood, his face clenched in racking agony.

Yet there was no blood welling out of his mouth anymore, and the great wound in his neck was—gone.

And Storm was getting to her feet with her face drawn and old, swaying and staggering, and throwing up her hands in a desperate magic that flung scores of weapons up into the air from the dead all around and whirled them at the mercenaries surging forward.

Screams and wet gurglings rent the air as the front ranks of the besiegers collapsed into wild butchery, blood spraying in all directions, as Storm turned grimly to Arclath, who was once more in Rune's fierce embrace, and said grimly, "It's past time that the two of you went into hiding—and *stayed* there."

"And leave you to die here? Leave Myth Drannor to fall?"

"Are we going to argue this?" Storm hissed fiercely, glaring at them both for just a moment before she found it prudent to whirl around and glare at the nearest mercenaries—those creeping around the edges of her spell to try to reach them.

"Y-yes," Rune managed, matching her glare for glare. "Don't think I'm ungrateful—"

"Oh, I don't," Storm replied, trading two swift parries with a mountain of a mercenary before dispatching him with a leaping thrust up through his mouth into his brain. "*I think you're being stupid. Just as I was stupid to bring you here.*"

She spun around and slashed another mercenary across his eyes, letting the force of her swing bring her back around to face them—and another mercenary, who stumbled back in alarm at her speed. "A mistake—"

She sprang to meet that stumbling mercenary, and at the last instant sidestepped and surprised the one beside him with a thrust through the man's leather-gloved sword hand. He shrieked, she twisted her steel free and fed it back to the stumbling man—right through his neck, just as Arclath had been wounded, something he winced at the sight of—and turned to add, "—I'll now—"

She spun around again, to strike aside a hurled spear, then pluck up a fallen mercenary with her hair and fling him at the ankles of a trio of advancing besiegers, forcing them into cursing falls, and added over her shoulder, "—rectify."

And without any warning at all she spun around again with her arms spread, and gathered Arclath and Amarune into a fierce hug.

Which became a tingling shroud of silver-blue fire, magic that snarled up into a rushing wind that flung all three of them aloft, soaring up in a great arc that tore through leaves and small branches to hurtle up into the sky, far above the countless helms and shoulders of the mercenary army below.

And on through air that was surprisingly chilly, high and far before it started to descend, the huge trunk of a gigantic shadowtop looming up to meet them—

Storm hissed something that snatched all three of them abruptly aside, to the left, to miss crashing into that huge tree.

Instead, they smashed into the bough of another tree with enough force to wind and daze all three of them, and break Storm's hug—so the three of them tumbled on through a bruising, buffeting, deafening chicane of torn and whirling leaves, shattering twigs, and dancing branches, plummeting down, down, and—

Through a tangle of vines and snapping, collapsing dead trees those vines had strangled, to crash at last to earth.

Or rather, several soft and mushy feet of dead leaves, to rebound out of muck that had a decidedly skunky smell, and roll to a painful stop in a thorn bush.

It was quite some time before Arclath had breath enough to groan. He rolled over, still moaning, and grunted, "Rune? Rune?"

"I'm fine," his beloved replied sourly. "More or less."

Arclath peered rather blearily in the direction Amarune's voice was coming from, and beheld a wincing Storm rolling over to her knees, his Rune tangled in the bard's long silver hair—and sliding off her back.

"While I," the bard informed Arclath gingerly, "have been better. Thank you for asking."

She got to her feet with a wince and a hiss of pain, her tresses setting Amarune upright with gentle care, and peered all around.

Distant mercenaries shouted, and they heard crashing as heavy-booted men hurried closer.

"Time," Storm announced, "to fly." And she reached out and hugged them again.

"Not like last time, I hope," Arclath managed, as magic swept them aloft again.

"No," Storm agreed firmly. "A moment ago I was making us all look like a catapult load, because some of yon hireswords will be itching to use the bows, which Myth Drannor's wards have been foiling, on *something*. This time, we'll be flying properly—with about as much control as a heavy, ungainly bird."

An arrow shivered off the nearby spreading branches of a dusk-wood, and Storm sighed and announced, "Change of plan. If arrows can fly, we're far enough from the wards to translocate."

"Translocate?" Arclath asked suspiciously.

"Teleport," Storm informed him—and blue light rose like a mist all around them, and fell over them like a cloak in the next instant.

Then they were falling through a soft blue void, all sounds of the forest gone, and . . . standing on a flagstone floor.

"My kitchen," Storm announced. "In my farmhouse, in Shadowdale."

Arclath and Amarune looked at each other, then with one accord started slowly turning as they gazed all around.

They were in a low-raftered room with fieldstone walls and wooden countertops inset with marble tiles and sinks, furnished in sturdy stools and thick plank-topped tables. Diamond-paned windows looked out into a choked garden, overhung with trees so that dappled sunlight lanced down through them to the flagstones.

"What a beautiful place," Rune said aloud.

"Good," Storm agreed briskly, "then you won't mind tarrying here a bit. Without me."

Arclath gave her a frown. "While you—?"

Storm held up one hand to silence him, and with the other reached to a nearby pillar—and tore it open, a concealed panel swinging open. She plucked out a tiny metal box that was tarnished black with age, flipped it open—and the room flooded with almost blinding light.

Wincing, Amarune tried to peer past it. She saw Storm's long fingers silhouetted against that brilliance for a moment as the bard plucked whatever was glowing so brightly up out of the box and into her mouth.

And then the light was gone, and Storm turned toward them a face that was young and unlined again. As she opened her mouth to speak, an echo of the blinding radiance winked inside her, just for a moment.

Rune gaped. What had she just seen? It looked like Storm had swallowed a tiny star. Some sort of ancient healing magic, or a spark of silver fire, or—?

"Later," Storm told her with a wry smile, "when the time is right. Full explanations, I promise."

"But—" Arclath started to protest.

She waved a flamboyant arm at him like a furious high priestess silencing a blasphemer.

"*Later*," she repeated sternly, and added, "Now *stay* here," she said, that order afire with a fierceness born of new vigor, then turned to Amarune, seeming somehow taller. Stronger. Renewed.

"If El and I and the rest fall," she said, "*you* are the future—the last Chosen of Mystra. She'll need you desperately. So stay. Please. The future of the Realms may depend on your obedience."

She spun to face Arclath, and commanded him as imperiously if she was the Queen of Cormyr. "See to it that she stays here—and defend her with your life."

"Lady," he replied, "that's not something you *ever* need to order me to do."

As he uttered the last two words, Arclath found that he was speaking to empty air.

Storm had whirled away from him to pluck a stone out of the nearest wall to reveal a niche, plucked a glowing blade from out of hiding there, blown them a kiss, and—winked into nothingness.

Arclath looked at the revealed niche, then looked away.

And then, as sudden silence stretched and deepened, and Amarune regarded him with a knowing smile, found he couldn't resist going to see what else might be hidden within it.

CHAPTER 13

So Suddenly Swept Away

THERE WAS A LOUD CLATTER AS MATTICK'S SCABBARD RAPPED against the door of the audience chamber of Thultanthar in his breathless haste.

Then he and his twin, Vattick, had burst through the doors and were sprinting across the room to where the High Prince of Thultanthar stood addressing a half moon of nine silently standing, dark-robed men. Arcanists. Their brother Aglarel stood like a watchful stone statue behind their father, hand on sword, as he watched their undignified arrival.

Then Telamont Tanthul turned to regard them, and his face was as friendly as frost-touched iron.

"W-we came as quickly as we could, Most High," Mattick gasped. Vattick was too winded to manage words, and could only nod.

"Was *personally* inspecting the den of dalliance established by your nieces Manarlume and Lelavdra so important, at this precise time?" Telamont asked coldly. "I would remind you that we are at war." He turned back to the arcanists, and added over his shoulder, "And before you protest that we're always at war, be advised that such an observation would be most unwise. At least you remembered your swords."

Telamont surveyed the carefully expressionless arcanists, and so did his twin sons.

Who saw that all nine were wearing identical crystal pendants—before their father leveled an imperious finger at one.

A thin line of ruby fire sped from his fingertip to strike that arcanist's crystal. It pulsed once, and then the fiery beam was gone and racing fire curled in swift loops within the stone—only to leap across the room and stab at the uppermost glass globe of the *tammaneth* rod. Its dark glass flared, and a moment later red fire whirled within it.

Mattick looked back at the arcanist's pendant. It was dark and clear once more; the fire that had visited it so fleetingly was gone. His father had already repeated the process with the next arcanist, and was starting on the third. Mattick noticed that the fire streaking from each pendant went to a different sphere of the rod than the previous one, but otherwise . . . he shrugged. Father's magic had always been well beyond him. He was happier with a blade in his hand, anyway, magic relegated to useful service such as keeping off the rain.

Eight, nine . . . the last arcanist's pendant had relinquished its fire to the rod. When he saw that, the Most High turned to his sons, satisfaction clear on his face.

"Our forces continue to advance through Myth Drannor, taking more and more of the city," he told them, "and letting us reach increasing numbers of elven burial crypts. You will accompany these loyal Shadovar, and protect them as they destroy guardian baelnorn, then seize and drain the magic of crypt after crypt. Guard these two"—he lifted a languid hand to point—"above the rest, for they know where most of the crypts are. Slaughter any disloyal and disobedient among them without hesitation."

The Most High turned back to the arcanists. "Obey these two princes as you would me."

Then he waved a hand, and the audience chamber was suddenly empty of arcanists and twin princes of Shade.

The High Prince of Thultanthar turned away and allowed himself a sigh.

From behind him, Aglarel asked quietly, "How much do you expect them to achieve?"

Telamont snorted. "Less mischief than if I left them idle. And the small victory of denying desperate elves the magics they might otherwise seize for valiant last stands against us."

He turned to face his most trustworthy surviving son. "It is time, and past time, for us to deliver to Shar what she desires. And claim our reward: dominion over all cities and lands of the Realms."

A smile rose to his lips. "There are *so many* of them I want to destroy."

If there was one thing he disliked more and more about serving Mystra with every passing year, it was all the damned *running*.

Elminster puffed and panted his way along, sprinting through Candlekeep with far more bruising haste than prudence. He doubted any of the Shadovar had ever seen their High Prince run before, but then again, that would mean they wouldn't know what Telamont Tanthul looked like when running.

He was trying to get well ahead of them, anyway, but even if he'd been young and fresh and not seeking to maintain a disguise of Art, Candlekeep's layout didn't make that an easy thing to do. Rooms gave in to rooms, with a minimum of passages, the lighting tended to be dim or worse, and there were always odd steps just where you didn't expect them or had forgotten there were any, and—

He burst out into a room where monks stood waiting. Six of them, grim faced, in front of open double doors at the far end, all facing him. He saw no weapons, but they were standing like veteran adventurers, well enough apart so no one would unintentionally get in the way of a comrade's sword being drawn in haste, and—

That one, dead ahead, shared a face with one of the corpses he'd found on his way into the keep. So, a false monk, and almost certainly *not* a Shadovar. Which left independent agents of all stripes, and—the Moonstars.

The six were glaring at him as he pounded up to them, their arms lifting and faces tightening—

El gave them a wide and genial smile and caused twelve tiny blue-white stars to wink into being in a circle around his face.

"Make way," he gasped, "please."

Three of the monks drew aside, but the one he knew to be false and the two monks on either side of that false monk stood their ground.

As, back behind El, the Shadovar started pelting into the room.

Elminster drew in a deep breath, threw back his head, and bellowed, *"Moonstars!* All of these!"

Then he threw all his will into wrapping himself in the wards of Candlekeep and bringing up his own mantle to its utmost inside those wards—as he crashed into the false monk shoulder first, got both hands on one of the man's elbows, and spun him around, hard. He'd be drawing a dagger or worse, of course, but any spell El should be able to hold at bay for a few moments at least, and hopefully—

The false monk did have a dagger out, but had made the mistake of raising his arm high to bring it down in a forceful stab, so all El had to do was shove the force of the wards into the man's face and throat and hold it there, to keep that arm from being brought down.

The elbow grab and spin had flung them both around to look back down the room El had just run the length of, and had done so in time to see the first Moonstar spells strike the Shadovar, and the swiftest Shadovar who weren't flung off their feet hurl magics of their own back at the Moonstars.

Great bright bursts of force erupted among the Shadovar, spattering some of them back against the walls—and then a full and proper spell battle was raging.

A scene that abruptly vanished in blue mists that El was softly and silently falling through, all alone.

Mists that were gone again just as abruptly as they'd come, leaving Elminster blinking away the half-seen cold smile and raised bony hand of Larloch, to stare around a room he knew.

So the Shadow King had just teleported him away from the battle between the Shadovar and the Moonstars—and right back into the tall chamber in Candlekeep with the wall of galleries.

El looked up. Much of the highest gallery was gone, blasted away, and its remaining stonework was scorched and crisscrossed by a webwork of cracks.

The surviving Prefects had descended a level, and were crowded in one corner of that lower gallery, keeping well away from the ruined end of the one above. Eleven strong, still in their robes and still clutching their rods and scepters. They were deep in angry, worried argument.

"May I remind you," the First Reader was snarling, "that they are all within our wards and walls! *Among* us! The fiercer the magic we hurl, the more we endanger tomes that *cannot* be replaced! The work of centuries!"

"Yet if we don't regain mastery of our halls swiftly and decisively," a Great Reader replied heatedly, "we risk losing our lives and all chance of expelling or defeating these foes—and then they'll have every last tome to take away or destroy at whim!"

"Fellow Avowed," the Chanter broke in, sounding genuinely anguished, "we don't even know who these intruders *are*! Most of them wear our faces, so they can obviously take on many guises by magic, and it follows that we can't even trust—"

"*Don't* say it!" another Great Reader interrupted. "That way lies madness! I *refuse* to let us be ensnared in the trap of none of us trusting an opinion or an observation because we think the mouth uttering it belongs to an impostor! It *is* possible to overthink everything, you know, and—"

"*Excuse* me," the Gatewarden broke in, his voice just a trifle below a bellow. His unaccustomed fury and volume drew every eye on the gallery—so they all saw that he was pointing down at the floor below, where all the Shadovar had been standing quite a short time ago. "We are not alone."

All of the Prefects looked down. Amid the litter of broken Shadovar bodies stood a lone man looking back up at them.

A man who looked like the High Prince of Thultanthar—but was melting, as they stared, into someone else.

Someone now holding up both hands in surrender or to show they were empty, and saying earnestly, "I come in peace!"

Wands and scepters were hurriedly trained on him. None of them were drawn back when his new likeness became apparent.

The Prefects stared down at the beak-nosed and white-bearded Sage of Shadowdale, and he stared back up at them, asking urgently, "Can we talk?"

"I suspect a trick," the First Reader announced coldly, "or a ruse to buy time or distraction for your fellows to attack us in circumstances most advantageous to them. In any case, I will *not* debate with anyone actively engaged in altering the wards of the keep, until they cease doing so."

"Such inflexibility is neither wise nor prudent," observed a cold voice from behind the Prefects, "but perhaps the Avowed of Candlekeep don't deserve the mastery of either that their reputation bestows upon them. Will you debate with someone who can destroy you at will, yet chooses not to do so?"

Even as the monks started to whirl around, they felt the wands and scepters they held snatched from their hands by irresistible rushing magic that numbed and paralyzed their hands in an instant.

Tingling, their arms flailing beyond their control, they lurched around to face the back of the gallery—and found themselves staring at a tall, withered, nigh skeletal figure, surrounded by the wands and scepters that had just been torn from them and were now floating in midair. Untouched by any hand they could see, each and every wand and scepter was aglow with risen power, and aimed directly at them.

"Well met, Prefects of Candlekeep. I am the one your lore tomes call Larloch. Or the Shadow King . . . or less fitting names."

The lich gave the monks a smile that was soft as it was grinningly sinister.

"Down below us is the man your books name 'Elminster Aumar.' Neither of us are Moonstars nor servants of Thultanthar. We are here for a nobler purpose than most visitors to Candlekeep, and we need *your* help, Avowed of the keep. We are trying to call on the age-old wards of the keep to stabilize the Weave."

Silence fell.

"The Weave?" Larloch added mildly. "I believe you've heard of it."

The First Reader was the first to rally. "Well, yes, of course, but—"

"This is *highly* irregular!" the Chanter protested.

"The more you live outside the routine and order that usually hold sway within these walls," the Shadow King replied, "the more you'll discover that high irregularity is frequent in most lives. Unwelcome to most, but frequent nonetheless. I am well aware that you embrace tradition, and seldom reach decisions swiftly, but our errand carries more than a little urgency. May we count upon your assistance?"

"Assistance *how*, exactly?" one of the Great Readers asked doubtfully.

"And by what right do you frame decisions and press us for answers within these walls?" asked another. "We serve the Binder, and only He can do that with our implicit and wholehearted acceptance. All others would seem to need to submit to *our* judgment."

"Elminster and I can proceed with this needful work with you," Larloch replied coldly, raising a hand meaningfully, "or without you."

Silence fell again.

"Well," ventured the Gatewarden, "when you put it *that* way . . ."

The Shadow King's smile was as soft as his purr: "I do. Oh, I do."

A Great Reader shuddered visibly, and the First Reader cleared his throat several times before he managed to say, "I believe that in these circumstances we can see the, ah, utility of aiding you. I know *I* can."

"Yes," several Prefects agreed.

"Then leave off attacking either of us, and sit down. Yes, here on the gallery floor. Lean back against the walls, be at ease, and bend your minds to the wards. Each of you Prefects is attuned to them. All you need do is will their power—the *thunder*, I believe your late and lamented Keeper of the Tomes called it; that silent and heavy weight that rests on your minds every moment you are within them—to slowly flow, like a tiny trough of water, into *this*, my mind-mouth held ready for you. As Elminster's vigilance keeps the flow both small and stable. Through me, the power will flow into the Weave, strengthening and reanchoring it, and I shall return it, in just as slow and careful a flow, back into the wards again. Leaving neither drained or lessened, but both restored. I am the only one here who knows how to do this, so I must be the focus, and none other. *This* is the service Candlekeep was founded to render, so long ago. This is the salvation you can bring to all Toril, both the lands of Faerûn around you and the distant lands across the seas. Yes, *you* can save the world."

One by one, eyes fixed on Larloch, the Prefects sat down, settled themselves against the wall, and acquired that head-bent stillness that accompanies intense and careful concentration upon the wards.

Larloch cast a look down at Elminster, and with it came the silent mind-message: *You make this possible by stabilizing their minds. Guiding them. Do it.*

The feel of Larloch's mind was somehow familiar.

Ah. *This* is who had quenched and compelled the wards from afar when he and Storm had been hiding in crone shape and working with Amarune on mending the Weave.

A fellow meddler. As if he'd needed more proof.

In his mind, El saw a door opening, and beyond it was a bright, swarming chaos of mental images and sounds, remembered conversations and moments. He was looking into the mind of one of the Great Readers. Across that whirling maelstrom another door opened as he watched, revealing a more ordered whirling mass of memories, this one driven by an insistent rhythm, a many-voiced chant that went on and on. Ah, yes—the Chanter's mind, of course. Beyond it, another door swung wide into greater chaos.

"Not too many doors, now!" Elminster mumbled warningly, more in his mind than with his mouth. "Let me master these, first . . ."

"Are Chosen of Mystra so much less than Chosen of Mystryl? I can ride them all, and at the same time watch over and command every last lich who serves me. And most of them have minds both stronger and *much* nastier than these monks. Surely, Old Mage, you can manage a mere eleven minds? Trained and disciplined—but sheltered—minds, at that?"

"Despite what ye may have heard, brutalizing minds is *not* something I have overmuch experience with," El growled.

"Ah, yes, you prefer to be loved. I find it far more efficient and practical to be feared. Do it your way, then—but no more slowly than you must. And forget this not: you will need to encompass all eleven before we're done."

Mind to mind, they gazed at each other, and Elminster gave the archlich a slow nod. Larloch smiled like a dragon surveying prey, and withdrew to the far end of the row of eleven imaginary rooms, leaving those vaults of whirling, flashing thoughts brighter in front of Elminster.

Who sighed, recalled a beautiful tune an elf had harped to him on a soft summer night far too long ago . . . and drifted gently into the first room.

The mind of Great Reader Albaeron Thalion, once of Athkatla, a calligrapher and artist who'd become a scribe and then heard the whispered summons of Oghma one night, in a dream drenched in moonlight and words written in moonfire crawling across empty air, a calling to Candlekeep on its rocky height overlooking the endless waves . . .

Thalion was aware of him now, as a softly stealing shadow in his own mind, and alarm welled up despite knowing who the intruder was and why he was here, warm red sharp-edged apprehension, rising . . .

Distantly, El felt his hair stand on end as more ward energy than he'd ever been able to tap on his own leaked into him. He stepped into and through that warm scarlet wash of apprehension, moving boldly deeper into the monk's mind. Only to find himself swimming among strands of darkening emotion that circled alongside him like gigantic sharks, wary and menacing and closing in.

Sharks Elminster needed to banish, to relax Albaeron Thalion enough to win trust enough to gain the secrets he sought without the winning of each one becoming a bruising battle that darkened the monk's mind a little more with each yielding . . .

For each monk must be set at ease, or at least given new confidence, so their mind would share what they knew of the Weave, and the Weave energies they controlled, rather than fighting to deny and deceive and keep that knowledge secret.

Gently, now . . .

Calm and smiling confidence to the fore . . .

El projected reassurance, envisaging it as a lantern coming softly to life, a small and brass-barred hand lantern like the one that had comforted Thalion as a child in his small bedchamber, a room the graying Great Reader still sadly missed, yearned to see again, the little bed and the stuccoed walls curving to a smooth arching cave-like ceiling close overheard, the precious street map of Athkatla on the wall with the important buildings drawn so clearly, prettier than they were in life . . .

El pushed the lantern ahead in Thalion's mind and drifted gently in its wake, going deeper now, past more recent memories and the excitement of discoveries in pages brittle with age, the revelations of discerning what was meant when two sages' screeds disagreed yet intersected, and on into the secrets the Great Reader had been thrilled to learn. Where certain tomes were hidden, and wands and scepters too, passwords that opened spell-locked doors, and (ah, *here*) the ways of taking hold of the wards of Candlekeep, and changing a paltry few of their settings . . . all that had been shown to Thalion. The Great Reader visualized the handles of the wards as a harness, a coach harness from the wealthier streets of Amn, that could be grasped here and here and *here*, thus, and altered by doing this . . . El made that alteration with Thalion, shadowy hands cupping the Great Reader's own imaginary one, and radiating thanks with the lantern light ere drifting on.

A thread of power loosed from the wards by Thalion rippled with him, and he passed on into the second chamber, the next monk's

231

mind, where the Endless Chant of Alaundo rose around Elminster and enfolded him in its insistent recitations, the deeper male voices dominating—the voices the Chanter, whose mind he'd entered, remembered from his first days in the keep, when he strode at the rear of the long procession, repeating more prophecies than were uttered these days. The current chant, quieter thanks to fewer voices and shorter with the fulfilled or false foretellings being lost, kept its own tireless refrain, looping around the older chant.

Of *course* this would be how the Chanter defended his mind against intrusion. El joined the older chant first and then the current one, moving with them and then drifting to one side of their relentless flow so as to move forward, deeper into the monk's mind, rather than boring through them and doing damage, but the ribbon of ward energy trailing El seemed to melt everything it touched in Nabeirion the Chanter's mind, and awakened bright flares of crimson anger that boiled up swiftly to tower like a great fist.

El darted at the base of the rage before any hammer blow could fall, and plunged into it, ricocheting and swirling down through a maze of razor-sharp flashing thoughts, sparks whirling up around him and traveling with him like a great billowing cloak of winking lights, every mote of it failing but not before being replaced by two or more tiny dancing stars. Light that was reflected warmly by thoughts ahead, thoughts El swooped at, though his invading shadow felt like it was being stabbed by thousands upon swift thousands of pins and needles, and burned feverish hot all over, yet as chill as ice down his back, a coldness that gnawed at the back of his neck and started to flood up his scalp and down his jaw.

Nabeirion the Chanter was angry indeed, because he took such pride in being a master of the Weave. To relinquish or share that was to lessen his special status—to lessen *him*. Or so he firmly believed, and was using the might of the Weave against this intruder—for only the flow of the Weave could deliver fire and ice at once in the same spot.

And only one who had worked so long and so closely with the Weave could survive that conjunction. But for how long?

El hastened on, worried that he might be overwhelmed before he could unleash the ward energies in this second mind—only to stumble upon the Chanter's memories of being shown the wards by a Keeper now dead, a blind monk, in the Chanter's memory, who could no longer read a word or recognize a face or banner, but who saw the wards like shifting, flowing golden lace in his dreams . . . something the Chanter himself was now getting his own fleeting glimpses of, mere echoes . . .

The beginnings of attunement. El seized on those memories and made them his own, for the Chanter had been shown much, more than El himself had ever guessed or been told or felt through the Weave.

Ah, there was a threefold lock, devised to foil Netherese arcanists and Thayan zulkirs and all those who habitually created their own spells—the Imaskari, for example—alike. A sigil had to be traced in the mind, not in the air or on stone, then a word written in the mind, then a second sigil traced—and then the first one redrawn, something just not done in any of the human traditions. Dwarves did that, but then dwarves murmured over runes and passed fire over runes and sprinkled blood or tears over runes—they did *nothing* without scratching runes first. Writing just the word, in the right place in the keep when someone else had half unlocked that place, allowed you to change a setting or even add a spell effect to the existing wards, but all three were needed to substantially alter the wards, shift their boundaries, or bring them down.

And now he, Elminster, had this control. He commanded the means of releasing great amounts of the ward flow without the

Chanter's assistance, or that of any other monk for that matter.

Yet he was not the sort to gloat or exult. That was for younger or more crazed-wits mages. El allowed himself a thin smile—and restricted himself to a deft, minor unleashing, gliding along that released power out of the Chanter's mind and traveling with it into the mind of another Great Reader, this one younger and full of himself, and so dark with resentment at the invasion into his mind.

Great. Think of young and crazed-wits, and behold! Faerûn obligingly presents such a one—so much for thin smiles! El fought his way through the dark thunder of resentment, and used what he'd learned from the Chanter to wrest ward energy from what this younger mind controlled without even asking for permission. Less friendly, but there was no welcome here at all, so it was best to save time, and just take and move on . . .

On into the fourth mind, which presented as a vault of darkness with real resistance, a stubborn and opposed will that thrust at his advancing shadow and the ward energies with a moving wall of darkness, rolling forward like one of the great storm-driven waves El had often seen racing at the Sword Coast, trying to halt El and shove him back into the unfriendliness of the mind behind him.

El called up his lantern again and made of it a blinding sphere, a brightness that seared and tore at the unyielding darkness, forcing it to shrink back and melt away and—collapse utterly as El hurled the radiance into the heart of it. That mind fled, shrieking, in all dark directions at once, leaving El wincing in the barren heart of it and wondering what damage he'd done.

He felt the cold edge of Larloch's amusement as he freed a carefully small amount of ward energy as quickly as he could, and raced on. Through a mind that wavered on the brink of collapse, clawing at Elminster until he dimly saw the chamber he was in again, and the source of that clawing.

(On the balcony, a Prefect shuddered, hands twitching and then clawing the air in a sudden frenzy, foam bursting from bitten-through lips as a whispering, wordless snarl erupted through clenched teeth, eyes staring at nothing as the head jerked from side to side, as if staring fixedly at things that were not there. The Avowed on either side of the stricken monk shrank away from him in fear and disgust—ere he collapsed into a lolling, almost lifeless heap.)

"Idiot," Larloch said in disgust.

El rode the echoes of the lich's comment onward out of the ruined mind, and plunged into two more monks' minds in swift succession that were both brighter and more cacophonous, yet fought him not. He swerved and banked and slowed at will in their chaotic midst, deftly unleashing trifling amounts of ward energy from each, to add to the flow already accompanying him, and raced on again, into a seventh mind.

And into a sudden mental assault, his heart pounding as maleficent dark lances of thought thrust into him, ward energy leaking like golden gore . . . El fed those blades silver fire and had the satisfaction of seeing them vanish into smoke, their shafts recoiling to a source that shrieked in pain. The wild screaming went on and on as the mind of its owner shuddered and yawed and shrank back in a wet, crimson retreat. Again El took what he wanted, quickly and ungently, and moved on.

He could see the end of his work ahead, just four minds remaining between him and the coldly waiting presence of Larloch, and could feel the power of the ward energy he was riding, the first sense he'd had of any sort of inevitability to his success. He was rolling into minds that weren't expecting to withstand him now—and so probably couldn't.

Another Great Reader, who was more fearful than anything else, and only too happy to let the invading shadow glide to where it needed to go, so it would be gone all the sooner.

Into a very different sentience. Pride here, and real power. The First Reader's mind was alert and watchful, aware of his every movement within it and accompanying the shadow that was El like a watchful armored sentry with spear held ready, keeping pace with El, crowding close to peer as the ward energies this mind controlled and was fully attuned to—only the Keeper of the Tomes had known more—were tapped, then ushering him carefully out, and on.

Into the mind of the Gatewarden, who was friendlier but no less aware and vigilant, escorting El's shadow like a smiling light. There was real power here, too, but it was might that was kept largely hidden, roiling and shifting and pursuing other matters at the same time as it shared ward secrets.

Last, El flowed into the mind of the Guide. This mind was both curious and suspicious at once, offering no resistance but massing so as to offer battle the moment it seemed needed. Some thoughts the Guide snatched away, to be kept hidden from the intruder, others the Guide advanced like armored knights to form a defensive wall. El glided past as much of it as he could, then proffered the bright lantern when he needed to turn into the massed-against-him wall and reach through those close-clustered thoughts to the ward memories. Which proved even more extensive and useful than the Chanter's: attunement plus mastery without the strong defenses of the First Reader or the Gatewarden.

He was almost done and out when the mind around him spasmed as if struck by a gale—and then blew apart in bright and terrible ribbons and the roaring blackness of lacerating annihilation whipping past.

The mind he'd been in had just died.

El flung the ward flow to Larloch, but spun his own consciousness up and out and away rather than plunging into the depths of that darkly waiting and coldly amused intellect. Seeing only enough of

Larloch's thinking to see a deeply hidden connection with . . . the mythal of distant Myth Drannor?

Oh, no! He had to . . . had to . . .

Return to himself enough to perceive what was happening in the chamber.

He did that, just in time to see what was left of the Guide's body—a head and limbs loosely attached to what had become a great hole of gore and burned robes and wet flesh—toppling from the gallery to splatter on the floor right in front of . . . himself.

El realized his neck was stiff, and his arms and shoulders felt numb. When he moved, to break off staring up at the gallery, he discovered why. He had been standing like a statue all this time, and now—

Now the room was full of angry Moonstars, different Moonstars than he had flung the Shadovar at, with Alustriel and Laeral at their head.

Their spells had slain the Guide, though their target had been Larloch, and the unfortunate Prefect merely the archlich's helpless shield. More spells were crashing into the gallery, shattering it as the gallery above it had been blasted. This was no safe place to stand, when all that stone came hurtling down.

And other spells were leaping at him!

El dashed them aside with the wards in an instant, but even as he did so, felt that there was something not quite right.

Something clawed at him, commanding his attention—ah! The ward flow he'd harvested, small rill by small rill, was a vigorous stream when it reached Larloch, and rushed through the Shadow King into the Weave. Yet after that—

El felt through the Weave to try to see what it was from another vantage than his own place along the flow, and saw what was amiss.

He'd been duped.

And Luse and Laer might have come too late.

The ward flow was reaching the Weave, but invigorating and brightening just this local bit of it—because Larloch controlled the entry of the ward energies, and their path, too—which was to circle in this fringe of the Weave and depart it right back into . . . Larloch!

The Shadow King had played him for a fool.

And won.

Larloch gave Elminster that soft, knowing smile, and with a spell, sent all the Prefects hurtling down out of the gallery. Then he released the spell that held up the shattered gallery, so its shards tumbled after the screaming monks.

Standing unconcernedly on empty air, the archlich gave El back some of the ward energies—in the form of a great, rolling wave of thrumming force that plummeted from the gallery to crash onto the floor where the Guide had landed, hurling Prefects through the air like dolls to smash down into Elminster, Alustriel, Laeral, and all the Moonstars, before dashing them all back against the far wall.

El slammed into a layer of several Prefects, and felt broken bones grating under the force of his solid arrival. Where the ward energies continued to pin him, the Moonstars, and the Prefects, holding them all helpless against the wall.

"I must thank you, all of you," Larloch told them mockingly, "for your assistance in giving me most of the power I need to remake the Weave as *I* see fit. I'll collect the rest in Myth Drannor. Farewell, fools."

And the tall, dark figure standing in midair abruptly vanished.

Leaving Elminster, Alustriel, and Laeral to stumble away from the wall caked in dead and dying Moonstars and Prefects, in a swiftly darkening room.

They all knew why the light was failing.

They could feel it.

The great wards of Candlekeep were gone.

CHAPTER 14

Seeking the Next Crypt

THE MOST HIGH LOOKED AS IMPRESSIVE AS EVER. SO CALM AND casual he was frightening. Behind him, the cavernous audience chamber looked as nigh empty as usual. Huge expanses of empty marble, around . . .

The great throne, of course, flanked by that bare metal table and the *tammaneth* rod, floating in its corner, its black spheres as empty and dark as always.

Gwelt had never seen anything on the table, nor any radiances of risen magic in the rod's spheres.

But then, he'd only been in the room a handful of times, and always when preoccupied by matters that frightened him and ensnared his attention far more than mere furniture.

He was deeply preoccupied right now. With trying to keep his own temper—and life—and yet make the High Prince of Thultanthar see that what had been done and decided thus far amounted to . . . sheer folly.

Why by the untasted delights of Shar were such things always left to *him*?

"Most High," Gwelt heard himself saying carefully, "it is with the utmost respect that I say this, but say it I must, however unwelcome.

You *must* be told of it, for the good of the city, and for our best hope of success and victory! We are on the wrong road!"

"Convince me, arcanist," Telamont Tanthul said coldly. "Persuade me how I and all the senior arcanists and she whom we all serve are mistaken, while just you are correct. It is in your own interest, I must warn you, to persuade me both well and swiftly."

"Forgive me, Most High, but I decry not the goals the Divine Mistress of the Night desires us to achieve, but the means—and *only* the means—by which we are attempting to reach them. Specifically, this siege of Myth Drannor."

"Be more specific, Gwelt."

"We seek the might of its mythal. As I see it, no host of unwashed mercenaries can master the Art to achieve this, so they must be mere distraction, occupying the elves so that those who can drain the mythal's power can work unhampered. Yet the siege itself will inevitably destroy much of the magic that is—yes?—our only reward for winning the city. After all, who but elves would want a good handful of old, poorly repaired buildings plus rather fewer new ones, in the heart of a deep and overgrown forest? It is so remote as to have no great strategic value, and hurling it down or capturing it is far less impressive to others than, say, the taking of Candlekeep or Athkatla would be. Why—"

Sudden black light flashed in the empty air to their left, and Gwelt's argument faltered. *Black* light? He turned in time to see a star of leaping rays that faded and dwindled as swiftly as they had appeared, to leave behind something floating upright in midair.

Something grisly. A dead, scorched man in what was left of the cassock of a lowly monk, his head lolling on a broken neck. The blackened head had lost all its hair, but the face was still clear enough.

It was Relvrak, a Shadovar arcanist of no small accomplishment, who had been Gwelt's tutor for a time, and was still his friend.

Until now. Relvrak's eyes were melted, as if by a fire that had raged within his skull. Even as Gwelt stared up at the ruined shell of his friend, one of those eyes slid out of its socket and began a slow slide down the blackened face, like the most bulbous of tears.

"Where was—?" Gwelt gasped.

"Candlekeep," came Telamont's calm reply.

"But-but—surely that's impossible! Do not the wards there prevent translocation magics from . . ."

Gwelt ran out of words, awed at the implication.

Telamont nodded expressionlessly. "Exactly. The wards must be gone." He turned to look at the great black rod floating in its corner, and saw that its globes remained empty and dark.

He added coldly, "And their might has not flowed into my hands."

He turned back to Gwelt. "Begone now. I have work to do. You can rant later, when I've time to pretend to care about it. Go."

"But—"

"Go."

Gwelt took one look at Telamont's face, then hastily bowed low and backed away. By the time he was passing out through the audience chamber doors, he was almost running.

The baelnorn did not bother to glow. There was no one to impress or frighten away from that which he guarded.

The passage around him was as deep and dark as ever, the air stale and undisturbed. Which was good.

The baelnorn was content, not bored. He had so much to contemplate, so many matters to weigh and speculate upon. When an intruder did come—and they always *did* come, in the end—he hoped to plumb their knowledge and memories of what the world now was, to compare his conjured possibilities of what might befall with what had actually occurred, so he could contemplate anew. Such thinking he greatly enjoyed, and had lacked time enough to indulge in, back in the busy, crowded, emotionally ruled days of his life.

Deep in these oldest crypts of Myth Drannor, there was no converse that was not with other baelnorns, and talk among baelnorns was rare and tended to be dry, for they shared the same ignorance of what had happened since the last interment in the halls they guarded.

Which had been long ago, even as tireless baelnorn judged passing time. So far as he knew—as everyone alive in Myth Drannor at the time of Aumarthra's passing had known—House Iluanmaurrel was extinct. There would be no new arrivals to come and rest behind the double doors sculpted with the two-headed dove whose wings were maple leaves, no new—

The baelnorn of House Iluanmaurrel faltered in his thoughts and flared a bright blue, startled as he had never been startled before.

The sealed double doors he had been sadly contemplating had started to open.

Dust swirled as the seals broke and crumbled. The doors were opening from within, one faster than the other, which meant they were being moved by unseen hands, rather than a spell.

Bewilderment giving way to rage, the baelnorn swooped toward the widening gap between the two doors, and darted between them, ready to—

Come to an abrupt and strangling halt, as bony hands that could somehow grasp the incorporeal undead as if they bore solid flesh took him by the throat. And tightened ruthlessly.

He did not know the owner of those hands, smiling into his fading face as he was throttled and drained, but Larloch gave the baelnorn of House Iluanmaurrel an almost merry smile and announced, "I'm discovering I quite like the taste of elven magic. Elegant craftings. Most elegant."

There was a horribly long groan from overhead, a groan that sank into a swift series of sharp cracks like the lashes of lightning strikes.

Elminster didn't waste time looking up, at a ceiling that had just shattered and would be starting to fall—in great chunks the size of wagons, by the sounds of things. He just rushed at Laeral and Alustriel with his arms spread wide to sweep them into his grasp—and rushed them out of the room, running hard.

They slammed through the doorway *just* in time. Behind them, the domed ceiling of the chamber crashed down with a mighty thunder that jarred teeth and shook the walls all around. The floor sprang up beneath their hurrying feet so hard and fast that they had fallen and bounced before they could even draw a breath.

The thunderous echoes died away swiftly, leaving them lying in a panting heap among eddying dust and gravel.

Elminster cleared his throat, and rolled off Alustriel's pleasantly soft chest. "'Tis not often," he growled, "that I must needs beg ye two, but now is very much one of those times. I beg ye to forgive my foolheadedness. I've been roundly duped. I use—Laer—ye were right, and I was wrong. *So* wrong."

"Heh," Laeral coughed, rolling over. "Have I waited a long time to hear *that*. Yet I'll not gloat, Old Mage, but merely ask: So, what now? Wrong, duped, and how to mend it? Just so we know if we must fight you to the death again to stop you, or not, what will you seek to do now?"

She conjured gentle handfire. Enough dust had swirled away that they could see each other's faces.

"Myth Drannor's mythal now *must* be destroyed," Elminster said grimly, "to keep Larloch or Telamont from gaining its energies. No matter what the cost to the Weave—or the world—from the flood of released magic."

"The things gods and villains must do to make this man see *sense*!" Alustriel joked, and the three of them laughed together in sheer relief at being able to be full friends and make common cause again.

Laeral stopped laughing first. "How do we stop him, El? Without the Lady, we are poor champions—and the Shadow King was powerful an age ago, and has built his power while we've been spending ours."

"He didn't help raise the mythal, nor repair it," El reminded them. "I did."

And he scrambled to his feet, slipping on loose rubble, and hastened along a passage he could barely see, through the drifting dust. The silver-haired sisters hastened to follow.

El looked back at them and growled, "Nor can he drain a mythal so swiftly and easily, alone, as he could the wards with my help. In the midst of a siege and in the presence of elves who'll fight fiercely to defend it, even if doing so dooms them. Come!"

"Certainly," Alustriel replied as they hastened along the passage, conjuring her own handfire to use like a lantern, "but come *where*? We can't teleport through the mythal!"

"No, but we can use a portal to get inside it."

"But the mythal now prevents . . . ," Laerel began, and then she started to chuckle. "Trust you. Didn't even tell the elves, did you?"

"Myth Drannor has fallen before. I knew they'd need a way out sometime," El replied. "If the coronal has looked in the right places, she'll have found my warning notes about it. So be prepared to face down guards, or some such."

Alustriel rolled her eyes. "The story of my life . . ."

"The other Moonstars—" Laeral said urgently, plucking at his arm.

244

"No *time*," El snarled. "I'll *not* be too late this time!"

He rushed down a stair, and they pelted after him. Through a door and—

Into a jakes.

Alustriel rolled her eyes. "Your sense of humor, El, needs work. Serious work."

The Old Mage snorted, by way of reply. As he clambered up to stand on the garderobe seat.

Where he bent his knees, and jumped high into the air.

He waved one arm wildly as he leaped—and a sudden blue-white glow enshrouded them all.

When he landed, El's boots were on quite different stones, with Alustriel and Laeral right behind him.

They seemed to be in quite a different privy. As deep and disused as the one they'd just left, but smelling more of forest earth, and less of the salty sea.

This one had many stalls, and great tree roots running overhead and plunging like pillars down between the stalls, into the tiled floor. Sea-blue tiles, as beautiful as—

"We're in Myth Drannor," Laeral observed.

"Aye, indeed, and come this way!" Elminster replied over his shoulder, hastening.

He led the two sisters to the entrance of the room, an archway that opened into a fork of two tunnel-like passages, both smelling even more strongly of damp forest earth and green growing things than the garderobe, and both veiled behind rich tapestries of royal blue inset with sparkling silver stars.

Stars that moved seemingly by themselves, and gave off the faintest of musical chimings.

"Well, that's different," Alustriel murmured. "I wouldn't mind having the likes of those in my—"

Stars boiled up from the tapestries and into a racing tangle of winking silver lights, hanging in midair and framed in that empty archway.

Then they coalesced into someone they'd not seen for some time, and the archway was empty no longer.

A diminutive, shapely female elf floated, facing them, surrounded by a nimbus of purple-white light.

"The Srinshee!" Laeral murmured in surprise.

The Srinshee smiled and nodded, but her face held more menace than mirth.

"*Going* somewhere?" she asked, her words a clear and sharp challenge.

The bored prince of Thultanthar at the head of the file of Shadovar walking along the stone-lined elven underways drew his sword and trailed it idly along one stone wall, making a grating, scraping sound.

His brother sighed.

"We can have haste *and* stealth, Brother," Prince Vattick reminded his twin a little testily. "The quieter we are, the farther we can get before we're battling elves at every step."

Prince Mattick sighed. "Yes, yes, but after all this time spent planning and posturing, I want to *smash* something."

"Oh, I've no doubt we'll have opportunities enough for that. More than we'll want, I'm thinking, and sooner than I'd prefer too."

"You're probably right, but it's been nigh deserted down here. Our hired armies are probably keeping the longears so desperately busy fighting for their lives that they can't spare the time nor swords to—"

From around a corner ahead, an elf in eerie blue armor floated, to bar the way in menacing silence, drawn swords raised in either hand.

Vattick gave Mattick a disgusted look. "You *had* to say it, didn't you? Couldn't just keep your jaws shut for once, could you?"

"Brother," Mattick replied, "*this* is what I've been waiting for." And he showed his teeth to the waiting baelnorn and drew his sword with a flourish, letting it sing and watching the runes crawl like black flames up and down its blade.

"Arcanists," he ordered, "have fun. Let fly!"

"Please do nothing of the kind," the baelnorn said sadly, its voice low and gentle yet carrying to every ear with clarity. "I'm charged to guard House Velanralyn, and I'll do just that. You proceed at your own peril."

"Well, of *course* we do." Mattick sneered. "Arcanists!" He pointed at the baelnorn with his sword. "Blast her down!"

Obediently the Shadovar spread out in the passage, took up stances, and hurled spells.

Only to shout in pain and reel back, staggering, as their own magic rebounded from the baelnorn's blades to strike at them. One arcanist blazed up like a torch, shrieking, and another was flung headlong back down the passage they'd traversed, to slam into an unyielding wall with a bone-shattering thud.

The baelnorn shook its head, sighed, and backed away around the corner.

Vattick looked disgusted. "Just a *little* care on our part would have avoided that." He watched the arcanist who'd slammed into the wall slide down, broken and senseless, then beheld the burnt arcanist toppling to the floor trailing wisps of smoke, little more than ashes around blackened bones. "Years of training gone to waste."

"Just when did you become such a wistful philosopher, Brother?" Prince Mattick demanded. "When you go to war, you know there'll be losses. The trick is making certain you're not one of them."

The baelnorn leaned back around the corner, pointing a sword as if it was some sort of wand. Blue-green fire spat from its tip, and Mattick sprang hastily back from its snarling beam with a curse, clutching the seared knuckles of his sword hand. The fire raced past him and slammed into the chest of an arcanist, who was driven back on his heels, and then fell, his despairing shout ending in a horrible wet wail as the fire roared into and through his face—and on into the arcanist behind.

More Shadovar spells were hurled, but the baelnorn was gone from view back around its corner again, and only a few of the magics swooped around it after the undead guardian.

"Idiots," Mattick growled at the arcanists. "Must we do this all ourselves?"

He strode to the wall and stalked along it toward where it turned the corner, muttering to himself as he worked a magic that would hurl any nastiness this undead guardian served up right back at her. Two could play such games, and this blade of his held some nasty powers of its own . . .

He thrust it before him, to round the corner first, but nothing happened. Still silence. Cautiously he peered with just one eye around the edge of stone, and saw the baelnorn floating in calm, deep blue silence, quite a few strides distant down its passage. Its upper armor, still glowing, hung floating behind it, leaving its body shrouded from the waist up in some sort of gauzy gown. Just behind its shoulder were the double doors the baelnorn was no doubt guarding.

Was this some sort of strange attempt at seduction? It was shapely, but an elf, and visibly beyond death at that. Not to his tastes. Perhaps this was some sort of strange elder elf custom.

Well, *pah*.

Prince Mattick had never heard of House Velanralyn before this day, and cared nothing for its history or former greatness. He had his father's orders; there was magical might here to be seized and drained, and the more he and Vattick took in, the more invincible they'd be when the *next* annoying elves showed up to offer battle. These arcanists were expendable. Unless too many of them fell through his folly, or his brother's. Then the Most High of Thultanthar would be too furious for comfort.

"Arcanists, attend me!" he ordered, trying for the calm coldness of his father's customary voice, as he strode grandly around the corner.

Let it try its worst, this lingering dross of elfkind. Then he could watch it humbled by its own battle spell, and step in for a little vicious hacking while it was still on its ghostly knees. This sword of his could cleave incorporeal undead as if they were solid meat; he'd enjoy its astonishment, for the fleeting moments before pain and death replaced that surprise.

Why—

The baelnorn was doing nothing as he strode up to it, nothing at all. Suspicious, Mattick slowed, bringing his blade up warily.

"Is there some problem, proud human?" the baelnorn asked, as gently as any Shadovar nurse. "Your own deceits disappoint you, so you expect some from me?"

"Oh, shut your over-clever *mouth*," Mattick snarled, slashing at it two handed, in a great swing that it parried with apparent difficulty. As both its swords clanged aside, struck wildly by the force of his blow, he grinned savagely—and thrust his sword home into its unprotected breast, low and angling up, up through ribs and through its heart and up into spine and brain.

"*Die*, elf bitch." He grinned into its face. Which, though he could see right through it to the dark stones of the passage beyond, showed gasping agony, dark eyes that clung to his in desperation and . . . was that *triumph*? He twisted his sword within it, shoving the blade in even farther—and felt nothing, of course. It was but a wraith to him, only his sword could slice the baelnorn as if it was wholly alive and solid.

With a sneer, he leaned forward until he could feel the chill of its undeath on his chin, could have thrust himself forward and kissed it if he'd wanted to.

"Does it hurt?" he whispered, smile widening, letting it see the cruel contempt he felt. "Does it?"

"Of course," the guardian breathed back—and kissed him.

The cold of that contact shocked Mattick's breath away, and he flung himself back, lips and face seared as if with ice. He tried to curse, and found his tongue a thick and then an unfeeling thing. He slashed furiously with his sword—and found that he was holding nothing but a hilt.

The stub of the blade was smoking, runes smoldering as they slid off steel that was no longer there, and collapsed into nothingness.

Prince Mattick stared at it in disbelief, stumbling back. The baelnorn was a brighter and more opaque blue than before, and it was smiling at him, sadly.

"I have descended to this," it whispered. "Still, you intend to do worse to me, and shall. I thank you for the energies in your blade, man—and your life-force. I'm well aware you didn't intend to yield either to me, but . . . I will do *anything* for House Velanralyn. That is my honor, and my curse."

Mattick flung down the hilt of his sword before the dark smoldering consuming it reached his fingers. He felt weak, sick . . . *hollow*.

He was, he was . . . suddenly no longer alone, as the five surviving arcanists led by his brother boiled around the corner and charged at the baelnorn.

Vattick stopped abruptly as he saw what had befallen his brother, ignoring the sudden flare of spells rocking the passage.

"Kisses of Shar!" he cursed in astonishment, grabbing Mattick by his elbow and towing him back around the corner. "You've no lower *face* left! How did it *do* this to you?"

Mattick shook his head helplessly, no longer able to speak. His heart was slowing, coldness was creeping across his chest, he couldn't breathe . . .

Vattick sighed, stepped back, and started casting spells.

"This should teach you," he began severely, between the second and the third. And then, when the sixth was done and Mattick was looking distinctly better and feeling his jaw and face wonderingly, Vattick sighed and added, "but it won't."

Mattick managed a grin. "Oh, I don't know. A few things stick, sometimes. I owe you thanks, Brother. And I am thankful, believe me. Now, let's see to this blasted baelnorn."

And he strode back around the corner.

The baelnorn had lost even more of its armor, and looked to be in pain again. The shards of one of its swords were circling it in midair, tumbling in slow leisure, but the guardian was holding its other blade high, looking more than ready to slay.

As it had been, and rather busily, it seemed. Only two arcanists were still standing, and one of them looked to be in pain, his clothing torn and burned away and scales appearing here and there on his revealed skin, before fading away to reappear somewhere else.

"Now *that's* interesting," Vattick told the baelnorn politely, pointing at the scales. "How did you manage that?"

He looked at Mattick, who was wincing at the carnage and muttering, "Father is going to be less than pleased."

Vattick nodded—and without looking at the baelnorn, unleashed something small and blindingly bright from his hand at it.

Mattick and the arcanists all shouted in pain and clutched at their watering eyes, dazed and blinded, but Vattick ignored them, turning to gaze hard at the writhing wisp of fading blue radiance that was the baelnorn.

It was gone from the waist up, consumed by his sunglow magic. He watched it sigh into oblivion with satisfaction that would have been greater if he hadn't known he had no more sunglows. And that his father had given it to him months ago in secret to use as a "last resort," not for this.

Oh, well . . .

"Can you see yet, Brother?" he asked wearily. "Why you feel the need to spend so much time playing the stone-headed fool is beyond me, but I'm yoked to you, great lout of Thultanthar!"

"I can see more or less," Mattick growled. "Pretty well for a stone-headed fool, anyway."

"Good. Then take this mace—what's left of Arthulniyr here certainly won't be needing it again—and breach the crypt doors. Have fun just hammering away at them. I'll stand ready, lest a trap or another guardian waits inside."

Mattick hefted the mace a few times, shook his head as if to clear it, passed a hand across his eyes as he worked a minor healing on them, and strode to the vault doors.

The entwined phoenixes of House Velanralyn didn't stand a chance.

The view out of Storm's kitchen windows into her herb garden was beautiful, even in mid-Marpenoth.

Yet with an exasperated sigh, Amarune suddenly turned away from it, fists clenched. "I know I can walk right out that door, and down to the gate, and out into all waiting Faerûn—but I *daren't*. I know not where to go, or what to do . . . this house is as warm and comforting as any place I've ever been in, yet it's a *prison* for us!"

Arclath set aside the old, thick book of recipes he'd been delving in, and hastened to wrap comforting arms around his beloved. "You want to be out there *doing*," he murmured soothingly. "That's my lady. A true however-many-greats granddaughter of Elminster."

"Lord Delcastle," Rune muttered into his chest, "are you patronizing me?"

"No! Gods, no! Your need to be out striving is a credit to you; you are a *true* noble, caring for the land and the folk in it, wanting to help. It's just that . . . staying here, where Storm knows where to find us, and you can survive if the Old Mage should fall, is the best service you can render just now."

Rune arched her back and shoved on his upper arms to put distance between them, so she could lift her chin and glare at her lord. "Oh? And who made *you* the all-knowing sage, between two beats of my heart? Hey?"

Arclath grinned. "There, you're even *sounding* noble."

"Oh, go ride a unicorn's horn!" she snarled, breaking free and striding across Storm's kitchen. She flung out an arm to bat a bundle of dried herbs down off its beam, then stopped herself, hands like claws, only to whirl back to him and say pleadingly, "Oh, forgive me, my love! It's just—not being part of what's going on *gnaws* at me!"

"I know," Arclath almost whispered. "I feel that same ache." He took her hand, as if he was going to whirl her into a dance across the smooth-worn flagstones of Storm's farmhouse kitchen, but instead drew her close and murmured, "But I must confess it's being overtaken swiftly by a deeper ache. Yawning hunger. Let's make some soup."

"*Soup*? At a time like this? Is *that* how Cormyr was founded, and defended, and made great? By the making of *soup*?"

"Doughty nobles ride into war best with full bellies," Arclath replied brightly, giving her a wide and false smile. When he batted his eyelashes at her like a dockside lowcoin lass, Rune found herself snorting in helpless amusement.

She wagged a reproving finger in his face. "*You*, my lord, are a *dangerous* man!"

"But of course," Arclath replied airily, twirling away from her into a full-flourish court bow. When he rose out of his crouch, he was holding a tureen and a large wooden spoon. "Soup?"

Amarune put her hands on her hips, shook her head, and then smiled wryly. "Soup," she confirmed.

"Good. Pull some leeks and parsnips while I prime the pump."

Rune arched an eyebrow. "My, but lords are very good at giving orders."

"'Tis what we do best," he replied airily. "Which really means most of us are hard-galloping disasters at doing anything else, but at least I'm one of the all too few who knows so, and will admit it. You chose well."

"*I* chose—? Lord Delcastle, may I remind you—"

"You may. Several times, and beating your points into me with yon spoon if you feel the need—*after* you get the leeks and parsnips."

Rune stopped in midretort, nodded, grinned, and went out the back door into the garden. Only to peer back through the door arch and ask warily, "You *do* know how to cook, yes?"

Arclath grinned. "Wise woman. Know ye: so long as we stick to the six—no, I lie, *seven*—dishes I was taught, down the years, behind my mother's back, I probably won't kill us both."

"Probably," Amarune echoed warily—and flashed him a grin before ducking out into the garden again.

Arclath found the pump didn't need priming, so he had the tureen full of water and the beginnings of a fire smoldering under it when his lady returned.

"Gods, what a garden," she murmured, joining him at the counter with its window looking out into the beanstalks. "I could learn to love it here."

"Storm told me generations of Harpers have stayed here, when they found the need," Arclath told her, inspecting what she'd brought and reaching for a trimming knife.

"You're strangely calm, considering the doom that may soon befall all Faerûn," Rune complained.

Her lord shrugged. "I can't do much, so I'm seizing this rare time of *not* running around swinging a sword to think. Yes, we nobles *do* think. Once or twice in our lives, between flagons and platters of whole roast boar."

For a moment, Rune's face told him she was going to say something saucy and stinging by way of reply, but then her face changed and she asked almost humbly, "And what are you thinking about just now, my lord?"

Arclath set down the knife, looked straight into her eyes, and replied, "When I was a child, my mother told me of a prophecy the High Herald Crescentcoat once shared with her. It impressed her so much that she wrote it down and often referred to it. I'm trying to remember it."

"Because?"

"It might bear on what's befalling right now. All I can recall of it, here and now, is the last half of it: 'That when two cities fall together, nobles across Faerûn must and shall renew the realms they serve.' So I find myself wondering if the prophecied time is nigh."

"Renew Cormyr?"

"*If* it's time. And if that be the case, and Myth Drannor is one of the cities that will fall, what's the other?"

Rune shrugged to indicate she hadn't the faintest. "Elminster has shown me that prophecies are put into the minds and mouths of mortals by the gods. They are what they want mortals to believe—wishful thinking, if you will—not firm destinies that can be fully understood beforehand, and counted on. That prophecy may be so many empty words, or—"

The front door of the kitchen swung open, and a man in worn leathers and homespun confronted them, drawn sword in hand.

"Who are you?" he growled. "And what're you up to?"

"Making soup," Arclath replied, bending to add some of Storm's split kindling to the fire, and wincing at how damp it was. "I hope."

The sword leveled at him didn't waver. "Neither of you are the Lady Storm—"

"No," Amarune replied calmly, "but she brought us here, and asked that we stay and await her."

"Oh? And what did she say might depend on your obedience?"

Rune and Arclath blinked at their gruff interrogator . . . and then Rune remembered Storm's words. "The future of the Realms," she replied triumphantly.

The man stared at her for a moment, then—very slowly—smiled, and his sword went down.

"Well met," he said. "I'm Braerogan, of Shadowdale. Next farm up. Heard your voices."

Arclath bowed. "I am Lord Arclath Delcastle, of Cormyr, and this is Lady Amarune Delcastle, my wife. We are . . . friends of the Lady Storm."

Braerogan lifted a bristling brow. "Lords and ladies, is it? Well, carry on. Didn't know nobility knew how to make their own soup, but . . . live and learn, live and learn. Any friend of the Lady Storm is a friend to all Shadowdale. And we need friends, what with all this fighting and tumult from one end of Faerûn to the other, and portents and priests muttering about Chosen, and I don't know *what* all."

He nodded, sheathed his sword, waved an uncertain salute in their direction, and went out, pulling the door closed behind him.

Rune stared at it in statuelike silence for long enough that Arclath had all the parsnips washed and chopped and into the tureen and was starting on the leeks before she exploded into pacing. Across the kitchen and back, across and back, whirling hard at each turn, and growling under her breath.

"Salt?" Arclath asked. "And share what you're snarling?"

His lady halted at the far end of the kitchen, hands on hips, and snapped, "We *shouldn't* be cowering here, when the Realms—literally, this time, not mere bardic overblown claims—hangs on the brink of utter destruction. Why should I keep myself safe to carry on tomorrow, when there won't *be* any tomorrow if Elminster, Storm, and the others fail?"

She marched across the kitchen to fetch up against Arclath's chest.

"Well, Lord Delcastle? Answer me that! Why are we languishing here when every blade and spell is needed? *Why?*"

"Because if they fall, you are their only hope. They can fight better knowing that, knowing you are out of harm's way."

"But I'm *not*, Arclath, and neither are you. The two of us can't even defend every door and window of *this kitchen*! We're safe only so long as none of the Shadovar or their hirelings and beasts notice us! The moment one of them so much as *looks* in this direction, or happens to blunder up yon path and through that door . . ."

Arclath stared at her, looking grim.

Rune put her arms around him, drew him so close that their noses touched, and stared into his eyes. "You haven't any answer for that, do you?" she asked softly.

Slowly, very slowly, Arclath shook his head.

CHAPTER 15

Attempting the Needful

BLUE LIGHTNING STABBED BRIEFLY OUT INTO THE PASSAGE AS THE last rubble fell away. Mattick and Vattick regarded each other across it, smiled, and when the lancing death was done, stepped through the archway with one accord, boots crunching on the rubble where Mattick had breached and shattered the crypt doors.

House Velanralyn had died out a long time ago, by the looks of things. Corpses sighed into dust at the most delicate of touches, and Vattick swiftly gave up on trying to see what sort of dead elf was wearing or holding what—he just started snatching things of magic as fast as his brother was, and draining them.

Briefly flaring blue glow after silent blue glow, they worked their way across the crypt. It was larger and dimmer than most, and they went to the highest, grandest biers and catafalques, one after another, leaving the lesser interments until later. The two arcanists watched uncertainly for a moment, and then one took up a guard's stance at the shattered entrance, and the other—the one afflicted with scales migrating around his body—joining the harvesting of magic items, collecting them rather than draining them as the two Tanthuls were.

As the draining went on, Mattick felt more powerful than ever in his life before, swollen and tingling and *itching* to hurl spells and blast screaming elf faces to nothingness. Then a stealthy movement seen out of the corner of his eye made him turn, in time to see the scaly arcanist slip a glowing blue ring into a belt pouch.

A moment later, the kneeling arcanist gasped and swayed forward—as the point of Vattick's sword burst out of his breast.

Mattick's brother had run the Shadovar through from behind. He twisted his blade to make the sobbing, convulsing arcanist feel more pain. Then pulled it out—and slid it back into the shade's body at a different angle and twisted it again.

The raw shrieks and gurglings were impressive.

The other arcanist came from the crypt entrance to watch, reluctant and white faced, as his scaly fellow Shadovar died slowly and horribly on Prince Vattick's magical sword.

When the thieving Thultanthan was still and silent at last, Vattick kicked the body off his steel, wiped the blade clean on the dead, staring face, and drawled, "I knew we'd have to make a lesson of someone. It was just a matter of who."

He slashed open the dead arcanist's pouch, hooked the ring on the tip of his sword, flung it into the air, and caught and drained it, letting the dust the ring crumbled into trickle out of his palm onto the dead man's face.

Mattick looked at the sole surviving arcanist. The man's face was the color of old bone, and he was swallowing repeatedly, as if something was caught in his throat.

A curse, probably.

"Next crypt," Mattick ordered him briskly, and followed his words with an impish smile.

The last arcanist shuddered and swallowed again. Hard.

"Beloved teacher," Elminster said gently, "we are indeed going somewhere. Up out of here, to the heart of Myth Drannor. I think ye know why."

The Srinshee nodded.

"The hour of need is come," she said sadly. "Being as *some* are contemplating destroying the mythal."

"Olue," El asked gravely, "ye aren't going to resist us, are ye?"

"No. What you are attempting is needful. It tears at my heart to lose this bright city again—oh, how it hurts—but I would lose a thousand Myth Drannors if the loss could save Faerûn. We elves can go to Semberholme, or find trees elsewhere. If the dwarves can abandon all their homes and travel far and do whatever is needful to endure, so can we. So *shall* we. Yes, El, I'm with you."

"Oh, thank *Mystra*!" El exclaimed in relief as he rushed to her, arms flung wide.

The Srinshee smiled, and burst into a rush of her own. They ended up in each other's arms, and El swept the small guardian off her feet in a fierce embrace.

Laeral gave her sister a sardonic look. "*This* is why he never gets any work done!"

"Oh, I'd not say that, Sister," Alustriel countered, watching El and the Srinshee weeping softly and murmuring to each other, rocking back and forth in each other's arms. "We all have our talents. I've accomplished much, doing that and more."

"This one yet lives," one Moonstar announced to another, who hastened across the high-vaulted and now blood-spattered room in Candlekeep, slipping on the rubble underfoot.

On all sides, glum-faced Moonstars were tending injured monks or moving the bodies of the dead.

"The wards gone . . . ," one muttered in head-shaking disbelief.

More than a few of his fellows peered at the stone walls soaring up into dimness above them, as if expecting Candlekeep to collapse on their heads without warning. Soon.

"I," said another quietly, "find myself wondering what we should all do, after these needs have been seen to . . . for what is to be done, now that we've failed?"

"Much," a new voice said firmly, from beyond a dark archway. A woman's voice, but deep and rich as many a man's. Moonstars all over the littered room looked up sharply, and more than one hand sought a sword hilt.

The speaker strode into the room, and they beheld a warrior woman, tall and broad shouldered and clad in silvery coat of plate. Her close-cropped hair was of the same hue. "If you would serve Khelben's vision still," she said, "and do great service to all the world, come with me now. There's still vital work to be done."

"And who, exactly, are you?" a Moonstar asked warily.

"I am Dove Falconhand. Of the Seven. Chosen of Mystra."

Several Moonstars stirred, and some of their faces darkened, but before any spoke, Dove added as sternly as any battle commander, "If we are to defeat the Three Who Wait in Darkness—the very purpose for which the Moonstars were formed—we must go to Myth Drannor and fight the Shadovar there. I understand there's no shortage of them there right now; there'll be foes enough for each of you."

"I lack the spells to take more than a handful of us there," another Moonstar objected.

Dove gave that man a smile. "Portals will serve us. I know three within the keep, all of them an easy stroll from here."

Another Moonstar frowned at her. "I've lived and worked in this monastery for more than thirty years, and have never seen nor heard of any working portals."

Dove winked. "That's what 'secret' means. Trust me."

"And if I don't?"

"Then stay behind. I might well be going to my death, and would rather not have someone at my shoulder who believes not in what we must do now."

"And what's that?"

"Die cheerfully, fighting hard, so our world may survive," Dove replied. "I know bards talk like that all the time, but I don't. I mean every word. And I'm not waiting. So stay, or come." And she turned and strode back through the archway.

Moonstars looked at each other doubtfully. Then one of them rose, drew his sword, and hurried after Dove.

Then another.

And another.

Then two in unison, swiftly followed by another pair, and then by the rest, in a sudden rush.

Leaving just one Moonstar, who gazed around the room surveying the corpses and the wounded monks, sighed, and announced to the empty air, "I'll miss this place."

He walked through the archway, following his fellow Moonstars. "Will the bards sing songs about us, I wonder?" he asked himself.

A few slow, faltering paces later, he stopped long enough to ask, "And if I'm dead, how will I ever get to hear them?"

Another pair of grand and firmly closed crypt doors, and another baelnorn standing in grim guardianship before them, bared long-sword in hand. The long, slender blade was studded with clear-cut gems that winked as the baelnorn lifted the war steel, facing the three Netherese as they strolled up to it.

"I am Prince Mattick, and this is my brother, Prince Vattick. We are Tanthuls of Thultanthar," Mattick announced almost jovially. "You won't have heard of us, but that matters not. Surrender or be destroyed."

He didn't bother to mention the lone surviving arcanist with them, but neither that Shadovar nor the baelnorn seemed to mind.

"I am the guardian of House Hualarydnym," it announced calmly. "I shall not surrender."

"You surprise me not," Vattick drawled, and lifted a finger, unleashing a roaring spell that howled around the doors of the Hualarydnym crypt like two talon-headed emerald serpents, then plunged through the seams around them—and exploded with a last ear-clawing bellow.

The doors shattered and burst outward, huge stony shards stabbing right through the baelnorn from behind. The other shards, large and small, hurtled past the guardian for a moment or two, then curved around in the air, every one of them, to race back at the baelnorn, impaling it from all sides.

Vattick's catlike smirk widened into a broad smile of delight as they watched the sharp stone fragments speed right through the glowing guardian, but leave their glows behind.

The baelnorn gasped and reeled, the magical auras the stone shards had borne now protruding from it in an ungainly, bristling array. It looked like a fitfully glowing, stumbling parody of a porcupine.

The guardian took several shuddering steps toward them, hissing in pain . . . and then darkened, gasping out puffs of glowing unlife as it sank into crouching, trembling agony.

And died, falling into a collapse of fading nothingness.

"Down after the first blow," Mattick remarked approvingly. "Nicely done."

"It's all this tomb magic we've been drinking," Vattick replied, beaming. "They crafted magic well; I'll give them that, these ancient elves."

He looked down at the stretch of scorched but empty smooth stone where the baelnorn had been, shook his head, and strode through the ravaged entrance of the crypt.

House Hualarydnym had not been a fertile family. Either that, or most of its fallen had been interred elsewhere. There was magic, right enough, but not much of it.

Mattick scowled. "Hardly worth the spell you spent on the door guard," he said to Vattick.

Who shrugged, still smiling, and replied, "That was one baelnorn-reaping I *enjoyed*."

"Hunh," was Mattick's eloquent reply to that, as he led the way back out into the passage. Vattick chuckled, but the lone arcanist left carefully said nothing at all, even when Mattick turned and glowered at him.

The passage wound its way around massive tree roots that protruded from the ceiling and descended into the floor like the sloping, half-buried bodies of gigantic snakes. Then the tunnel-like way started to ascend, until Mattick could see leaf-dappled daylight and hear the distant din of battle. Its walls held no more doors.

"Damned longears," the prince growled. "They can't have built a city this big with just the families we've found so far; there have to be more crypts—but the passages that lead to them could be *anywhere*. And if we follow this one to the light, we'll soon be up to our necks in squalling elves trying to lash us with spells we've never learned any counters to! While we blunder about in the heart of a battle searching for ways back down again! Shar *spit*!"

"She does, I'll grant," Vattick agreed, "and a trifle too often for my pleasure, but as it happens, we don't face the doom you fear. Father didn't want us to run out of crypts so soon."

Mattick swung around sharply. "What?"

The silent arcanist deftly stepped to one side, eyes downcast.

Vattick watched the Shadovar's maneuver with obvious amusement before he met Mattick's gaze again, and said gravely, "The Most High impressed a map of sorts into my mind. I know where other nearby crypts can be found."

Mattick stared at his brother in still silence, a deepening frown spreading across his face. Both the last arcanist and Prince Vattick knew, as clearly as if he'd shouted the words, that he was thinking "Why Vattick and not me?"

Mattick said nothing, however, until he abruptly turned away and flung back over his shoulder curtly, "Tell me, Brother: Did the Most High share anything else with you that you've neglected to mention until now? Orders, perhaps?"

Vattick's laugh was brief and harsh. "No, Brother. On that, you can trust me."

Those words fell like stones into a bottomless well of deepening silence as Mattick strode to the nearest tree root and bounced a clenched fist off it, making no reply.

When he turned around again, Vattick was strolling back down the passage the way they'd come, the arcanist walking uncertainly in his wake.

Mattick swallowed a growl and hastened to catch up.

Rocks and trees unrolled swiftly below. The breeze was stiff, and the clouds scudded like ships driven by a gale; Thultanthar was flying at speed.

"It won't be long now," Aglarel commented, leaning out between two merlons to peer ahead, though he knew they were still too far away to see any sign of Myth Drannor in the great sweep of Faerûn spread out below and ahead.

His father didn't bother to reply.

Or rather, as Aglarel saw a moment later, the Most High's attention was fixed on something in the air above them.

A black line where there should be none, in the hitherto-empty sky.

A line swiftly broadening into a dark rift—that became a black star, low overhead and seemingly of about the same size as the many-spired city flying beneath it, a star that for just a moment seemed to be one dark, coldly knowing, somehow feminine eye.

It was an orb Aglarel felt would freeze his heart if it happened to turn and gaze upon him, and he knew the deity it belonged to was aware of him—knowledge that made his heart sink into deeper despair, in that instant, than he'd ever felt in his life before.

Shar was manifesting in midair to his father. This *must* be urgent.

"How can you be so *patient?*" Amarune burst out. "The world may be shattered before nightfall, and you're sitting there calmly reading *recipes!*"

"Not calmly," Arclath whispered, looking up from the heap of old books he'd fetched down off dusty shelves onto Storm's kitchen table, and she saw that his hands were shaking. "Just feigning calm. Something nobles are taught young. Pretend to be calm, keep your true emotions off your face, and cultivate patience."

"Thank the *gods* I'm not noble!"

"Ah, but you are now." Lord Arclath Delcastle set the book aside and rose to go to his lady and embrace her. The look he gave her, once they were in each other's arms, was more grim than grave. "And if there's someone in this room who must learn patience to keep the world from being shattered, probably many times in the years ahead of us, it's you, Rune. Haven't you noticed that it's one of Elminster's best weapons?"

"No. I guess all the kingdom-shattering spell-hurling he does distracted me."

"Misdirection," Arclath replied, with the faintest ghost of a smile, "is another of his best weapons. That and his sense of humor."

Rune gave him a dark look, and warned, "Don't you say *one word*, Lord Delcastle, about how I'm related to him, and have inherited this or that. Just don't."

"All right, I won't." Arclath smoothly disengaged her clasping arms, returned to the table, and said, "There's an interesting recipe here for turtle soup—"

And being noble, he watched anyone standing near out of the corner of his eye, and so was ready to duck aside as she hurled a handy onion at him.

The great black eye floating in the sky above the flying city blinked. It and its dark rays and the rift they had appeared through were all gone in an instant, and bright sun banished the temporary gloom that had fallen on the battlements.

Sunlight that lit the High Prince of Thultanthar like a torch as he turned to Aglarel in sudden haste.

"Go," he ordered, "and fetch my herald. Don't hurry."

His most loyal son bowed and backed away, but was taken aback and didn't try to hide it. "Your herald? Who—?"

"The arcanist Gwelt," Telamont snapped. "*Go.*"

Aglarel turned away, cloak swirling. "Since when have you had a herald?" he muttered, as he hastened away.

The Most High shrugged. "I've always needed one," he replied, knowing his magic would take that quiet reply to his son's ears.

Then he strode down a stair and along a passage, passed through a door and spell-sealed it behind him with the wave of a hand, and hurried to his innermost spellchamber.

He sealed its doors too, warding himself within a room that was colder and darker than it should be.

When he turned around from the doors, she was waiting for him.

There'd been a secret door in the wall of the passage just outside the doors of the second crypt they'd plundered. The time-worn stone steps beyond had come up inside a hollow tree—or rather, the crumbling stump of a long-dead and fallen shadowtop, the roofless room inside its ring as large around as a good-sized turret.

Vattick worked a disguising spell on himself without slowing that left him looking like an elf high mage, and his brother and the lone surviving arcanist hastened to follow suit. Vattick seemed to know the way onward unerringly. He went to a cleft in the stump, stepping through it into a drift of dead leaves as if walking along a passage he took every day.

Mattick and the arcanist kept close behind him, as they strode past armed elves rushing here and there through the trees, the drifting smoke of a fire, and the screams and clangor of battle that wasn't far off at all.

They strode along like men bent on business, who had every right to be there, ignoring all elves and walking with brisk purpose. Soon enough they ducked between two old and mighty duskwoods and down into a passage so old its ceiling had collapsed, leaving it as a deep trench in the forest, open to the sky—yet shielded by the thick forest canopy high overhead, and here and there by the small trunks of fallen saplings and the living nets of forest creepers.

Vattick led the way as sure-footedly as if the rotten-leaf-strewn ditch was very familiar, and soon enough it curved to the right and angled down underground into darkness. Dirt-and-root walls soon gave way to stone every bit as ancient as the underways they'd been traversing from crypt to crypt earlier.

Ahead, something ghostly and deep blue glided into their path, to bar their way.

Vattick never slowed, even when all three elf high mage disguises melted from them to the accompaniment of a hiss of disgust from the guardian ahead.

"So, what family bones do you guard?" he asked it cheerfully.

"Human, you intrude upon the resting place of House Alavalae," the baelnorn replied coldly. "Halt, and go back, or face mortal peril."

"Indeed," Vattick smiled—and let fly with the same spell he'd used on the last guardian. Not at the doors of a crypt, this time, but at the baelnorn itself, two talon-headed serpents of emerald force that the guardian countered almost casually, with some sort of barrier that held the prince's spell at bay in front of it, writhing and clawing and spitting emerald fury in all directions.

Vattick waved to his twin as if he was directing him to a seat at a feast table—and Mattick strode forward with a smile whose malice would have done credit to any ruthless wolf, and unleashed some of the magic he'd drained from the crypts of Myth Drannor.

His ravening magical fire snarled around in a great arc to stab at the undead guardian from behind.

It backed away hastily to avoid being caught between two destroying spells at once—but the doors it was bound to guard were all too near, robbing it of space enough to flee into.

Its blue glow seemed to catch fire, going red and emerald green and then boiling up inky black—until it managed some sort of more powerful warding, and forced the princes' contemptuously hurled magics back.

That was when the arcanist dared to step forward and add his spell to the fray, a careful casting that shattered the warding, consuming itself in doing so.

The spells the twin princes had cast crashed in on the guardian from either side—and it winked out of visibility, letting the spells crash together and roil angrily in midair.

When they were spent, the last force rolling away from their meeting to strike the walls and rebound, like a wave striking a rocky shore, the guardian faded back into visibility—much closer to the three Shadovar than it had been before.

Mattick spat a curse and Vattick ducked hastily aside as he worked a spell, but the baelnorn had guarded this spot for centuries, and had made some preparations. It spread hands that pulsed with blue fire—and flat, sharp-edged stones burst free of the walls all around and whirled at the human trio like whirling blades.

Scores of stones, a volley that Mattick and Vattick flung themselves to the floor to try to survive, arms cradling their heads.

The arcanist wasn't swift enough in joining them. He staggered, his skull shattered and his arms and ribs breaking with sickening thuds under the barrage of piercing stone . . . and then he fell over backward, his throat crushed and his head lolling limply.

The stones flashed through the air with unabated force, ricocheting off one another and the walls amid deafening *krrracks* and sprays of small shards as one after another broke apart. They flashed through the baelnorn without doing it any harm, but the two groaning, crawling princes of Thultanthar weren't so lucky.

Vattick finally managed to cast something that flung all the stones at the ceiling, then sent them racing at the floor, and then back at the ceiling again. At each thunderous meeting of hurtling stone with immoveable floor or ceiling, more shatterings spat clouds of curling dust and sprays of pebble-like shards everywhere.

And then, at last, it was done, and Mattick and Vattick surged painfully to their feet, teeth clenched, and advanced on the baelnorn.

Who gave them a serene smile, and worked the same magic again.

This time, Mattick—who'd half suspected such a tactic, for all his snarling rage—had enough warning to work a strong ward shield. Vattick's went up more slowly, but protected him against the worst whirling shards—and when the second stone storm died away, he did something that caught the baelnorn by surprise.

He gave his own ward shield a slicing edge of pure force, and slashed the undead guardian with it, as if it was a great drover's whip.

Causing the baelnorn to waver, leaking blue fire in all directions and reeling back—right into Mattick's flames of the sun spell, that made its undeath burn like a pyre.

It blazed up with a sudden roar, and was gone before the two princes could draw another breath.

Mattick and Vattick regarded each other sourly over the last wisps of the vanishing baelnorn. They were both bruised, cut, and bleeding, their contempt for elves gone and anger in its place.

"You look like an arcanist who's just won his first spell duel by sheer luck," Mattick panted.

Vattick nodded grimly, and spent some of the elven magic they'd drained on a healing that left him gasping, trembling, and leaking blue fire from his dozens of cuts—but standing straighter and freed from pain when it was done.

Mattick did the same thing. Then they both looked back at the sprawled corpse of the last arcanist, with his shattered hands dangling from his splintered wrists, shrugged in unison, and turned to the now-unguarded doors of House Alavalae. Two rampant pegasi faced each other, wings and hooves raised, but neither of the twin princes was in the mood to appreciate skilled elven sculpting.

They each flung out a hand and sent blasting blue fire at the doors. The stone shuddered, wavered, and swung open a trifle.

Vattick sidestepped as he advanced, and sent another spell against the now-exposed lip of one of the doors, driving it fully open with a heavy grinding rumble.

Revealing a line—no, a *wall*—of blue fire in the dim interior of the crypt. Literally heaps of magic.

"Ah," Mattick purred, striding eagerly forward, "*that's* more like it."

Vattick hastened too. Only for the blue fire to fall away like a cascade of spilled water, revealing the grim-faced Coronal of Myth Drannor flanked by a quartet of elf mages.

Without wasting a word on greeting, parley, or challenge, they all hurled ravening spells into the faces of the twin princes of Shade.

The purple-eyed face hanging in the darkness was almost as large as the wall Telamont could no longer see behind it, and was wreathed in restlessly whipping and coiling black tresses like the tentacles of the giant octopi sometimes called "the Devourers of the Deeps." Shar's choice to give that face the features of one of Telamont's first loves, dead and gone centuries ago, was merely her usual cruelty; that she'd chosen to manifest in person to speak to him rather than her usual mindspeech in his head was a measure of her fury. Even her nimbus of awful darkness wasn't as bone chilling as usual, thanks to the warmth of her anger.

"Both of your agents have failed," the goddess told her servant coldly. "For all their training, they accomplished little. So now, amuse me: *try* to justify your failure in Candlekeep."

"I cannot justify, Mistress of the Night," Telamont said swiftly, "but I *can* explain. Even without Maerandor, our agents among the Avowed could, I believe, have accomplished what we intended *and* overcome our enemies among the monks, had not an unforeseen power moved against us."

"The meddler Elminster was *not* unforeseen," Shar snapped. "He is always present, at nigh every great play of power in Toril, outside of Thay, these last four centuries. Such is the chaos he wreaks that I never send servitors directly against him, for time and again he furthers discord, and visits loss, despair, and destruction on many, *better than those sworn to me*. Prate not to me of Elminster."

Telamont Tanthul dared to raise his voice to his goddess. "I did *not* presume to blame Elminster, and do not. By 'unforeseen power,' I meant the one called Larloch. The Last Chosen of Mystryl."

"Who has never deserved that title, but let it pass. Why did you not foresee his involvement? *I* expected it."

"I, too, anticipated that he would take a hand—but I foresaw that he'd work through his servitor liches, to seize what books and items of magic could be stolen amid the chaos, as he's reported to have often done in the past. I had no idea he'd try to seize the power of the wards of Candlekeep for his own, to share the folly of the most crazed arcanists of Netheril and try to make himself into a god!"

"The wards of Candlekeep might make a toad or a pixie a guardian demigod of Candlekeep, but no more."

Telamont shook his head. "Larloch goes now to Myth Drannor, or is there already, seeking to snatch its mythal. With that much power, he seeks to remake the Weave and root it in himself, and so ascend."

"That, I did *not* foresee," Shar admitted, her words rolling across the room as if from a great distance. "So, Telamont Tanthul, your fear tells me you believe he can achieve this. That he is likely to achieve this."

Telamont started to pace, cursing softly under his breath without thinking, though his every oath was an insult barbed against Shar. The coldness around him seemed somehow amused as his profanity faltered, then quickly gave way to an admission.

"The archlich has always been stronger in the Art than I am—possibly stronger than all the massed arcanists of this city, even without the liches who serve him. Goading him out of his seclusion and researches by the bold actions we've taken was always a risk . . . which we're now facing."

"You don't seem to relish the coming confrontation, High Prince of Thultanthar."

"*No,*" Telamont whispered fiercely, turning away.

Not that it was possible to turn his back on the Mistress of the Night, in a chamber filled with her dark presence.

What do you seek to run from, Telamont Tanthul? Her whisper was far louder and more terrible than his, seeming to sigh through his head like a tidal wave racing across hard-day's ride after hard-day's ride of unprotected fields.

"Goddess," the ruler of the Shadovar mumbled miserably, "I am afraid of Larloch."

"Fear is the lash, the goad," Shar told him, as gently as any mother. "Freeze and cower not when it descends on you, but embrace it, and know me more closely, and use the fear you feel to spur you to greater service."

Telamont winced, nodding but still hunched, his teeth set.

"Show me your mettle, High Prince. Show me why I should still rely on you to serve me."

The clear warning in those last words took Telamont by the throat and shook him out of his dark fear.

He straightened, flung out an arm as if he could dash down mountains with it, and snapped, "Your intentions are *not* thwarted by the archlich, Divine One. If I can drain the mythal before Larloch can, it should be power enough to raise the Shadow Weave."

"It should," Shar agreed, her approval an arm of warm darkness that seemed to wrap around his shoulders amid silent thunder.

"See that you succeed," she added, drawing away again.

"H-have you any instructions?" Telamont asked quickly, sensing Shar's presence receding.

"No one is unexpendable, Telamont, son of Harathroven," the goddess warned softly, as if from a great distance.

And with that, she was gone, leaving the Most High of Thultanthar standing alone in empty darkness, sweating and pale.

"This—this is *utter* chaos!" a Moonstar protested, white faced in revulsion. Amid the trees, the smoke of countless fires drifted, some of them reeking pyres of the dead. Bodies were heaped and strewn everywhere, swarming flies buzzed, and from all sides arose the clangor, shouts, and shrieks of battle.

"Do as yon elves are doing," Dove commanded over her shoulder, as she strode toward the nearest skirmish, sword drawn. "Slay all non-elves you see attacking elves, or advancing to the heart of Myth Drannor."

"Yes," another Moonstar agreed, espying a good blade among the fallen and snatching it up to heft and swing experimentally, "but who *are* all these warriors? Whence came they here?"

"From all over Sembia, and Inner Sea ports where the Shadovar sent ships and recruiters," Dove replied. "It seems the Thultanthans never foresaw their command of the siege of Myth Drannor could slip from 'absolute,' and so gave their hirelings no battle cries to shout to keep friendly steel from butchering allies."

"So this siege has become an utter confusion of scattered skirmishes," a third Moonstar said disgustedly. "Yet the hireswords seem *endless*."

"*Seem* endless," Dove replied. "Ever planted seedlings? No tossing and walking on; you must root and tamp every one, one after another, until the task is done. The hewing of mercenaries must be like that for us, if this siege is to be broken. One after another, and just keep at it until the task is done. If—"

She was interrupted by a ragged shout, as a dozen human warriors in motley armor came crashing hastily through saplings and dead leaves, waving swords and spears and axes.

"Let's start with these handy targets," Dove added cheerfully, and strode to meet them, dagger in one hand and long and ready blade in the other.

Moonstars hesitated—but Dove waded cheerfully into the fray, one woman alone against the dozen. Steel clanged on steel; she danced and ducked and sprang like a festival tumbler, and it was mercenaries who fell, not the lone woman darting about in their midst. "Surrender and be spared," she chanted in their faces as she parried hard enough that sparks flew, and dealt death. "Surrender and be spared!"

The last few mercenaries fled from her, crashing wildly through the forest, but the din of their flight was drowned out by the arrival of more of the besieging army, from two directions through the trees—hundreds of them.

They came on at a trot, flooding through the saplings, swarming up and around Dove, who never faltered in her demands that they surrender, though they closed in around her, thrusting and hacking viciously.

Several Moonstars rushed to her aid, charging determinedly through all the offered steel, but others yelled, "Fall back!" or just hastened away.

More warriors came through the trees, scores of them, and it wasn't long before a Moonstar fell. And then another.

Even Dove was being driven back by the sheer force of new arrivals, charging in to try to get at her, their rush shoving back the forefront of the bloody fray.

A high, clear horncall rang out through the trees, and suddenly there were elves darting in among the mercenaries, their long swords gleaming.

A Moonstar reared up, transfixed by two mercenary blades, shrieking in agony—and right beside him, as he crashed down in his last fall, choking on his own blood, an elf charge swept away most of the Shadovar forces surrounding Dove and the handful of Moonstars standing with her.

And came at Dove and those Moonstars with the same slaying ferocity that they'd shown to the besiegers.

Dove thrust them away with a swift spell, shouting, "Can you not tell friend from foe?"

Whatever reply the elves she was facing might have tried to make was lost in another horncall, this one three notes winded at once.

The signal for a retreat.

In an instant, the elves fell back again, running back into the trees. After a wavering moment, the besiegers let out a ragged chorus of yells and went after them.

Leaving Dove and her Moonstars behind, forgotten.

She peered through the trees, grimacing. The elves were surrendering more and more of their city.

Given what she knew of their pride, their ranks must have been thinned indeed, worn down in this siege, for this to happen.

"Well?" one of the Moonstars asked, looking to her.

"Aye, what now?" asked another, wiping at blood that was streaming down the side of his face. "Where shall we throw our lives away?"

Dove snorted like a horse in dismissal of his words, but had no others to give him.

"So pass two princes of Thultanthar," the Coronal of Myth Drannor said bitterly. "Would that they had kept to their own city and their own Art, and left ours alone. What they've destroyed can never be replaced . . . like so much of what all *Tel'Quess* have lost, these last few centuries."

She turned away from the smoking ashes of what had been Mattick and Vattick Tanthul, and signaled wordlessly to one of the high mages. He bowed and obeyed, beginning to cast an intricate spell over the remains of their fallen foes that would ensure no one successfully brought them back to life or unlife.

His three fellow mages turned to obey commands she'd given earlier, resealing the crypt of House Alavalae.

Ilsevele Miritar, the Coronal of Myth Drannor, watched them, and sighed. How long would it be before the next tomb robbers came down this passage, bent on taking what they could and destroying all that was left of a proud elf family?

They had won this battle, but it didn't feel like any sort of victory.

The mages all looked to her, their castings done.

"Come," she commanded softly, and led the way along the passage. There was another crypt, around two bends of the way ahead, and these plunderers might have sent others . . .

They found its doors intact, but the door warden of House Felaeraun was a flickering blue flame in the passage before them, weeping inconsolably.

"Gone!" was all they could get out of the baelnorn. "*Gone!*"

At a gesture from their coronal, two of the high mages unsealed the doors with careful spells, working gently—and just as gently, opened the doors wide.

Into still darkness.

The last resting place of House Felaeraun had been drained *from within*. All of its honored dead were now dust, their magic gone.

CHAPTER 16

Slain Qualms and Worse

I HAVE AN IDEA," ELMINSTER ANNOUNCED SUDDENLY.

"Of *course* you do," the Srinshee, Alustriel, and Laeral all replied in unintentional unison—something that startled them into gales of laughter.

El overrode them all with a firm, "*Heed me!*" And then added, "For I'll be needing aid—mind-steadying—from all of ye."

"El," Laeral told him crisply, "you've needed that for *years.*"

That brought a chuckle from the man himself, amid fresh mirth from the others, but then he said, "I've magically bound more than a few beings over the years. Some, I'm thinking, could wreak much havoc among the armies of Thultanthar gathered here."

"*And* against the battered few *Tel'Quess* still fighting for our city," the Srinshee said sharply.

"Only if they break through all the massed mercenaries I'm thinking of putting them right into the midst of."

"What *sort* of bound beings?" Alustriel asked suspiciously.

"Dracoliches, dragons, beholders, and the like. Usually I thrust them into stasis, where they've been caught ever since, but in a few cases I bound them to a particular place, so they could no longer wander and maraud at will."

"Dragons . . . beholders," the Srinshee murmured, shaking her head. "And this will help my people *how*? By sending them to their graves all the sooner?"

"If you help me transform the bindings I've laid on them into prohibitions to keep them from translocating or flying," El explained, "we'll keep most of them ground ridden. Beholders dragging themselves along, dragons and dracoliches stalking like cats—they'll be caught in the thick of well-armed hireswords who can hit back, and hit hard. Lots of hireswords. The armies far too numerous for the *Tel'Quess* of Myth Drannor to stand against. Think of these beasts as *our* army."

Laeral winced. "I have some ethical qualms . . . convince me, El."

"I bind nothing and no one lightly. These bound creatures are all menaces—and if I fall in battle, they'll all be loosed anyway, wherever they are on Toril, without heralding nor any watch over where they go and what they do. Which will undoubtedly be to slaughter and despoil and devour. Why not have that havoc be visited on warriors who've taken coin to do butchery on others, in a forest-locked city far from what any of them hold dear, whose inhabitants have threatened them not at all? Let them earn their blood-coins for once. And if all this should thin the ranks of mercenaries, so be it. Better they fall, and all lands be somewhat the safer for the lack of so cheap and plentiful means of making war, than Myth Drannor fall and Shar or Larloch or something worse prevail, the Weave crash, and a new Spellplague or worse race like wildfire across the world, and countless beings be plunged into fear and misery and lives of desperate savagery, fighting every day just to stay alive in the face of—"

"*Enough*," Laeral said firmly. "You've slain my qualms, not to mention any more qualms I may entertain for the next season or so. Let's be loosing your beasts—only with precision."

"Of course," Elminster agreed. "*That* is what I need the three of ye to help with. I need ye to steady and guide me, so we translocate each beast to the best spot at the right time."

"Though every moment we spend means more of my people fall," the Srinshee said firmly, "we are going to begin by taking time enough to swiftly survey the strength of the foe, and just where they're scattered. Fortunately, this was a survey I was already undertaking when you arrived. Sit down, all of you."

"I—"

"*Sit down*. Or lie down; whatever brings most ease. Linking hands, all of us, in a ring. Attune to me."

Both Alustriel and Laeral opened their mouths as if to protest, then nodded, sat, and reached out for Elminster—who was grinning at the Srinshee's sudden fire—and for the Srinshee herself.

It took a moment for their minds to mesh, four so spirited and long-lived individuals, but when the inevitable tugging and surging subsided into a comfortable union, their linked minds flashed out to several pairs of small, darting forest birds, and rode their tiny minds and all-seeing eyes through the trees, sweeping over the Shadovar army ringing Myth Drannor. Everywhere within the city, there were skirmishes and fires and rushing armed bands . . . but not far off, there were thousands of mercenaries encamped, or waiting orders to advance into the city.

Elminster and the two sisters could feel the Srinshee's despair growing as she saw just how many hireswords there were—and how few elves were left to stand against them.

"Do it," she snapped at last. "A good big dragon *there*, and a dracolich there, and beholders here and *here*. So anyone fleeing will rush into the fearful running from another peril, not off by themselves to straggle through the forest for days and regroup to do mischief. Hem them in with terror. Then we watch, and unbind more beasts only as some of those fall. Yes?"

"Yes," three mind-voices agreed, and plunged into Elminster's memories, following him down to the black elder wyrm Harlotharaur, bound in a deep mountain cavern on the northern edge of Amn after it had gloated to El that nothing and no one could stop it poisoning the wells of human cities and the streams that watered mountain villages, to destroy humans in their tens of thousands, and so rid the land of a pest that endangered all other creatures.

The bindings on the dragon were thus and so . . . Alustriel and Laeral twisted them, and when the roused Harlotharaur stretched its wings and sat up in fell glee to smite the bindings and win its freedom, the Srinshee smilingly plunged into the dragon's mind, pinned its every muscle, and held it immobile as she translocated it to precisely the spot she'd chosen— and then flung it into a daze.

When the wyrm recovered, not all that many handfuls of moments later, all trace of the four minds that had so violated it were gone, but it was ringed by angry and fearful humans who were even now assailing it with everything they could swing, hurl, or thrust.

Almost gleefully it gave battle, rearing up and lashing out in one titanic surge. Broken bodies were flung high into the air, or sent spattering off trees all around—and Harlotharaur roared in exulting challenge, and set about harvesting more bodies to hurl. It gathered itself for a bound into the air, and flung out its wings for one great beat—only to feel nothing. The muscles that should coil and let it bound into the air twitched and spasmed instead of obeying, and the wings drooped; they could spread but not beat down with any force at all, nor hold an edge . . .

In baffled rage Harlotharaur tried again and again, throwing back its head and howling its fury. And then it lowered its head and reached out with its claws and jaws, and dug into the armed humans around it, savaging them and scattering them like dried leaves, and then savaging them some more.

By then, the Srinshee was already rooting through Elminster's deep memories, dismissing the seething pain it caused him with a brisk, "The sooner we're in and out and done, the sooner you can start mending your mind—something you *should* have given more thought to long ago."

Finding the dracolich he wanted her to find, the Srinshee pounced.

Its cold eyes stared around vainly in the lightless, frigid water and swirling mud. El, Srinshee, Laeral, and Alustriel could all feel its puzzlement, and now, as they drifted in more closely to its flashing thoughts, could hear what it was thinking.

Who *were* these awakeners? They were—they were *in its own mind*, nowhere to be seen . . .

Anger and fear blossomed and rose in the bone dragon's thoughts. It was Tlossarylathaunglar by name, one of the oldest and most fell creations of the Cult of the Dragon, long frozen by El's will and Art in the silted depths of a frigid Underdark lake after it refused to stop using its spells and undead brawn to cause collapse after collapse in the Realms Below, crushing entire deep gnome cities and flooding a huge network of caverns that were home to drow, duergar, and dwarves alike by shattering lake basins in the bedrock above them. All for the delight of slaying and the goal of opening vast subterranean caverns it could fly through, and rule over . . .

Now, Tlossaryl was aroused.

It was appalled to find itself in the grip of a mind far mightier than its own, enraged to feel the attentive awareness of that other, hated mind that had bound it, and frightened to discover that two other minds of power were also in contact with it. Its struggles were feeble—or rather, crushed before they could amount to anything—until it was suddenly elsewhere, in the blinding light and warmth, in air instead of water, and surrounded by so many angry and excited minds that the dracolich was overwhelmed anew, and frankly cowered.

Then the four minds that had gripped it so powerfully were gone, and it was free. Attacked by thousands of armed humans rushing at it from all sides, but unhampered at last—at *last!*—and so, free to give battle. It beat its bony wings, shattering trees and swiftly learning how entangled by the forest it was—and also discovering that it had lost the power to fly; that part of its undeath and magic had been stripped from it.

That plunged it into a darker, deeper rage than it had ever felt in all its life and unlife, and it lost no time in venting that fury. The minds all around it flared up into fresh rages of their own—and fear. Fear that Tlossaryl reveled in, as it slew, maimed, and slew some more.

By then, the Srinshee was thrusting ruthless mental barbs—long black lances of her contempt and revulsion—deep into the mind of the eye tyrant Xoraulkyr, shattering its arrogant confidence that it was superior to all other minds, and had been ensnared by the human Elminster only through luck and deceit. While it was still reeling mentally, too aghast at being so wounded to gather the will to slap down any of the four minds riding it, it was suddenly no longer in the bricked-up Waterdhavian cellar Elminster had put it into stasis in, but—elsewhere.

Specifically, a glade in deep shade, roofed over by the interwoven branches of a thick stand of duskwoods, where shades and arcanists of Thultanthar were arguing over where to send their "idiot troops" to most swiftly smash what elf resistance remained.

"I've always hated commanders who led from the rear," the Srinshee whispered into Xoraulkyr's mind confidingly, her words carrying into the thoughts of her three companions. "Let them taste unleashed beholder, and learn a little!"

An instant later, Xoraulkyr thudded heavily to the trodden moss of the forest floor, eyestalks writhing in pain. It sought to soar, to lash out at these astonished humans before they could work the magics they were even now frantically calling up—but found, as the Thultanthans scattered, fleeing for the encircling trees, that it couldn't even rise off the ground. At all. It was what it had always been: a beholder of massive size for its kind, a sphere the size of a small human coach. Which meant it was so heavy that if it rolled without great care, it crushed its own eyestalks under its bulk.

Xoraulkyr painfully rediscovered this very flaw just before the first spells tore into it. Their force awakened agony and flung it away in a clumsy, bouncing roll, to fetch up against the trunk of a large duskwood where the eye tyrant rested, stretching its eyestalks in a swift wild spasm and then unleashing its magic back at those who'd just harmed it.

The glade erupted in magic so ferocious that trees started to topple, or were blasted to shards that were flung far away through the forest.

By then, the Srinshee was dumping another beholder into another group of commanders, a gathering of mercenary war captains who were strolling and chatting idly, pursuing war in far idler fashion than the shades and arcanists. To a man—and they were all men, ruthless louts of veteran killers, every one—they were most interested, at the moment, in emptying wineskins as fast as their servants could pour them into flagons. The war captains were toasting their guests, a dozen hired mages, but the Srinshee made sure none of those wizards would be fleeing with all that much alacrity, by breaking one ankle of each mage she saw.

And then she let go of El's hand to break the ring and give them all a moment to breathe and collect their own wits, while she called on the mythal she'd helped shape, to let her far scry the four centers of mayhem they'd just kindled.

"Mayhem," she commented with some satisfaction, after she'd looked for a few moments at each fray, "is certainly spreading. It might just become widespread among the besiegers of Myth Drannor, if you can find us four more champions as powerful as *that* quartet among your bindings, El."

"I believe I can," Elminster replied, managing a slow grin. It felt good to be rid of burdens, and he was carrying *so* many.

"Good. Do so. Then I'll leave you three to get on with destroying Weave anchors, and—"

"*Destroying* Weave anchors?" El came to his feet in a wild rush, aghast. "We've been renewing them, and crafting new ones! Why, the Weave may collapse, and cause all magic to go wild, if we take away its anchors! What—"

"Madness is this? Desperate times, desperate measures, my firesword! You're right about the danger, of course, but Larloch—and Shar—expect you to rush around strengthening anchors. They are depending on it. Only if the Weave holds strong here, around the mythal, can they drain the one and take over the other. They *need* someone else to hold the Weave steady so they can snatch it all, whereas if you sever it from its local anchors here, it becomes not a target stretched and held taut for their snatching, but a ragged bit of cloth blowing in wild winds that they can scarce see, let alone seize, as they rush past. Trust me."

El winced.

"Yes," the Srinshee told him softly, "I know you have just trusted and been betrayed, but I am no Larloch. Trust *me*. Destroy anchors, just hereabouts, as swiftly as you can—but take care to choose and destroy those that anchor both the mythal *and* the Weave, first. Wise crafters would have overlapped none, but . . . elves and humans alike are all too often unwise."

"And lazy," said Laeral.

"And in a hurry," Alustriel added.

"Indeed," the Srinshee agreed. "And have not all of us been all of those things, betimes? Yet let us not be those things today. Too much rides on victory. Which is why I've come back. Myth Drannor stands imperiled, so I am here."

Laeral regarded her unsmilingly. "You truly believe the city can be saved?"

The Srinshee shrugged. "Buildings are just that—buildings. The community has already been lost, turned from lives unfolding freely into waging constant war . . . but the people can be saved, some of them, to return and refound and rebuild once this threat is past. I'm here to salvage what *Tel'Quess* I can, and friends to the elves too. I came back because I could not bear to see it all be lost, while I did nothing. You three have brought me hope; with your meddling, perhaps Shar and the Shadovar who serve her, and Larloch who seeks to exalt himself, shall not prevail."

She looked into their eyes, one after another, and then added, "Now enough grand words. El, yield me up some more monsters!"

And she plunged right through his eyes into his mind, plucking at the minds of the two silver-haired sisters as she passed, and dragging them down and into the warm and familiar murk of Elminster's busy mind along with her. Images flashed past them, one melting through another with bewildering rapidity, some half familiar, some very strange. El steered the racing meteor that was the Srinshee, taking her down, down to where runes glowed and wrote themselves over and over in his remembrances, secret words were whispered, hiding places under stones and behind concealing spells were revealed, and—a mind flayer came striding.

It had baleful eyes, as it reached out its tentacles in another place and another time, uncoiling to stab into both Elminster's ears, to feed—but was instead ensnared in his waiting trap, stiffening in dismayed disbelief as its intrusion plunged into waiting magic meant to hook it alone, setting mental barbs deep so that to tear away would be to lose the greater part of its intellect. It tried to tear free anyway, tasting terror for the first occasion in a long time, but the leaking chaos washing across its thoughts, that lessened it and bewildered it, left it powerless to resist the tightening spell . . . and so it was that the illithid Qhelaraxxalarr was frozen, its mind whirling in an endless loop, its muscles locked. Shoved into a closet, hooded, and as the endless darkness began, sunk into a torpor by a chilling spell it had never felt before, even as it heard the thudding echoes of the closet being boarded up, blows that seemed to come from a vast distance, and that were followed by fainter hammerings that went on for a much longer time, as a false wall was built in front of the closet.

"Perfect," the Srinshee decreed. "Mind-wounded beyond recovery, but goaded by fear and anger into the feeding hunger. It won't last long, the moment the mercenaries see what's in their midst and any Shadovar with them decree it not of their recruiting." She whirled it away as Laeral and Alustriel worked busily on lifting Elminster's spells, and it was gone.

"Next!" she commanded briskly.

"How about another dragon? Only a little one, but deadly. It can't fly, having no wings—nor does it have a breath weapon—both thanks to arcanists of Thultanthar, as it happens, and their eagerness to experiment on dragonkind. But it can take human shape, and once it escaped the arcanists and went on a slaying spree, slaughtering any human mage it could find. 'Ware the poisonous stinging tail."

"You do have quite the menagerie, don't you?"

And so the unleashing went on, El groaning at the upheaval in his memories as long-forgotten oaths and sealing spells and bindings were dredged up.

"Hurts," he gasped several times, and by the time the last bound creature—a one-armed lich that wielded some *very* creative magics—was set among an encampment of the besiegers, El was staggering in a murk of his own making, lost to the world.

When he ran into his third tree, gentle but firm arms embraced him and sat him down, and from somewhere nearby he heard Alustriel murmur, "He's not doing well. A little silver fire?"

"*No*," the Srinshee said emphatically. "That'll draw arcanists galore down on us, and quite likely Larloch too. No, just let me . . ."

She murmured something, and cool, blessed relief flooded through Elminster's roiling thoughts like dappled sunlight dancing through leaves and falling through high windows onto the dark floor of his mind.

He was barely aware that he was being lifted and carried, by Laeral and Alustriel, who grunted and staggered from time to time under his dead weight and the awkwardness of conveying him over tree roots and the uneven forest floor. More than once, he felt a magical force thrust up beneath him out of nowhere, as if the air had suddenly become a firm and solid hand, to hold him up over the roughest stretches, or where the trees stood so thick and close that he had to be turned on his side and slid through and around boughs and trunks, to . . .

A place where he started to tingle all over. A Weave anchor!

He was propped against a tree trunk—a shadowtop, by the feel of the bark, and as large across as the wall of a good-sized cottage—and left there, as Laeral and Alustriel and the Srinshee moved to form a box, with each of them and himself as a corner. The magic they worked then roused his mind out of the Srinshee's healing mist, into full awareness of the forest around him again, and of what they were doing.

Destroying a Weave anchor, that was also one of the places the mythal of Myth Drannor was rooted. It was like shifting a downspout while storm rain was racing down it, rain that tugged at him and tore a little of his essence away.

Shocking him utterly awake. He blinked and groaned.

"Get up!" The Srinshee was shoving at his chest and armpits, trying to make him stand from where he'd slumped down the tree trunk. "*Up*! The sooner you're on your feet and able to think, the sooner I can be fighting! I can win you more time by defending my city than helping you three do away with anchors—which must be done with care, remember, or the Weave *will* be lost!"

"And Mystra," Alustriel warned.

"Not necessarily. That's the foremost reason Mystra is hiding from the wider world—to withdraw herself from the Weave as much as possible. She told me so, and said her other important reason is to not provoke Shar into taking a hand openly—lest the Dark Goddess sweep the most important mortals who oppose her off the board before we have a chance to play."

"This isn't a *game*," Laeral flared.

The Srinshee turned to her. "Isn't it? To Shar, it certainly is. Remember that. She doesn't want to destroy the prize to win it, or she'd have done so long ago. Playing the game is what sustains her, not winning."

The sisters both stared at her, openmouthed, as Elminster tried to remember how to nod. And managed it with some satisfaction.

"After she destroys or enthralls all mortals," the Srinshee added, almost fiercely, "where will she gain the loss, forgetfulness, and oblivion she feeds upon? Did you never ponder why the world hadn't been destroyed by the gods who feed on destruction long before any of us could have been born? It never ends—it's not meant to. If we defeat Shar's pawns now, she'll withdraw and seduce new ones and scheme anew. If you think of her thus, and talk not of 'forever' and other absolutes, it becomes easier to bear—and easier to correctly foresee what any deity will do. Even the mad ones."

"Especially the mad ones," Elminster muttered.

"Which, from the point of view of most crofters and shopkeepers, is every last one of them," Laeral said wryly.

Alustriel, however, was frowning at the Srinshee. "How can you be sure of what Shar will do?"

"I *know* her," came the bleak reply. "Far better than I care to. I was the Herald of Mystra before El was—stars and seas, before any of you were *born*. I met many of the gods, often." The Srinshee shook her head and added in a whisper, "I am . . . too old for this now."

She turned away. "So come on. If he can't walk straight yet, bring him."

Elminster waved away helping hands, started striding after the Srinshee—and fell flat on his face.

Grinning and shaking their heads, Laeral and Alustriel hauled him to his feet, put their arms around his shoulders, and started walking him through the forest. Six stumbling steps later they lost patience, exchanged glances, slid long locks of silver hair under their burden's thighs from behind, and boosted him off his feet into a chair lift.

Enthroned, Elminster was whisked over a wooded ridge, across a tangled ravine beyond, and over a second ridge. Where mercenaries came charging out of the trees with a triumphal roar.

The Srinshee sighed, waved one arm without slowing, and paid no attention at all to the startled cries of pain—or the thuds and abruptly-cut-off yells that followed, when the weapons and bucklers racing away from her towed their mercenary owners into swift and brutal meetings with trees.

Not a single besieger reached the two silver-haired women and the bearded old man bouncing between them.

"Here!" said the Srinshee, a ridge later, as they came upon an ancient stump the size of a large coach, with a tiny spring fountaining out between its rotting roots. "Triangle, the three of us, and put El between us. When the anchor breaks, mind you thrust the leakage into him!"

It was Laeral's turn to frown. "But won't that—?"

The Srinshee gave her a look that was somewhere between patiently polite and withering.

"Ah." Laeral winced. "You've done this before. Yes."

The anchor gave way with frightening ease, and Elminster's body arched and bucked as Weave and mythal energies snarled through him, leaking out of his mouth as brief blue flames.

He rolled over, coughing weakly.

The Srinshee clapped him on the back, kissed the startled face he raised to her, and announced briskly, "Right, only forty-two more to go! I'm off!"

And she hurled herself away through the air like a sling stone—to slam into an arcanist who was just stepping out from behind a tree to hurl a blasting spell at Elminster and the two sisters. He was flung backward into an awkward stagger, and the Srinshee pursued him, slicing his throat open with a dagger as she flashed past.

About then, she noticed the arcanist she'd felled was just the foremost of a dozen more hastening through the trees to investigate the magical turmoil of the anchor being destroyed.

She fetched up on a high bough, rebounded off the trunk it had grown out of to reclaim her balance, and cast a spell of her own.

As El, Laeral, and Alustriel watched, the Srinshee's working became a mighty explosion in the heart of those approaching arcanists. Tattered bodies—some collapsing into disembodied heads, limbs, and hands in midair—hurtled in all spattering directions.

Then, with a cheery wave, she was gone.

"Well," Alustriel said rather ruefully, "that seems to be that. We're on our own."

"Which means," El agreed, "that we'd best be finding the next anchor. *She* remembers where they all are. I . . . recall a few. Luse, Laer, 'tis done like thi—"

Laeral gave him a withering look, and pointed through the trees.

"Ah," Elminster said hastily, "my apologies."

"Accepted, *Old* Mage," she replied pointedly, leading the way.

Which meant the Shadovar warriors who burst out of the next thicket came at her first, thrusting bills and glaives that she easily turned aside with her hair.

Alustriel's swarm of a dozen racing blue-white bolts arced and swooped into as many faces—and Elminster contributed an echo spell that followed up the magic missiles with stunning lightning.

Most of the mercenaries fell, but a few snarled in pain and kept coming, swinging swords and axes rather unsteadily.

The three Chosen met them blade to blade.

"After this anchor, we need only take care of forty-two more, remember," Elminster panted, amid the clang and clash of steel. "That should be enough to collapse the mythal at our bidding."

"Only?" Alustriel asked archly, as her tresses dashed two helms together hard enough to crumple metal. "Your words delight me."

"We must all find our delights where we can these days," Laeral commented, ducking under a vicious axe swing and slamming the pommel of her blade hard into the ear of her would-be butcher. Who reeled right into Elminster's backswing.

Laeral sprang away from the gory result. "*Don't* get blood on this, you! It *never* all comes out!"

A mercenary was startled enough by her complaint to turn and gape at her, just for an instant—and that was all Elminster needed.

"Back in brawling form?" Alustriel grinned at him, as he rose from downing that last man and saw that there were no more mercenaries left to fight.

El smiled and shrugged. "Got my wind back, at least. Help me remember, you two; if we see the coronal, we *must* tell her where the portal that brought us here is located. When the city falls, it and the other portals nearby will be the only ways she'll be able to get any *Tel'Quess* out."

Laeral laid a hand on his arm. "You think any of us will get out, El?" she asked softly.

El shrugged. "Acting as if I know we all will is always best."

Laeral gave him a wry smile. "So you're always bluffing, no matter the danger?"

Elminster drew himself up and made a dignified reply. "Manipulating, *please*. 'Bluffing' is such a crass word. Merely bending others to do as I'd like them to do, by means of a little acting. Ye learn these things, when ye've lived through as many falls of cities and utter Realms-rending disasters as I have . . ."

Luse and Laer stared at him, then burst into wild, helpless laughter.

The Wizard of War and the six Purple Dragons with him came to a stop in the dingy back street in Suzail, all of them wearing deepening frowns.

"So just where is this treason you speak of?" The young mage's tone was openly suspicious. "This looks like all too good a place for an ambush, if you ask—"

"I didn't," the fat and wheezing man in the well-worn and food-stained clothing and the flopping wrecks of old seaboots interrupted, "and you needn't worry. I'll be going first." And he flung open the nearest door.

"Yes," the wizard snapped, "but how do we know you aren't working with some miscreants, and leading us right into their clutches?"

Mirt caught hold of a good fistful of the young war wizard's splendid doublet and dragged him down until they were nose to nose.

"You can come with me, young fearfulguts," he growled, "because I'll be needing you. But mind this: *no* casting spells, and *no* yelling at enemies of the Crown, until I say so, hear? You may have standing orders and the shiny authority of the Dragon Throne—but I've managed to keep myself alive for more years than you've seen, *without* having spells down both arms and stuffed up my backside to resort to! So, do we have an agreement?"

"W-we do," Narancel replied, with as much dignity as he could muster. He made a little show of brushing the breast of his doublet smooth again with apparent unconcern.

"Good." Mirt grinned at him. "Then follow me up these stairs *quietly*."

"But—but this building's been cleared out for a tenday, after two clerks came down with blacktongue! We—"

Mirt's withering look reduced the protesting mage to silence, and he followed the rotund and wheezing merchant up the narrow and dim back stairs as quietly as possible. As he did, Narancel wondered why they didn't just go in the front way, but he took care to wonder it mutely.

Two flights up, he heard voices. Mens' voices where there should be none. Mirt turned with a warning finger held straight up against his lips, then went on. The wizard followed, taking great care to be as quiet as he could.

They were close enough, now, to hear what was being said.

"So you see, I'm prepared to pay you this handsomely *just to do your duty*. Nothing beyond the rules, nothing that can get you in trouble. You are *supposed* to inspect noble estates—and their city properties too—from time to time, without warning, to make sure what they tell the Crown tax clerks to be so is, in fact, so. Oh, the particular nobles on my little list, here . . . ah, *your* little list, yes? . . . will be less than pleased, but then, they always are, aren't they?"

"It's—if anyone higher finds out—" That voice was anxious, and was echoed by the wordless murmurs of others. Worried others.

"Ah, but they won't, if none of you talk. See how short that list is? All you have to do is remember *one* name each from it—just one—and it becomes your choice, and I destroy the list, and—behold!—there's no evidence left, at all! Now, what say you?"

"I—I—oh, I don't know . . . ," the worried voice mumbled, sounding very unhappy.

Which was when Mirt laid a firm hand on the war wizard's arm, tugged meaningfully, and let go to lurch and wheeze his way through the door and around the corner to give the room of startled men—six palace courtiers and one Manshoon—a nod of greeting and a lopsided grin.

"Well *done*, men of Cormyr! Well done!" he told them heartily. "You passed this little test as Cormyreans staunch and true! Proving yer honesty and loyalty to the Crown as boldly as any battle-tested Purple Dragon! The Forest Kingdom is proud of you!"

Clasping his hands behind his back, he started to stroll. Mainly to make sure the tremulous young fool of a war wizard had indeed dared to follow him into the room—aye, he had, thank all the gods for small beneficences—but also to put one or two courtiers between him and any little magic an annoyed Manshoon might hurl.

"You rightly saw through the stratagem our peerless actor here"—he waved at the glowering Manshoon—"was so smoothly attempting to recruit you into abetting. It would create dissent among certain noble families whose support the Dragon Throne sorely needs right now. You didn't know it, but more than a dozen Wizards of War have been watching and listening to it all! Worry not; every last one of you has impressed them. Young Narancel here will escort you back to your offices now, and will echo my praise. Cormyr's future is bright in your hands!"

Mirt swung around to give Narancel a look. Damned if the young pup wasn't shaking like a sapling in a fall wind, but at least he knew his cue, and nodded, waving to the courtiers to come with him.

They bolted, almost upsetting their chairs in their relieved haste, and were gone in a door-banging trice. Leaving Mirt alone with a seething Manshoon. The onetime ruler of Zhentil Keep and of Westgate, founder and longtime leader of the Zhentarim—and a vampire, to boot.

Who would kill him in an instant or three if he so much as suspected it was all a ruse, and those more than a dozen war wizards were so much utter fiction.

Manshoon's smile was as hard as cold crypt stone. "I can think of no magical defenses you can have, fat man," he remarked with menacing softness, "that will protect you against me if I choose to destroy you now. In slow, writhing agony."

Mirt chuckled, and took the seat right across from Manshoon. "Ah, so you still can't think—clearly enough and ahead far enough. Yer usual problem, if you don't mind me pointing it out. The salient point on the table between us right now is this: you don't *know* what defenses I have. I, however, obviously do. Care to be foolish enough to think I'm bluffing?"

Manshoon scowled, then shook his head.

Mirt produced a belt flask with two metal flagons clipped to it, and poured them both wine.

He handed one flagon across the table to Manshoon, who regarded it dubiously. Mirt took it back, drank deeply from it, and handed Manshoon the other, still-full flagon.

Slowly, Manshoon put out his hand, took it, sipped—and then smiled. The wine was splendid.

He sipped again and savored it, sitting back and letting it roll around on his tongue.

Mirt leaned forward and rumbled, "So, Scourge of Westgate and Zhentil Keep and the gods alone know how many other places . . . why don't we sit this one out, the two of us? Hmm? At least until half Toril is done tearing itself apart?"

Manshoon regarded the fat and battered man across the table thoughtfully for a long, silent time before he said, "Convince me."

He sipped again. "More of this wine ought to do it."

CHAPTER 17

A Good Day to Butcher Elves

I N THE THIRD OF STORM'S KITCHEN CUPBOARDS HE ROOTED through, Arclath made a discovery. He drew the square, human-head-sized wooden box out into the light, set it on the kitchen table, and used his dagger to warily undo the latches and flip the lid, then peered in.

Rune watched him tensely from across the room, where she was washing radishes in one of the sinks.

Arclath relaxed with a pleased little crow of satisfaction.

"Well?" Rune asked, daring to relax a little.

Triumphantly, Lord Delcastle lifted something large and round out of the box, drew aside the soft black cloth swaddling it, and held it up. A crystal ball.

"We *shouldn't*," Rune told him, though she knew she was looking at it longingly.

"You need to know what's happening," her man replied. "It's eating you, not knowing. I can see that. Hells, anyone could see that."

"Put it back in the box," Rune told him firmly. "For now. But leave the box out."

"While I scour all the rest of the cupboards?"

"Lord Delcastle," Amarune replied, assuming the manner of a mildly peeved noble Cormyrean matron, "do you really think it prudent to plunder the secrets, if nothing more, of so gracious—and powerful—a host? *I* hardly do."

Arclath shrugged. "Prudence, my *good* lady, has never been one of my strengths. If the Dragon Throne values me at all, it is this well-known lack of prudence that they cherish. So . . ." He advanced on the next bank of cupboards, but couldn't resist glancing over his shoulder to see Rune's reaction.

In doing so, his gaze fell upon the pantry door. Or rather, upon its frame. Where his thoughts seemed to linger.

"I wonder . . . ," he said thoughtfully.

"What?" Rune asked, finishing with the radishes and reaching for a hand cloth to dry her hands.

His only reply was to open the pantry door, stand back, and peer at the revealed lintel, threshold, and standing frame. Then he reached out warily, wrapped his fingertips around the lines of the molding, and tugged gently.

And with the softest of sighs, the door frame swung open on hidden hinges, to reveal a hidden cupboard behind. The narrowest of cupboards, within the thickness of the stone wall, its door only a finger's width or two wider than the palm of his hand. It was full of bone tubes with carved end caps.

Cautiously, he drew one out. There was a word graven on the nearest end cap, and repeated on the side.

"Teleport," Rune read aloud, over his shoulder, thankful she could move with swift silence when she wanted to. She snaked her arm under his and deftly snatched the tube out of Arclath's fingers. "We'll be needing this."

Arclath grinned, but also crooked an eyebrow. "Can you pull off a spell like that?"

301

Amarune gave him her best cold glare. Under its weight, he added hastily and falteringly, "I mean—so powerful, need practice, wizards of much experience, usually . . ."

"I am Elminster's heir. His new Chosen One," Rune reminded him icily. "I can do *anything*."

Her man decided it was his turn to tender a withering look.

Rune smiled wryly, but didn't blush. "Magically, that is," she admitted, "and in all this spell chaos, perhaps as well as any caster can."

She lifted her chin in determination. "If I have to, I have to. There is no 'fail,' or we *all* fail."

Arclath shook his head, smiling at her in obvious admiration.

"Stop mooning over me and hand me that crystal ball," Rune snapped. "And *don't* drop it."

Arclath put it into her hands with exaggerated care. "You've used one before, of course?" he asked, as gently as any deferential servant.

"You *know* I haven't," she flared. "Stop trying to be helpful and—and eat some radishes!"

And she set the sphere—gods, but it was heavy, far heavier than she'd expected—on the table on its swaddling cloth that she tugged into a ring around it.

That did nothing at all to stop the crystal rolling. The hand-carved and well-worn tabletop was a little less than level. She put out a hand to pin the sphere in place, but sighed. She couldn't use it while holding it, could she?

Without a word, Arclath reached into the box, brought out a thick slab of wood with a bowl-shaped depression sculpted into it, and set the sphere into this rest that had obviously been made for it.

Amarune thanked him with a grimace, flung her arms wide to clear her head, and leaned forward to peer into the empty, colorless depths of the crystal.

Not empty, no, there was something there after all . . . stirring . . .

She had to focus on people—well, Storm, of course—or places. That is, memorable fixtures that sat in one spot unmoving, like trees. The problem with people, she half remembered something Elminster had mentioned in passing, was that they moved, and had thoughts of their own, and so were hard to "settle on."

So it was with Storm. To call to her to mind was to see Rune's own memories, of Storm turning to smile, Storm speaking sharply, Storm looking impish as her hair reared up like a snake about to strike, Storm . . . Rune sighed. She could call Storm to mind vividly enough, but her parade of memories did nothing at all to the crystal.

So, then, places, or rather, things in places. That distinctive rotten stump, the one the size of a large oval dining table that Arclath had scrambled over to . . .

She could remember it, all right, and something stirred in the crystal, its heart going milk white, but then her sharpening concentration *veered*, as if she was on a racing horse that decided on its own to turn sharply to the right.

Well, then, that sapling she'd put her hand on, to catch her breath, after . . . no, the same thing was happening. Veering to the left this time, mind, but . . .

Something was blocking her.

Oh.

The mythal.

Of course.

So, focus on something outside the mythal. Downdragon Tor.

And the milky hue in the depths of the crystal spun, winked, flashed, and Rune was seeing the same view she and Arclath had enjoyed upon their arrival there. Just like that.

Not by night and moonlit, this time, but the same vast carpet of green treetops, spread out before her and stretching into the misty distance.

A bird flew past, startling her. This was no still picture; she was seeing Downdragon as it was right now.

Nice, but she needed something nearer the siege. If the mythal was weakening as badly as she'd feared it was, she might be able to use trees and ridges she'd glimpsed while they were fighting in the forest. Wait, that dead, leafless duskwood, silhouetted against the bit of sky that had gone orange from the Shadovar spell . . . yes . . .

Yes! There it was, in the crystal! With drifting smoke from some campfires beyond it, the scene in the crystal moving and alive . . . which should mean she could look at something—those two dark, entwined trees—at the far left of what she was seeing, make them the center of her view, then look left again, and so face Myth Drannor.

Or what was left of it.

She'd half expected to see a milky shroud blocking any clear view of the city, but there was nothing like that. Just scorched towers and splintered and smoldering trees and a few still-beautiful, leaping bridges arcing between them, cascading gardens of flowing water and lush, spreading plants—and corpses. Everywhere the dead, heaped and strewn and being trodden underfoot by hurrying still-alive elves in blood-besmirched armor, and inexorably tramping mercenaries. Some bridges were broken, abrupt jagged ends thrusting out into empty air, and others trailed what had seemed at first glance to be creeping vines, but that Rune now saw were dangling bodies.

The besieging Shadovar forces were tightening their grip, the exhausted elf defenders ceding more and more of their city—which was being hurled down by the spells of arcanists, tower by tower and bridge by bridge crashing to the forest floor.

And just *there*, Rune saw, was the lashing tail of an angry *dragon* that was crawling around, seemingly unable to fly and obviously seething with rage!

"We *have* to be there," she told Arclath. "Every last sword and spell is needed. If I could somehow snatch up all the Purple Dragons on duty in Cormyr right now and set them down in the heart of that siege, I'd do it." She turned to give her beloved a hard look. "But I can't, so you'll have to be all of them."

"Lady," her lord replied, eyes bright with unshed tears, "command me."

"We go back to Myth Drannor. Now."

Arclath nodded, and then spoke like an imperious noble. "Use the jakes first," he ordered briskly. "Both of us. Then finish this soup. We don't know when we'll next—"

"Now I know how the endlessly annoying nobles of Cormyr continue to lord it over the Forest Kingdom," Amarune snapped, smiling despite herself. "They always finish their soup."

Arclath bowed low, indicating the garderobe door with a courtly flourish. Then he held it open for her.

She lifted her chin, for all the world as if she'd been born noble, and in one of the haughtiest houses at that, and went in, reading the teleport scroll to herself.

He closed the door behind her, regarded its dark and polished wood, and murmured, "All gods bear witness, I *love* you, Rune. Was ever a man so fortunate as I?"

"Yes," a ghostly voice answered him, from somewhere behind him in the room.

Arclath spun around, sword half out, staring everywhere, shocked into silence.

The voice—gentle and low, coming out of nowhere, a woman's tones—added, "Yet lovers are so easily lost. Treasure every moment you have left together."

"Who—who *are* you?" he asked, sword out as he peered around, trying to see where the voice was coming from.

"Once, I was Syluné. Eldest of the Seven. They called me the Witch of Shadowdale. Now I am but an echo in the Weave. Your Amarune is doing the right thing, young lord of Cormyr. May victory be yours." The voice faded steadily as it spoke, and by that last victory wish, Arclath could hear it no more.

The garderobe door swung open. Amarune peered out, frowning. "Who were you talking to?"

"A-a ghost," Arclath replied, as he rushed to embrace her.

Their kiss was fierce and deep, but brief—as Rune broke free and whirled away from him, to point at the door and command, "Hurry!"

It was dimly blue wherever they looked, and everywhere they beheld blue leaves and green glowing softly against the dark brown of old dead leaves and the brown-black of forest soil. On all sides the great dark pillars of duskwoods and blueleaf trees soared up to an almost unbroken blue-green canopy. In every direction, over gentle hills cloaked in endless trees, the vista looked much the same.

"Where by Shar's howling holy darkness *are* we?" Mattick snapped. "These *tluining* trees!"

He slashed at the nearest leaves in his temper, sending them spiraling down to the moss-girt fallen trunks underfoot.

"Still in the forest," Vattick offered, mock-helpfully.

They'd been fleeing wildly through the seemingly endless deep woods around Myth Drannor for some time now, just the two of them. Both were scorched, breathless, and bedraggled.

They'd escaped death by the proverbial hair-slicing thickness of a sharp sword blade's edge, by both desperately working the same last-moment spell to forcibly swap places with Shadovar arcanists elsewhere in the siege.

306

So two bewildered unfortunates had almost certainly died in the spells hurled by the coronal and her four high mages, while Mattick and Vattick, wounded and more frightened than they'd been in battle for a long time, had found themselves out in the forest surrounded by startled mercenaries.

Whom they'd departed from the company of immediately, for they were interested now only in getting away. To Shar's never-seen rump with their father's grand plans, and with butchering their ways through this old and overgrown elf city they'd never seen before and didn't care one whit if they ever saw again! It was time to get gone, far and fast, and—and seek their own lives, for as long as they could.

Oh, the Most High would find them soon enough, and that meeting would be less than pleasant, but in the meantime they were still alive, and—

"I," Mattick vowed, crashing through some dead branches and seeking a little open ground to stride through, "am going to get me some folk *I* can lord it over, for once. I'm done with all of this conquer worlds upon worlds for the greater glory of Shar!"

"And the greater satisfaction of Telamont Tanthul," Vattick agreed, before he came to a frowning stop.

"Brother," he added, "I thought we were leaving Myth Drannor behind, but look."

He pointed with his sword through the trees ahead.

Mattick peered and swore.

"Elves! *More* bloody elves! Everywhere we go, it's rutting, fluting-voiced, tree-swinging elves!"

The twin princes strengthened their wards and strode to meet these new foes, who likewise stalked through the trees to meet them.

As they got closer, both princes could see bodies, both human and elf, strewn here and there, and some shattered walls and towers that were now mostly heaps of rubble.

"We must have got turned around, somehow," Vattick mused. "That, or Myth Drannor spreads through the forest farther than I'd thought, with far-flung clusters of buildings and wild forest between them."

"I," declared Mattick, "am beyond caring about elf architecture or settlement patterns. I just want to hew me some longears! Yeeeeee*arrrgh*!"

And with that sudden bellow, he launched himself into a wildly swinging charge. Vattick planted his sword in the soft forest mold beside him and worked magic instead—and as the elf warriors closed in, limp bodies and blocks of rubble rose into the air behind them, to whirl forward in silent haste and dash the elves to the ground.

Preparing to hack his way into half a dozen foes, Mattick found them all writhing helplessly at his feet, so it was ease itself to ruthlessly stab through the backs of their necks, one by one.

Only one determined elf reached him upright, and that was after four elf corpses had slammed into that elf from behind. Off-balance and winded, the elf could only parry desperately as Mattick slashed at his face. Which left him vulnerable to the prince's hearty crotch kick.

As the elf was propelled into the air, mewing in shocked pain, Mattick moved to where he could hack the falling body viciously—and did so. The elf's neck broke at his second blow, and its owner slammed heavily into the ground, loose limbed and dead or dying.

Mattick regarded his work with some satisfaction, but Vattick slapped his arm on the way past and hissed, "Come *on*. There'll be plenty more showing up if we tarry!"

Mattick sighed, nodded, and followed his brother over a heavily wooded ridge, and down into a little dell ringed by the smooth-curved walls of elf buildings that looked more like gigantic garden plantings than dwellings. Fearful-faced elf children and wrinkled elders emerged from the arched doorways of some of the buildings, all heading off to the princes' left.

A lot of children, but only a few withered elders—and no other sort of elves at all.

The two princes looked at each other, then nodded in unison, hefted their swords, and started forward.

"It's *always* a good day to butcher elves," Vattick hissed, as they began their charge.

Storm was fighting hard in the teeth of the fray.

She was drenched with blood not her own, and despite subsuming the spark of silver fire she'd swallowed in her kitchen—the spark that had once belonged to her fallen sister Syluné—she was more than tired. She kept her matted silver tresses plucking up fallen daggers whenever she saw them and hurling them at the hireswords she couldn't reach, the ones crowding to get at her from behind the men she was busy killing at the moment.

And those men seemed endless. The Myth Drannor still in elf hands was down to just a few buildings, the battered and weary defenders dwindling to mere hand counts—and *still* the Shadovar hirelings came pouring out of the trees, a forest of moving helmed heads that outnumbered the trees within sight.

There could be only one end to this, and it might well come very soon.

Slashing open a warrior's throat and kicking his body down off the high stump he'd joined her atop won her a few moments to draw breath and twirl for a proper scan all around.

That whirlwind of dying mercenaries was Fflar and three or four elf knights fighting with him, and—

There. That was the coronal. Fighting hard, too, with none too many knights and not a single high mage left to stand with her in battle.

"Sorry, saers—must run!" Storm called merrily to the besiegers warily approaching her stump, and she sprang down to hit the ground sprinting. She might as well get as close to the coronal as she could before she had to stop and hack and hew the rest of the way.

Storm could still run like the wind when she had to, and got surprisingly far, but her reward for that was to have a score of silver-plate-armored armsmen converge on her. Obviously all stalwarts hailing from the same elite mercenary company.

All that gleaming armor gave her an idea, but she would have to time things *just* right. When the foremost trio of the shiny helms reached her, Storm backed away hastily, looking scared.

And as she'd hoped, one of them fell for her ruse, sneering at her and swaggering forward, drawing back a great war axe for a cleaving blow.

Storm sprang at him like a panther, reversing her sword and dagger so two hard pommels slammed into the axeman's nearest elbow, driving his swing farther back than he'd intended. He overbalanced with a profanely startled yell—and crashed back into the knees of his fellow full-plate mercenaries, driving them back in turn. One crashed back into the hurrying man behind him, and the other fell unopposed to the ground but bounced and flailed, tripping another mercenary who was at a full run, charging to get at Storm.

Which meant all these stalwarts were in clanging contact, so it was time.

Storm spent a tiny spurt of silver fire—as chain lightning.

And saw it leap and crack from man to man, back along the colliding stream of them.

Grunts became screams, but she hadn't time to watch the fun; she needed all the time their disablement and brief careers as spasming, helplessly convulsing armored barriers would buy her to get to the coronal.

As it happened, Ilsevele Miritar was no fool in battle, and between foes, she constantly snatched moments to glance around her. So she saw Storm while the blood-drenched Chosen was still far off, but sprinting her way, and turned to slash her own route to meet Storm.

She hewed her way through five besiegers—then six—the last one a tall hulk of a man in bright armor that didn't fit him, sobbing his way down into death. Falling to reveal another dying, sagging mercenary beyond him, dying in the arms of . . . Storm Silverhand.

"Well met!" Ilsevele greeted her, and they traded wry smiles. Both knew things were far from well for the defenders, and would rapidly get very worse.

"You must get all the *Tel'Quess* out you can, *now*!" Storm panted. "The city is lost!"

"I know," the coronal agreed grimly. "We're doing that already. The youngest ones first, with the weakest of our elders—to guide and teach them, should the rest of us fall. You know Iymurr's Gate?"

Storm nodded.

"Find the door in its tallest tower adorned with a diagonal line of four star gems. Pluck them out, reverse each one and put it back in, and a portal will form, right there—if the mythal is too weak to prevent it." And with a sigh, the coronal added, "And I've been feeling the mythal weakening more and more, as the day draws on."

Storm nodded again, but said not a word. This must be heartbreaking for Ilsevele; she wasn't going to say anything to make it worse.

"That way leads to Semberholme," the coronal went on. "But if the portal won't open, then any who gather to take it will be trapped there and doomed if these Shadovar-serving slaycoins take that end of the city. There'll be no other way out."

Storm shrugged and hefted her sword. "With this I'll make one, if I have to. May we all live to see another dawn."

They embraced, kissed, then whirled and rushed their separate ways, back into the hard-fought slaughter.

Some of the arcanists were reluctant to leave their towers. Thultanthar was now close enough to Myth Drannor that nine or more rising pillars of smoke, where some of the mercenaries had set fires, could clearly be seen from high windows and balconies of their city—and they wanted to miss nothing.

"Accursed spectators," Gwelt muttered darkly. "They'd sit and watch the world get devoured, and never lift a hand to defend it, for fear of spoiling the spectacle."

Aglarel gave Gwelt a grim half smile as he nodded, but he said not a word. His attention was on the arcanists hastening to obey the summons of the Most High and assemble in the great courtyard below. There would be few better moments for treachery than this one, with the High Prince of Thultanthar walking among most of the city's arcanists, arranging them to stand in the best places for the spell-linkage.

So the great mythal-draining magic could begin.

It would take the services of most of the arcanists of the city, and they were streaming into the courtyard, converging on the Most High. Telamont was warded and mantled, of course, but such defenses do little against a spellcaster standing so close as to be within all wards and mantles. Wherefore Prince Aglarel was worried and intent on seeing every person, at every last moment.

"I'll happily attend you later, Gwelt," he muttered almost absently, moving to a better vantage point. "When I have rather fewer duties to perform all at once."

"Of course," Gwelt agreed quickly, backing away.

He took great care to step behind several hurrying arcanists, so Aglarel—and the prince's father too, for that matter—wouldn't see him slip away from the swiftly growing assembly.

Not that he need have bothered. Aglarel had already spotted something that alarmed him—the patiently inexorable way another arcanist was stalking toward the Most High—and was hurrying to deal with it.

The commander of the Most High's personal bodyguard was fast, and imposing enough with his height and manner and well-known obsidian armor that arcanists hastily got out of his way, yet even so he was almost too late.

The suspicious arcanist threw up both hands and sent a shrapnel-star spell rushing across the heads of his fellows. A magic that would have sent jagged blades of steel thrusting in all directions among the assembled Thultanthans.

Even before Aglarel's hasty counterspell sent the shrapnel star veering away, its creator had started to bellow.

"Fellow citizens of Thultanthar! I call on you to refrain from what is contemplated here, to not assist in this draining of great magic! For this is madness, madness I tell you, and imperils our city! If we do this, our own Thultanthar will in turn be destroyed! I—*eyyyurkkh!*"

Aglarel's sword met the shouting man's skull hard but cleanly.

It was like cleaving a large and wet melon, but Aglarel cared not how much he got splattered, or how many fellow Thultanthans got covered in blood. He went right on brutally beheading the man from behind.

313

The body reeled, spurting blood in all directions, and Aglarel sprang atop it and bore it bloodily to the flagstones, holding it down as its writhing became sluggish . . . and then stopped altogether.

He looked up, drenched in blood, and beheld his father, regarding him down a long open path that had almost magically opened in the jostling ranks of the arcanists.

Telamont looked calm, but impatient, as if expecting an explanation.

"Order," Aglarel told him, "has been restored."

His father nodded gravely, something that might have been thanks and might merely have been satisfaction in his eyes, and worked the swift and simple spell that would take his words to every ear.

Then he lifted his chin, looked at the arcanists all around him, and raised both arms.

"This," the Most High of Thultanthar announced calmly, "is how we shall begin . . ."

There were only six Moonstars still standing beside Dove, and they were as bloody, weary, and wounded as she was.

And they'd retreated, step by hard-fought step, until they could retreat no more. The central buildings of Myth Drannor stood on all sides, and not far behind their backs were the backs of the thin line of elf defenders facing the other way—who were somehow holding back besiegers still numerous enough to stretch back through the trees as far as the eye could see.

Dove suspected that "somehow" had a name, and it was Fflar. He'd been everywhere, smiting swiftly and moving on, blunting every mercenary charge.

She couldn't hope to match him. Her handful knew they were doomed, and were grimly leaning on their grounded blades and gasping for breath as they watched a fresh wave of mercenaries coming for them out of the forest.

Scores of them, hundreds . . . their slayers, and soon now. They had no hope at all of withstanding so many. The Shadovar coffers had been deep, and—

Something hissed horribly, off to the left, much nearer than the oncoming mercenaries.

Then it came into view around a many-towered elven mansion, writhing and struggling, and Dove gaped at it along with all the surviving Moonstars.

It was a black dragon of great size, an elder wyrm. It had been so badly—and recently—hacked at that it had no wings left, and limped heavily, one foot missing and the stump weeping blood, and the other legs crisscrossed by deep cuts. It moved more like a serpent, on its belly, than a great cat, whose gaits most of the dragons Dove had met resembled.

Its attention was bent on the mercenaries, and it struggled to meet them, hissing again in agonized rage.

Spears and glaives and shouts were all raised—and then it was among them, snarling a challenge, biting with its great jaws, and rolling to crush men by the score.

And after it, through the air, came a creature that made more than one Moonstar moan in dismay.

A floating sphere the size of a small wagon, from which projected a moving, serpentine forest of eyestalks. It was emitting horrible, hissing laughter.

"Free!" it exulted, fairly dancing in the air. "Free again at last! Blast me with all the spells you want, elves, if that's the result! Hahahahaha!"

"A *beholder*?" one Moonstar gasped. "Ye gods, what *next*?"

The eye tyrant glided to where it could hang above the lunging, rolling, biting dragon, and from that vantage point above the fray sent its eyebeams lancing down into the mercenaries. Who started to shriek in terror, and tried to flee—right through the gathered ranks of their fellows.

Turmoil spread.

Dove allowed herself one mirthless smile at that, before she turned to look in other directions. She half expected another menace to come creeping up while she and the Moonstars watched these two monsters who shouldn't be anywhere near here maraud through the foe.

The elf knights defending in the other direction were still holding, a fresh fire billowed up from somewhere beyond buildings to her right, and just a little way to the left of them she could see . . . the heads of running elves! The rest of the fleeing *Tel'Quess* were hidden from her, down in a dell.

Dove trotted to the nearest tree and scaled it until she was high enough to see who was running, and why.

She beheld ancient, wizened elves, elders, shooing and shepherding elf children in some haste from her right to her left. Beyond them, farther off but getting closer fast, were two shades with drawn swords in their hands. They were rushing at the elves, with clearly fell intent.

Dove flung herself from the tree and landed sprinting, heading for the dell as fast as she could. If anything could be salvaged from this dark day, it must be those children, the future of the *Tel'Quess* of this part of Faerûn . . .

"To me!" she shouted to the Moonstars, but didn't slow for a moment to see if they'd heeded or were following.

Down the long years, her way had not been that of the spell. Daughter of Mystra or not, the sword and a skilled tongue and the making and keeping of friendships had always served her better. Yet she'd studied her share of dusty tomes, even in the dim chambers of Candlekeep a time or two, and remembered some things.

Badly, for the most part, and never really thinking she'd need them. But now, as she sprinted over tree roots and through wet leaves and over slippery moss, Dove Falconhand gasped out what snatches she could remember of an ancient spell she'd read in one of Candlekeep's inner rooms, more than a few centuries ago.

It was a last resort magic of the elves, to be used when doom was imminent.

A spell that would summon baelnorn.

Lord and Lady Delcastle faced each other across the pleasant farm-house kitchen of Storm Silverhand, their faces grim.

"Lady mine," Arclath said gravely, "please misunderstand me not. I don't wish to dissuade you in what you attempt, nor mar what we have between us or your needed concentration. Yet I must ask: Are you ready for this? Do you know what you are doing?"

Amarune sighed gustily, neither in anger nor resignation, but to steady and calm herself, and told her beloved, "Yes. Yes, I think I do."

She gave him a little grin, then pointed at a particular flagstone in front of her and added sharply, "Now go and stand *just* there and belt up while I read the scroll through once more, and then read it aloud. We have to be touching, but mind, Lord Delcastle, this is no time for tickling me or otherwise amusing yourself."

"I understand that," Arclath told her dryly, moving to the indicated spot. "Yet I do have another question: How are you going to keep the scroll from rolling itself up?"

"I—" Rune ran out of answers, and stared at him helplessly.

"And we're going to rescue besieged Myth Drannor," Arclath told the ceiling. Then met her eyes, grinned, and suggested, "Why not have me stand on two corners of the scroll, unroll it, then you stand on the other two corners? Then you can look down between us, and read."

His lady nodded slowly. "That'll work," she said—and *just* managed not to sound surprised.

And so it was that Arclath Delcastle was grinning fondly at his ladylove when Storm's kitchen went away in sudden blue mists, and they fell out of that eerie sapphire place into . . . a forest where the dead and the flies were everywhere, and an army was tightening in a ring around the tall spires of a few buildings, and monsters of nightmare and legend were harrying that army . . .

And a spired stone city floated in the sky, vast and dark and blotting out the sunlight as it came scudding menacingly overhead.

CHAPTER 18

Low Cunning Prevails

DOVE SHOOK HER HEAD. IT WAS NO USE. SHE'D REMEMBERED the entire spell, she was sure—but nothing had happened. Whatever baelnorn still guarded their crypts somewhere beneath her would remain there. She'd have to do this alone.

As usual.

And her luck was turning for the worse. Also as usual.

She'd cast a look back to see if any of the Moonstars were following her—they weren't, only gawping in bewilderment at her sudden sprint across the landscape—and had seen that someone else was following her.

The big beholder who'd been hovering above the wounded black dragon happily slaying Shadovar mercenaries was drifting in her direction, eyestalks writhing menacingly.

And though she couldn't place from where, the creature seemed somehow familiar.

"Stars and spells, Mother!" Dove cursed aloud, "why now? How is it that *monsters* are here—here in the farruking mythal-guarded heart of Myth Drannor—to settle old scores, right in the midst of the elves' latest last stand?"

And with those words, running as hard as ever, she plunged over the edge.

Down into the dell, a green and pleasant place. There were the elves, the youngest sobbing in fear, and—

There they were, the pursuers. Wearing broad and arrogant grins as they came, striding unhurriedly, *enjoying* this. Two tall and muscular shades, twins—and *Tanthuls*, by the looks of them!

"Well, now," she panted aloud. "Princes of Shade! I'm honored. I think."

She'd be able to get between the two and the fleeing elves; that was what mattered. As she hastened to do that, Dove cast a swift look back over her shoulder, and saw what she'd expected to see.

The beholder didn't have to run over uneven ground or down steep slopes, and had glided serenely closer. The baleful gaze of its central eye was fixed on her.

"Hunh," she gasped at it. "Wait your turn."

And then she had no more breath to speak, because damned if these two running princes of Shade hadn't sped up, to try to run past before she could reach them.

Dove sprinted beyond breathlessness, putting on a burst of speed that left her staggering as they came rushing up, swinging their swords.

She ducked, feinted with her hips, saw the foremost shade's gaze follow her movement, swung her sword aloft to distract him further—and threw a perfect cross-body block across his midriff.

They slammed together like two charging bulls, Dove's hip sinking deep into a yielding gut—and the prince went helplessly cartwheeling.

Whereupon the other shade gleefully ran her through.

His steel felt like ice inside her, but he made the mistake of twisting his blade to do her more agony, rather than pulling it out of her to use again, making sure of her death. Instead, he turned the hilt sadistically as he made a sneering speech.

"I am Prince Vattick of Thultanthar, and your doom! So tell me, foolish wench, who are you?"

Dove kept her feet moving, and clawed her way up his blade before he could withdraw it. Which meant she was close enough to use the sharpest and strongest run of her own sword, the length just above the hilt. Her first slash almost took the prince's free hand off, and while he was busy screaming about that, she chopped at his sword hand.

Prince Vattick of Thultanthar promptly lost his grip on his blade, which meant she could lurch back far enough to swing—and slice his head off.

She turned, as it bounced in the dust, wearing a look of pained disbelief, to see what had become of the other prince, but the agony flaring inside her took her to her knees.

She shuddered, still impaled on the dead prince's sword, the sword that was now propping her up, its point caught on the backplate of her armor.

Mother Mystra, but it hurt!

The air above her darkened.

Of course.

Dove looked up through the welling pain. The beholder loomed above her, its wide and many-toothed smile gloating. "Dove Falconhand," it hissed, "do you remember me?"

She did, but still couldn't recall its name.

And then she did. "Glormorglulla," she gasped, her blood iron and fire in her mouth.

"The same," the eye tyrant purred. "And do you recall our last meeting?"

"No," she told it honestly, looking past it to try to see what had become of the fleeing elf children and elders and the other prince, but finding her vision was blurring, and everything was going dim.

She could hear screams and cries, but they sounded human, not elf.

"No," she said again, drifting through memories she hadn't brought to mind for a long time, but finding no scene nor recollection with Glormorglulla in it.

"You helped the accursed Elminster capture me," the beholder spat. "With your spells, you aided him, when he lacked the might to overcome me alone. *You* were responsible for my imprisonment. Yet fate and chance are sometimes wondrous—and now, at long last, I shall have my revenge."

"So be it," Dove hissed up at it, spitting out blood and feeling more flooding up into her mouth than she could hope to swallow.

She spat hastily, and managed to ask, "I wonder if you'll escape the curse I worked on you?"

"*What* curse?" the beholder asked, swooping down until its great eye towered over her. "What is this you speak of?"

It was a lie, an empty ruse, but Glormorglulla was close enough now for even her dying, agony-sapped mind to reach.

Dove glared up through the blood, and locked gazes and minds with the eye tyrant.

"*Saerevros,*" she murmured, and so sealed the blood lock.

The beholder could easily break free when she was dead, but until then it could win free of where she held it only if its mind could break hers.

"Not a chance," she mumbled aloud, as the first hint of horror dawned in Glormorglulla's fell gaze.

Dove held that dark and malevolent mind in thrall.

The eye tyrant struggled, at first furiously and then in growing terror, tugging—but failing. It couldn't move away, and couldn't use the powers of its eyes, thanks to her willing otherwise, but it could and did roll over and over in midair, and flail the passing breeze and her face and shoulders alike with its eyestalks.

Thrice it tried to devour her, its great jaws gaping, but she held it back with her strength of will, its fetid fangs clashing right in front of her nose as their minds wrestled.

She was dying, and her mind was weakening, and they both knew it. The frightened and furious Glormorglulla dared to hope, and anticipate, and even to gloat.

Whereupon she let it feel her full rage, and the silver fire that had started to spill from her weakening constraints.

Fire the beholder sought greedily to take from her, for was it not the fabled all-consuming power that humbled all magics? Would not an eye tyrant wielding silver fire be able to conquer all, and rule every last tree and river of Faerûn it desired?

Dove smiled bleakly into its great eye, and gave it what it wanted. Silver fire, unleashed and raging.

Rushing through the mind she was locked to, boiling and melting remorselessly, destroying so swiftly it barely had time to know true terror.

An awful reek rose around her as the malevolent beholder's brains fried.

Until Glormorglulla could think no more.

One by one, the small orbs at the ends of its writhing eyestalks burst, popping out gooey matter and then weeping a dark ichor. Then the great eye darkened and shriveled, until it looked like the largest raisin Dove had ever seen.

About then, her mind-hold failed. She was going fast.

Dully, she watched the husk of the great eye tyrant drift aimlessly away.

Well, she'd taken down one prince. Those elf elders would have to deal with his surviving brother.

"Florin," Dove gasped with her last breath, still draped over the sword that had slain her, tongues of silver fire blazing out between her lips. "I'm coming. Coming at last."

Magnificence and a dream restored in the heart of the forest, the City of Song—but the song was faint and faltering now.

It had all come down to this bitter end, here in this fiery blue cleft amid a last paltry handful of spired buildings. So fair and so doomed.

"Females first," the coronal ordered the elf knights around her briskly. "Young and old together—pair them if you can, but waste no time trying to do so."

Blue fire lit her face in flash after flash; the pulsing blue glow of the portal was reflecting back off the knights' armor, wherever it wasn't covered with gore.

"Of course," the eldest knight agreed, and spun away to see it done.

"You, you, and you," the coronal said, pointing at other knights, "with me!" And she started to run, down along the ragged and lengthening line of children and elders, to take a stand at its end, in case the last line of defenders—pitifully few they were too—was overwhelmed.

She got there just in time. "Mages!" she called over her shoulder, and pointed at the surging besiegers, as they overbore two elves—several spears and glaives thrusting through each—and poured forward.

The coronal strode to meet them, and the knights with her grimaced and rushed to get in front of her, to shield her with their lives.

They were still a few strides apart from the foremost mercenaries when the elf line broke in another place. With a ragged roar of triumph, the Shadovar-hired mercenaries charged, heading around the coronal and her handful so they could fall upon the largely undefended line of children and elders.

The coronal turned and rushed to intercept them. "Old lives for young!" she cried to the loyal elves running with her. "Win a future for our younglings with our own blood!"

As she chose the highest ground, to stop and make her stand, Ilsevele Miritar saw that she'd been shouting to only six *Tel'Quess*—and the grinning and eager foe closing on them were beyond counting.

Yet the slope between her and the human hireswords was suddenly shrouded in blue-green mist. A spell, obviously, but not one she recognized. Nothing the handful of high mages here could cast, of that she was sure.

The mercenaries boiled up the hill—but out of the ground in front of their boots, up through the coiling mists, rose a line of baelnorn.

Tall and gaunt and terrible, eyes aglow and withered bodies clutching long curved swords and scepters that shone with risen magic.

"Dove hath called, and we answer," the tallest of them announced, and raised her scepter.

The line of blue-white fire smashed a dozen mercenaries as if a stone had been dashed into a heap of raw eggs. Torn bodies flew through the air, and the screaming began. Then other scepters spat, and the slaughter *really* began.

Sapphire-blue hair swirled, dark eyes blazed, and the lone petite elf slashed with a sword that was not there, a bloody edge of sharp force sweeping through the air and cleaving flesh, bone, armor and blade alike.

It cut a bloody swath through shouting, shrieking mercenaries—and then she was gone, darting like a hummingbird across the glade to thrust and slice anew.

This time she swooped and stabbed among arcanists, haughty and bewildered shades of Thultanthar who, until a moment ago, had been relaxing in the secure knowledge that they were far in the rear of the besieging army, on the winning side, with not a foe who could reach them anywhere near.

"Who the—?" one arcanist shouted, watching the diminutive figure dart away again through the trees.

"Blast it down, whatever it is!" snarled another. "*Quickly*, or—"

He'd meant to say before this unlooked-for solo attacker was out of range and lost to them in the endless trees of the deep forest, but before he could frame the words, she was back, and he saw what he was facing.

A small and shapely female elf, brows and hair of sapphire, clingingly clad in high soft leather boots and a leather harness of indigo hue. Whose hands seemed empty, yet sliced as if she swung a weightless, invisible sword four times as long as her slender arm, and whose eyes were ablaze with anger.

She looked . . . splendid, he had to concede. Her beauty was the last thing he saw, before his own blood blinded him, cloven skull and nose cut open and much of his face torn bloodily off in the wake of her slash.

Her unseen blade claimed the throat of the arcanist standing beside him, and several fingers from the next Thultanthan beyond, and then she was gone again into the trees, swooping and darting.

Not that he could see her, choking on his own blood and going down. He bounced as he hit the ground, and the pain was enough to jolt him to his senses for long enough to hear the oldest arcanist in the glade shout, "The Srinshee! It's their undead ruler, or whatever she is! Every arcanist still standing, to me! *To me now!*"

That bellow ended in a rough, wordless scream that cut off abruptly.

It was replaced by something loud and booming and teeth-jarringly deep—the roar of a large and angry dragon.

It, too, ended with brutal suddenness, rising into a yip of startled pain.

The Srinshee didn't unleash herself often, but right now was one of those rare times.

Prince Mattick Tanthul was two ridges away, slowing warily as he saw more and more high mages and baelnorn between himself and those elf children. They were no longer easy kills.

He turned and sought higher ground, the natural refuge of the close-clustered trunks of soaring shadowtops where he could catch his breath and take a good look around.

He was still a few panting breaths from reaching them when he saw a thousand-some mercenaries coming out of the trees in a huge flood of armored humans, heading for that last beleaguered cluster of elves.

Well, it should be a short slaughter, but an entertaining one.

And then he saw something cleaving a furrow through all those hireswords, something too small to be easily seen, yet as devastating as a swooping dragon. He blinked at all the screaming and the reeling, falling dead. Was it a spell? If so, from where, and what magic could do this—and cast by whom?

He certainly couldn't wreak that sort of havoc with just one spell. Yet perhaps it was a succession of identical magics, cast along the same path, and—

Then he saw it—no, *her*. A tiny flying figure, impossibly blue hair streaming out behind her in a streaming tail, wheeling in the air at the end of the great channel of death she'd just sliced through an army, and now plunging right back into the armored ranks, just behind the foremost mercenaries, cleaving through them and leaving a chaos of dying and maimed men behind.

He saw an arcanist blast at her with a spell, down the trail of the dead in her wake. His magic rebounded on him, hurling him broken limbed and limp into the nearest tree, while his flying target hacked and hewed her way on.

Prince Mattick of Thultanthar swallowed, shook his head—and just turned and ran.

The courtyard was eerily quiet. Only the fast-scudding clouds betrayed the fact that Thultanthar was flying through the air in a killing plummet beneath all their feet.

The vast and usually open space was crowded, seemingly filled with robed and cowled pillars standing almost shoulder to shoulder: the assembled arcanists of the city. Each of them held still, in the precise spot chosen for him or her by the Most High, and every face was set with the strain of intense concentration.

Telamont's great draining magic was underway, and the fear and awe the younger arcanists felt at being part of such a meld, working in concert with so many other minds of power, was starting to subside as the dark and driving force of the Most High's will really took hold.

Overhead and all around, in the hitherto empty air, an impossibly complex and glowing tangle slowly faded into view, lines of racing white fire tinged with gold, ever changing but growing steadily brighter.

The Weave had become a visible thing.

From high windows all over the city, lesser Thultanthans exclaimed in startled wonder as the shining network spread. Filling the sky above the city and stretching into vast distances through the clouds and everywhere below—including the white spires ahead, poking through the great green carpet of trees that marked the heart of embattled Myth Drannor.

And along those strands of racing force, leaping up from those spires, rose a thin, soft, high-pitched, ethereal song. Singing that swelled, mournful and defiant.

As the baelnorn who'd guarded elf crypts for so long fought the hiresword army converging on the last few spires of the city still in elf hands, the elf dead in their now unguarded tombs beneath Myth Drannor were singing.

The City of Shadow was coming to the City of Song.

"Well," Elminster growled, as they reeled away from the sighing collapse of a half-magical pillar, breaking the human triangle they'd formed around it, "at least they're hurting less, with each one we destroy."

Laeral gave him a smile. "Stop looking so *worried*, El. This either works—or it doesn't. If we fail, we've done the best we could. And at least we haven't done nothing."

"Which is how so much evil crawls unchecked in this world for so long," Alustriel put in. "Good folk tending to their own lives and concerns, and doing nothing for their neighbors, their villages, their realms. Leaving the hard and distasteful work for someone else."

"Aye," El grunted. "Us."

"How many anchors is that now? I've lost count," Alustriel asked.

Laeral grinned. "Is now a good time to admit I've never been able to keep track of coins, or numbers of any sort, above about seven at once?"

El grinned at her. "A serious failing in a ruler, I'd say. And one that I share."

Laeral turned to her sister. "Well, High Lady of Silverymoon? And whatever-they-called-you, of Luruar?"

Alustriel gave her a wry look. "*I* generally lose count somewhere around forty-odd. And we passed that many anchors destroyed, long ago. Speaking of which, the next one is over that way, about—" She broke off, her face changing, and asked, "What's *that?*"

They could all feel it. A tugging in the air, an invisible pull rising in its silently tremulous force. It clawed at them, seeming to want to drag them up into the air, angling up into the sky, northward.

Up to the floating stone city of Thultanthar, now hanging tall and dark in the sky, still drifting closer.

"They want the mythal, those arcanists," Elminster said, peering up at the city, then down at its spreading shadow over the trees. "Perhaps we should give it to them."

"Not freely, I take it," Laeral said dryly.

"Oh, freely indeed—but all at once, in a rush, like a great fist of force. Mayhap we could shatter it."

"Quite a rain of destruction that would be," Alustriel commented, peering up at the dark stone city. "You think we can manage it?"

El sighed. "No. No, I don't, though I wish I could answer thee otherwise."

"Take too long?" Laeral asked softly. "Might go awry?"

"Both of those," the Sage of Shadowdale said shortly. "Take too much crucial time, I'm almost certain . . . so this draining magic may well succeed."

"*Ignore* it, El," Alustriel counseled grimly. "Let's just go on destroying anchors. You can't be everywhere, do everything, and save everyone—and you should have stopped trying centuries ago."

"And how much less fun would that have been?" Laeral countered. "For old weirdbeard here *and* all the rest of Faerûn?"

"Ah," her sister granted, nodding her head and letting her long silver tresses writhe and swirl freely about her shoulders. "You have a point there. That many have felt the sharp end of these last twelve centuries or so."

"Or so?"

Alustriel grinned and shrugged. "As I said, I lose count."

"I wish I could," Elminster whispered fervently, and stalked off in the direction of the next anchor.

The two sisters exchanged worried glances and followed.

With their every step, the tugging grew stronger.

Storm Silverhand trudged past perhaps her sixteen thousandth tree of the day, reeling on her feet with weariness. She was alone and blood drenched and trailing her sword, glad of the wrist thong that tethered it to her numbed sword hand.

Was there *no* end to these Shadovar-hired mercenaries? She'd slain hundreds herself, today, and clambered over thousands slain by others—and they were *still* as thick as the swarming blow-flies, coming through the trees by their dozens and scores and even hundreds.

As if her thoughts had alerted a lot of someones that their battlefield cue was upon them, she saw sunlight glinting off bright armor in the trees.

She sighed and started looking around for a good place to make a stand. Against the broad trunk of yon duskwood would have to do . . .

By the time she reached it, her foes were out in the open, walking steadily toward her in a wedge of gleaming shields, helms, and armor. No spears or glaives, but plenty of long swords and battle-axes. Fresh troops, hundreds of them.

And at their head strode two warriors who must have been seven feet tall and three feet across at their shoulders—half-orcs or half-giants or some such; it was hard to see their features through their menacing beak-faced war helms. Between them walked a young Shadovar arcanist in his robes, his face as haughty as any Zhentarim or Red Wizard Storm had ever met.

"Well met, elf-lover," he greeted her. "If you beg for your life, I *might* spare you for a time. Long enough to serve as a reward for those under my command here who fight outstandingly today. But I warn you, you must choose your fate *right now*. We're in a hurry; if we tarry, there might not be any elves left."

Leaning on her sword with the duskwood at her back, Storm gave him a wintry smile. "An interesting bargain, Thultanthan, but I offer you a different one. There's been enough killing this day. Surrender or depart, and I'll spare you."

The arcanist gaped at her, then sneered. "*You* presume to try to stop me?"

"It's what I do," Storm told him grimly, and started to stalk toward him, sword raised.

Contemptuously he cast slaying lightning at her—only to see it meet a sudden gout of silver fire from her mouth. It spiraled around that silvern flame, into her, and she hissed in pain—but kept right on striding.

Before he could do anything else, she sprang, a great swing of her blade sending one of his gigantic bodyguards sprawling. She came down in a squat and launched herself at the other one, who swung his blade in time to meet hers in midair with a great clang and shower of sparks, and spill her to the ground on her behind.

On her way down, her sword flicked out—and sliced off all the fingers on one of the arcanist's hands.

He screamed in shock and pain, staggering back as Storm's blood-matted hair swiped the feet out from under the second bodyguard, and her sword cut deep into the goliath's neck as he fell. He bounced, writhed, clawed the air feebly . . . and fell back into a bleeding heap.

As she turned to face the arcanist again, he stared at her in disbelief. "You—how did you—?"

"Old, gray experience and low cunning prevails over youthful overconfidence," she replied crisply, bounding forward and swinging her sword. "Again."

Her slash took out his throat.

As the arcanist toppled, she looked past his falling body at the rest of the mercenaries he'd been leading. They stared back at her uncertainly, not advancing, their swords and axes raised.

Storm Silverhand gave them a sweet smile.

"Run," she suggested softly.

And obediently, they turned and fled back into the forest, every last warrior of them.

It had been some time since the young war wizard and a handful of Purple Dragons had bolted from this upper room off a back street in Suzail; Mirt's flagon was almost empty now.

And that was bad, for his drinking companion was not in any mellow good humor.

"Fat man," Manshoon said coldly across the table, "I have acquired a certain sneaking respect for you, truly I have. Yet know this: what is unfolding across Faerûn right now offers too many and too great opportunities to seize power for me to resist—even if I wasn't as restless as I am. I enjoy drinking your wine, I have gone so far as to refrain from blasting you to ashes for foiling my plots, and I intend to depart this place leaving you alive and unharmed. Yet I will *not* tarry here longer, like an idle noble of Cormyr, too dunderheaded or too hampered by timidity or ignorance of how the fanged and clawed real world beyond these ornate walls works to stir from my chair and the endless parade of succulent feasting platters set before me. I go. Try to prevent me at your peril."

Mirt looked across the table sadly, let out a great belch that rattled the door handle Manshoon was reaching for, and replied, "Worry not, Lord Manshoon; I intend to do nothing of the sort. I doubt I could hold my own against a vampire for half a breath, anyroad—to say nothing of an archmage of yer accomplishments."

Manshoon sneered and wrenched open the door—to find the way blocked by two elderly but mighty-looking priests with glowing rods in their hands.

The other doors in the room opened then, and more high priests of various faiths, with quite an arsenal of enchanted items roused and aglow in their hands, came into the room. Followed by more than a dozen Wizards of War, holding all manner of dangerous-looking items of magic.

"That's why," Mirt added mildly, "I admitted my limitations for once, and called in the—er, cavalry."

A cold-faced woman came up behind the fat man's chair then, staring with flinty eyes at Manshoon. "Are you calling me a horse, Mirt?" she snapped.

Mirt chuckled. "No need, when I happen to know yer name. Thanks for coming, Glathra."

Wizard of War Glathra Barcantle shrugged. "I did it for Cormyr, not for you." There was an ugly, ungainly spiderlike creature on her shoulder with a human-seeming head that looked far too big for its splayed, segmented legs.

Manshoon peered at the spider-thing's face, and frowned. "Vangerdahast?"

"The same," the spider-thing rasped. "You haven't been keeping up with events, Lord Manshoon. A serious failing in a vampire who desires continued existence, I'd say."

"Is that a threat?" Manshoon asked silkily.

"I don't make threats," Vangerdahast replied. "These days, I deal in promises."

Power was beginning to flow to the arcanists in Thultanthar, invisible energies dragged up from the besieged city below. Slowly, very slowly those energies came, the mythal seemingly reluctant to yield its shape and anything of its might.

The things the mythal of Myth Drannor could do, and the things it could thwart, were many, and most of them came with intricate commands and contingencies and attunements, a flood of half-seen memories and silent instructions and magical lore, the very things that fascinated most arcanists, that left them lusting for more. A hundred or more minds wavered, craving to know more, to study and see and master . . . and like a dark-eyed storm front rolling inexorably into their minds with cold patience but a grip like tightening iron, the High Prince of Thultanthar quelled their straying and dragged them back to the shared work of breaking down the resistance of the mythal and draining its energies.

Settling back into the shared concentration, they felt the power flowing, slow but vast, more and more on the move, coming to them, coming . . .

Stopping cold. There was a moment of chaos, of many minds separately plunging into shocked realization that their mighty shared ritual hadn't ended, but rather had been abruptly halted by something more powerful.

Then the dark will of the Most High rose through them again, rallying them, turning them to collectively face and examine whatever it was that had stopped the draining—and walled away the energies they'd already sapped from the intricate and many-layered mythal.

The mysterious impediment loomed in their collective regard as a dark wall, but it was a dark wall that seemed to smile, and not nicely—in the brief instant before a barbed and many-clawed energy boiled out of the wall and lashed into their minds in a malicious slap, a bludgeoning blow of mental power that overwhelmed many of them.

All over the courtyard, arcanists toppled, bleeding from mouths and nostrils, unconsciousness as they fell. Others reeled, drooling or keening in dazed mental ruin. One fell to his knees and started trying to eat his own hands, biting and gnawing.

The great collective faltered.

Those who were still standing, mentally, recoiled in involuntary unison when the dark wall became a smiling, nigh skeletal face.

Fools and idiots, the undead being's voice rolled mockingly into their heads, *well met.*

Half a hundred minds dared to ask, without any words at all, *Who* are *you?*

Some of the others knew, or guessed, and to them came the mental equivalent of a wink, dividing them from their fellows.

Shades of the City of Shadow, the voice echoed in their heads, far deeper and louder than the Most High's had ever been, *I am the Shadow King. I, alone, blocked all of your minds. A trifle, when one is Master of the Weave and Devourer of the Wards of Candlekeep. You*

336

prate of your power, and smugly hold yourselves to be mightier than the wizards of this world you have returned to. You preen, arcanists of Thultanthar, and exult in your power. And all the while, you know nothing of real power.

Another mental slap felled more arcanists, and left others clutching their heads and screaming, their minds collapsing into shattered darkness.

That is but a taste of what I can do casually, in an idle moment. As one would slap an irritating insect. As anyone responsible would slap down someone too ignorant and reckless to be trusted with the power you so arrogantly presume to seize. Shadovar, know this: if anyone in this world is going to be so arrogantly presumptuous, it will be me. Because I, Larloch, can—and can gainsay you and all other hollow pretenders.

And then that terrible mind turned from the cowering, gibbering, or droolingly ruined arcanists to bear down on just one mind. The sentience of Telamont Tanthul, High Prince of Thultanthar. What Larloch said to the Most High of the city, he let—nay, forced—every mind in the city to hear. It was a biting rebuke.

If you were a tenth the wielder of the Art you presume to be, you might have succeeded in this. If, that is, I decided not to prevent you.

Larloch ended his address with a contemptuous surge of power that shattered the draining spell and left Telamont Tanthul leaking mental pain into the heads of those arcanists still conscious and sane.

Then, the dark and awful mind was abruptly gone.

Leaving the Most High of Thultanthar aghast, standing in a courtyard littered with ruined arcanists.

Telamont Tanthul stared around wildly, hearing wild bab-blings, keening, and even doglike barking from some arcanists on their knees.

Then he turned and ran for the doors that would lead most directly to his throne, desperate to get to it and unleash all of the magics in that chamber, to try to destroy Larloch.

Before Larloch decided to destroy him.

Prince Aglarel lay sprawled and senseless in front of the doors.

Telamont kicked desperately at his son's body, to try to shift it so he could get at least one door far enough open to slip through.

In the courtyard behind him, some of the arcanists started to howl and bay at the sun.

CHAPTER 19

Descent, Destruction, and Endgame

THE DOOR BANGED OPEN.

Manarlume and Lelavdra whirled from their table of maps and tomes and rune tiles, hands rising to hurl dread magic.

The arcanist Gwelt stood panting on the threshold.

"Madness!" he gasped, "sheer madness! And the Most High is paying for it right now!"

"What madness?" Lelavdra snapped.

"T-the draining spell! Of hundreds of arcanists, working in concert with the High Prince, together seeking to draw the power of the elf city's mythal to us, and so master the Weave, for the greater glory of Shar! He—"

"Yes, yes, we've heard the grand and glorious plan," Manarlume said dismissively. "Mythal down, Weave our servant, hot suppers for everyone with a snap of our fingers, new gowns whenever we turn around, *yes*. What 'madness' is involved, and High Prince Tanthul is 'paying for it' *how*, exactly?"

"The one called Larloch—the archlich served by many liches—got to the mythal first. And blocked the shielding, sending deadly magic along it that's felled many arcanists, mind-ruining them or worse! He's calling himself the Shadow King, and he taunted the

Most High, and said he prevented us all by himself, and could stop anything we tried. Called us fools, presumptuous fools who know nothing of real power."

"Oh? And how fared *you* against Larloch's attack?"

"I . . . I was not touched. I was there, but not part of the meshed minds of the spell."

Manarlume stared at the arcanist coldly. "So you played traitor, when the Most High most needed your loyalty and service."

"No! No, I am no traitor! I foresaw the folly and tried to warn Prince Aglarel; he told me he'd hear me out when the spell was done."

"So *you* are now the judge of folly and best policy in Thultanthar?" Manarlume flung at him, eyes flashing as she strode at him.

Gwelt stood his ground. "No! That is to say . . ."

"Gwelt, I am enraged. I am disgusted. Stand aside! I'm off to report your treachery to the Most High right now!"

"*No!* No, hear me! Whatever you think of me and want to say about me, tarry for a day—*please!*"

"Why?" Lelavdra asked bluntly. "Why should my sister delay on your say-so, when our city's safeguarding and bright future are at stake?"

"For her own safety! He suffered mind-wounding and a terrible humiliation; when last I saw him, he was *kicking* Prince Aglarel! Stay away from him right now, I beg you! It's not *safe!*"

"And why do *you* care what happens to me?" Manarlume flared. Tense silence fell, as they all stared at each other.

"Well?" she snapped. Lelavdra stepped to her side, folding her arms across her chest and adding her glare to that of her sister's.

Gwelt flushed a deep crimson under the hard weight of their regard, and muttered, "I . . . I love you, Ladies Tanthul. Both of you."

Manarlume and Lelavdra stared at him.

Then, slowly, they both grew the same catlike smile.

Larloch was talking to himself. Again.

"For a long time I contented myself with studying the Art, taking it further than any one entity had done before," he purred, "and letting Toril attend to itself. I cared for no realm nor ruler nor cabal, and was content to be left alone. And the world grew no better, and petty tyrants meddled ever more recklessly with magic, from the dupes of Shar to those fools in Zhentil Keep and Thay, and now these arrogant returned bumblers of Thultanthar. It is time, and long past time, to intervene. Not to rule the high and the low, trying to make laws and enforce them in matters ever so petty—but to slap down the worst parasites and vandals, and let commoners and oxen alike *breathe* once more! A city should have a ruler pitted against guilds and street gangs and the wealthiest families—but above that, there should be no one but the gods, and their priesthoods locked ever in opposition. Let there be an end to kings. Let there be only . . . Larloch."

Elminster rolled his eyes. Alustriel and Laeral both wagged fingers at him in mock reproof.

The Weave anchor between them hummed on, intact. A mythal anchor had been entwined around it, like a thriving vine, and when they'd trudged up to the Weave anchor, amid the moss-carpeted roots of a thriving duskwood, they'd felt the mythal anchor, and heard Larloch's voice thrumming along it. He must be somewhere near.

Or perhaps not. He could be anywhere else that the mythal of the city extended. Far beyond the few buildings the elves still held against the tightening ring of Shadovar besiegers.

They could see him through the anchor, as well as hear him; a flickering, translucent, miniature image of the tall, gaunt archlich in his robes. He was gloating, head thrown back, concentration turned inward, bent on drawing the mythal's power into himself—and as they watched, he was growing larger, and larger, and starting to glow . . .

Elminster beckoned Alustriel and Laeral close. When they bent their heads to his, he whispered, "Anchor *me*."

Frowning—what was the Old Mage up to *now*?—they nodded and wrapped their arms around him from either side. He sat down, drawing them down with him onto the forest moss, and closed his eyes, waiting for their minds to settle into full and calm contact with his. When that happened, El called on the connection to the mythal Larloch had inadvertently shown him back in Candlekeep when the death of the Guide had wrenched him out of the monks' minds.

He called on that connection ever so gently, not wanting Larloch to sense him doing so.

The mythal was flowing into the archlich's vast, dark, and starless mind, slowly but ever faster, draining away from the City of Song.

El didn't try to fight that flow, nor divert it. Not yet. Not until he had need of its power. First, he called on his command of the Weave, that far greater web of magical might, wrapping himself in all the thrumming power he could stand—his body shuddering and then shaking violently in the firm grip of the sisters—and then reaching up and out with that gathered power.

Power that stretched out like so many soft and unseen tentacles to nestle among the enchantments that knit together the stones of the flying city of Thultanthar, and held it aloft, and controlled the moisture that reached it, and governed the temperature within and around its buildings. Making those contacts into bindings, knitting them into the very fabric of all those thousandfold enchantments; turning them into so many hooks for him to pull on.

Then, tentatively at first, and then insistently, Elminster set about pulling the floating city of Thultanthar down out of the sky.

Alustriel and Laeral, their faces almost touching his, stared at him in dawning awe, feeling what he was doing through their link with him.

Then, each of them accepted what must be, and bolstered him with their will.

And silently, through the clouds, the great floating city started to descend.

Arclath looked up at the great dark bulk of the Netherese city, floating so large overhead. It was blotting out most of the sun, and it was getting larger.

"It's definitely getting lower," he reported, and then added inevitably, "Are you sure it was wise to come here?"

"Wise?" His lady's eyes flashed. "Of *course* it wasn't wise, Lord Delcastle!"

Arclath winced. Uh-oh. And me without a shield.

"It was, however," Rune snapped, "the *right* thing to do! And the gods take all wisdom and prudence if riding under their banner means a life of renouncing or shirking what is right!"

And perhaps, just perhaps, a life of longer duration.

Arclath was careful to think that, but say no word nor hint of it. If he was going to get killed or maimed this day, let it *not* be by the lady he loved.

Who was now tugging at his arm and pointing. "There! Elves, more than a dozen of them!"

"With what looks to be several thousand mercenary warriors trying to slaughter them," Arclath pointed out.

"Yes, those elves!" Rune said fiercely. "We go to reinforce them!"

"Of *course* we do," Lord Delcastle replied. Lifting his chin, he hefted his sword and started running, his beloved right beside him.

The flows of power were thunderously obvious, and Larloch looked along them at their commander.

And saw what Elminster was doing.

The archlich smirked, smiled broadly, then burst into laughter. "You amuse me with your strivings, petty meddler!" he told the Old Mage. "Destroy all the architecture you want! Soon you shall have a new master, and your dances will be to my command—you and every last archmage and hedge wizard, from one end of this world to the other!"

"Oooh," Elminster replied mildly. "Won't that be nice?"

The lights of Larloch's eyes blazed up. "Man, do you mock me?"

"Archlich, I mock everyone. Myself, most of all. It's how I guard my heart against the flailing lashings of life. And you?"

The archlich regarded him in still silence for an uncomfortably long time. And then sighed and said, "You *do* understand. I need such as you. I have all too few friends."

Elminster looked steadily back along the flows, into Larloch's distant face.

"Me too," he said.

The doors of the audience chamber were barred and spell-sealed, and one man sat alone on that high seat.

All around him, things of beauty and power summoned from all over Thultanthar floated in the air, drifting in slow orbits around the throne. Staves, rods, scepters, crowns, rings, keys, wands, pairs of boots, and many smaller, odder things, from tiny pouch coffers to ornate lamp statuettes, hundreds of them were slowly circling the throne.

And as they drifted on their unhurried journeys, they darkened and crumbled as their magic was drained from them, and the vivid and crackling blue-white auras surrounding the slumping items and becoming bright lines of force that stabbed at the arms of the throne. And as those arms shone an ominous blue beneath the clenched fingers of the man seated on the throne, and stray bolts and tendrils of unleashed force snarled up his arms, item after item became drifting black ashes . . . that then tumbled into powder, and in time became finer dust.

The Most High of Thultanthar sat on his throne like a statue; stone faced, his eyes closed, patiently brooding. Letting the magic build within him.

When all the circling items were gone, Telamont Tanthul opened his eyes. They had become two blue-white stars.

He crooked a finger, and the air before him came alive with the bright and moving hues of a scrying scene that filled the room from wall to wall, reflecting off the polished marble.

The air above a vast green forest was filled with crisscrossing, shifting, racing lines of bright force that formed an impossibly complex and ever changing weaving—the Weave, made visible, and beneath it . . .

A panorama of a few desperate elves in shining armor, battling to protect the flickering blue upright oval of a portal on a terrace between two tall, fair, slender-towered buildings. All around them were their foes, human mercenaries in motley armor who pressed inexorably forward over their own dead, a dozen of them to replace each of their fellows who fell, a score to drag aside the limp dead to keep them from becoming walls the elves could defend.

Myth Drannor had all but fallen—and now this.

"No!" Telamont Tanthul spat suddenly, bringing one hand down on the arm of the throne in a fist. "Never, lich! No Tanthul shall serve the likes of you!"

He sprang to his feet and flung his arms wide, exulting in the power now surging through him. "I shall destroy you, dead wizard!"

The doors of the room boomed open, and magic howled through them, summoned from all over the city.

Draining wards and craftings that should not be drained, but . . . there comes a time for strong measures, and it was here.

The High Prince of Thultanthar laughed wildly as more and more power flooded into him.

The shadow of the descending city loomed larger and larger above the dwindling section of central Myth Drannor the elves still commanded, blotting out the sunlight.

Storm saw something flying like a vengeful arrow. It plunged into the mercenaries waiting to get at her and the rest of the surviving elves, opening a great furrow through the startled warriors. It was an elf whose sapphire-blue hair trailed behind her like a comet as she flashed through mercenaries, slicing as she went.

All the way to Storm, where she hissed, "Get all the *Tel'Quess* out of here! *Now!*"

And she was gone, racing away through clanging steel and more reeling, falling warriors.

Storm felled four foes with as many vicious slashes, then turned and sprinted to the coronal.

"Get them out!" she screamed. "Every last one of your people! *Now!*"

And she lunged forward to strike down the mercenaries hacking at the coronal and at Fflar beside her, to give them both time to think. They looked at her, then up at Thultanthar darkening the sky—and started shouting orders, directing a fighting withdrawal through the portal.

Storm whirled away from them, thrust an elbow into the thrumming magic that outlined the portal, and called on the Weave.

It flung her through the forest in the direction she desired, over the heads of the mercenaries, to land in a corpse-strewn courtyard that the elves had yielded a day ago. Where a spell had just sent lightning lashing through the rearmost mercenaries.

Storm ran for its source.

Amarune Whitewave, with Lord Arclath Delcastle standing like a bodyguard in front of her, sword ready. They both gaped at her.

"Well met!" she greeted them, still sprinting hard. "You two are as blithely disobedient as I expected you to be. What? Why the astonishment? Haven't you ever seen a Chosen of Mystra who's been bathing all day in blood before?"

"Storm!" Rune's stare was anxious. "Where are you headed?"

"This way, and I need you both with me! *Come!*"

Some of the rearmost mercenaries were turning now, and running toward them.

Amarune and Arclath glanced at them, then back at Storm. Who spread her arms and gathered them in. "Come *on!*"

More of the besiegers were running now, and the sky was growing dimmer overhead, the floating city lower and nearer.

"Where're we headed?" Rune gasped. "A portal?"

"No!" Storm panted. "No magic! Want to be far away from all magic, when—"

The flash of blinding, deep blue light from behind them came with a shock wave that lifted every last running being—not to mention shrubs and sapling—and flung them onward.

"Noooo!" everyone heard two voices shout, out of different directions in the empty air: Telamont Tanthul and the archlich Larloch, united in dismay.

Yes, another voice replied fiercely, out of the heart of the light. *I, the Srinshee, have made my choice, so that my people shall live. In a Realms* not *bound to tyrants of darkness. So whenever you smile into the fresh winds of freedom, remember me.*

In a dark corner of the exclusive upper room in the Memories of Queen Fee, the most fashionable and expensive club of the clubs that overlooked the great Promenade in Suzail, a tall and darkly handsome man suddenly stood bolt upright. His surge upset goblets and tallglasses in profusion, not to mention a side table bristling with expensively filled decanters. Nobles exclaimed in exasperated irritation.

"Dolt!"

"What's got into you? Have a care, man!"

"Such a *waste*! Sirrah, I'm *talking* to you!"

Manshoon ignored them all. His eyes were wide, not seeing the room around him, but struggling to far scry an elf city far away across a mountain range—and failing. His magic was failing him.

"Something's happening," he snapped, still struggling. "Great power—"

As everyone stared, he cried out in pain, blue light flashed from his eyes in actual spurts of flame, and he collapsed across the table.

Mirt deftly whisked his own drink safely out of the way, regarded the senseless man almost in his lap, and muttered, "Never *liked* wizards. Damned excitable idiots. Swords now, and sly tongues . . . with them, I know where I stand."

There were suddenly armed and uniformed men in the room, peering around, hands on sword hilts. A Purple Dragon patrol.

Noble lords of Cormyr looked up from their drinks to regard the Dragons sourly. "Even *here?*" one of them rumbled. "Aren't there murders you could be solving? Thieves to catch?"

"We got a report that the wanted wizard called Manshoon was here," the leader of the patrol snapped.

"A man *claiming* to be Manshoon, aye," another noble replied, pointing at the senseless man draped across the table. "Me, I think he was just trying to get out of paying for his drinks."

The Dragon officer looked at Mirt, who growled, "I'll cover his owing. And stand all of you yer favorite slake too. Now go put yer love of country to better use."

Out of the blue light, a face swam. The Srinshee.

She blew Elminster a kiss and said tenderly into his mind *Farewell, old friend.*

Then the face exploded into a racing blue flame that stabbed across the air between them and coursed into El, imparting such raging power that it lifted him a few feet into the air—sitting on nothing, Alustriel and Laeral clinging to him and elevated with him—and made every hair on his body stand out stiffly, his eyes become spitting blue flames.

Alustriel and Laeral were flung away from him, shocked and numbed, and landed hard. They stared at him, aghast, as he rose, standing on nothing, now about the height of a tall man off the ground, trembling. Small blue flames spurted from his stiffly spread fingertips.

The Old Mage hung in the air, helpless, as all of the Srinshee's magical might and life-force flooded through him—and through the linking flows of power, to stab into Larloch.

Whose shrieks, as he burned, clawed the ears of everyone in Myth Drannor and Thultanthar.

It took a long time for those screams to dwindle as the archlich was whirled away, his hold on power lost.

The mythal collapsed into Elminster, and exploded out of him in all directions, flooding the Weave nearby with its energy.

The air shone brightly, and sang, loud and bright.

As the city of Thultanthar crushed elven spires as if they were made of sand and came inexorably down, down atop Myth Drannor.

The Most High of Thultanthar looked around wildly. The city was heading for the ground, faster and faster, the very stones around and beneath him groaning deep and awful with the strain—and there was nothing, *nothing* he could do to stop it.

He'd flung all of his gathered power to tug against the downward pull, in utter vain, then turned it to trying to twist what few spells he could see in the minds of nearby Thultanthans—for there was no time at all to craft a new magic—into a severing force, to slice free of that pull . . . and failed.

His city was doomed.

Telamont snarled a heartfelt curse, and gathered all his newfound power to flee—but the empty air in front of his throne fell away like a curtain, to reveal a bearded and weathered face staring at him with eyes that held no shred of mercy.

Force flooded out of those eyes in a torrent, slamming Telamont Tanthul back on his throne and pinning him there.

They gazed at each other, High Prince and Old Mage, while the tyrant of Thultanthar tried a dozen swift spells of escape or destruction, and Elminster casually shattered them all in the instant of their forming, one after another. Until Telamont Tanthul ran out of ideas and relevant magic. As he racked his wits desperately, trying to think of how to escape, Elminster said flatly, "*Enough*, Tanthul. Ye've misused thine Art for centuries, and grown more arrogant rather than wiser. The Realms are far better off without ye. Reap now the reward that should have been thine long, long ago."

And the almighty crash that came then shattered bones and toppled walls and pillars, even before the Most High of Thultanthar was flung up at the ceiling and his upthrust throne pinned him there and then drove him through it, in broken pulped pieces that leaked magic in all directions.

The floating city and hapless Myth Drannor beneath it smashed and ground together and were both destroyed, ancient elven magics exploding here, there, and everywhere amid the roiling field of tumbling stone.

And Telamont Tanthul died, already in bodily agony, shrieking in terror as his mind broke like a toppled wineglass. Elminster Aumar held the shade's cracking and disintegrating body on his cracking and disintegrating throne throughout, and the Shadovar's mind clamped tightly with his own, to make *very* sure.

So it was that he tasted Telamont's destruction, and very nearly shared it.

Lost in tears, reeling, mentally exposed and exhausted, Elminster swam in and out of consciousness . . . and lay helpless beneath the coming of the Mistress of the Night.

Shar raged, vast and dark and terrible in the sky above the broken cities, glaring down out of her own nightfall at the floating, slumped Elminster, her darkness rolling down, down, reaching out with great dark tentacles . . .

That vanished in a flood of silver light, a sloping wall of silver fire like an impossibly tall tidal wave, sweeping up into the sky and growing a face.

Mystra, bright and powerful and whole, smilingly defying the dark goddess.

"Let us, for once, not go too far, Goddess of Night," Mystra said gently, her eyes two silver flames of understanding, warning, and grim promise.

Shar snarled in rage and turned away in a swirling of shadows, and the day came back again.

One moment the coronal was fighting desperately against too many mercenaries to count, in deepening darkness as the floating city came down on all their heads, fighting to guard Fflar's back and keep him alive as he worked miracles of deft bladework to hold back hireswords beyond counting, and helping elf knight after wounded elf knight through the portal—

And the next, she was somewhere else.

Somewhere green and forested and familiar, that lacked tall spires and human butchers-for-coin beyond number and fallen *Tel'Quess* everywhere.

She blinked. Semberholme, that's where she was.

There were elves everywhere around her, in bloody armor, swords in their hands, weeping and embracing. Her people, the last Myth Drannans who'd fought beside her, she who was now coronal of nowhere.

Through the sobbing, hugging crowd, she saw Fflar, her Fflar, in his hacked and rent armor, sword still in hand, stalking wearily toward her.

"The Srinshee," he said hoarsely. "She saved every one of us." And burst into tears.

They plunged into each other's arms.

352

The breeze was icy, up on so high a ledge of the Thunder Peaks, but it afforded them the view they needed—once augmented by their spells, of course—and they simply *had* to see.

It's not every day you watch your home and most of your kin and people destroyed, all at one stroke.

Gwelt, Manarlume, and Lelavdra stood together in stunned silence as the debacle unfolded.

It was a long time before Gwelt stirred.

"Your grandsire was a mighty man, but a proud one," he said grimly. "Too proud, in the end."

"He was a proud *fool*," Lelavdra replied scornfully.

"There are worse things to be," said Manarlume, "but yes, let us strive not to be so proud."

"Or foolish," Gwelt added.

"And keep far from the company of those who are," Lelavdra said bitterly.

Manarlume sighed. "So shall we shiver on some mountaintop? Shrivel dry at the heart of some vast desert? Or drown on a rock far out in the trackless seas?"

The three Shadovar looked at each other—and then burst into rueful laughter.

It was so late on this night of the thirteenth of Marpenoth that it had really become early on the fourteenth, and outside was chill darkness and glittering stars.

Yet Storm's kitchen was a warm welter of noise, delightful aromas, and dancing candlelight from a dozen lanterns. It was hot and getting hotter, and Amarune and Arclath were trying their best to help their whirlwind of a host prepare a feast. Storm preferred to stir and sample the soups herself, but there were roasts to be wrestled onto spits and then turned by someone who could kick fresh logs into the hearth beneath them without having all the flaming firewood roll right back out (Arclath's job, and he was learning mastery of it fast, though his boots would never be the same), and bread to be hauled out of ovens (Amarune's task).

She blew clinging hair off her forehead with a mighty puff, slid her hands into the padded gloves Storm had tossed her way, and picked up a pry bar to do battle with the bread-oven doors.

"How do you *know* they're done?" Arclath asked her.

"See that line of bread dough all around the edge of the door, sealing it?" Rune asked tartly. "It's done, yes? Well, then, so are the loaves inside."

"And you became an expert on baking bread when?"

"When Storm told me about that trick, while you were raiding the pantry," Amarune admitted, and when Arclath looked over his shoulder, he saw Storm watching them with a broad grin.

"You're a couple, all right," she murmured happily.

"We're cooking enough for an *army*," Rune pointed out, chipping baked bread away from one door. "How can you be sure they'll come?"

"I *know* them," Storm replied. "Saving the world makes you hungry."

And it was only one dropped loaf and one slopped soup cauldron later that the kitchen door opened without knock or warning, and two tall silver-haired women arrived.

"Luse! Laer! Wine yonder!" Storm greeted them, not leaving her pots.

Alustriel and Laeral smiled and waved at her, and Alustriel asked, "Anything we can help with?"

"Eating and drinking," Storm told them, "*and* settling your behinds down in the chairs that end of the table, out of the way."

"Fair enough. Oh, we've brought along some friends," Laeral announced, and stood aside to introduce, with a flourish that would have done credit to any herald, a bewildered-looking Lady Glathra Barcantle of Cormyr, with a spiderlike, human-headed *thing*—the former Royal Magician Vangerdahast—riding on her shoulder.

"Well," it was telling Glathra rather testily, "*I* think the Rune Lords are—oh." It stared at everyone in the room, and blinked in surprise.

"Welcome!" Storm said with a smile, and then looked at Vangerdahast and added, "You should have come visiting more often down the years, Vangey. Affairs of state make more sense when discussed over broth—or something stronger—in a farmhouse kitchen."

Vangerdahast bowed his head, looking a little abashed, but whatever reply he might have made was lost in the banging of the door.

It flew open with force enough to make Storm lay hand on the fireplace poker beside the cauldron she was paying most attention to, ready to hurl it—but through it lurched no foe, but a familiar bedraggled wizard.

Looking more exhausted than usual, if that was possible.

"Elminster!" Amarune exclaimed delightedly.

He gave her a smile that twinkled. "Well, now, *that's* a pleasant change! Well met, dearest!"

The Old Mage blew Storm a kiss, gave Arclath a cheery wave, then nodded to Vangey and said, "Ao's finished toying with us all, Abeir and Toril are apart and getting more so, the Sundering is done—and I believe I need a drink! Oh, and *here's* a lady 'tis high time I spoke cordially with, rather than sparring over the safety and good governance of Cormyr with!"

Glathra, who'd said nothing at all and looked like she intended to go right on doing so, ducked her head and blushed.

Then Elminster turned to the two women who stood down at the far end of the table, flagons in their hands.

"El?" Alustriel asked tentatively.

"Luse! Laer!" Elminster rushed to them, spreading his arms wide, and they hastily set their flagons down and fell into his arms.

They rocked together for a few moments, murmuring things and chuckling, before El said briskly, "I perceive I seem to have arrived at the right time!"

"As usual," Storm commented archly, waving a ladle at him.

"Lady fair," he said gravely, "point ye not that thing at me!"

"Or you'll . . . *what*?" she challenged him, hands on hips and a mock glower settling onto her face.

"Or I'll eat one last feast at thy board, burst of a surfeit of everything, and expire at last!" he replied, crossing the kitchen and sweeping her into his arms. "After all, I have a successor now!"

And he pointed at Amarune, who blinked back sudden tears as she reached out an imploring hand to him, fingers far too short to touch him from clear across the room. "*Don't* say that! I'm not ready for—for any of it. Yet . . . you've been meddling and fighting and striving for centuries! As those you love are born, live their lives, grow old, and die, again and again, leaving you alone at sunset, time after time. You must be so *tired* of it all!"

Storm and Elminster looked at her, their arms around each other. Then they regarded each other, nose to nose—and with a smile and a squeeze, Storm silently bade the last living prince of vanished Athalantar to make reply.

And he smiled back at his too-many-greats-granddaughter with a touch of sadness and a much larger measure of pride, and said, "Yes, dearest, oh yes, but don't ye see? 'Tis what ye haven't done that torments ye, in life. And it's always been the love given me that sustains me—and ye still give it, all of ye. So I cannot stop, until I drop."

356

"If you get any more poetic," Alustriel murmured, "I'm going to gag."

El chuckled. "Ye see? The love never ends."

At that moment, there came a knock on the door. Two raps, gentle and widely spaced. "Now who might that be?" Arclath asked, drawing his sword.

El spun something swift and unseen from the Weave that anyone watching might have suspected was some sort of magical shield, and beat the young noble to the door, mainly because he was closest.

"Duth Braerogan from the next farm, quite likely," Storm told them, looking up from a pot that was right at the stage where it shouldn't be left alone, with no one to stir it. "He keeps a fairly good watch over the place, and I—"

Elminster opened the door, ready for anything.

And the room silently flooded with deep blue light shot through with a thousand thousand tiny, twinkling silver stars.

Those stars were coming from the eyes of a dark-haired, slender woman who stood almost shyly on the threshold.

"May I come in?" she whispered, but her voice held a deep thunder that set Arclath's blood thrumming in his veins. He lowered his sword—it seemed to be shrouded in countless swarming stars—and stared.

"Well met," the woman said to him, and as their eyes met something happened to Arclath. His heart sang, yes, but was he—? He *was*! He was floating, drifting gently back from her, the soles of his boots no longer touching the ground.

"Oh, yes! Be welcome, Mother," Storm said in a tremulous voice, as if she was on the verge of tears. "You are *always* welcome here."

"Mother?" Amarune asked, bewildered.

Arclath looked back at her and saw happy tears streaming down the faces of all five Chosen in the room. Among them, Vangerdahast was frozen, openmouthed in dumbfounded awe—suddenly a spider-thing no longer, but a man again, dark robes and all, and looking down at himself and back up at the woman in the doorway and back down at himself again, in utter disbelief—and beside him, Glathra was out of her chair and on her knees, cowering.

It occurred to Arclath Delcastle that he should be kneeling too, if this was who he thought it was, but he was still drifting, unable to go to the floor. That didn't stop him trying.

"An inherited title I still feel unworthy of," the woman answered Rune, and seemed to *flow* into the room rather than walking. "I am Mystra. Yes, *that* Mystra. And I've come to give my deepest thanks to all of you—and to be who I used to be for a little while, if you'll let me."

Her eyes twinkled as she looked at Storm. "You see, I've never forgotten your cooking."

"So You'll be wanting me to stick around and cook a meal or two for You every century or so?" the Bard of Shadowdale asked, her silver tresses stirring around her shoulders like the tails of so many contented cats.

"Please," the goddess of magic said simply, and the room fairly crackled with benevolent power.

"Not without my El," Storm replied gently, staring into Mystra's eyes.

Whereupon the goddess turned to Elminster, who still stood by the door, his hand raised and surrounded by the faint shimmering of his shield. In sudden silence, everyone else looked at him too.

The Old Mage smiled back at them all.

"Well, look ye, I've wanted to die for a long time now. But no longer. Now, I want to stay and see the Realms healed."